THE
WILDE
ONE

CLAIRE CONTRERAS

DEDICATION

For the broken ones—

Don't give up.
Giving up is easy.
The fight will be worth it.

For you, depression—
Thank you for making me somewhat of a decent writer.
And also, fuck you.

"They say you'll find yourself
one of these days,
as if they know I'm lost
and can never be saved."

—Phillip Phillips

PROLOGUE

8 years ago

My eyes burn from tears that mask my eyes but refuse to fall as I stare out into the ocean. Focusing on the waves crashing the rocks below, my eyes trail along the water. A body of blue so big and wondrous that I can't decide where it begins and where it ends, because it doesn't—the ocean doesn't have a beginning and an ending, it just is. Much like me, it just is. Except I do have an end, and that ocean is it for me. I clutch the red bars before me when sobs threaten to overtake me, thoughts of the hell I've been living seeping through my memories. Closing my eyes, I see his strawberry hair and the light freckles that paint over his beautiful smile, and the pain stabs me harder.

The reality of what I did spreads through me as the sobs consume me. I killed him. *I killed him.* The only person who was ever there for me, the one that showed me what love was supposed to be, and I killed him. Tears stain my face and my dyed blonde hair, wild from the turbulent wind, sticks to it. I try to swallow back my broken cries as I look around, my eyes squinting at the sign beside me that reads: Hope. My shoulders shake as new tears rise and my throat opens up with cries that refuse to be held back.

Then I see him, or he sees me. I close my eyes to the wind once more, relishing the feel of its caress against my skin before opening them and looking into the pools in his eyes.

"What are you doing here?" he asks.

I mirror his question, unable to find my own thoughts.

"Looking for you," he mutters, rendering me speechless.

I open my mouth to speak again but uncontrollable shivers invade my body making it impossible for me to form words. My eyes roll back shakily and panic floods through me because I can't see him anymore. I can't see the boy that found me.

I can only see the one I failed.
The one no longer here.
He's gone ... and so am I.

CHAPTER ONE

When I was six years old, my father held both my arms and shook me so that I would look into his eyes.

"Who do you want to stay with, Brooklyn?" he seethed. "Who do you choose? Me or your mom?"

I looked between both him and my mother. She was standing there with tears running down her face, her hands covering her mouth, and her eyes screaming what her mouth wouldn't. I didn't want to choose between them. Truthfully, they were both a terrible option, even in my six-year-old mind I knew that. They were always arguing, always fighting, always screaming—my mother always throwing items at my father. But they were my parents and I loved them both. They were all I knew.

In the end, I never had to end up choosing because they chose each other. They always did. One thing I learned from seeing my parents is that some people would rather stay in a toxic relationship than experience the fear of the unknown. I understand that now. They chose that life and I have made an effort to choose to *not* become that with anybody. As much as I have to love them because they're my parents, I never want to marry someone like my father, and I sure as hell never want to become my mother. I've tried so hard to distance myself from them and their exuberant lives, yet here I am, waiting to speak to my father. Waiting to see what favor he's going to ask of me, because there's always a favor to ask. That's the thing about my parents: I love them because they gave me life but in return love me under conditions—always theirs. And they don't leave room for interpretation when I don't agree to their favors. They threaten me with taking away things like my education. My mother is the queen of threats, amongst other things, and she uses that to her advantage. Boyfriends, cars, concerts, school, clothing, friends ... you name it, she has taken it away from me.

At the sound of heels clinking on the marble floor, I rise out of my seat.

"Your father will see you now," Sherry, his assistant informs me as she turns to usher me to his office.

I roll my eyes at her when she turns around. I don't need somebody to walk me to his damn office. I've been coming here since I was a child. Despite the three mansions he owns, this building (along with three others) is where my father lives. Sherry suddenly jolts to a stop, the short red bob that frames her face swaying into her eyes. She pushes it back quickly and presses down on her earpiece to speak.

"Yes, sir. I'll be right down," she says to whomever is on the other end then she turns and smiles at me. "You can make your way in now, Brooklyn."

"Thanks," I mutter as I push the two massive iron doors open to enter the foyer that leads to my father's lair. When I reach the threshold of his office, I stop and look around. Everything is as manicured as it always is: the wooden shelves filled with LPs that adorn the right side of his office are spotless, matching the larger-than-life stark wooden desk that sits in the middle. It's simple yet masculine, but the thing I love the most about his offices, all three of them, is the stunning view that the floor-to-ceiling windows hold. This one is the most impressive, in my opinion, as it showcases Hollywood. The bold iconic letters on the canyon are as clear as a postcard from here. I've always been drawn to those letters. That sign is the one thing that makes me smile, despite the burden the word holds.

"Hey, Baby Girl," my father croons as he swivels his chair to face me.

"Hey, Pops," I say, retuning his smile as I round his desk to greet him.

He opens his arms for me, as he always has, his green eyes bright as he examines my face. The thing about my father is that as much as I want to despise him for some of the things he's said to me in the past, and for making me feel like I'll never be good enough for … anything, I freaking love him. I return his hug and breathe him in; he smells like cigarettes and honey. He always smells like honey for some reason, I think it's the shampoo he uses. When I pull back I dust some little white flakes from his light brown wavy hair and smile.

"What's up?" I perch up on the edge of his desk.

He exhales a long breath. "Are you still dead set on that microphone company?"

The swinging of my legs die down as I wait for the impending question. Because in my family, there's always a question. A favor, usually. I blink away the tears I know are bound to form in my eyes.

Blink. Blink. Blink.

I have an issue when speaking to authority. For some reason my eyes well up when they speak to me. I can sit here and psychoanalyze myself the way I've done, the way others have done, and say that it's because the authoritative people in my life never paid attention to me when I was a child, but that would be an odd reason for the water in my eyes. Regardless of what the reason behind it is, they're there, swimming in my sockets, burning before my iris, and threatening to spill out. Blinking one last time, I tear my gaze away from his face and look out into the horizon. My parents know how to twist my arm hard enough to see that I agree to what they ask of me, so it's not as if delaying this any longer will make a difference. Growing up, my mother wanted me to follow in her footsteps and be a model, as if anybody can just snap their fingers and become one. When she saw that I didn't have a model body like her, despite her efforts in making me diet from a young age, she gave up on me—with much dismay, I might add. I decided to study business because I wanted to start my own empire—of anything. I just wanted to be part of something big that I could call my own.

Petty dreams, I guess, even for an eighteen-year-old that had just gotten out of a stint at rehab. When I declared my major to be business, I had to convince my mother that I would use it in fashion one way or another. That was the only way she would agree to continue paying my tuition. My father, of course, defended me, saying that business was a great option. He didn't care much about what I did, he had my older brother to hound and make an employee of his. Still, the fact remained that as much as I hated the music industry, I was good at it. At scouting for talent, anyway. I was responsible for signing most of your favorite artists, though you'd never know it. Dad's label, Harmon Records, takes all the credit.

"The microphones, Brooklyn. You still set on that?"

"Yes," I say, my voice steady. "We're doing really well. I really believe in my brand."

I've been working with my best friend Allie on a line of

microphones. Obviously, my parents think it's a joke, but ever since one of the biggest entertainers, Shea Cruz, started using them, our line has taken off.

"I know that, sweetheart. It's an amazing brand." He exhales. "But I need you in Harmon."

I turn my face back to him, feeling those words like a jab in the gut. "You know, all my life I've done everything I've thought you guys wanted me to do." I pause when he raises an eyebrow and gives me a look. "I've done these things hoping you guys would notice me, be proud of me. And it's never mattered because everything I've ever done gets overlooked. I know that I'll never be as good as Hendrix, but anytime I find something that I think I can finally excel at, one of you takes it away from me. When will you be happy with what I've done? What do I have to do?"

He walks over, moving his seat in front of me. When he stops before me, he cups my chin so that I'll look into his serious eyes. "Bee, I am proud of you! We're all proud of you! Look at how far you've come in just a few years. You turned your life around. You quit all your bad habits and got back on your feet. Do you know how hard it is for some people to do that in this city? It's because of how much I value you that I need your help. I need you to help me find new artists ..."

He lets the question hang between us. His eyes tell me that he's not really asking me to do this—he's telling me that I will. I roll my neck and look outside again. The sunny sky that's slowly clouding, the cars stuck in traffic on the highway, the nightclubs that I used to frequent, the streets that made me crazy once and restored me to believe in myself again.

"What do you want me to do?"

"I need you to move to New York. You can work out of there. Hey, maybe on your free time you can work with your

Aunt Mireya. She can help you out with that line of yours," he offers with a smile.

"How thoughtful of you," I quip.

"Always the smart alec." He chuckles. "You can leave to-morrow. I'll have the plane ready for you. You can stay at our place in the city, and your brother will walk you through any-thing he needs you to do in the office. What time can you be ready?" he asks, getting up from his chair and shrugging on his suit jacket.

He's effectively dismissing me, knowing he just got me to agree to something that I never concretely said yes to. Knowing that he's asking me to give up everything I've been working on. For a second I wonder what would happen if I turn him down, and then I have a flashback to things that have happened when I've turned him down in the past. I know it's not worth it.

"Good seeing you, Dad," I mutter, turning to walk out of his office.

I hear his footsteps follow me and stiffen when he grabs my bicep and turns me around to face him. "Hey. Be happy, you're going to change people's lives."

I guess in a sense he's right, I do change people's lives when I offer them a chance to sign with Harmon Records. I also ef-fectively screw over a lot of them, but I try not to dwell on that thought.

"I'll be ready at ten," I say, in response to his previous ques-tion. "I'll call Hendrix to let him know I'm coming."

He smiles his empty yet charismatic smile. "He already knows you are."

That doesn't surprise me and as I turn to walk away, one last thing occurs to me. I turn around and ask him before I lose my nerve. "Can we maybe not tell anybody in the company who I am?"

His eyebrows furrow. "You don't want people to know that you're my daughter?"

"Nope. I want to do this for me, to prove myself worthy of working there."

His mouth pops open and I know he wasn't expecting that one. The first chance he got, my brother Hendrix took the job of CCO and ran with it, never looking back or wondering whether or not he was a good candidate for it.

"But you're a Harmon, of course you're worthy of working here. It's your company, Brooklyn," he says, frowning.

I shake my head. "No, Dad, it's your company. The artists that I sign from here on out are my artists."

. "Are you saying you want a commission? Because that's already assumed, Brooklyn, you'll get a commission."

"I never did before," I say quietly with a slight shrug.

He lets out a laugh. "Whose commission would you have wanted, BK? Let me guess … Shea?"

I grind my teeth together in hopes that I won't lash out.

"From what I remember, you got a lot more than signing brags with Shea," he says. He knows he's hitting a nerve there, and it's a low blow, even for him.

"I can't believe you just said that," I say, my voice a broken whisper as I take a step back.

"Yeah, well, it is what it is, right? Be at the airport tomorrow by nine." He shoots the last part over his shoulder as he turns and walks away. I hear him tell Sherry he's headed to his next meeting.

The difference in the way he treats me and all of his employees is incredible, you would think he fathered them and not me. I don't call him out on it though. I just let it be like. My best friend Ryan used to get mad at me for that, but somehow I always find a way to excuse his behavior and berate my mother's instead. She is much worse, after all. My father comes from nothing; he's the oldest of three children of a cocaine addict and a deceased father. Growing up in Brooklyn wasn't a walk in the park for him and he doesn't take anything he has for granted. I think he's done a pretty good job in instilling those morals on to us. My mother, on the other hand, thinks everything is owed to her. The air she breathes should pay her because she allows it to go into her golden lungs, that's how she sees it. I've always wondered what attracted my father to her to begin with because I just don't see it.

I take a moment to gather my breath and make sure my tears aren't going to spill over before I begin to walk quickly. He stops to pick up some papers from Sherry and I make my way to the elevators. I know he has to walk by me on his way to the conference room, so I take a deep breath and click the down button when I see him approaching.

"Hey, Dad," I call out and wait for him to acknowledge me. "For the record, nobody knows I signed Shea. I gave you all the credit."

Thankfully the elevator door closes before I get a chance to glimpse his face one last time. It's not like he would ever apologize to me. He'll never tell me I'm right, and he'll never thank me. And I think I'm okay with that now.

CHAPTER TWO

I read somewhere that by the age of twenty-five, women are more sure of themselves, more comfortable in their own skin. Sometimes I want to find the person that wrote that and stab her in the eye with a rusty fork. I've been twenty-five for six months and that sureness of myself hasn't hit me yet. I hope that when it does, it washes over me like a wave, hard and fast, taking all of my insecurities with it to a place unknown. I'm not an idiot, I know why I feel this way about myself and I know I need to suck it up and get over it because nobody cares, not that they should. The only people that should care are the reason I feel this way to begin with.

I sigh and rest my head on the headrest of my car. Seven years ago I couldn't wait to get out of LA and now I'm hesitant to leave. I run a mental checklist through my mind of the pros and cons of moving to New York, not that I'll change my mind at this point. Pros: my brother Hendrix is over there most of the time and I love him to pieces. My uncle Robert lives there with his husband. My cousin Nina is over there. Her mom, Mireya, lives there and can brainstorm with me on new designs on my "free time", as my father calls it. Getting away from all the memories of things I shared with Ryan and finally getting a fresh start.

Cons: My niece, Melody lives here with her mom (my brother and Sarah have been separated for almost a year now and she works out of LA). I'm going to miss my little monster to death if I make New York permanent. My best friend and business partner, Allie, also lives here with her husband and she wouldn't leave for anything in the world.

My parents travel between New York, LA, and Miami constantly, but I don't even consider them when I run through my pros and cons list because they don't count. Other than Allie, the few friends I have here are either married or socialites. They won't really miss me, even though they pretended to be sad when I called to tell them I was leaving. Truth is, for the past four years I've kept a really low profile, opting to go to parties and small gatherings instead of clubs. I've been focusing my time on expanding my knowledge of fashion, which is how Fab came to be. It's not much yet, but the microphone line and possible headphones could definitely be going somewhere. Baby steps.

When I get to the airport, I drive into the private entrance, where the hangers for the private jets are, and park in the lot. My heart feels heavy as I get my things out of my two-door Audi. It's stupid, missing something tangible like a car, but I can't help it. I lock it and drag my suitcase to the small building. I notice that the airplane is missing from the runway and wonder where it could be. The Harmon jet is used mostly by my father, but I know he lends it out to the artists signed to the label here and there.

Once inside, I hand my bag to the nice lady at the front desk and take a seat to wait for the plane to arrive. As I scroll through my phone and check my email, I type a message to Allie letting her know I'll call her when I land. Then I call my brother because I still have no idea who's picking me up.

"Hey, BK," Hendrix answers on the second ring.

"Hey, are you picking me up at the airport?" I ask. I wish I didn't sound as hopeful as I know I do, but I haven't seen my brother in a couple of months and I truly miss him.

He pauses and I hear him shuffling papers in the background. I begin to twirl the skull and anchor rings on my fingers out of habit as I wait for a response.

"It's okay if you can't," I offer quietly.

He sighs after a moment. "Sorry, Bee. I'm gonna try. If I can't, I'll send a driver. Love you, sis, can't wait to see you."

"Love you too," I reply as he hangs up on me. Staying in the same city as my brother again will be interesting. We were never close growing up, even as kids we both did our own things. He's only four years older than me, but our parents had us both in completely different things. While Hendrix went to karate, I was stuck in piano lessons. While he was in fencing, I was in ballet. Even as children our parents made sure to always keep us busy and out of the house which meant little time together. As we grew up and developed different interests, we drifted our own ways. I think Hendrix regrets that now and wishes that he would have been there for me more than he was, but we both know it wouldn't have made much of a difference. My demons are my own and they would have probably developed regardless of his presence.

"Sorry, Miss Harmon, the plane should be here soon, then it refuels and we're ready for you," the nice lady says, interrupting my thoughts.

I thank her and glance down at my watch. It's eight forty-five, which means the flight will be late. I wonder who's using the plane this time. Dad didn't mention anything about any bands or my mom using it, but somebody must have.

"Excuse me," I say as I walk over to the counter. "Do you know where it's coming from?" I glance at her nametag: Farrah. She looks like a Farrah with her blonde hair and fair skin.

"San Francisco," she responds with a smile. "Should be here any minute."

Even though I haven't been there in years, a shiver runs through me at the mention of that city and the awful memories I have there. I push my negative thoughts away when I see the blue Harmon plane approaching the gate. I haven't been excited about my move to New York until this moment, and I allow myself to smile and revel in it. I am moving to New York City! I'm starting over. I'm going to give talented people the opportunity to make a name for themselves. I should be ecstatic about this change, and I will be. I pick some lint from my sweater off of my black skinny jeans and stand up to walk to the window, in hopes of catching a glimpse of who used the plane. It doesn't matter, and I figure that it can't be anybody too famous since there were no paparazzi or fans waiting outside. This part of the airport is definitely hidden, but not enough that the vultures won't find you.

As soon as the staircase is settled in front of the plane and the doors open, my phone signals a text message. I sort through my purse to look for it.

Nina: When do you get here? Get ready to party, bitch.

I laugh at my cousin's message and type in a response as I look up to see who's walking down the stairs of the plane. A blonde girl, about my age, is wearing a black maxi dress and her hair is tied up in a messy knot. I squint my eyes to see if I recognize her, but I don't. Walking behind her is a tall well-built guy, maybe a little older than me, wearing dark washed jeans and a fitted black V-neck shirt. Aviator sunglasses sit on top of his light brown faux hawk, which he snaps down to shield his eyes as he drapes an arm on the girl's shoulder.

I notice that she's much shorter than he is, and they both have amazing tans. He drops his arm from her as quickly as he put it there and stretches over his head. My eyes drop to his exposed torso, which is freaking ripped and has musical notes tattooed along his ribs. I wonder what the notes are for. Does he sing? Does he play? Who is this guy?

My phone rings in my hands, making me jump. I look away from the couple and frown when I see my cousin's face on my screen.

"What happened?" I ask, confused, looking back up as I wait for her response.

"What the hell was that message?" she asks.

"What message?"

"Your text back to me! It was gibberish, you dork."

My frown deepens as I try to figure out what she's talking about, not that I'm really paying attention, because I'm still looking at the hottie in black and his girlfriend.

"I don't know what you're talking about," I murmur.

"Are you on the plane?" she asks. "Brooklyn! What the hell are you doing?" she shouts.

"God, Nina, what do you want?"

"Rude. I was just calling because you're taking so long to reply and I want to make sure you're still coming today!"

"Yeah, soon," I respond distractedly.

"Okay, I can tell you're busy. Call me later!" she says, sounding annoyed at my lack of interaction.

I don't pay much attention to it because Nina is the type of person that constantly needs undivided attention. I swear, she picked the perfect career for herself: Broadway actress.

"Yeah, bye," I respond aimlessly after she hangs up on me. My eyes are still glued to the couple outside.

They're still standing right by the door, and I'm assuming they're waiting for their bags, until I see two more people get out of the airplane. This time my jaw completely drops, along with my heart and every other organ in my body. Another guy walks out, wearing a baseball cap, a white T-shirt and worn jeans. He tucks his hands into the pockets of his jeans, leaving his heavily tattooed caramel arms exposed. A huge smile breaks out on his face as the guy in the black shirt yells something at him. It's not his good looks or his tattoos that get my attention, it's the fact that I didn't expect to see him. I usually like to prepare myself before seeing an ex-boyfriend. You know, give myself the whole "you can do this, you're totally over him" pep talk. I hate being caught off guard like this. It makes the inside of my brain turn into complete mush. It's stupid, really, since Shea and I are still friends and talk often. I am completely over him but I would've preferred a little warning. I bury my face in my hands and take a deep breath. *I can do this. I've seen him a million times before. I've seen him with a million girls before. I'm fine.*

Despite my hesitation for seeing him, Shea is more than just an ex-boyfriend to me; he's one of my closest friends. He's seen me at my lowest point and stuck by me, which is something I'm forever grateful for. Nonetheless, when I'm caught off guard and see him out of the blue, my heart skips a beat, mainly out of habit. It's a habit that's been fully explored in the past nine years, which is how long I've known him. After our second break up, we both realized that we didn't want to be in a relationship, but that didn't mean we didn't continue winding up in each other's beds-or dressing rooms, for that matter.

Still, it doesn't erase the fact that I don't trust him turn down groupies and he doesn't want to make me the main object of his affection.

In hindsight, the smartest thing I did was putting an end to the whole friends with benefits thing we had going. He has a gazillion fuck buddies all around the world, and being with him was hazardous to my health in more ways than I care to think about. I know Shea doesn't miss me in that way, in fact, he has an arm draped over his newest conquest right this instant. A very pretty and very famous one whom I'm still unsure how I feel about. Gia Reynolds was actually one of the first reasons I wanted to end things with Shea.

I've been around the music industry my entire life and have always known the pressure and temptations it brings. I was with Shea before he hit it big, hell, I was one of the reasons he made it there to begin with. I know he loves me in his own way, but I'm not a moron, I know what a twenty-something year old is going to be offered on the road. Especially one that looks, sings, and moves like Shea.

As for Gia, she's going on tour with Shea soon, but she's been trying to sink her claws into him for a long time. I was in the studio with him one day when she barged in there like she owned the place. She'd been recording her own record in a neighboring studio and took it upon herself to go introduce herself to Shea. It took everything in me to step out of the room that day. When I close my eyes I can remember it vividly. *Gia had her wild dyed blonde hair down to her waist and was wearing cut out shorts that she probably bought at Justice. Her mile-long legs looked perfect in them, not one ounce of cellulite, which made me hate her a little. I remember looking down at my own legs that looked chubby in comparison and noticing that unlike my thighs that had a never-ending love affair with each other, hers didn't even touch. The way she looked at him through her lashes and laughed loudly as she slapped him playfully on the arm made my stomach sink. She looked like she was ten seconds from offering him a blow job and he looked like he was two seconds from asking for one. I knew then that I couldn't do it. I just couldn't be with him anymore. I had known throughout our little fling that he had other women, but I never saw it. That day, seeing them, I just knew I couldn't stomach it any longer.*

Maybe it was for the best. Who knows, maybe Shea would actually settle down with somebody like Gia. The thought makes my stomach turn because it would only prove, once again, that I'm not good enough. And even though I don't want him anymore, in that way, nobody wants to acknowledge that they're not good enough for somebody.

Plopping down on my seat, I look around, wondering if I should go to the bathroom while they check in so that I won't have to face them. *That's stupid, he's your friend, dammit.* As I mull over my options, two more guys step out of the airplane and my shoulders drop at the thought of not saying hi to them. Leo and Fern are part of Shea's band and I've known them since I was a teenager. I can't pass up the opportunity to say hi to them just because he's with Gia freaking Reynolds. I can't hide from him every time he has another girl on his arm just because it makes me feel like I'm in an uncomfortable situation. It's funny how things are, I can speak to him on the phone and hear girls giggling in the background and it doesn't bother me anymore, but seeing him actually show affection to another girl in front of me is off putting.

I groan loud enough that Farrah turns her head toward me. "Just a couple more minutes, Miss Harmon."

"Sure."

The door swings open and the guy in black walks in with

the blonde. He looks around the room, one of his arms curled upward showing the cuts on it. I can see a scripted tattoo in his inner bicep, though I can't read it. My eyes trail his folded arm up to his defined jaw that has a shadow of hair on it. His eyes, the bluest of blues I've seen, continue to scan the room until he spots me. He looks at me for a moment too long. In that moment, the way his eyes burn into me, my entire body hums. Swallowing loudly, I tear my gaze away from his and notice his forearms flex as he drops his hand from the bag over his shoulder and tucks the tips of his fingers into his pockets. I dare myself to look into his eyes again, just for a second and find intense eyes still on me, unmoving, unnerving.

"No fucking way!" Leo booms as he opens the door, snapping me out of my reverie. "Brooklyn!"

My heart is still rattling, but I'm smiling as I stand and walk toward him, throwing my arms around his neck and letting him lift me up into his arms, swinging me from side to side.

"What! I didn't know my girl was here," Shea says excitedly from behind us.

"Hey, Shea," I greet quietly as he reaches over to hug me.

He hugs me tight and I exhale into his chest, feeling loved for a couple of seconds before he backs away and holds both sides of my face to look at me. I lose myself in his twinkling muddy green eyes as he searches my eyes, my face, and for a moment I want to back further away at the thought that he might kiss me. He doesn't, which I'm glad for because that means I got through to him with our "no more kissing on the lips either" talk the last time I saw him.

"How have you been?" he asks as he draws circles on my cheeks. My breath stalls at the weight of those words coming from his mouth. If anybody else asked me that I wouldn't get upset, but it's Shea, the person who's seen me at my worst, and it does affect me. Besides, the way he's looking at me with such concern, and touching my face, it feels like too much for me to handle right now.

I blink back the tears that I feel forming, embarrassed that I'm feeling emotional in front of a group of people. I've never been a crier, but the few times I allow myself to break down, I do so in private. "I've been good. Fine. You know." I shrug.

"You know you can call me anytime, right? I know I'm an asshole and haven't really been in touch much lately, but I've been so swamped, Bee."

I smile at him. I love it when he calls me Bee. He usually calls me BK, Bee is something he saves for when he's regretful or want to be loving. I always appreciate it when he uses that nickname.

"I know, Shea, I know. I'm the last person you need to explain that to."

He gives me his signature Shea smile, the one he uses on stage, the one he uses to make all the girl's panties melt, and I shake my head. My eyes drop down to Shea's wrist where the tattoo of my name sits. I look at it for a moment and smile again. He didn't get that tattoo for me, but the fact that he has it there still makes me smile.

"So, you're the one going to New York?" he asks, his dark eyebrows knitting. I always thought he looked so cute when he was trying to figure something out, like a kid trying to figure out how much money he has for ice cream.

"Yep. Daddy Dearest asked me to work for him," I say, tracing the tattoo with the tip of my finger. I look around and notice that everybody else is speaking amongst themselves and before I look back at Shea, the guy in the black shirt snaps his head up and looks at me. I tear my gaze quickly from his, hoping he doesn't think I was staring at him or anything.

"What the fuck?" Shea snaps, making my eyes widen as I look back to him, wondering if he's mad that I was looking at the unknown guy. "Is that what you want?" he continues. "Your mics are boomin', Bee."

"Hey, Brooklyn!" Gia interrupts as she walks over to us, giving me a genuine smile. "He's right. I loooove my microphone! It's so cute and different."

"Hey, I'm glad to hear it!"

And I am. Gia is my first "real" client. I sent Shea his black matte microphone knowing he would love it and use it because it was from me, but I didn't expect him to tell everybody and their mother about it. I'm so glad he did, though, it makes me happy to know that at least somebody is genuinely proud of me and supports me.

"It's not just me, everyone does. Everybody keeps asking us where they can get one," she adds. "Well, Shea-bay, guys, Brooklyn, I'll catch you later. I have a meeting at eleven I have to get to." Gia blows air kisses to all of us and walks out of the airport.

"Shea-bay?" I ask him with a raised eyebrow when Gia is out of earshot.

"Girls, you know how they are," Shea mutters, rolling his eyes.

I laugh. "Yeah, I am one, so I think I do."

He shakes his head. "So tell me, why are you gonna go work for him?"

"I don't really wanna talk about it right now," I say with a shrug, looking around. I say hi to Fern and look back at the guy in the black shirt, who catches my wandering eyes, and I curse myself for looking at him. *He has a freaking girlfriend, Brooklyn, and you're being rude.*

"Oh snap, my bad. Brooklyn, this is my boy Nick Wilde. He's producing my CD," Shea says, signaling the guy in the black shirt to walk closer to us.

Nick steps forward, his potent blue eyes never swaying from mine. The way he moves and the way he lets his eyes drift and slowly checks me out as he makes the walk over causes my heart to thump wildly inside my chest. I know this guy is trouble, I can feel it and he hasn't even said a word to me yet. He extends his hand when he reaches me and says something, but I can't hear it through the sound of my heart that's clogging up my ears. I acknowledge his introduction by putting my hand in his, shaking it along with his moving arm.

Shea continues talking while I'm swimming in Nick's blue eyes. The color reminds me of the water in the beaches of Maldives. They're not your ordinary blue. They're the most perfect shade of the color. The blue that makes you want to name a crayon because it's so magnificent. The shade that makes you want to dive in. Of course, I know there's a great white shark waiting for me in that beautiful water if I dare to take the leap. I contemplate that for a while as we stand there hand in hand. About whether or not I could swim with a shark. Would it dance around me? Would it take a chunk from me and leave me to bleed out ...

Nick lets go of my hand, clearing his throat and drops his head, scratching his neck with his hand. I take a breath, clearing my own throat and shake away my thoughts.

"I'm Brooklyn," I explain dumbly.

He chuckles, a deep, raspy chuckle that makes my heart skip a beat and makes me wish I could sit down because suddenly I don't think my stiletto booties can hold me up.

"I got that," he says and winks at me. Freaking winks at me.

"I'm Stephanie," the blonde beside him says, snapping

me out of my fantasy about swimming with dangerous sea creatures.

I plaster on the smile I've perfected over the years. "I'm Brooklyn. Nice to meet you, Stephanie," I say, shaking her hand.

"So, BK, what else is new? I feel like we haven't spoken in forever," Leo says.

"That's because we haven't," I respond, placing my hand on my hip and pursing my lips.

Leo laughs. "Aw, don't be that way! You know I love you."

"Mmm-hmm," I reply but can't keep from laughing when he lunges at me with a hug.

"Miss, the aircraft is ready for you," Farrah informs me.

Leo lets go of me and places a kiss on my head promising me he'll call me when he goes to New York in a couple of weeks.

I give Fern a hug, wave goodbye to Nick and Stephanie and lean into Shea's open arms.

"Be careful over there and call me if you need anything. I'll be there in a couple of weeks and I wanna talk to you about something."

I shoot him a confused look. "Okay?"

"In private," Shea says quietly.

"Okay, call me."

I turn around and yelp, staggering a couple of steps in my heels when he unexpectedly smacks me in the ass.

"Shea," I reprimand, narrowing my eyes at him while he just laughs and puts his hands up in mock surrender.

"What? Your ass looks great in those jeans. I couldn't help myself," Shea says innocently.

I shake my head as I turn around and head toward the airplane wondering what the hell he needs to talk to me about in private. Surely he can't want to start hooking up again, can he? I glance over my shoulder one last time and catch Nick standing beside Shea. They're so different that comparing them is pointless, but I do it anyway. Shea is shorter and has the "you know you want to fuck me" swagger going for him with his hazel eyes, messy hair under his ball cap, and rugged edge. Nick is tall, more built, and looks all man in contrast to Shea's boyish charm. The gleam in his eyes practically screams: "I know who I am and I'll make it impossible for you to forget me." His sureness of himself literally makes me shiver.

They're both looking at me, but my gaze gets caught in the intensity of Nick's eyes. When he looks at me I can almost hear him daring me to look away, and that's what locks me in. That's what makes Shea's figure look like a blur beside him. I force myself to look away as I get on the airplane and wave one last time. As I walk in, I'm greeted by Eleanor, an older lady with paper white hair that's been working for my dad for a long time. It warms me to see her. After saying hello to her, I dump my oversized purse on one of the first leather seats to the right and walk to the back. I settle into my dad's favorite seat, the biggest, most comfortable one. I snuggle into the seat and look around the plane, my eyes tracing the cherry wooden panels and the big leather seats, and the television that's currently blank. I turn my head and notice the door to the bedroom is open and wonder if Shea took a nap during the flight then cringe, my face twisting in disgust when I think about what Shea and Gia might've been doing in there. *Where did Nick sit?* I wonder. *Beside his girlfriend, dumbass,* my own mind replies. I have never been one to take an interest in anybody's significant other, but something about him makes me want to know more about him. *Where did he come from? How have I never heard of him producing? Who hired him to produce Shea's entire album? Is Stephanie his girlfriend? He never really specified.*

CHAPTER THREE

To my surprise, Hendrix's black Escalade is waiting for me by the hanger when the plane lands in New York. I throw my bag over my shoulder and thank Eleanor before galloping over to my brother and throwing myself into his welcoming arms.

"God, I feel like I haven't seen you in years," Hendrix mumbles into my hair.

The feeling is mutual. The last time we saw each other was for my mom's birthday in April, which was four months ago. Four months isn't a long time, but it feels like ages when the only person who feels like family to you is thousands of miles away. I'm really glad that'll change now that I'm going to be living here for a while.

"I know, too long," I respond, tearing myself from his embrace so that I can take a good look at him.

Hendrix smiles and shakes his head at me as I hold him at arms' length. He always says I'm like a mother hen and treat him like a child, even though he's three years older than me. He's probably right about that. I'm a nurturer. Clearly by nature.

"Have you been working out?" I ask, squeezing his arms.

My brother is really tall and equally as lanky. He has dark blond hair like my father and caramel brown eyes like my mother. He's the perfect mix of both of my parents, and I've always been jealous of that. It's kind of dumb to be jealous of how skinny your brother is, even I know that, but it still bothers me that he got the skinny gene. And I'm not saying that I'm fat because deep down I know I'm not, but it's still something that I struggle with even years after the number my mom pulled on me when I was younger. I've been to countless therapy sessions for all of my "issues" but I always seem to have a load of them left over.

Hendrix chuckles. "Actually, I have been working out. How the hell can you even tell when I'm wearing a suit?"

I shrug. "I dunno. It's a woman's thing, I guess."

His driver, Marcus, opens the door for me and I slide in while Hendrix runs to get my suitcase.

"Who are you and what have you done to my sister? Did you not bring clothes?" Hendrix asks, unbuttoning his suit jacket and shrugging it off as he climbs into the car.

I don't know what's funnier, his bemused expression or the fact that it's a valid question since I like to travel with my entire closet.

"I only brought my purses," I answer after my laughter dies down.

He frowns. "What?"

"I only brought my purses," I repeat slowly. "Daddy snapped his finger and ordered me to do something, which of course I freaking agreed to, so I figured if I was going to drop my entire life to cater to him, he might as well buy me a whole new wardrobe." I shrug to show him how nonchalant I am about it, but in reality this entire thing terrifies me a little—from the small fact that I have no clothes to call my own and no apartment to my name, which means I'll have to stay at my parents' or Hendrix's, and no car that I can drive freely anywhere. I'm actually really terrified. The only thing keeping me together is the knowledge that my brother, cousin, favorite uncle and aunt are here. Family. Finally.

"Wait, wait, wait," Hendrix says, his face still puzzled. "You didn't even bring underwear?"

I laugh loudly, throwing my head back and slapping my thigh. "Of course you would ask that! I brought a pair."

"So what are you expecting to do? Buy some Hanes in Duane Reed?"

My eyes knit together. "Why would I do that? There must be a Victoria's Secret around here somewhere ..."

"That's not the point, Bee. You should always be prepared. I can't believe you didn't bring underwear," he says, but he's laughing. "You're too fucking much."

I wink at him. "Don't I know it. Oh! Before I forget!" I open my purse and sort around in it.

"I don't understand why women have such big purses. You can never find anything in them," Hendrix mutters under his breath.

My eyes shoot up to him and I'm about to tell him to mind his own business when I see that he's already on his phone. "Found it! Here!" I say excitedly, shoving a folded piece of paper in his face.

He pushes his head back and smacks my arm down, snatching the sheet of paper from my hand and opening it. The biggest smile takes over his face and I snap a picture. His daughter, Melody, sent him a paper that says, "I love you and miss you, Daddy."

"She wrote it herself," I explain.

"Thank you for bringing it," he says, his voice low and quiet.

I know he misses her so much and I hate that he lives so far away from her. It's not fair, but it's his fault and I know I can't push him on it. I've tried enough times to get him to try and fix things with his ex Sarah, but he just won't budge.

"She misses you, you know," I whisper.

He looks at me and blinks rapidly a couple of times before he clears his throat. "I miss her too."

I wonder if we're talking about the same person, but it doesn't matter, there's no need to specify. Both girls miss him and I know he misses them both terribly.

"Do you think love really conquers all things?" I ask him quietly, resting my head on his shoulder as we drive into a tunnel.

"I think it conquers most things," he responds. "Why?"

I sit upright and look at him; the reflection of the tunnel's orange lights making his eyes look like lava. "Do you think you're in love with Sarah or do you just love her because she's comfortable?"

I watch as his Adam's apple bobs up and down a couple of times. "I think you've asked me this before and I think the answer to such a question is: you can be in love with someone and comfortable with them and it won't make a difference if life throws obstacles at you that you can't push through together."

I nod and rest my head back on his shoulder. "Where are you taking me? I don't even know where I'm staying. I swear, Drix, this is the last thing I'm doing for them."

He chuckles and ruffles my hair, which makes me scowl and sit upright again so that I can finger comb it. "You said that last time, Bee. And the time before that." He leans in and ruffles the top of my hair again and I slap his hand away.

"Will you freaking stop that? Not everybody has naturally straight non-frizzy hair, you asshole."

Hendrix laughs his obnoxious carefree laugh, which is only obnoxious when it's at my expense. "You're such a clown, Bee. And to answer your previous question, I figured you would wanna stay at my place. Unless you want me to take you to Mom and Dad's, it's not like they'll be there ... I just didn't think you would want to be there."

"Your place is perfect."

I check my phone while Hendrix takes a call and see a couple of text messages. The first one is from my best friend Allie.

Al: Bee, let me know when you land! I hope you have a safe flight. I love you! xo

I respond back, letting her know that I made it and I'll call her later. The second one is from my cousin Nina.

Nina: Hey, whorebag. Are you here yet? Drinks tonight? Shopping? Let me know, I'm free!

Me: In car w/Hen. Have to go buy underwear and clothes.

She replies immediately.

Underwear? WTF? How did you lose that? Didn't you take a private flight? Tell Hen he's an asshole for not going to my play last week.

I laugh loudly and Hendrix shoots me a look that tells me to shut the eff up, so I do as I type back a response.

Me: I didn't bring clothes, only purses. He's on phone so I can't tell him.

Nina: Fk. He'll probably cut my tits off if I call you then. No shoes either?

Me: Nope. Nothing. Only the clothes on my back.

Nina: Ballsy. I like it. U staying with the Hen?

I laugh again and cringe when Hendrix tells me to "shhh." We call him "the Hen" when we want to piss him off.

Me: Yeah.

Nina: FML. He's gonna try to control your every move. Forget about taking a guy home.

I shake my head because of course my cousin would be thinking about that.

Me: Not worried about that.

Nina: I forgot. You're a fucking nun.

Me: Please.

Nina: I'll pick you up in an hour. Shopping and dick hunting.

I'm not surprised that those are the two things on her mind.

Me: You're insane.

Hendrix gets off the phone and looks at me expectantly. "Who the hell are you talking to?"

"Nina." My smile is so bright not even his foul mood can damper it right now.

He rolls his eyes. "Shoulda figured. What did the little slut want?"

My mouth drops open. "Hendrix! She's our cousin!"

"Yeah, and?" He blinks as if he's missing the point.

"You can't call her that."

"Whatever. Did you know she invited me to watch her stupid play? I went and left two seconds into it, before the fucking curtains even went up because I read the bill, THANK GOD, and noticed it was a NUDE play?"

I cover my mouth to keep laughter from spilling out, but it's no use. "No, it wasn't."

He gives me a *don't be stupid* look.

"I can't believe that," I say, laughing.

"She's a moron. Why the fuck would I want to see her naked?"

I shake my head and dry my tears, gasping for air as I picture my brother sitting in a tiny dark room waiting for my cousin's show only to find out she would be naked.

"Who did you go with?"

"By myself, thank God. I would've freaking died of embarrassment if I had taken a date. Can you imagine? 'Hey, let's go watch my brilliant cousin act.' 'Oh, which one is she?' 'The naked one.'"

My laughter rises again and this time I double over in it, tears streaming down my face and he joins me.

"She's such an idiot," I say, laughing too hard for the words to be intelligible.

"She really is," he says as his laughter dies down.

I text Nina back because I cannot wait until I see her.

You were in a nude play and you invite the Hen to watch!

**Nina: OMG! I WAS NOT NUDE! HE'S SUCH A DICK!
IS HE SICK? GOD. WHAT IS WRONG WITH YOU
PEOPLE!**

I laugh and show Hendrix the screen. He laughs and then glares at me. "The Hen? Are you fucking kidding me? You still call me that shit?"

"Only when you're being an asshole about things."

My reply earns me a pinch on the arm, which I yelp at. We make it into Manhattan at six o'clock and I'm starving. I look out the window as we drive around, watching all the suits and women in work attire shuffle through the streets, clearly dying to get home after a long day. I turn my head to look at my brother and smile, thankful that he took part of his work-day to pick me up at the airport. He's a workaholic just like my father, so I know how hard it is for him to be out of the office on a weekday. And a Tuesday at that, since it's the day albums release. He's been on his phone like a hawk the entire car ride, so I'm sure he's either checking numbers or emailing people about staying on top of sales.

When I face the window again, a huge billboard of a half naked Shea startles me. His dark brown hair is ruffled, look-ing like he just got out of bed. His tattooed arms and torso are exposed, the lines on his tan stomach more visible than usual with the oil they put over him. His hands are tucked into his jeans and the band of the brand of underwear he's modeling for is out. He's looking at the camera with a smirk on his face, his muddy green eyes practically eating me as I stare back at the photo.

"Crazy, right?" Hendrix says beside me.

I nod slowly in response and clear my throat. "I saw him today. The Harmon jet flew from San Fran to LA and landed while I was waiting."

I turn my head to face Hendrix when I hear him chuckle. "That must've been something. He was there with Gia, right?"

"Yeah."

Hendrix's lips twist and he sucks his teeth. "I don't know what you saw in that guy." He cuts me off before I get a chance to defend Shea. "Don't get me wrong, he's a cool guy, he's a great person … but he's not someone I want my little sister going out with."

"I agree, which is why I'm not going out with him. He would've never settled to be with me anyway," I say. It's the truth, but it sucks to speak the words aloud.

"He's an idiot, Bee. He doesn't know what he's missing. Funny thing about that is, when he is finally ready to settle down, he'll come back and you'll be gone."

I stare at him for a long time, processing his words, knowing he's completely right. What is it about no longer having somebody and seeing them happy without us that makes us want them more? It just shocks me to hear Hendrix say it because that's pretty much where he's headed. He's completely pushing Sarah in that direction and he obviously knows it. Men can be such clueless assholes sometimes.

"You're one to talk," I mutter, turning my head away.

"Have you spoken to Mom lately?" he asks, jabbing me harder than I got him.

My teeth clench at the question. I've never been one of

those people that can't take what she dishes out, but that one little question is a hell of a sucker punch.

"Nope."

Hendrix exhales loudly. "Bee, I know she's a bitch sometimes, but she's still your mom."

I swallow, holding back the rude remarks that are dying to spill out of my mouth, and turn my face to look at him. "I know that, but for the first time in a long time I feel like I'm healthy. I'm not obsessing over my diet or what creams to use on my face or what shampoo makes my hair shinier. I'm not worried about not fitting into size two jeans. I'm finally coming around to accept that my ass is never going to be small enough to fit sample designer clothing, and I'm okay with that. I can't talk to her because every time I do, she makes me feel like shit. She makes me feel worthless and fat and hideous, and I can't go back to being the person that believed her."

By the time I finish my rant, the tears that have been pricking my eyes are flowing freely. My brother is silent as he listens to me, but the sure look on his face has crumbled. He slides over and wraps his arms around me, pulling my face to his chest.

"I'm sorry," he whispers against my hair.

"It's fine," I reply, blinking rapidly to get rid of my tears. I hate that I let myself cry. I hate that I let her affect me this way even when she's merely mentioned. I used to look back on what my life has been, the choices I've made and the losses I've dealt with, and blame myself. Now I blame her. Now I hate her. I hate her for being so cruel to me, my father for letting her, my brother for being too busy, God for forsaking me when I felt I needed him most, and myself for being weak and giving into the bullshit I make myself believe about it all.

"We're home," Hendrix murmurs when the car pulls up to his luxurious building.

Is this home? I want to ask him. I've never had a concrete meaning for the word. I've never had a place that I truly considered home because I've always felt like a burden in all of my parents' homes. When we get upstairs and I put my purse down, I take a moment to assess his place. I've been here countless times, but it's never struck me as a homey place. Looking around I see everything a home should have: furniture, artwork, a kitchen, bathrooms, bedrooms, but there's something missing, specifically in this one. He doesn't have Melody or Sarah here to greet him when he gets in from a long day at work. He comes home to this humongous space, kicks off his shoes and hangs out by himself most nights. I just don't understand it. I walk around, picking up the picture frames he has laid out on his side table and hold one with an outline of a heart. The picture is of Melody's first birthday. Sarah's carrying Melody on her hip, Sarah's blonde hair was cut short then, her green eyes are smiling as bright as her lips as she looks at Hendrix with the most adoring expression on her face. Hendrix is looking back at her with his arm wrapped around her shoulder, and Melody is holding her hands out to touch her Minnie Mouse cake. I can't help but wonder: if your heart is in LA, how could your home be in Manhattan? And where is mine? I seem to have misplaced my heart so long ago and I don't know where to even begin looking for it.

CHAPTER FOUR

The loud buzzing sound of my alarm clock stirs me out of the amazing dream I'm having. I groan loudly as I tap my hand on the nightstand in an effort to make it stop.

"For the love of god, shut that thing up!" Nina mumbles beside me. She ended up staying over after our shopping trip turned into us going to a restaurant and her downing a bottle of wine by herself.

I sit up and throw the covers off of me, pressing the off button as I make my way to the bathroom.

"Gotta get ready for work," I say over my shoulder as I shut the door behind me and begin to strip off my Snoopy pajamas.

Hendrix told me that the dress code they go by is business casual, which can mean a lot of things. I didn't want to risk it and look like the only idiot wearing flats, so I ended up buying a lot of skirts, matching frilly blouses and dress pumps. After dressing in a blue knee length skirt that hugs my hips and a white blouse with a navy-blue collar, I step into a pair of navy patented pumps, finish my makeup and fluff up the ends of my wavy hair. I take a look in the mirror and nod, happy with what I did in thirty-five minutes. Nina is simultaneously pulling on the jeans she wore last night and checking her phone when I step out of the bathroom. She's muttering something as she scrolls down her screen but stops when she looks up and sees me.

"I told you those skirts would look good on you!"

I smile back. "I like them."

"You look like sex, you know that, right?" she says.

"I didn't realize sex had a look."

She nods, pursing her lips. "It does. You see something and you think: sex. That's the look you got going with the way that skirt hugs your hips. Turn around, your ass probably looks amazing too."

I turn around exaggeratedly and shake my butt for her, which earns me a short laugh.

She groans. "I hate you. I wish I had an ass like that."

"Like what? Full of cellulite?"

"Shut up. You don't have cellulite. You make it sound like you have a cheese ass or something. It looks good as hell, Bee," she says when I make a face.

"Whatever. The grass is always greener on the other side and all that jazz. I would kill to look like you," I respond.

Nina has the perfect body, in my eyes. She's thin with slight curves, she doesn't have much of a butt, but it's shapely, and her boobs are a perfect C cup. Basically, she looks good in everything. My mother always said I should work out harder so that I could have a body like Nina's. I tried hard to do that for a while, until it took a toll on me. It's exhausting to watch what you eat and throw up what you know you shouldn't but couldn't help eating anyway.

"You're so blind, Bee. I love you, but you can't possibly look in the mirror and not be happy with what you see. You have beautiful curves, and you need to embrace that shit and own it. Our bodies aren't all that different. I just have the boobs and you have the butt. We're backwards." She walks to the bathroom and turns around when she's standing in the threshold. "You should see the way people look at you when you walk by them. Pay attention. And consider yourself lucky. At least you can get a boob job. Do you know you can't sit down for weeks if you get ass implants? Trust me, I Googled that shit."

I laugh and grab my purse on my way out of my room. I walk down the stairs and round the corner to the kitchen, pausing right before I get there when I hear my brother talking on the phone. His back is facing me, but I know he heard my loud heels clicking on the hardwood floor. I don't want to purposely eavesdrop, but from the tone of his voice I know he's speaking to my mother, and I'm curious about their conversation.

"Yep. She'll do great. I know. All right, Mom, I'll talk to you later. Sure, I'll tell her," Hendrix says, turning around to face me as he hangs up. "Morning. Mom said to wish you good luck at work."

"Awesome," I reply shortly.

He exhales and runs his fingers through his wavy hair but doesn't make any further comments on the topic as he hands me a coffee mug. "Did Nina sleep here? I heard you guys get in pretty late," he says after a while.

"Yeah, she decided she wanted to close down the little bar we went to in The Village," I murmur distractedly as I sort through the cereal boxes in his pantry.

"Hmm. Were you drinking?" he asks as nonchalantly as he can, but the edge in his voice makes me pause on the box of Fruit Loops and turn to face him. His caramel eyes are looking at me with both questions and concern and I wish he had no reason to do either.

"No, Hen," I respond, turning around to pull out the box of Frosted Flakes. "I don't usually drink. But I can, you know? Drinking has never really been an issue for me." *It's what I do after I've had the countless amount of drinks.*

"Yeah, but still. I've heard that any kind of addict is an addict," he says, cringing as soon as the last word leaves his mouth.

"It's okay. We can talk about it," I assure him. "And I'm not really an addict, Hen. I was going through a lot of shit."

"Still, Brooklyn ..."

"Hendrix. I'm not an addict."

"You went to rehab. You go to meetings a couple of times a year. You had a sponsor," he says quickly, before I can cut him off.

"I went to rehab because I was scared shitless. I go to meetings because I want to help others that may be in the same shoes I was in, and they're not all meetings for addicts, you know that. And I had a sponsor because she and I understood each other and she helped me deal with a lot of my emotions," I say calmly, getting the milk out of the fridge and sitting down to eat my breakfast as I explain myself.

"You take medication," he says, sitting on the barstool in front of me.

"I haven't in a year and that was for my depression, not for my supposed addiction. What the hell, Hendrix?"

He's starting to irritate the shit out of me. I'm trying to keep my cool, but it's hard when I'm being given the third degree this early in the morning on a day that I'm already nervous about as it is. A nagging feeling tells me this has something to do with his conversation with my mother, but if I ask him and he confirms that, I will go ape shit, so I would rather not know.

"Sorry. Sorry. I just worry, and for some reason it's easier to worry about you when you're on the other side of the country. I can pretend that you're just sitting at home working on microphone designs every night and not out with friends at bars and stuff," he says with a long exhale, running his hand over his hair again.

"It's fine. It's just ... it's really early for this. I'm already freaking out about work and doing a good job and hoping people like me—not that it matters because either way I'll be stuck there and now everyone is gonna think I'm only there because I'm your sister and I get everything handed to me on a silver platter—and it sucks because this isn't even anything I wanted to do. I've never done this openly and for real, and now that I am, I'm thinking I might suck at it or maybe I've lost my touch and can't find anybody good. I'm going to end up letting everybody down and Daddy's going to think I suck and tell Mom and she's gonna rub it in my face."

My words are pouring out of me quickly and my heart is hammering just as fast. In this moment I feel absolutely lost and afraid, and not for the first time I wonder what the hell I let my father talk me into. Hendrix's face falls and he shakes his head slowly, standing up and walking around the table to hug me to his side.

"You're going to be fine, Bee. You're going to be more than fine. And let people think whatever they want to think. Everyone thinks I'm the CCO because I'm Dad's kid, and though that may be true, I also worked my ass off in school and have been working my ass off for years to get to where I am. So fuck 'em, let 'em say whatever they wanna say."

I nod and take a deep breath. "Thanks."

Nina joins us, wearing one of the T-shirts I bought yesterday. Her dark hair is pulled into a high ponytail and she's barefoot, lazily swinging the black stilettos she wore last night in her left hand.

"What's up, bitches?" she greets. "You got coffee? Or are hens not domesticated?"

Hendrix grumbles something that sounds like "fucking moron" under his breath as he reaches in the cabinet to get her a mug.

"Sweeeet," Nina says, placing her mug on the table and serving herself coffee. "I like this mug, you asshole."

I laugh, covering my mouth with both hands to keep the cereal from sputtering out of my mouth when I read the mug he handed her: **I am surrounded by fucking idiots.**

"You can thank Bee, she gave it to me for Christmas," Hendrix says.

Nina rolls her big brown eyes at us. "Why do I hang out with you? You guys are so fucking weird."

"Because you have no friends," Hendrix comments.

"Because you love us," I say at the same time.

Hendrix makes a face. "That's not corny."

I shrug and continue eating while they talk about Nina's plays and the lack of clothing in the one she invited him to watch. I tune them out as I begin to worry about the day and how it'll be to work with my brother every day. I make mental notes of things I have to do as soon as I get a break. Call Allie and ask her about the two pending microphones. Figure out what wholesaler we can get the earphones from. Find out who can put us in contact with a supplier for recording studios to see if bedazzled earphones are even a good option for us. I know I need to simmer down so I don't stress myself out more than I am, but it's so hard when I know I have things to do.

"You'll have to go to my next one, Hen," Nina says. "It's not nude. It's actually a rockstar themed musical. You'd love it."

"Cool. I'll go to that. Has Uncle Rob gone at all lately?" I ask, chiming into their conversation.

"Sometimes. He's been busy helping Victor set up his new store, so he hasn't been by in a couple of months," Nina explains as she slips her shoes on. "All right guys, have a good day at work. Bee, call me later and tell me how it went."

Hendrix and I get our stuff and leave shortly after Nina does, and he explains to me that he always tries to leave at the same time because even though the building is only ten blocks away, it's taken him over an hour to get there sometimes. I've been to New York countless times, but I've never had to worry about how long it takes to get somewhere in the mornings, so this bit of information is shocking. My eyes are glued to the sidewalk where hundreds of people are walking and talking on their phones and texting. It amazes me that only a handful of them actually speak to each other and not the device in their hand. Not that I'm one to talk because I'm always on my phone, but it kind of makes me wonder how many landmarks and things are unappreciated by the people who walk past them daily.

My phone vibrates in my lap, which makes me laugh quietly, and I see an email from Allie with images of the microphones she's assembled. I practically squeal at the sight of them. Every time I see my little logo on a new one, the happiness in my heart blooms a little more. It's a little bee with a crown on it, simple but elegant, and more importantly it's very personal to me. It's the little image that my best friend Ryan used to draw for me whenever we exchanged notes in the hallways in school. All of the little notes had that little bee on them. It's the same little bee I have tattooed on my back in honor of him. Having it displayed on our line of microphones doesn't take the pain of him being gone away, but it definitely makes me feel like I'm keeping his memory alive.

I reply back to Allie and hit send right as we're pulling up to the Harmon Records building. Waiting for Marcus to open the door for me, I check my face in my compact mirror one last time, making sure that I don't embarrass myself by having food between my teeth or something. I snap it shut just as my door is being opened and slide out, Hendrix following closely behind.

"Welcome to your new home away from home," Hendrix says, draping his arm over my shoulder.

"Yep. God, I should've taken a shot of something before coming here," I say, shaking my head when I feel Hendrix stiffen beside me.

"Geez, Hen, it was a joke and please don't make me repeat my whole spiel again," I counter.

"All right, I'll drop it," he mutters ushering me toward the elevators. "I'll give you the tour now since we're on our way up anyway. Not much has changed since you last came, but we've added a couple of wings that I know you haven't seen since, well, when you come you usually go straight to my office and right back out."

We move toward the back, making space for the people stepping into the elevator and ride up to the forty-third floor in silence, only listening to the chatter around us. A couple of men and women say hi to Hendrix as they spot him, but other than that, we remain uninterrupted. Most people get off as we ascend, leaving only a handful of Harmon employees to continue the ride with us. When the elevator is more comfortable, we move away from each other, and Hendrix starts talking to one of the guys standing beside us. The guy is in his early twenties, I think, and keeps eyeing me as he talks to my brother. I offer him a small smile as I stand there awkwardly, waiting for my brother to either stop talking or introduce us. Thankfully, we make it to the forty-second floor and Hendrix tells "Bradley" that he'll "catch him later" as he pulls me out of the elevator, which catches me off guard since this isn't our stop.

"All right, you remember how Dad was thinking about building a gym so that the employees could just use the facilities here?" Hendrix asks as we walk to the right.

I nod, remembering how my father was on a health trip a couple of years ago after he had a heart scare. I know in most families the mother is what keeps the household together, she's usually the driving force behind things and holds down the front while the father busies himself with work and other things, but in our family our strength is my father. In my eyes he is anyway, and I realized it the day Hendrix called to tell me that Dad had been taken to the hospital because of shortness of breath and chest pains. It happened in Los Angeles so I got in my car after I got out of a Micromanagement class I was taking and drove straight over there.

On my way to see him so many things flashed through my head. Would I be okay if he died? Did I feel like I told him everything I needed to? Would I feel the way I felt when I lost my best friend Ryan? I knew the answer to that question was hell no because I didn't see my father enough for his death to affect me in that magnitude. As sad as it sounds, and even I realize it's a terrible thing to say, but the loss of my best friend was definitely more hurtful to me than the loss of either one of my parents would be. I'm certain about one thing—if my father died, I would have absolutely no relationship with my mother.

"Yeah, I know he built a nice gym in here. I saw the plans," I respond just as Hendrix stops in front of a glass door, pulling it open and letting me step in first. Even though I had seen the architectural plans for the gym, seeing it in person is much more magnificent than I could have imagined. All of the walls are glass so you can see the machines and the people working out regardless of where in the gym they are. When I walk to the back, where the treadmills are, my breath leaves my body for a moment. The view of Manhattan is breathtaking from here.

"Wow. I would totally work out here." I breathe as my eyes scan over the Empire State Building and Central Park.

Hendrix chuckles. "That's the idea. This way, employees can get here early, or come during break, or even after work. Between you and me, I think Dad built this to make the studios more enticing to work in, not that anybody is going to want to work out while they're recording, but whatever."

"Hen," I say, putting a hand up. "You're killing my vibe. Let me enjoy the view for five more minutes without all the blabbing."

"You're such a brat," he says with a laugh. "What do you think your view is going to be like from your office?"

My eyes widen at that and I turn my head to look at him, trying to gage whether or not he's serious. He only nods, which makes me giddy but I contain it, only offering him a smile.

We walk around and then move up to the floor above, which holds twenty recording studios. It's big enough to have double that, but that's what makes Studios Forty-Four exclusive. Well, that and the fact that it's in the Harmon Records building. Artists from all labels love to record their projects here in hopes of running into others and possibly collaborating with them.

We see a couple of familiar faces and wave as we walk the halls before taking the elevator up one more time. When the doors open again, we reach the floor of Hendrix's office and my new place of employment. A sense of pride washes over me when I see the big silver letters on the wall behind the receptionist that read: Harmon Records. My dad may be a jerk, but he's built an empire that nobody can touch or tarnish. And for that, I respect him. I smile at the girl behind the desk. Her jet-black hair is teased up into an Afro that is shaped like a snow cone. Her eyes are big and brown and the eyeliner around them enhances their almond shape. When she stands and sorts through the papers on her desk, I notice that she's wearing an outfit similar to mine, except her top is teal and enhances the color of her dark skin.

She smiles a welcoming smile as she extends a folder to Hendrix.

"Mornin', Hendrix," she says. Her voice is husky and smooth. She sounds a lot like Beyonce when she speaks. "Here are the files you asked Bradley to get for you."

"Thank you, Kina." Hendrix smiles at her and takes the files from her hand. "You're looking extra pretty today. Special occasion?"

"Husband's birthday," she explains with a shy smile. "Going to lunch with him on break."

"That's nice. Be sure to wish him a happy birthday from me," Hendrix says as he turns to me. "This is my sister, Brooklyn. She'll be working here for a while. I already showed her most of the place, but I want to show her this floor so she can get acquainted. Is Stacey in yet?"

Kina looks at me and smiles warmly as she replies to Hendrix. "She should be in her office. Pleased to meet you, Brooklyn."

"Likewise," I say, offering her my hand. "Have a good lunch," I call over my shoulder as Hendrix and I walk away.

For some reason my brother's interaction with the receptionist makes me happy. One thing our father taught us was to always be kind to others and treat them, whoever they are, with the same respect you would want to be treated.

"You never know when your ladder is going to wobble or break," he would say. *"So no matter how high up you are, you need to be mindful of the ones holding the legs on the ground. They have the power to pull you down or help you if you fall. And more importantly, you never know when you'll be the one at the bottom of that ladder, because that happens—tables can turn quickly in life."*

Hendrix walks me down a long corridor that I know well. At the end of the hall is my father's massive office. To the right of my dad's office is Hendrix's, but instead of turning that way he walks the other way and goes into Stacey's office. Stacey's blue eyes immediately pop up and she smiles. Her smile brightens when she sees that I'm standing beside my brother.

"Brooklyn! So good to see you. Hendrix told me you would be here for a while," she says, walking over to me and throwing her arms around me.

Stacey is one of the few people that can get away with hugging the crap out of anybody. She just has that friendly, but not so overly friendly that she's creepy vibe to her that makes people instantly comfortable with her. She's short and a little on the heavier size for her height, but she's gorgeous. She's in her mid-thirties and has been a friend of the family since we were kids. Now she has her own kids, one of which Hendrix and Sarah are godparents of. Stacey is also one of the only people that can put up with our attitudes. My father's, Hendrix's, my mother's and mine—because we all have terrible attitudes sometimes. Save for my mother, she *always* has a bad attitude. Stacey has a gift in how she deals with us, though.

"So good to see you too! How's Zach? How are the babies?" I ask.

"Zach is good, the babies are great! You have to go by and

see them sometime now that you're here for good."

"I will!"

"Stace, I need you to send Kina's husband a gift. I just don't know what … fuck … maybe tickets to the Jets game this Sunday?" Hendrix says distractedly as he sorts through the file in his hand.

"Sure. The opener?" Stacey asks as she rounds her desk and takes a seat again.

"Yeah, I guess. Good seats, though. I don't want him sitting nosebleed," Hendrix specifies.

Stacey rolls her eyes. "Obviously."

"Good. See you later. Hold my calls for the next half hour, I gotta show Brooklyn some stuff."

We walk to the office beside his and he opens the door. He doesn't need to switch the light on because the sun that bathes the room is perfect. I hear myself gasp as I take it all in. It's not the size of the office that I'm amazed by because it's much smaller than my father's and Hendrix's. It's not even the view, which is absolutely stunning, just as he promised. The office must be directly below the wing of the gym that I was looking at earlier because I get the same view of Central Park and the Empire State. The floors are dark wood and the desk is a modern white with a matching chair. It looks totally girly but chic, and I wonder whose idea it was to throw this together for me. There's a chandelier suspended from the ceiling that reminds me a lot of one I had in my childhood room. To the right there's a big wooden shelf, and that's what really takes my breath away. The shelf must hold hundreds, if not thousands of vinyl records, which is what gives the room a mix of wood and a scent that I can instantly correlate to my father and the times he'd lay my head on his chest while he listened to his old Marvin Gaye albums.

In this moment I realize how much small things matter because no matter how many hurtful things that man has said to me in the past, something that he may not have thought was such a big deal like this, makes me feel like I'm home. And for once home doesn't feel like such a bad place, after all.

CHAPTER FIVE

"**S**o you mean to tell me that you have no going out clothes?" Nina shouts, so loudly that I have to hold the phone away from my ear.

"Geez, will you simmer the fuck down?" I groan.

"You simmer the fuck down! No! You pipe the fuck up, actually! It's seven o'clock right now. You still have time to go to the store and buy a little black dress. DO. IT. BROOKLYN."

I let out another frustrated groan, throwing my head back. I placate her by telling her that I'll go as soon as I shower and hang up the phone. Nina's been talking about going to a club all week. She insists that it has to be today since she rarely gets weekends off and her "kind of nude, but not really" play just wrapped up. She's using the end of my first week of work as her excuse to get me to go with her, which is fine, but I really wish she would be okay with getting a drink at a low-key bar instead. As it is, I have to go check out a local band at a hole in the wall bar tomorrow because they impressed me on a video I caught of them on YouTube the other day.

In reality all I want to do is have some wine, kick my feet

up, and watch old Curb Your Enthusiasm episodes. I relax into the dark leather recliner and pop up the foot stand, covering myself with the Lakers fleece throw that Hendrix adorns his couch with as I snuggle into the headrest. As soon as I close my eyes, my phone rings again and I want to die. I begrudgingly open my eyes and stretch my arm to look at it. When I see that it's Allie, I swipe my finger over the screen with a smile.

"Hey," I answer.

"Hey, you. You busy?" Allie asks.

She has one of those childlike voices, like her vocal chords didn't develop past age six. I used to think it was annoying when I first met her, but over time I began to find it endearing. It's cute and it suits her tiny little frame.

"Nope, just lounging."

"Cool. Hendrix is over here, right?" she asks.

"Yeah."

Hendrix left for LA last night to meet with a client. He's bringing Melody back for the week, which I'm really excited about. I already Googled places to take her to play, explore, and eat. It should be fun having her here.

"I'll have to call so I can meet up with him and send you some stuff. No big plans for tonight? It's your first weekend there, I'm sure Nina has something up her sleeve," Allie says with a laugh.

Allie is very familiar with Nina's antics from our younger and wilder days. Allie and I grew up. Nina did too, but in a different way. She still lives her carefree life. Allie married her high school sweetheart, Craig, and I ... well, I've just been floating around trying to survive.

"Yeah, she's ... she wants me to go to a club with her, so no big deal. I'm kind of glad that Hen isn't here tonight because he probably wouldn't even let me go out," I say, exhaling. "I swear, he thinks I'm a child."

Allie snort laughs. "He wouldn't *not* let you go, Bee! He's probably just worried about you. You put him through a lot, you know."

I groan, knowing she's right. "Al, that was years ago. The other day he seriously asked me if I drank wine with Nina. Fucking wine, Allie!"

Allie's laugh gets louder and her snorts get more repetitive as that sinks in.

"You done?" I ask, annoyed but smiling.

"Yes, sorry," she says as she winds down. "Anyway, so you know that Sinatra microphone you designed—you wanted to know if we could get them on stands?"

My eyes are wide as I nod excitedly even though she can't see me. "Yes, yes, yes. What about them?"

"I'm sending one with Hendrix so you can approve it." She squeals the last words, knowing how much this design means to me.

I screech and clap my hands wildly, dropping my phone in the process. "Ohmygod! You're kidding! That was so …"

"Fast?" she finishes. "I know! I'm so freaking excited for you to see this one. You know who's going to want one? Shea! For freaking sure. This is such a Shea mic!"

"Yeah, I think so too. I think he'd like it," I agree quietly.

"Bee, he'd love it. You have to send him a picture of it."

"Ha … funny thing about that … he's supposed to come visit soon."

The words hang between us for a moment, like I knew they would.

Allie exhales loudly into the line. "So you saw him the other day and he told you he wanted to see you again?"

"Yeah. But it's not like that. He just wants to talk business,

I think."

"I can't even … I can't even tell you what I think about that. He's a good friend, he's a good guy, but you know he's no good for you," she reprimands softly.

"I know."

"'Kay, girlie, I'll talk to you later. Go have fun!"

I smile widely. "I will."

Hours after Marcus drives me to a few stores, I finally make it back home with three short dresses: two black and one teal. The black ones are both short and form fitting, but the teal one shows more skin because it's cutout in Vs where my ribcage is on either side. I decide on that one and a gold pair of heels. I leave my thick dark hair to cascade down my back. I sort out the loose curls that hit the small of my back and apply my makeup. Once I'm finished, I walk to the standing mirror outside of the bathroom and do a turn, feeling good about how I look. The combination of the gold eye shadow and teal dress make my emerald green eyes look bigger and brighter, and I love the way the dress fits. I just hope my feet survive the night in these heels. They're the most uncomfortable pair I own but they're too perfect not to wear.

When I hear the doorbell ring a dozen times in under a minute, I grab my clutch and run downstairs. By the time I hit the first floor, I am totally regretting these heels, which is not a good sign.

"Holy crap," Nina says as I swing the door open. She's wearing a short little black dress that I doubt covers her entire ass and black stilettos. "You look hot, Bee!"

"So do you," I respond.

"You really wanna wear your hair down?" she asks as twirls a loose curl around her fingers before tugging it. I'm constantly straightening my naturally curly hair, but today I decided not to tame it much. It's not a mess, it's mostly straight except for the tips that curl, which is much better than the way it looked before the gazillion straightening treatments it's been through. Either way, the more you touch it, the worse you make it.

I shoo her hand away. "Stop. Yeah, worse case I'll put it up," I say with a shrug as I lock the door. I look at her and shoot her a confused look. "Your hair is down too."

Nina presses her lips together to contain a smile. I roll my eyes, knowing what's coming before she even says the words. "Yeah, but my hair isn't as long … and it doesn't get frizzy like yours."

"God, you're a dumb bitch. Why do I even hang out with you?" I mutter, walking past her toward the elevators.

"Because you looove me," she croons.

"Yeah, whatever."

Marcus drives us to the Meatpacking District, which is where Provocateur is, the nightclub Nina has been raving about all week. She's on the phone the entire ride there, talking to a friend of hers that's getting us in through the VIP entrance. Marcus drives around the front of the nightclub, and I shake my head at the amount of people in line waiting to get in. I've never had to wait to get in anywhere and I don't think I would if I had to. I stopped coming to places like this when I was nineteen. I'd been going to them since I was sixteen, so I guess I had enough of the nightlife by then. I prefer house parties, even big ones. Partying in dim lighting with sweaty bodies around me isn't really something I'm interested in anymore.

I do love to dance though, and I love hanging out with my cousin. One night of this nonsense isn't going to kill me. Marcus parks and goes around the car to open the door for us when we reach the side entrance, helping us hop down before telling us he'll meet us inside. We don't really need him hanging out with us, we're nobody, but Hendrix being the hen that he is, gave Marcus instructions to not let us out of his sight. We flash our smiles to the security as they check our IDs, and Nina starts yapping about how she's going to get Marcus to leave us alone for the night. I tune her out as we walk into the dark hallways and shiver at the difference in temperature from the outside heat.

"This place is jammin'," Nina shrieks as she sways her hips to the latest Pitbull song. "Let's go find Sky!"

I shrug, letting her lead the way. I can't say I'm not curious to see which one of her uber-artsy friends would have connections at a nightclub like this. Nina says it's one of the most impossible places to get into unless you're somebody, know somebody, or have loads of money, which in turn means you know numerous somebodies. I bob my head side to side as I pick up my feet in a sort of dance/walk behind my equally bouncy cousin. I look around the place, which really is *jammin'*, as she called it. There are people everywhere, dancing, drinking and grinding under the glowing purple haze that the lights emit.

"We got here at the perfect time," Nina shouts over her shoulder, her brown eyes giving off an up-to-no-good gleam I know all too well. I raise a questioning eyebrow, wondering what she's alluding to. She steps beside me, bumping into a leggy blonde dancing behind us as she wraps her arm around my shoulder. "A bunch of hot guys just stepped into the VIP," she shouts in my ear.

I cringe, stepping away from her hold. "You're going to bust one of my ear drums!" I reprimand as I follow her line of sight. I see the group of guys she's talking about. They're all dressed similarly: a couple in jeans and long sleeves, a couple in slacks and long sleeves. I purse my lips and shrug at her, not impressed. She throws her head back and laughs.

"We soooo need to get you a drink ... or twelve! I can't believe you didn't drink before coming!"

Nina is all about pre-gaming and probably had that amount to drink before coming out tonight. I really don't think it's sunk in her head that I'm trying not to be the wild child I used to be.

"One drink," I say loudly.

Nina squeals and lets go of my hand as she propels forward and wraps her arms around a tall guy. He smiles widely and receives the hug, crushing her onto him. I can't see her face, but his looks like the definition of happiness, which stuns me enough that I stop walking. Nina has never had a long-term boyfriend. All of her relationships are fleeting moments of pretend love or opportunities. The guy she's clinging onto has long shoulder-length dark hair, piercing blue eyes, and a scruffy beard. He's totally not her type and completely my type. I usually go for what Nina calls *the grungy look*—dirty looking but totally hot, her words.

She steps away from grungy guy's hold and turns to me with a huge smile on her face and I know this means they're just friends. Or in reality, he's just a friend to her; she probably means more to him though.

"Bee, this is Sky!" Nina says, pulling my arm so forcefully that I stumble a little as I walk to her. Sky steadies my other arm and looks at me with a bemused expression.

"Sorry," I say, embarrassed even though I didn't fall, and even if I would've it wouldn't have been my fault. "Hi, Sky. I'm Brooklyn."

He collects a handful of his hair and swipes it back on his head, letting me see his face better under the pulsating lights. His eyes are clear blue, like the sky, and I wonder if that's why his parents named him that or if it's a nickname in reference to it. He has light stubble over his jaw and thin lips that are turned up.

"Brooklyn, I love that name," he says, leaning in to give me a peck on the cheek. "I'm Skylar."

"Skylar," I repeat with a smile as I nod in appreciation. "I like that name too."

Skylar wiggles his eyebrows playfully and I laugh. "You ladies wanna sit down?"

"Sure," I shrug.

"Bee needs a drink, Sky!" Nina booms. "Like ... yesterday. She's really uptight if she doesn't have one."

I gape at her. "I am so not uptight!"

I'm really not. And I had wine earlier; I just refuse to tell her that so that she won't make fun of me. Nina has this thing: wine is for old people, beer is for frat people, cool people drink tequila. I so do not drink tequila.

We sink into the low couches in the VIP section and I ask the waitress for a vodka tonic, hoping that'll ease Nina's pestering.

"Good girl," she says brightly and proceeds to drape one of her legs over Skylar's lap.

Oh my God. She's going to flash everybody. I close my eyes and scoot closer to her, pulling down her dress a little.

"You see? Uptight," she says with a laugh.

"Oh, I'm sorry. Are you purposely flashing your vagina?" I ask incredulously.

She groans and lowers her leg, shifting in her seat. "Anyway, Bee, Sky is the playwright I was telling you about ..."

I nod, not knowing what the heck she's talking about, but playing along for her benefit. I completely understand now, though, why she's all over him. He's one of her "opportunities." I wish my cousin would be a little bit harder to get sometimes.

It's not that she's slutty, like Hendrix pegs her to be, but she definitely takes what she has and uses it. Skylar gets up and walks away, saying something I don't catch.

"You know he's totally into you, right?" I ask her as we watch him leave.

"Yeah, but he's just a friend."

"Yeah, right."

"I swear! I haven't fucked him and I don't plan on it," she says, seemingly annoyed that I would think she was.

"Is he married?" I ask. She has a thing for married or taken men. That is her downfall and that's the one thing we always argue about. As much as I love her, it's so wrong that she does it and I cannot get over it. It's a subject that makes me uneasy.

"Nope. Live-in girlfriend," she says.

"And you're not fucking him?" I ask curiously. "That's … new."

She exhales. "I choose wisely. Sky and I would never work. He's too emotional for me."

I nod, now thinking we're hanging out with a psychotic emo guy, but say nothing about it. I scan over the VIP area again and see a couple of familiar faces: models, actors. My eyes stop when I reach the group of guys we previously saw and this time I feel my blood drain from my body. It happens quickly; the blood drains and rises, causing my heart to sputter rapidly and my breath to hitch.

"What? What happened?" Nina asks, her voice alarmed. "You're fucking killing me, Bee."

I register her words and let go of the grip I have on her arm. "Sorry," I say, but my eyes are still on the guy looking at me. With the dim lighting I can't see their real color, I can't see the richness of them or the waves they have, but I can feel the intensity and the heat they let out as they pin me.

"You know him?" Nina asks.

I nod, still looking. "His name is Nick. I met him the other day."

Nick, seemingly reading my lips, smiles. It's a very slow and sensual smile that takes over his face. It's not really a heart-warming smile, even though it does warm parts of my body.

"He's looking at you like he wants to eat you," Nina comments.

My heart is still pumping at a ridiculous pace, and for some reason, I cannot look away. I can't even play it cool and pretend I didn't see him or that I'm not completely attracted to him.

"Your drink," Skylar says, stepping in front of me and blocking my view of Nick, and I'm oddly thankful for this.

"Thank you!"

"No problem." He sits down closely beside me, his thighs touching mine, as he takes a sip of his own drink. He leans in to speak so that I can hear him. "So, you were living in LA before you moved here? That must be an ... interesting transition?" he asks, his voice light.

I shift to look at him and our foreheads bump, making us cringe and move apart. I hadn't realized how close we were sitting. "Yeah, in a good way though," I respond with a smile.

"You say that now, wait until winter hits," Skylar says, tossing his drink back.

I laugh. "You're right."

Nina pulls me close to her. "I just saw my friend Priscilla get here," she says and points at a short girl in zebra print pants. "I'm going to say hi. Be right back!" She leaves before I can say anything else.

"She's a social butterfly, that one," Skylar says, shaking his head with a smile, totally checking out Nina's ass as she walks away.

"She's … something all right," I offer.

Skylar laughs. He has a fun laugh that makes me smile. His Adam's apple bobs as he does it. He reminds me of my brother in a strange way, maybe because they're both tall and skinny. Skylar is obviously hotter than my brother, to me anyway.

"So you're a playwright? You look like you play in a band or something," I say, taking a sip of my drink.

"Eh, I used to until I realized I was going to die of starvation if I didn't do something else," he says.

I laugh. "So you chose to write plays for small income venues?" I ask, raising an eyebrow.

"Touché. I'm good at it though, and it's actually paying the bills quite nicely," he says, a smug grin spreading over his face.

"You don't look like the clubbing type either," I point out.

Skylar throws his head back in laughter. "You don't like to generalize at all, do you?"

I cringe and laugh along with him. "Sorry! It's kind of true though!"

"It is true," Sky says with a chuckle. "My brother owns the place, so I come hang out here sometimes. Usually upstairs in his office, but since Nina was coming …" He lets his words drown in the music as he turns his face away from me to look at my cousin.

"Cool." I don't know whether or not I should bring up Nina. I want to continue talking to him so I can get my mind off of Nick and the fact that his stare is burning a hole on the side of my face.

"You want another drink?" Skylar asks, standing up.

I jiggle my glass to show him I still have plenty and watch him walk off to the bar. I bite down on my lip and readjust the bottom of my dress before opening my clutch purse and taking out my phone. I write a text message to Allie letting her know I caved and went out with Nina, because that's what you do when you're sitting by yourself and don't want to look awkward. The leather seat dips beside me and I jump slightly, whipping my head to look at who sat next to me.

"Brooklyn," Nick says, tilting his head to appraise me, his eyes cataloging every inch of my face. "I'm Nick, we met the other day."

"Yeah, I remember. How are you?" I say, offering him a smile, hoping he doesn't realize that having him sitting so close to me makes me feel like a bowl of Jell-O.

"I'm great," he says, his mouth quirking up, calling my attention. My eyes stay stuck on the fullness of his lips as I watch him speak. "What a small world, huh?"

I nod slowly, bringing my eyes back to his. God, those fucking eyes are so expressive. I swear he's telling me he wants to fuck me. I'm not kidding, I'm not imagining it. He's really telling me that with his eyes.

"Yeah, small world." I all but squeak.

"You come here a lot?" he asks, bumping his knees against mine as he scoots closer to me. The rough denim of his jeans against my bare legs is causing goose bumps to break out over my skin. I rub my legs over with my hands and notice how his eyes stay glued to them.

"Nope. First time."

He tears his eyes away from my legs and looks into my eyes again.

"Shea mentioned you were going to be working at Harmon?"

My eyebrows furrow, wondering where this conversation is going. "Yeah …"

He flashes me a smile. "Cool. I'll see you around then. I have to get back to some people. Maybe I'll catch you later."

I smile. "Have fun."

He nods, pursing his lips as if to contain a smile. "You too."

He stands, picking up his cup from the table in front of us and walks back to his table. The checkered dress shirt he's wearing leaves no room to wonder whether or not he's fit. His back is broad and I can tell he has toned arms just by looking at his forearms. I look back, catching Skylar as he walks toward me and almost feel the urge to laugh. He's the typical guy I go for and he absolutely pales in comparison to Nick.

"Dance?" Skylar asks when he reaches me.

I shrug. "Sure." That's what I came for, after all.

Skylar offers me his hand as I stand, holding my skirt down so that I won't give everybody the free vagina show Nina was offering, and he leads me out onto the dance floor. We bump into a couple of shoulders trying to get to an empty spot, and when we reach it, Skylar turns to face me and begins to dance. He's holding my hands, not my hips, which is unusual for the song, but I go with it. It's a funny place, a dance club. You go there to dance with complete strangers. You let them touch all up on you and grind all over you, but heaven forbid the same person that has their penis pressed to your back tries to make a grab at your ass the next day in broad daylight. It's such a strange concept and it's even weirder that I feel so at home in this setting. I've always let myself get lost in music, in dancing. I live the lyrics. I fly with the beat.

Nina joins Skylar and me as the next song starts. She picks my hand up as she jumps excitedly when Rihanna begins to sing about finding love in a hopeless place, which again, is pretty fitting for where we are. I smile at my thoughts and close my eyes, throwing my arms over my head and swaying my hips to and fro. I'm so absorbed in the music that I don't even register hands on my hips or the way the person behind me, whom from the size of his hands I assume is a man, is mirroring my movements with his own hips. As the song transitions into Robert DeLong's Global Concepts, the large hands on my hips inch up to my waist where the V cuts of my dress reveal the flesh over my ribcage. I shiver at the feel of his hands and open my eyes as I grab his hands and peel them away from me. Pivoting around, my face lands on Nick's hard chest. He smells like a mix of cigarette smoke and masculine divinity. That's the only word that comes to mind in describing his scent, and even in my mind it sounds corny. I take a step back, giving us the only space the people around us allow, and look at his face. The moment our eyes meet, I feel like my heart is going to explode. The only thoughts running through my mind are: if this is how it feels to look at him up close, what the hell would it feel like to kiss him?

My thoughts turn to mush when his head dips toward mine, and I find myself automatically closing my eyes and parting my lips for his. We've completely stopped moving now and the bodies swarming around us are bumping us from all sides, but I don't care.

The feel of his breath leaves me quickly but his lips never touch mine so I open my eyes.

"What?" I breathe.

He smirks and shakes his head before leaning in and placing his mouth over my ear. "Why'd you stop dancing?" he asks, his voice is raspy and low and I unwillingly close my eyes again.

I stand on my tiptoes and hold onto his biceps, to steady myself, feeling his muscles flex under my fingers as I lean into his ear.

"Because you were getting frisky," I respond, letting go of him and standing back to look at him again.

His mouth quirks up again and he snakes an arm around

my waist, pulling me flush against his chest until all I can do is gasp in his smell. When he begins to sway his hips against mine, I automatically move along with him. He lets go of me just long enough to bring my arms up to his neck before holding me against his hard body again. His intense gaze never leaves mine as he takes my hands and spins me so that my back is on his chest and both of his arms are around the front of my body.

"I think you like it," he says, making my breath hitch as his bottom lip trails over the shell of my ear.

I'm suddenly finding it hard to breathe and it has nothing to do with the dancing. I look around and catch Nina's profile as she speaks to Skylar over by the bar. She's completely enthralled in her conversation and I wonder if she even remembers I'm here. When Nick lifts up my hair from my back and drapes it over one of my shoulders, I close my eyes, completely forgetting about Nina. Nick wipes the beads of sweat on the back of my neck and blows on me. He may think he's cooling me, but his breath on my neck is making me shiver heat.

I feel him brush the spot in between my shoulder blades with his lips, and I throw my head back to his chest. We're still swaying along to the beat of the music, but it feels like our dance is much more sensual than the music that's playing. His hands begin to inch upward again, and again I place my hands over them, effectively stopping him.

"I'm not going to cop a feel, Brooklyn. You can relax," he says, his voice husky.

I shake my head letting him know I won't relax, even though my eyes are still closed and my head is lulled against him. I turn myself around to face him again when the song comes to an end and he dips his head close enough that I can see his beautiful ocean eyes before he places a kiss on my cheek. I suck in a breath as he brushes his lips softly up to my ear.

"You look beautiful, by the way. The most gorgeous girl in this place," he murmurs as he lets go of my arm and turns to leave.

I stand in place, stunned by his words and the feel of his lips on my cheek. I don't even try to will my heart to go back to normal as I weed through the crowd to find Nina.

"Hey, ready to go?" I ask when I reach her.

"Are you?" she shouts excitedly. "Are you leaving with that hot ass guy you were dancing with?"

My mouth pops open, then shut, then open, then shut. "No!"

Skylar laughs loudly at my reaction and Nina turns to him. "I told you, she's uptight when she's sober!"

"Ugh. Can we just go?"

Nina laughs and nudges me with her elbow. "You didn't look so uptight out there, though. Maybe you should take him home and have some fun for the night. The Hen is gone for the weekend …"

"Nina! I am not doing that! Are you insane?"

She rolls her eyes. "Fine," she groans. "Bye, my Sky, I'll see you on Sunday!"

"Bye, babe. Bye, Brooklyn, good to meet you," Skylar says, giving me a hug. "I'll just walk you out."

The strangest sensation runs through me as I follow Nina out of the club. Sky has his arm draped over my shoulder, so I can't see much, but I feel like I have to look back. When I do, I find Nick's probing eyes. He's standing by the railing of the VIP area, watching me leave. His jaw is clenched and his lips are set in a straight line, his expression is the complete opposite of how it was when he was dancing with me. I'm about to wave at him when I see a girl walk up to him and say something. He looks at me for a moment longer and finally grabs the hand she's offering him and goes out to the dance floor with her. I swallow the uneasy feeling that takes over the pit of my stomach and walk out the door, already regretting not staying those extra five minutes.

CHAPTER SIX

Loud pounding on the door stirs me from my slumber, making me groggily wipe my eyes as I throw the covers off of me. I walk toward my door still blinking away sleep and yawning.

"What?" I mumble.

"Aunt Brooklyyyn," Melody sings from the other side.

I let out a groan and throw my head back. I love my niece to pieces, but she has the bad habit of waking everybody up at seven in the morning. I'm especially not after having two long nights in a row. Friday's clubbing and last night's shows completely drained me. I wipe my face with both hands and smile as I open the door.

"Hi, Little Miss Sunshine," I say.

She laughs and shakes her head. I started calling her that after I saw the movie, not that she knows that, but Hendrix gets a laugh out of it. The family in the movie has nothing on our dysfunctional mess, though, and that's saying a lot.

"Daddy made pancakes. You want?" she asks, shifting on her little feet.

"Sure. I'll be right out."

I turn to the bathroom and get ready as quickly as I can. When I come back out, I find Melody lying in my bed with an iPad in her hands.

"Is that mine?" I ask. Melody also has a habit of breaking iPads, and I really don't want to go to the Apple store on a Sunday.

"Mine," she says, going back to whatever she's doing.

"Let's go eat."

As we walk down the stairs, Melody tells me how her mom is doing, which of course she has a short answer for. Even when she's broken down, usually courtesy of my idiotic brother, Sarah holds up a strong front for Melody.

"Are you excited to start Kindergarten this year?" I ask, scooping Melody up in my arms and pushing her long blonde curly hair from her face.

Her green eyes widen as bright as her smile and she hugs the iPad to her chest. "Yes! I know how to write my first and last name!"

"Wow, you're ahead of your class already? Good girl." I kiss her forehead and set her down on a barstool when we get to the kitchen.

"Mornin'," Hendrix says as he plates the pancakes he made.

"Mornin' to you too. Thanks for sending Cinderella to wake me up," I say with a shake of my head.

Hendrix laughs. "You know how it is. You had a late night, huh?"

I shrug. "Not as late as Friday, but yeah. I went to the tiniest hole in the wall bar out in the Village and saw a couple of bands."

"Anything good?"

"Eh." I shrug.

The truth is, the bands I saw were good, but not good enough. There's so much untouched talent out there, and I'm sure somebody in my position could have gone to the bar last night and come home raving, but I know the difference between good and gotta have it. The three bands I saw were good but nothing that I felt would be amazing, even though I wish them all the luck in the world.

"Well, you know I trust you implicitly when it comes to sh … stuff like this," Hendrix says, shooting a quick smile to Melody.

I sigh, knowing that this is probably the only thing he and my father trust me on, but I can't even be mad at them. Through the years I've learned that you reap what you sew, and I've sewn a lot of stupid shit in my life, so I can't blame people for underestimating me. I just wish they would give me the chance to prove them wrong in other aspects of my life. *C'est la vie.*

"I know. I'm the best," I say with a shrug and laugh when he gives me a disbelieving look.

"So modest," he says.

"I learned from the best."

We spend the rest of our morning walking around Central Park, until we're so exhausted from running around and the heat that we have to take a break. We cross the street and duck into a small restaurant called Sarabeth's that Hendrix swears is amazing. Judging from the amount of people in here, I would think he has the right idea. Then again, the place is as small as the kitchen in Hendrix's penthouse, and there are over thirty people in here so it's not that difficult to get the out of this world illusion from it.

Hendrix asks for somebody and five minutes later we're sitting down, leaving the line of people that were on the waiting list before us fuming. My brother seems nonchalant about it, as he always does, because he's used to getting the five star treatment everywhere he goes. *He is so the son of my parents.* I think what separates me from them is the troubles I've encountered because of all the shit I reap due to all the shit I've sewn. If it weren't for that, I would probably feel the same sense of entitlement the rest of the Harmon family seems to be stuck on. I love my family because they're the only one I have and the only one I know, but their actions are questionable most of the time.

We eat until we're stuffed and walk back to Hendrix's place, swinging Melody in between us until she gets tired and he has to carry her.

"She's going to pass out as soon as we get in," Hendrix says over her little blonde head.

I smile, watching the way her blue eyes are unwillingly fluttering closed. "She's already about to pass out."

I hold onto my brother's arm as we walk and snuggle into it so I can be closer to Melody's angelic face. Whenever I'm with her I feel like I need to enjoy every second of it. I feel like I need to show her everything that I wish was shown to me when I was a kid just so that I can selfishly experience it through her eyes for the first time. I stroke her hair softly when we get to a stoplight and just watch her, wishing I could take all the bad in the world out so that she never has to worry about being hurt or suffering. But most of all I watch her and wish she could stay innocent forever. I would kill to have that innocence back. The kind where you don't question things or people's motives a hundred times before you decide that you can trust them. Kids just trust without question, and it's such a beautiful thing. A beautiful yet naïve thing to do, and as naïve as it is, I wish I could get it back.

Letting out a wistful sigh, I turn my head from her face and look across the street straight into the face of Nick, gasping at the unexpected sight of him. He's crouched down with his hands on his knees and catching his breath from a jog, it seems. I can see the sweat glistening over his forehead before he wipes it with his forearm. His dark blond hair is styled in his typical faux hawk and he's wearing a sleeveless black shirt with black basketball shorts. His arms, which are usually covered, are exposed for once and the visuals I've had of how they might look don't disappoint. He has an even golden tan and his arms are shapely, the muscles ridging in and out from his shoulders to his triceps. When he stands fully, he snaps his ear buds out of his ear and smiles slightly at me, his piercing eyes jumping from me to Hendrix and back to me. I can see the question in them, but I choose not to answer. I smile back and offer him a small wave right before the cross light flips on and we begin to walk toward each other.

I'm wearing my Tory flats today, my feet still suffering from the other night, and there are enough people walking around us for me to miss him, but I don't. Nick never takes his eyes off of me as he crosses the street. He walks around a group of people, purposely stepping to my side. There's no time for formal hellos in the middle of the street, and I'm glad for that because I don't want to introduce him to my brother and do the whole shebang in a crowded street. My smile is fixed on my face as he approaches, also smiling at me, his eyes crinkling in mischief. When he brushes past me, he takes my hand and squeezes it slightly. It's just a squeeze. Just. But it's enough to get my heart pumping, my blood tingling, and my eyes widening as if I've been caught doing something wrong, which I know is ridiculous, but that's how his touch makes me feel.

CHAPTER SEVEN

Monday, Monday. Nobody likes you Monday. Nobody likes you when they need to go to school and nobody likes you when they need to go to work. So, Monday, you freaking suck. Take a day off.

I groan, getting out of bed when my alarm clock chimes for me to get up. As exhausted as I feel, I have to smile when I hear Melody's footsteps pattering on the hardwood floor and her giggles bouncing off the walls. I can't imagine having such a bright, beautiful little girl and not seeing her daily. I don't know how my brother does it, or if it even affects him the way I would imagine it does. He's an amazing brother and a great father, but he is a man and men feel differently about these things. Then again, my mother is a woman and she completely wipes her ass with me, so I guess it depends on the person.

Once I'm ready for work, I switch my phone on and make myself coffee. I sort through my brother's endless funny mugs and find a decent enough one to take with me. It says: I LIKE BIG MUGS AND I CANNOT LIE. My brother, mug connoisseur.

"You ready?" Hendrix asks, stepping into the kitchen with Melody trailing behind.

"Ready. Is Mel going to work with us?" I ask.

I wonder if he thinks these things through when he brings her for the week. I'm guessing he does, but still, I wonder how much thought goes into what she's going to be doing while he's at work.

"Umm no. Well, she is, but Uncle Rob is picking her up there," Hendrix responds, checking his huge silver watch. "He should be there soon. Let's go."

I take charge of strapping Melody into her booster chair, while Hendrix works out details of a meeting he has. On the way to Harmon, I show Melody the pictures Allie sent me of the newest microphones and let her hold the sample of the one I have in my purse.

"It's heavy," Melody says with a giggle.

"It is. It's made of gold," I joke.

Her blue eyes widen like saucers and she gasps. "Gold? Like Golden Doubloons?"

I smile with a confused frown. "Golden the what?"

Hendrix turns in his seat. "It's from Jake and the Never Land Pirates. Some gold coins."

"They're not gold coins, Daddy! They're Golden Doubloons," Melody insists, shaking her head in dismay at him before turning her pretty round face back to me. "You get them when you solve problems."

I nod my appreciation. "Cool. I like that. Golden Doubloons. I'll Google them so I can see what they look like."

"They look like coins," Hendrix chimes in again.

Melody groans. "They're not coins like quarters," she whispers to me.

I laugh, kiss her round cheeks, and place the gold

microphone in the case in my purse. When we get to Harmon, we find our uncle, Rob, waiting for us outside. My smile magnifies when I see the excited smile on his face. Uncle Rob is my favorite member of my mom's family, aside from Nina's mom, Mireya. He's the one freest of judgment, and the most loving and giving human being I have ever met. Not that I've met many of those.

I wrap my arms around my uncle, who's exactly my height in heels, and he squeezes me tightly.

"Oh my God, I've missed you!" Uncle Rob says into my hair. "You look so good. Let me see you!" He lets go of me and holds me at arms' length. "Giiirl, you work the hell out of that dress!"

I laugh loudly, throwing my head back and slap him playfully on the chest. I'm wearing a very fitted navy blue dress with white buttons down one side. It ends just at my knees, so it looks professional yet sexy.

"Don't tell me you still don't know how to take a compliment," he chides.

I roll my eyes, smiling. "Please. You look great too, crazy. How's Vic?"

My uncle's brown eyes light up. "Good. Very good! You'll have to come over soon."

My uncle and his longtime boyfriend, Victor got legally married recently and they are over the moon. They've been together for over ten years, so it's not like they weren't married before, but making it legal made them feel like they were accepted. I know, at least for my uncle, that's a huge feat.

Hendrix and I say goodbye to Melody and Uncle Rob. Hendrix promises he'll pick her up as early as he can.

"Oh, don't worry. You know this little gal and I get along just right. We're going to the American Girl store. We're going to get ice cream. We're going to have a pizza party." With every word that comes out of Uncle Rob's mouth, Melody's smile stretches wider, and I can tell they're going to have a great time.

"Shit, I wish I was going with them," I mope quietly as Hendrix ushers me inside the building.

He laughs loudly. "Of course you do."

"Ice cream, shopping, pizza—what more can a girl want?" I say, placing my hands over my heart with a dreamy sigh, making Hendrix laugh louder.

We're still bumping shoulders and laughing at our own stupidities when we step into the elevator, which is a lot less crowded than last Monday and holds a very, very hot looking Nick and a very, very fine looking Shea. My mouth drops when I see Nick, or Shea, or both, I don't even know, but my mouth is on the floor. I have to blink a couple of times to snap myself out of it.

"What the hell?" I say, coming to a standstill in the threshold of the elevator and stumbling forward when Hendrix bumps into me from behind. Both Nick and Shea lurch forward and steady me to keep from tripping over my own feet.

"Brooklyn! What the fuck?" Hendrix growls as he drops his cell phone.

"Sorry," I say, cringing as my face colors in embarrassment. "I got caught off guard."

"Jesus," Hendrix mutters, straightening out his suit. "'Sup, Shea?"

Shea bumps fists with Hendrix and leans in to give me a kiss on the cheek. "I told you I was coming."

I raise my eyebrows, looking at Nick over Shea's shoulder. "Yeah, I didn't realize you were going to come talk to me at work unannounced."

"What?" Shea asks and then laughs. "Oh! No!" He laughs

some more, shaking his head. His muddy green eyes look just as amused as Nick's intense aqua pools. "We're going up to the studios ... new album ... remember?"

"Oh," I say when realization dawns on me. "Oh. Of course!"

Shea takes a step back and looks at me, scratching the barely there stubble over his chin. "There are definite benefits to recording here now, though," he says, his tone playful, but I know what he's doing. I know he's trying to see how far he can push this and it's tempting. It's very tempting. He's standing there wearing his signature white T-shirt that shows off his heavily tattooed sculpted yet lean arms, a beanie cap over his untamed curly dark hair that peeks out at the bottom, and his snug in the right places jeans. Very tempting, but not happening. Not anymore.

"Shea," Hendrix warns, not looking up from his phone.

"What do you think, BK?" Shea asks, ignoring my brother's warning and grabbing my chin to look at him. I'm wearing heels so he doesn't have to tilt my face; we're almost the same height. He may have an inch on me, if anything.

My eyes flick from Shea to Nick, who hasn't stopped looking at me. I've felt the weight of his stare on me the same way I felt it since the day I met him at the airport. It's a hot *I'll take what I want, and I want you* stare that he gives me and it makes me shiver every single time. I swallow loudly when my eyes meet his serious blue eyes and I wonder what he could be thinking. I can't tell what could be going on inside his head, and it kills me.

"I think that you need to focus on your album and keep your *member* in your pants," I respond with a smile.

Shea laughs, as does Hendrix, but Nick just continues to look at me. His lips quirk up slightly at my joke, but his eyes continue to trail slowly down my body. The fire in his gaze while he does it makes me hold my breath as I wait for those beautiful blue eyes to land on my face again. And when they do, I can't even let go of my breath because of the smoldering look he's giving me. My heart starts ricocheting in my ribs, making me bite down on my lip and shift beside Shea so that he can't see my face. I don't take my eyes off of Nick's though. He's daring me to. I know he is, so I don't. I don't think I could even if I wanted to. I just want to get lost in those eyes and never be found.

After what seems like an eternity and stopping on every single floor, the elevator finally reaches the forty-fourth floor.

"See you later," Shea says, bumping Hendrix's fist before looking back at me. "I'll go up there when I get a break. Or come down, we'll be in ten."

I smile. "Sure."

"Hendrix, man. I didn't ask you if-"

Hendrix interrupts him by stepping out of the elevator for him to follow and signals me to get out with them, so I do.

"What's up?" Hendrix asks, tucking his phone in his pocket.

"I didn't introduce you to my producer, Nick," Shea says, signaling from Nick to Hendrix. "Nick, Hendrix Harmon. Hendrix, Nick Wilde."

Hendrix watches Nick for a moment and then nods slowly, a smile creeping up on his face. "Wilde. Nick Wilde. Holy shit. I've heard nothing but good things about you," he says, extending his hand out for Nick to shake.

They shake hands and exchange words while I stand there watching them, not knowing what to do. Shea finally steps in and re-introduces Nick and me.

"Oh that's right, you guys met in the airport," Shea says.

Nick and I nod and smile, looking at each other until

Hendrix clears his throat and tells them he'll join them in the studio at some point today.

"Yeah, come down whenever," Shea says, bumping Hendrix's fist, bumping my fist and walking away. "Number ten," he calls out over his shoulder.

"Catch you later," Hendrix says to Nick before he walks to the elevator again.

"Sure," Nick replies. He looks at me for a moment and opens his mouth to say something but thinks better of it and closes it again. "See you later," he says.

I smile. "Yep. Guess you'll have to."

I turn and begin to walk toward my brother, who's on the phone again.

"You look sinful in that dress," Nick murmurs in my ear, making me jump at his unexpected nearness.

Before I can even formulate words to thank him, he walks away, leaving me to stare at his broad shoulders and the way his arms swing when he walks. I come to the conclusion that he must have been an athlete before. What kind, I have no idea. The kind that was tall with perfectly structured muscles that melded around their perfectly built bones.

"Bee?" Hendrix says.

Blinking away my thoughts, I follow him into the elevator.

The rest of the day is similar to the previous week: I listen to endless demos, bang my head against the desk three times—purposely, and pray that I will stumble upon one artist that will blow my mind. I've come to the conclusion that work is only fun when it's not mandatory. I guess in a sense it's kind of like cooking. Everybody loves to cook until they actually have to cook every day. I don't know how to cook and I've never had to do it, but I would imagine it's as tedious as what I'm doing.

My phone rings around one o'clock when I'm just about to

doze off, and I jump from my seat and pick it up.

"Hello?" I answer on the second ring, feeling anxious even though I know it's probably Hendrix.

"Hey," Hendrix says. "You wanna go down with me to the studio? The guys are going to get lunch. I know you're hungry."

"Sure."

I hang up and stretch my arms over my head just as Hendrix is barging into my office.

"You could knock," I say.

"Sure, next time. Let's go. I only have thirty minutes to spare and I need to make sure Shea is actually working down there."

"When is the CD due?" I ask.

Hendrix raises his eyebrows. "Two months."

My mouth drops just as the elevator chime sounds. "What!" I try to process what that means. Two months to complete an entire album is insane, and I know for a fact Shea hasn't even started recording anything. "He's going on tour in like a week."

"Yeah. Why do you think he brought in Wilde?" Hendrix asks, pushing down the button to the forty-fourth.

I shrug. "I dunno. I've never heard of him before."

Hendrix frowns and turns to me as the doors open back up and we step out. "You've never heard of him? You? How can you never have heard of him?"

I roll my eyes. "If you're trying to make me feel like I've been living under a rock, you're succeeding. Who has he worked with?"

He chuckles and stands outside of studio ten looking in. "Everyone, Bee. You won't see his name on CDs though … he goes by the name *Shadow*." Hendrix tilts his head to look at me.

My mouth forms an "O" when realization sinks in. Of course I've heard of Shadow. He seems to be the go-to producer right now. My sister-in-law has gone on and on about what a genius he is. She obviously failed to mention how freaking hot he is.

"Sarah loves him," I comment.

He nods. "She does. Everyone does. He's the crème de la crème."

I watch Shea's head bobbing slowly inside the recording booth and Nick sitting in front of the soundboards with his back facing us. His hands move over the board, touching the knobs, turning here, tweaking there, and my mind wanders to places I wish wouldn't be in the realm of my imagination.

"I guess the name suits him if he doesn't wanna be seen, right?" I muse quietly.

"Guess so. Or maybe he plays on it since he lives under his father's shadow," Hendrix states as he opens the door, shutting out any further questions I may have about Nick.

"Good?" Hendrix asks Shea as he steps out of the booth.

"Yeah," Shea says, taking a swig of his water bottle. "We'll get it done."

I walk toward Shea and stand in front of him, tugging his arm to step away from Nick and Hendrix.

"He says you have to have this done in two months," I say, concerned. I really wish they wouldn't put this kind of pressure on artists. It kills me that they do.

"I know," Shea says, his green eyes dim. He falls back to the couch behind him and pulls me down with him, holding me to his chest. "I can do it."

"I can see if we can get an extension," I suggest quietly, hoping Hendrix doesn't hear me, even though I doubt he can since he's speaking to Nick.

"Nah, BK, I'm good. Just tired. Let's go to sleep together like old times," he murmurs as his eyes flutter shut.

I take a deep breath and adjust myself so that my weight doesn't crush him.

"He's gonna take a nap?" Hendrix asks, amused.

I shrug with my free shoulder. "He's exhausted, Hen. Leave him alone," I plead.

Hendrix shakes his head. "Doesn't matter to me, it's lunch time anyway. I'll be right back." He walks out of the studio and heads toward the elevators, leaving me sitting on the couch with Shea's arm draped around me and Nick sitting a couple of feet away by the soundboard. He still has his headphones on and I assume he's going over whatever they recorded today. I disentangle myself from Shea and walk over to where Nick is sitting, sinking into the seat beside him.

"How many tracks did you record today?" I ask, nodding at the recording booth.

"One so far. We're aiming for two," Nick says, not looking at me. I don't know why it bothers me so much that he hasn't looked at me since I walked in the room. It really shouldn't bother me since he did a whole lot of looking earlier.

"How many do you think you can record in a week?" I ask, swiveling my chair side to side and hitting his thighs with my knees. "Sorry."

Nick takes off the headphones and places them on the board, turning his seat to face me. "I'm not sure. It depends on him, really. We've been working on them—we just need to get them recorded. We should be fine by the end of the month. He has a lot of hits on here."

I smile, feeling a sense of pride in knowing I had something to do with Shea's success. Leaning forward, I run the tips of my finger over the knobs, careful not to move any of them. I can feel Nick looking at me and see his body move forward from the corner of my eye. His hands soon appear beside mine on the knobs and he slides one of the buttons down.

"You can touch now. You won't mess anything up. Put these on if you want," he suggests, sliding his earphones to me.

I pick them up and look at them for a moment. They're big, and I know they're comfortable and the sound is amazing because I have a similar pair of Beats of my own. Nick's are bigger, though, and they're more cushioned than the standard ones we have in our studios here in Harmon. I get a thrill placing them over my head, as if I'm uncovering another tiny little puzzle to who Nick Wilde is. I tilt my head to look at him and find his eyes searching my face. He looks from my hair to my eyes to my covered ears and finally back to my eyes and smiles. It's not the panty dropping smile I'm used to getting from him, it's a boyish-boy next door-I can't believe the hottest girl in high school is talking to me-kind of smile. And I fucking love it.

When I smile back, he leans into the microphone in front of him and clicks a button.

"Why don't you wear a ring?" His whisper is loud in my ears and I'm so surprised by it that I turn my head to look around the room, eyes wide. I see him chuckle, but don't hear it, so I assume anything he says into the microphone is only heard by me.

I frown, not understanding his question, but I'm scared to ask because I don't know how loud I'll sound. I don't want to wake up Shea.

Nick clicks the button again and runs the tips of his pointer down my hand slowly, making my breath hitch as he slides it up and down my ring finger.

"A ring, why don't you wear one?" he repeats, his eyes losing their playfulness the longer he looks into mine.

I open my mouth and close it, suddenly understanding why he would think that I would be married. I move my hands from under his and take the earphones off, untangling the cord from my hair.

"I'm not married," I respond, still trying to rid myself of the earphones.

He leans in and holds them, helping me take it out of my hair. "I thought you were … I heard somebody call you Mrs. Harmon this morning. And then yesterday in the street …"

I smile at the memory. "So what? You actively pursue married women?"

Nick presses his lips together to contain a smile. "Only the really beautiful ones that I can't stop thinking about."

I shake my head, still smiling. "How's Stephanie?"

Boom. *Okay, so that's probably not exactly what I should've said, but damn him if he thinks he's going to use me the same way guys apparently want to use me. I'm so sick of being second to everybody.*

Then he does something I don't expect: he erupts in laughter. His laugh is low and husky and has the most beautiful ring to it that I've ever heard. And the way his aqua eyes light up and he dips his head and throws it back, showing his straight white teeth makes me smile, despite the fact that he's laughing at something I don't understand.

"Damn. You're good," he says when he comes down from his laughing high.

I shake my head and exhale, looking back at Shea who's still lying on the couch looking like a rag doll.

"Maybe I should wake him up," I suggest, placing both hands on either side of my chair to stand. Nick covers the hand closest to his, stopping me. His face is serious; his light brown eyebrows drawn together when I look at him.

"You never answered me about Hendrix."

"You never answered me about Stephanie."

He exhales. "Are you always this stubborn?"

"Are you?" I counter with a raised eyebrow.

He chuckles and shakes his head. "Stephanie ... she's ... I don't know. We're not really in a relationship."

I roll my eyes and groan, wondering if that's how Shea used to describe me to the girls he used to screw along the way.

"Fair enough. Hendrix is my brother. The beautiful little girl is my niece."

Nick looks visibly shocked by this information, but says nothing more. I yank my hand from under his and stand, walking over to Shea.

"What about Shea? What is he?" Nick asks, his question stopping me from walking further.

I look over my shoulder and smile. "He's my best friend."

Nick's eyebrows rise as if he wasn't expecting that answer and I can see the disbelief written all over his face. I wish I could take Whiteout and go to town on it, but I would hate to erase any of his gorgeous features.

"Shea," I whisper, shaking him. "You have to wake up so you can eat something."

Shea mumbles and groans something about not getting enough sleep.

"Just let him sleep," Nick suggests. "I'll just keep setting up as many songs as I can to record on."

He shrugs as if it's no big deal for him to do this, and maybe it's not, but to me it is a huge deal that he would act so nice about it. Most of the "big time producers" that I've met are eye-roll worthy. They're all so nice in interviews and so humble in front of cameras, but you get them in a studio and they're all about work no play, as they should be. Anybody else would have gone all diva over Shea taking a nap during his recording time and Nick hasn't.

"What's your deal?" I ask, walking back to sit beside Nick. "Why are you so nice?"

The side of his lip turns up. "You think I'm nice?"

I shrug. "Well, yeah."

His eyebrows raise as he shakes his head. "You really haven't heard much about me, have you?"

"You haven't heard much about me either," I reply.

"True ... so let's remedy that. Tell me more," he says, shifting in his seat and crossing his ankle over his leg.

I laugh. "There's not much to tell. I just meant because you didn't know I was Hendrix's sister."

Nick nods. "What else are you?"

I shrug. "Chris and Roxana Harmon's daughter," I mutter, exhaling loudly and turning my head to look away. I hate having people know who my parents are. I wish it were something I could be proud of. I guess it should be since they both work hard and are so successful at what they do, but I can't bring myself to be happy for any of it. Most of the time when people find out whose daughter I am, they leach on to me to better their own agenda.

"I didn't ask who your family is, Brooklyn. I asked you who you are. I don't give a fuck about who your parents are."

I look back at him, stunned. Not because he doesn't care about who my parents are but because it gives me nostalgia about the last person who said that to me.

"I have to go," I say, standing quickly.

"You okay?" Nick asks, visibly confused.

"Yeah," I whisper. "I just remembered something I have to do."

I walk out before tears pool in my eyes.

CHAPTER EIGHT

Past

It was a hot summer day and I was lying out by the pool of my parents' Beverly Hills house waiting for my cousin Nina to wake up. Nina was staying with us for the summer, which I loved because nobody was ever home. My brother was seventeen at the time and wanted nothing to do with hanging out with thirteen-year-olds. I couldn't blame him. I knew how annoying we could be sometimes. My mother had just fired the longest nanny I'd had, Mildred, saying that she was trying to seduce my father. Mildred was fifty-five years old and my mother was delusional. I had a feeling that the real reason she let her go was because she heard me refer to her as my mother one night. To me that was what Mildred was, though. She was more of a mother to me than my own. She had been ever since she started looking after me when I was six years old. Roxana, on the other hand, gave birth to me. But giving birth doesn't make you a mother, much less a good one.

When Nina woke up, she found me by the pool, dozing off

as I let the rays hit my back.

"What are we going to do today?" she asked. "Mall?"

"Okay," I replied sleepily.

I told my driver, Todd, that we needed to go to the mall to shop for a party we were attending that night. One of the kids in school was having a birthday party and invited me. It was the first evening birthday party I would attend, so I was extra excited about it. After shopping we went back home and tried everything on. My mother barged into my room while I was pulling on a purple tube top.

"Oh, Brooklyn, how many cookies have you had this week?" she asked.

My excited face instantly fell. "I haven't had any," I lied. I'd only had two—how could she tell?

"Sure," she scoffed. "If you keep that up, I'll be able to pinch your fat."

I looked in the full-length mirror in front of me, horrified. I'd heard the way my mother spoke about muffin tops and "cellulite covered thighs." I'd heard the disapproval in her voice whenever she saw a friend of hers for the first time after a long time and she'd gained weight. "Wanda," she'd say, "you look so … fat." Just like that. The filter over my mother's mouth wasn't broken. She was just a bitch. That was something I'd learned from an early age.

"Yeah," I muttered quietly, wishing I didn't have to constantly diet to earn her approval, not that I would have it even if I looked like a skeleton.

"Where are you two going tonight, anyway?" my mother asked airily.

"Donovan's party," I replied.

"Donovan … Matthews?" she asked, seeming more interested.

"Yes."

My mother nodded, a smile spreading over her face that made me wonder what she was thinking. Of course she never said, she just turned around, her perfectly wavy, frizz-less hair bouncing as she did, and walked out. My mother walked with a grace one could only hope to perfect in one lifetime. She'd been in countless fashion shows and modeled for numerous designers. She was still, even at her age, one of the most sought out models. She had long dark hair like mine, honey brown eyes like my brother's, and a lean figure that made her look taller than she was. She had legs for days, my father loved to say. I always wished I did. The only thing I had for days was my ass, and I hoped to grow into it as I kept developing because it was calling a lot of unwanted attention from much older men.

When we got to Donovan's party that night, Nina went off to flirt with the first cute guy she spotted. I walked around talking to the girls from my class, ignoring the way they began to whisper to each other as soon as I walked away. A couple of them asked me if my brother was coming over, which I hated. I hated that the girls in my grade and the grade above mine had such big crushes on him. And I hated that the guys in my class all called my mom a MILF. It didn't disgust me more than it bothered me. I just hated that they paid attention to her but didn't even give me a second glance.

Sighing, I stepped outside and wandered off to sit by the pool, grabbing a soda on my way there.

"You here alone?" Ryan, a tall lanky kid in my class asked.

"With my cousin Nina," I replied.

"Oh. Nina. Yeah," he said with a laugh.

"What?" I asked confused.

He shook his head. His hair was strawberry blond, matching the strawberry freckles that bathed his cheeks. He had nice green eyes, big ones that always looked like they were in awe of one thing or another.

"She was trying to hit on me," he explained as he sunk down to the grass beside me.

"Ohhhh," I said, laughing. "Sorry about that."

He shrugged. "No biggie."

We sat there in comfortable silence, listening to the music pouring out of the speakers and the loud squeals of laughter emitted from the girls that were dancing and jumping around. I never understood the whole *shriek when I see my friend even though I just saw her yesterday in school*, so I just sat there rolling my eyes most of the night.

"Can I ask you for a favor?" Ryan said after a while.

I closed my eyes and lay down beside him on the grass. I didn't want to be rude because he was always so nice to me, but I felt like screaming, "Why? Why do people always want something from me?"

"Sure," I replied instead.

"Will you be my pretend girlfriend?" he asked.

My eyes popped open and I turned to him. "Pretend girlfriend?" I asked, completely shocked by what he was asking. "Why *pretend*?" I was annoyed and a little hurt. I didn't want a boyfriend. I didn't even like Ryan in that way, but why did it have to be a pretend thing? "Is it because of my parents? You want to pretend you're my boyfriend so people can say 'Oh, look how cool Ryan is. He's Brooklyn's boyfriend. He gets to go to her house and see her mom all the time.'" I imitated with a goofy voice even though my blood was boiling. I sat up quickly, too pissed off to sit there any longer.

He grabbed my arm to keep me from standing. "No! I don't give a fuck who your parents are, Brooklyn!" My eyes widened at his use of word. We didn't usually say bad words, even though some of the other kids in our class spoke like sailors behind the teachers' backs. "I need you to pretend because my father asked me if I was gay, and I said no, but I know he doesn't believe me."

My shoulders slumped. "Oh," I said. "I guess … are you?"

He shrugged. His eyes looked sad, all the light that was previously there had gone out. "I don't know," he whispered. "I think so."

I looked around, not knowing what to say or do. "Do … do you want to find out?" I finally asked.

His blond eyebrows crinkled. "How?"

"I dunno, maybe if you kiss me you'll see that you're not gay?" I suggested with a shrug.

Ryan laughed. "Okay."

So we did. We both leaned in, our lips touching ever so slightly until they met. That's as far as it got before we both pulled away, both looking equally as disturbed and disgusted.

"No?" I asked.

"No," he confirmed.

We shared a laugh and lay back down beside each other for the rest of the night.

"Well, boyfriend, I think I'm going to go home now," I said when I saw Nina walk outside.

Ryan smiled brightly. "So that's a yes? You'll be my girlfriend?"

I laughed and bumped him with my elbow. "Are gay guys supposed to be that excited about having a girlfriend?"

"A pretend one, yeah," he said, laughing as well.

"So I guess that's a yes," I said. It's not like I had anything to lose.

"Brooklyn," he said, standing and helping me up. "This will be the beginning of a beautiful pretend relationship."

I shook my head, unable to contain my smile. "I believe you."

And that was how my friendship with Ryan went from "just friends that talk here and there" to "pretend boyfriend and girlfriend that don't let each other breathe because we talked so much." And I loved it. Every moment of my relationship with Ryan was full of joy.

For a while.

Much like non-pretend relationships.

CHAPTER NINE

Present

I'm expecting Shea to call me at any moment. He's been in the studios downstairs for the past week and a half and has yet to tell me what he wants to talk to me about. I've made it a point to stay out of his way so he can focus on his album. We've been to lunch a couple of times, but other than that it's been hi and bye. Even when I leave for the day, he and Nick are holed up in the office working their asses off.

As if hearing my thoughts, my phone rings in my hand as I walk into the Harmon building. I glance down at my screen and see a text message from Sarah. I swipe it to read the entire thing, which is a thank you and a picture of Melody with the American Girl doll we bought when she was here. I smile, replying to her quickly and stuff my phone in my purse. I'll just go up and see Shea on my way to my office.

The elevator ride is, as usual, eternally long with all of the stops it makes on the way up. I'm fidgeting with the mustache scarf I wore today when we finally reach the forty-fourth floor.

It's a half-day for me today, so I dressed casual. It's not really a half-day of *work*, just a half-day of work in the office. I have a meeting with a band later today, but because I'm meeting them at a pub for lunch, I figured I would dress down.

"Heeey, look at you," Shea says as he holds the door open to the studio.

I smile and pick up the pace as I walk toward him, wrapping my arms around his middle to hug him. He smells of strong cigarettes so I know he's just coming back from a break.

"Yeah, I'm meeting some guys later," I explain, stepping out of the hug to look at him.

As usual, his dark hair is messy but sexy. His eyes are exhausted, but look happy to see me, which in turn makes me happy to have come by.

He leans against the door, pushing it further open and waits for me to walk past him. The scripted tattoo on his wrist catches my eye and I sigh. Every time I see it I remember the day he got it.

"I'm getting your name tatted on my chest," he joked.

"No, you're not!" I squealed, turning my naked body away from his.

"Yes, I am. I never want to let you go," he'd said before bringing me back to face him and kissing me into silence.

He did get the tattoo, which may be a reminder of me, but is mainly a stamp to remind him of his roots and where he came from.

"You always did like it," Shea says, smiling when he catches my eyes.

I smile back. "You did say it was for me, didn't you?" I joke.

He laughs his throaty laugh and ruffles his hair a couple of times. "It was a joke when I said it, but don't think it doesn't remind me of you every time I look at my hand." His voice is serious even though he's smiling, and I can feel my conflicted emotions brewing.

"Hey, Brooklyn," Nick says, his husky voice snapping me out of my reverie.

He's standing beside the bathroom door, stretching his arms over his head, letting the faded black Led Zeppelin shirt he has on ride above the dip of his ab muscles. Victorious V, Nina calls that. She says that as soon as a guy takes off his shirt and exhibits the Victorious V, you're done for. Usually I laugh at that, mainly since I've been with guys that have it. Shea sort of has one, but he's thin. Nick's is the meaning of a Victorious V. My mouth is watering just thinking about tracing it and the defined muscles above it with my tongue. He has what I like to call washboard abs. With that and his golden tan, ocean blue eyes, and dark blond hair that he styles into the perfect faux hawk he looks like he could be on the cover of a magazine.

"I like your style today," Nick adds, his lips stretching into a knowing smile, like he knows exactly what kind of dirty thoughts I'm having of him. I blink rapidly and swallow my desire for his arrogant ass and smile.

"Hey, Nick," I say, smiling back. "What is your tattoo of?" I ask, pointing at his now covered ribcage.

"You seem to really like that tattoo, huh?" he asks, pressing his lips together to contain a smile.

"BK loves tats," Shea says, stepping in. "She has some nice ones … but they're in very private areas," he adds in a tone that leaves no question as to if he's seen them, which makes my face instantly hot.

Nick's face darkens at this, his jaw tensing as he looks away toward the soundboard before looking back at me. "I'm sure they're very nice," he says, clearing his throat.

I almost call bullshit because they are not in very private

areas. I have one on my pelvis, the other one is by my ankle. I don't correct Shea, though, for some reason I kind of like seeing the look on Nick's face when Shea pushes my buttons, even though I don't know why the look is there to begin with.

When Nick takes a seat in front of the soundboard and busies himself, I shoot Shea a dirty look and punch him in the arm.

"What?" Shea asks with a laugh. "What'd I do?"

"You're an asshole," I huff.

Shea laughs, plops down on the couch and takes out a Philly wrapper and some marijuana.

I gape at him. "You're seriously going to roll a joint in here?"

Shea shrugs. "You act like the people in studios one through eight aren't coked out."

My mouth drops open, but I pick it up quickly because it truly doesn't surprise me that they are. "Is that all you're doing?" I ask quietly. I don't have to specify what I mean by that because he knows exactly what I'm asking him.

Shea stops rolling and narrows his eyes at me. "Of course it is!"

I shake my head. "Just asking."

"A little weed never killed anybody, Brooklyn," Shea says in a defensive tone.

I roll my eyes. "Save it for somebody who hasn't been to-" I stop short, remembering that we're not alone, and look over my shoulder to find Nick watching me intently. "Whatever. What did you need to talk to me about?" I ask Shea.

"Oh. I want you to go on tour with me," he says nonchalantly.

I hear Nick drop something loud behind me, but I'm too struck by what Shea's just asked me to look back.

"*What?*" I ask, completely bewildered. When Shea lights

up his joint and takes a drag, looking at me like he doesn't understand why I'm shocked, I know he's serious. That's when I start laughing hysterically. "You are completely out of your mind."

He blows out smoke, the powerful smell of freshly cut wet grass filling the air immediately. "Why? It'll only be for a few shows. I'm doing you a favor," he says.

My eyebrows crinkle. "How?" I ask, picking up my long hair and holding it away from my face, hoping that I don't smell like a pothead when I get out of this room, but knowing that I'll most likely smell like Bob Marley himself.

"Because," he says, inhaling and exhaling again, "we have a lot of opening acts that are unsigned in some of our shows."

I shake my head in disbelief. "That makes no sense."

"It's true," Nick says. I turn around, crossing my arms against my chest, waiting for him to continue. "There are a couple in California."

I nod. "There's talent everywhere, though. Why would I travel to California when I just came from there? I know about a lot of them, they're good ... but not good enough."

Nick shrugs with one shoulder and turns back to the turntable, dismissing me. I let out a breath and look at Shea again. His muddy green eyes are becoming glossy and content. I mumble my goodbyes and walk toward the door.

"You haven't heard of Slate," Shea says, effectively stopping me from walking out.

My shoulders slump and I let go of the door handle. "I'm listening."

"There's a group of guys out there—they'll be in our show in San Francisco," Shea starts. I stiffen and immediately shake my head. There's no way in hell I'm going there. "Hear me out, Bee. Please," Shea pleads quietly. I jump at his proximity. I was completely unaware that he'd gotten up and walked over to me.

"I can't, Shea." My voice is wavering as I say the words.

Shea turns my body to face him and wraps his arms around me, pulling me to his chest. The smell of weed doesn't even bother me as I inhale. Because I'm wearing flats I'm eye level to his cheek. None of the guys I've been with are much taller than me. My eyes are filling with tears as he holds me so I begin to blink rapidly, unwilling to let my feelings show, but it's too late, I realize as I look over his shoulders and into Nick's eyes.

I can tell he's uncomfortable with this. His eyes are unreadable, but I can see it in the way he's sitting. His posture looks stiff. His forearms are clutching the sides of his seat as if it's the only thing from keeping him there. He frowns at me, silently asking me if I'm okay. That's when I decide this is too much for me. I cannot allow myself to cry in front of them.

Clearing my throat, I step away from Shea's arms. "I'll think about it, okay?"

Sighing loudly, Shea pulls on the ends of his hair. "You're not gonna go. I know you."

"I'm sure they'll perform somewhere else," I counter.

"No, Bee, they won't. Not everyone has the luxury of traveling to perform. You know that," he insists.

I throw my head back with a groan. "I'll let you know by tonight. I gotta go. I have things to take care of before I meet with this band today."

Shea pulls me into a tight hug and lets go quickly. "You know you're my girl, right?" he says.

"Shea, let's get moving," Nick booms, interrupting my reply.

I walk out of the studio and go upstairs with my heart in my throat, unsure of what to do. If Shea is insisting that I see the artists, it means they're good. He knows how picky I am.

And I want to get as much new talent as I can. I just don't know if I'm willing to open old wounds in order to get them.

"I can't just go," I protest to Nina over drinks. I called her when I got out of my meeting with the band, who seemed very enthusiastic to meet with me and give me their demo. I promised them I would call them in a couple of days, and I tried to give them my full attention throughout our meal together, but my mind just wasn't there. The only thing I've thought about all day is my conversation with Shea.

"I actually agree with you," Nina says, picking at the shrimp appetizer we're sharing. "What are you supposed to do? Stay on the bus?"

I shrug. "I don't know—we didn't talk specifics."

Nina's brown eyes go wide. "That's the first thing you need to do. Set boundaries and shit."

I let out a laugh at her "and shit" because those ugly little words hold so much promise in them. I know she's right, though.

"He wants me to go to California with him," I say under my breath, half hoping she doesn't even hear me.

"Aha?" she probes.

I let out a breath and close my eyes. "He wants me to go to San Fran ... specifically."

Nina gasps and drops her fork. "Holy shit," she breathes.

I open my eyes and nod. "Yep."

"Damn ... you want me to go with you?" she asks.

Exhaling, I shake my head. "Thanks. I can do it. I just have to mentally prepare myself. But I can do it."

She nods, giving me a small smile as she leans in to hold

my hand. "You're so strong, Bee. Much stronger than the girl who last went there. You'll be fine."

I continue to nod and swallow the lump in my throat. "I know."

Throughout our meal I send Hendrix's driver, Marcus, a text message letting him know to pick me up soon. Nina insists that she's going to accompany me to Harmon so she can be there when I tell Shea my decision to go. I roll my eyes at her and tell her she's stupid, but I'm too curious to see how this is going to play out to stop her.

When we finish eating, I text message Shea to make sure he's still recording and when he doesn't respond, I take it as a yes.

"This should be fun," Nina comments with a smile on our drive over.

I laugh. "You're so bad. I can practically see the bitchy schemes going on inside your head."

Nina nods, twisting her lip. "Hell yeah. I haven't seen that fucker in six months."

I shake my head and bite down on my smiling lip. "I wonder what will happen with the album … I guess he'll have to record on the road. That royally sucks. It's not like they can finish in a week."

Nina purses her lip again. "You're royally fucked," she throws at me. "You're going on the road with Shea AND his hot ass producer? What do you think Shea would say if you hooked up with him?"

I shrug. "Who knows? He'll probably act like he cares until he finds another floozy."

She sniggers. "Floozy. Mom calls me that sometimes."

"With good reason," I mutter.

She slaps me on the arm. "You're such an asshole."

I shrug in response.

"Turn around," she says suddenly. "I wanna fix your hair. It's a complete mess."

I turn and close my eyes as she massages my scalp and uncoils my curls from one another.

"You have the prettiest hair, Bee," she muses, twirling my hair around her fingers.

"Thanks. I could totally fall asleep right now," I mumble drowsily.

"Well, we're here."

"Of course we are," I groan. I have one good thing happen to me today and it's cut short.

When I see the elevator shutting, I shout for them to hold it, knowing what a pain it is to wait for one. I don't factor in the time, and am a little embarrassed when we're only greeted by two guys, both known rappers, going up to the studios. They laugh and joke about my screaming for a second before they start trying to flirt with us.

"Well, if you're into plays you can go see mine," Nina suggests as we step out.

"Is it another naked play?" I ask with a laugh, laughing harder when a blush begins to creep up on her face.

Nina rolls her eyes exaggeratedly. "I wasn't naked, dammit!"

The guys are very much into the conversation now that they've heard the word *naked*. They continue to sweet talk all the way to the tenth door, which is where I stop.

"Oh you're here to see Shea?" Cam asks, detangling one of his long flashy chains from the other.

"Yep," I respond. "Well, it was good meeting you guys," I say, holding the doorknob.

"Oh, it's like that?" Cam asks, moving closer to me now.

His dark eyes move down my body and stay glued to my

butt and I let out an annoyed breath. It's such a wondrous thing, the mind of a man. They don't care what your body language is saying because the only thing they take the time to actually look at is your body, not the way it's turning them down. They see tits and ass and they're blind. Not that I have tits, but my ass makes up for that … or so I've been told by the perverted men that are awed by it.

"What's it supposed to be like?" I ask, raising an eyebrow.

Nina is still yapping her mouth off to the other guy about her naked and non-naked plays. I swear the girl doesn't know how to shut the hell up. Once she starts talking about herself, it's over. The doorknob turns from inside and I stumble back slightly into a hard body.

"Yeah, it's like that, motherfucker," Nick booms behind me, making my eyes widen at his tone, which has a different effect on Cam, seeing his eyes light up like he's seeing Santa Claus.

"Holy shit! Dame, did you know Shadow was up in this bitch?" he says excitedly. Both guys completely forget about Nina and me and have a freaking fan-guy moment over Nick "Shadow" Wilde.

Nina shoots me a confused look like she doesn't understand how talking to Nick could possibly be more exciting than listening to her talk about herself. I smile and reach for her arm, pulling her in behind me.

"When will you be done with the one with the fine ass? I know how fast you get bored, boss," Cam says to Nick. I stop walking toward the booth and turn around to look at Nick and listen to his answer. I don't care what he tells him, it doesn't matter to me either way, but I'm curious to see what he'll say.

Nick's blue eyes bore into mine as he answers. "I haven't even gotten started with that one." My heart, which is clearly at odds with my thoughts, does an unwanted skip.

Cam and Dame laugh and throw some "Ooohs" in there, slapping each other like it's the funniest thing they've heard. A part of me wants to be upset at their little talk, but I've been around this kind of thing too long to let it bother me.

"Well, sweetheart, you call me when you need a shoulder," Cam says, addressing me now.

"Not gonna happen," I snap. I don't even want to turn around because I don't want him looking at my ass again. Nina's busy on her phone so she's not even paying attention anymore, and I want to strangle her for always abandoning ship when it's fucking sinking.

"All right, guys, I'll see you later," Nick says, closing the door.

"Remember, offer stands," Cam calls out.

"Give it a rest, Cam," Nick says, the threat in his voice unmistakable. "The only person she's calling is me." He closes the door, putting an end to the debacle, and I can still see the guys laughing and bumping fists as they walk off.

"Guys are such fucking pigs," I mutter.

Nick lets out a laugh. "Yeah, they are. Maybe the next one you choose will be a man, not a guy," he says, emphasizing the words slowly.

I narrow my eyes. "And let me guess … you know just the right person?"

He shrugs. "I have two brothers. I'm sure one of them is your type."

I try really, really hard to not look surprised at his words, but my mouth drops open on its own accord.

"Oh, that's it," Nina chimes in from the couch, finally putting her phone away. "You two are meant for each other."

Nick laughs his carefree boyish laugh, and even though I feel like an idiot, I find myself laughing along with him because his laughter is contagious. His entire demeanor changes and his eyes light up in such a way that they remind me of the sun reflecting the beach on a sunny day, it's spellbinding.

"What's up? BK! Nina-licious," Shea greets us excitedly, causing me to tear my eyes away from Nick's and walk over to him, rolling my eyes at his nickname for my cousin.

"Hey," I say, giving him a half hug.

Nina walks up to us and greets Shea with the same half hug before letting go and looking at him for a moment. "You're smoking again?" she snaps, then looks at me pissed off. "Nope. You're not going."

I laugh. "What are you, my mother?" I ask.

"Your mother," Nina scoffs with an eye roll. "Please."

"Touché," I mutter.

"I would never let her touch that shit, Nina!" Shea says loudly.

"Yeah, just like you would never-"

"Both of you, shut up! I am an adult!" I scream, stopping her from finishing the rant she's about to go on. "Jesus. What is wrong with you people?" I say, shaking my head. I'm interrupted by my ringing phone, which I take out and look at, frowning when I see my dad's number on my screen. "I'll be back, gotta take this."

I sprint outside and shut the door behind me and answer the phone. "Hey, Dad."

"It's about goddamn time you answer your phone!" he huffs.

Here we go. I exhale, hating the way my stomach drops when he reprimands me. "This is the first call I've gotten from you."

"Well, this is the third time I've called. What are you doing? Did you meet with the band? Did you hear the demos I sent yesterday? Are you scheduled with anyone else this week? What happened at that bar on Saturday?" He spits out question after question not even pausing to give me enough time to answer him. I know from the sound of his voice that he's exhausted and has been pissed off ten ways to Sunday today, so I tread carefully and wait until I know he's finished.

"How was your day?" I ask. "How have you been for the past two weeks? How are you settling in? Are you getting along with your brother?" I say, not letting my voice sound as pissed off as I am. I'm more upset at the saddening realization that my parents just do not give a shit about me, but rather than start crying over it, I've learned to accept it. Accepting it doesn't loosen the grip on my throat, though.

He exhales loudly. "How's everything, Brooklyn?" he mutters, completely uninterested.

"I did meet with the band. I liked them, but not enough. You would hate them. I heard the demos—there were three that stood out. I'm already on those. I'll have meetings set up by tomorrow afternoon. The bar band was fine, nothing outrageous." Tears prick my eyes as I talk and I continue swallowing them down, speaking slowly so the dam doesn't burst while I'm on the phone.

"Good. Good. At least some people around here are reliable. All right, baby girl, I'll talk to you soon," he says, cooing the last part, I'm sure for my benefit.

"Okay," I respond quietly, blinking rapidly. "How's Mom?" I ask, wishing I didn't care.

"She's fine. Spoke to her last night. She should be getting back at the end of the week so I'm sure you'll hear from her then," he says. "I gotta go."

He hangs up and because our conversation was two minutes worth of nothing personal, I feel empty. Shoving the phone in the back pocket of my jeans, I walk to the window on the other side of the elevator. I place my fingertips on it and look at the darkening sky over me, taking deep breaths to keep my emotions at bay.

"Everything okay?" Nick asks, behind me.

I nod, still looking outside, not daring to turn around and face him. I can't let him see the hurt look I know I have on my face.

"Fine," I reply, my voice steady. "Why'd you come out here?"

He scoffs. "I wasn't going to stand around and listen to more of that bickering. Jesus. Your cousin acts like a ninety-year-old cat lady with no friends."

Laughter sputters out of my lips and I finally bring myself to turn around. His face is downcast, but he brings his eyes up to me and gives me a small smile that tells me the joke was for my benefit, though I have no doubt that Nina yapping away.

"She kind of is like that, huh?" I say, taking one last deep breath.

Nick nods and exhales. "So you're going?"

I look down the hallway and back at him with questioning eyes.

"No, I mean on tour," he clarifies.

Down casting my eyes from his, I twirl the ends of my hair, shifting my feet. "It's only for a couple of days here and there," I say nonchalantly.

"You realize he's still into you, right?" Nick says.

I bring my gaze back to his probing eyes. "It doesn't matter."

He raises an eyebrow and leans against the wall behind him, swinging one ankle on top of the other and crossing his arms. "No?"

I shake my head slowly, trying to figure out why I feel like

I need to explain myself to him. "We dated, if you can even call it that, a while ago. A whiiiile ago," I say. Nick nods for me to continue. "When we were teenagers. Like I said, long time ago. Over the years he's always been my constant."

"Your booty call," Nick says.

I cringe, hating how that sounds coming out of his mouth for some reason. "Exactly."

"And you ended things? Or he did?" he asks.

"I did," I say. "Why are you so interested in this, anyway?"

Nick laughs lightly. "For the same reason that you're entertaining my questions."

I frown, thinking about that and look at him, not understanding what that means.

He shakes his head slowly, pushing himself off of the wall and strides towards me. I just stand here, watching the way he moves. He's so graceful. I don't understand how such a tall, defined body can move that gracefully, as if he's practiced the walk countless times. *Maybe he used to model underwear or something.* It's a dumb thought, but it's the only one that comes to mind. He stops when he's standing so close to me that I have to crane my head to look at him. His blue eyes are heated, burning into mine and making my breath hitch.

"Oh shit, sorry," Nina says.

I slump my shoulders and Nick shakes his head with a low chuckle. I start walking back toward the studio, my heart still beating wildly at the possibilities of what might've happened if we hadn't been interrupted.

"Fifty cats," he says quietly behind me, making me laugh.

When we all walk back into the studio, Nina and Shea are getting along again, but from the look on Shea's face I know Nina laid it down for him. He looks pissed off at me and I'm wondering what the hell she's told him. It can't be that bad. I mean, what have I told her? Holy shit, did she tell him about Nick? Not that there's anything to tell. Damn it, why does this guy make me feel like a child with my hand in the cookie jar?

"What?" I ask Shea.

"Nothing. Nina pisses me the fuck off like no other. She thinks you need a fucking mother to fill in for the sorry ass one you have. She apparently doesn't realize that you've done well all by yourself," he spits, shooting daggers at Nina.

She rolls her eyes. "Whatever. I just don't want her to be around drugs. Big fucking deal."

"Don't worry, Shea will have Gia to keep him busy," I say, smiling at Shea, who looks even madder that I brought her up. "Oh, what? You got bored of her too?"

Shea narrows his eyes at me. "I never got bored of you!"

My eyes widen at his outburst. I look over my shoulder but see that Nick has earphones on and is playing with knobs so he can't hear us.

"Shhh!" I reprimand.

"Oh, this is rich. You have a thing for Shadow?" Shea asks with a laugh. "This gets better by the second."

"I don't have a thing for anybody, Shea. I'm going to check out the stupid people you want me to check out and then I'm done."

Shea shrugs. "Whatever. Are we done? We're wasting precious recording time here."

Nina and I both nod. Nina gets up and slaps the back of his head before giving him a kiss and walks up to Nick to say goodbye. I follow behind but don't even say goodbye to Shea, I'm that mad at his pissy attitude with me. He's telling me he's doing me a favor by introducing me to the acts he wants me to see, but I'm doing him the favor by going.

Shea comes up behind me and grabs my arm, pulling me

into a hug. "I'm sorry, Bee. I just got a lot going on."

I nod against him. "Yeah, well, stop being a douchebag. I don't care how big of a favor you think you're doing for me. It's hard for me to go back there."

Shea nods, his cheek brushing against mine. "I know. I know."

He lets go and walks into the recording booth, signaling to Nick that he's ready.

"I'll see you, then," I say to Nick, who looks up at me for a second before going back to what he's doing.

"Yeah. Until we meet again," he says, gazing at me again for less than a second.

I don't know what it is about him that makes me want to grab his face in place so that he'll never look at anything but me. I'm not sure what bothers me more: the realization or the fact that I can't remember feeling this way about anybody before him.

I keep hearing hype about this girl, Christina Ferucci, and have been dying to catch her performance. She's supposed to be in a little place called The Bitter End tonight, which hosts a lot of open mics for new artists, and that's how I find myself pulling up to the small venue on Bleecker Street. A lot of amazing artists have performed here in the past. I caught a Lady Gaga show here before she was "The Lady Gaga." It's always nice when you get to see people sing before they become household names. When somebody stood in front of Harmon the other day handing out flyers, I knew it was a sign for me to catch a show here.

As I walk through the old wooden doors, I spot a small table in the dark towards the back and make a beeline toward

thoughts. I hate that my heart is painted in my eyes for all to see. He tugs my hair again softly and moves closer to me.

"Professionally," he adds, near my ear again in a way that makes my insides tingle at his voice.

"I didn't say anything," I protest quietly.

"You didn't have to," he responds just as low.

I breathe out through my nose, pursing my lips, wishing that he would move away from me so that my heart can roll back into my chest from the place in my throat it's perched on.

We speak a little more about music, about siblings, about random things—nothing of real significance, even though everything is significant. And then Paige walks on stage with her guitar, introducing herself before she begins to sing, and I forget that Nick is beside me. The strumming of her guitar and her soulful voice make me want to smile, cry, and cheer at the same time. The combination speaks that much to me. It's that beautiful. Nick doesn't say a word; he seems as submerged as I am. We both, maybe out of coincidence, turn our faces to each other at the same time when Paige sings: *You've tied yourself, through and through, my skin, my bones.*

Our hands inch closer together below the table as we look into each other's eyes, the tips of our fingers barely touching. We listen to the rest of her song like that, looking into each other's eyes, singers brushing against each other but not close enough to hold hands. And when it ends and the crowd begins to clap, he blinks, I blink, and we begin to clap as well. A moment gone, just like that. But the stupid seed of hope has been planted. Just like that.

CHAPTER TEN

Even though it's been a couple of days since the bar incident, I'm still smiling over it. Walking through the Harmon doors, I add a little speed to my steps and step into the elevators just before they begin to shut.

"Close call," Nick comments behind me, the sound of his voice making my blood pump faster.

I let the strap of my oversized purse fall and position it between my legs so that it doesn't bump anyone before letting myself turn to face him. His dark blond hair is styled into a messier faux hawk than usual and he has sprinkles of stubble along his chiseled jaw. My fingers twitch to touch his face, to let the tiny hairs prickle my fingertips, so I curl them tighter on the strap of my purse. Nick's eyes have a seductive hooded look as he peers down at me, a look that makes my heart run marathons inside my chest. Jesus, that stare could make anybody crumble.

"Hi," I say, my voice barely audible over the chatter going on around us. The elevator stops and some people push to get out, making me stumble onto Nick's chest.

"Hi," he whispers, holding my arms as he steadies me. I hear an apologetic mutter behind me but can't turn away from Nick's eyes to acknowledge it.

"Hi," I respond again, stupidly. How many times can we say hello to each other in six seconds?

Nick chuckles and I close my eyes, relishing the sound of it. I realize, as I have my eyes closed, that even though I'm not looking at him anymore, I'm still completely immersed in him. His scent overpowers my senses and for a moment I feel like I can't possibly in New York City because I'm breathing such fresh air. He tugs on my hair once, making me open my eyes and I see him watching me with a bemused expression. He grins at me after a moment.

"What are you doing for lunch?" he asks.

"Nothing of importance," I respond as the elevator opens again.

Nick moves out of the way, his body switching places with mine so that he can get out. He lowers his face to mine, brushing his lips against my cheek and I think he's going to kiss me goodbye, but his lips continue to my ear. "Lunch at one." He doesn't ask, he tells, and then he steps out, not turning back around to see my face or hear my answer. He knows I'm going. I don't know whether to smile or frown, so I do both.

I'm having a shit day. My father ripped me a new one for not being able to close a deal with one rock band. The band was fine, but the lead singer was a complete jerk off and wouldn't agree to anything. He stormed off after Hendrix told him that he needed to use a bus for his tour just like everybody else. The rest of the band stuck around for a while with their manager and decided to reschedule when they could get on the same page. As soon as I leave the conference room, I get a text from Allie telling me that the last microphone we were waiting on doesn't look anything like my design.

So by the time my office phone rings, I'm practically crying at my desk.

"Hello?" I answer, wondering why Stacey let any call go through after I asked her not to.

"Hey, beautiful, it's one o'clock," Nick says on the other end, his voice low and husky. My heart speeds up.

"I don't think I'll be good company right now," I mumble helplessly.

"Bad day?" he asks.

"You have no idea."

"I can make it better for you," he says, his voice dropping down a notch, making my breath hitch.

"Yeah? How?" I ask, humoring him.

"Hmmm … so many ways. Do I have to pick one?"

God, I wish I could just record his voice. Record it and make a podcast out of it so I can listen to it every morning. And afternoon. And evening. Definitely evening.

"Just one," I whisper, my voice a little breathy.

"First, I'm going to pick you up, even if that means I have to wrap those sexy legs around me and hitch up that tight black skirt you're wearing up to your waist. Then, I'm going to take you," he pauses. I close my eyes at the idea. "Downstairs. I'm going to toss you in the back of a cab and squeeze myself inside." He pauses again and his voice is deeper, more sensual. The way he's accentuating every word he speaks is making it hard for me to breathe. "Beside you. And last, I'm going to take you to the best little Indian restaurant I know, where they have the most delicious curry you will ever have. So good, you'll be licking your fingers. And if you're really lucky, I'll be licking your fingers."

I swallow loudly. "Okay."

I can hear the smile in his voice when he says, "Okay. See you soon."

There's a knock on my door shortly after and Nick walks in, his eyes sweeping over my space quickly before they land on mine and stay there.

"Ready?" he asks.

"Ready." I nod with a smile as I get up and grab my purse.

When we step outside, we catch Hendrix and Shea talking in the hallway, and before we know it, it turns into a part of four. Instead of Indian like we originally planned, we end up going for pizza, Hendrix's favorite. Nick tells Hendrix where his apartment building is, which is right by Hendrix's place and that gets my brother to go off on a tangent about the real estate market right now. Shea is looking at his phone, Hendrix is talking like he swallowed a parrot and Nick and I continue to steal glances at each other throughout our walk.

We take a stroll by Central Park when we're finished and stand by some of the carriages. Shea is going on and on about how the only time he rode one of the carriages was with me and how cold it was that night. I vaguely remember the night he's talking about, so I just nod and smile. When I look at Nick, he's staring at the horse in front of us, his jaw clenched. The horse sneezes a little too close for comfort, and we back away immediately.

"Totally not how I planned on this going," Nick says under his breath.

I laugh. "I'd say. Pizza is a far cry from that delicious curry you promised."

He turns to me; the hungry look in his eyes making my insides clench. "I would've licked the grease of the pizza off your fingers if I didn't think your brother would start a fight."

My heart stammers in my chest and I'm rendered speechless.

"How's the microphone thing going?" Shea asks, interrupting us.

"Good," I say with a shrug.

"Do you only design microphones?" Nick asks as we fall into an easy stride.

"Really nice ones," Shea offers, pretending to be nonchalant, but I know he's following our conversation because I can feel his eyes on us every time Hendrix stops talking to him.

"For now. I want to work on headphones too," I say shyly. I'm not sure why talking about this with him makes me feel like a schoolgirl telling her science teacher she wants to work for NASA.

Nick cocks his head as he studies me and a sly grin spreads. "Really? Are you going to custom make one for me?"

I raise an eyebrow. "You'll have to wait in line."

He playfully pouts his lower lip and I have to force myself not to look at it for too long. "I'm not one of your VIPs?" he asks, his voice soft, making me squint my eyes against the sun to look at his face again, to make sure that his question is just a joke.

I smile, seeing the small smile tugging the corners of his mouth. "Not yet," I answer, shaking my head.

"We'll have to work on that then. I don't like being just a regular customer," he says, his voice low again, with a hint of seduction. The way he's looking at me makes me think he's talking about something else entirely.

"Maybe you're not just a regular customer," I counter, not knowing what the hell I'm talking about or doing.

We stop walking at a red light and Nick moves closer to me so that his chest touches my arm when he turns to me. "Yeah, but how do I get the VIP status?" he asks, over my ear now, making me shiver.

I purse my lips as if I have to think about this really hard. As if he's not affecting me the way he knows he is. "You have to work for it."

"Oh, I plan on it," Nick says, stepping back so that I can see the mischievous streak in his eyes.

Somehow I manage to whisper a "we'll see" that makes him laugh.

"It's the banter, that's what it is," Allie, whom I haven't spoken to in days, tells me about Nick and my attraction to him. "The newness of it. You know how it is in the beginning."

But that's the thing, I don't know how it is in the beginning because the only "real" thing I have to compare it to is Shea. Other than Shea, I've dated two guys and they weren't what I considered to be boyfriends. There was no "let's get to know each other" phase with them. It was more like we liked the same things, hung out with the same crowds, so we hooked up. Literally. That's all we did. I can't even give you an example of a real conversation I had with either one of them other than "So, is your dad looking for new talent? Because I'm in this band and ..." That's usually how it goes, so I've always been cautious to let guys in. It's not that I think they only want to be with me for who my father is, but more times than not they don't even try to hide it. I'm not interested in being anybody's pretend girlfriend. I already did that once and that didn't turn out so well in the end.

"Maybe. I dunno," I answer, taking a bite of my apple and holding the phone away so I can chew.

"Will you be able to make it to the meeting?" Allie asks hopefully.

I try not to groan outwardly. I had completely forgotten about the damn meeting we have scheduled with a company that's interested in selling the microphones in their store. It would be huge for Fab so I know I need to make the time. With my job at Harmon and now this tour thing with Shea, I'm not sure how I can do it.

"I'm really going to try, Al," I promise quietly.

I know this is the last thing she wants to hear right now. As it is, she's been taking the brunt of the workload. I don't even bother to tell her all the stuff I've had going on at Harmon. The only thing worse than having to hear an apology one hundred times is listening to the lame excuses it comes with. Seriously, if excuses are butts, apologies are like the whores they belong to: overused.

Allie exhales loudly. "I know you're busy, Bee, but this is supposed to be a partnership."

My shoulders slump at that and I nod slowly, tossing the rest of my apple aside. "I know," I whisper. "I swear I'll try to be there."

After discussing the earphone line we want to launch soon, we change the subject and start talking about lighter things, which takes a huge weight off my chest … until she brings up Shea's tour again.

"So you're really going to do it?" she asks hesitantly.

"It's only a couple of shows. I don't know why everyone is so worried about it," I say, sounding a little annoyed. I'm not annoyed at her, and I'm sure she knows it. It doesn't matter, she's used to me being a bitch sometimes.

"I'm just saying," she starts.

"Please don't," I groan. "I swear, if I have to hear the drug talk one more time I'm going to shoot myself. I mean, seriously, I feel like I'm in fifth fucking grade and going through the damn TRUTH program all over again."

Allie laughs. "You're such a clown. It's true though, Bee. It's scary—you know why we're worried," she says seriously.

I sigh. "I know. I get it, but why isn't anybody worried about Shea? He's around crazy things all the time and he gets by."

"Because nobody cares about Shea, Brooklyn, we care about *you*," she chimes.

It breaks my heart to hear her say something like that about Shea. He's been friends with Allie almost as long as I have and she knows that he doesn't have many people that care about him at all. Shea's mother is there for him, but mainly to collect a paycheck. She's as big of a gold digger as my mother, which is probably why they get along so well.

"Yeah, thanks," I mumble half-heartedly. "I'll email you the designs I owe you tomorrow. We'll talk soon. Sorry about the workload, Al."

"You know I'm fine with it, Bee. I'll let you know when it gets to be too much," Allie says and I can hear the smile in her voice.

I am so thankful for this girl it's not even funny.

After hanging up with her, I get moving and sort through the demos I have yet to listen to. I took the day off from working at the office so I could listen to them at home instead. I like being holed up in dark places while I listen to music with my eyes closed, it's the only way I can truly feel it. Even when I go to concerts, I find myself closing my eyes the majority of the show. You would think that defeats the purpose of the ticket price, but it makes it more enjoyable for me. It emphasizes the tone in their voice and the way they hit each note. I *live* music when I listen to it that way. I click the button to lower the motorized shades in my room. I can tell it has rarely been used by the squeak it does when it begins to descend. I'm sure most people would rather bask in the sun and enjoy the sense of hope you're supposed to feel as you look out into the perfect New York skyline from this high up.

It's a view that has been painted and photographed count-less times. Postcards are adorned with this view and sent all over the world with all kinds of messages: mainly happy, hope-ful, and probably delusional messages. That's the lovely thing about big cities—the thing that I love most about them—they have this way of wrapping you up and comforting you in their blanket of beautiful lies. I guess I can relate because that's much of how my own life has been: a basket of beautiful lies. One I've learned to carry around, even though I don't like to pick from it. The moment I do, I become anguished, and when I become her I lose myself.

Closing my eyes, I fall back onto my bed, letting the dark-ness cocoon me while I listen to the woman I've decided is my new favorite artist, thanks to Nick: Paige Chaplin. Her voice is so melodic and filled with a sorrow that matches my own. I take a deep breath and get lost in her lyrics, letting her take me back to a time where there was very little light left in me. A time that I thought I wouldn't survive. A time where I didn't care if I did.

CHAPTER ELEVEN

Past

I was holding Ryan's hand when we barged through the door of my house that afternoon. I swung the door carelessly behind us, letting it shut with a loud thump that made us both jump and laugh.

"Brooklyn!" my mother reprimanded from down the hall.

Groaning, I rolled my eyes. "Sorry, Mom!"

Ryan rolled his eyes back at me, mimicking my annoyed face. I let go of his hand and pinched his cheeks the way he hated, and he moved away, laughing.

"Ryan?" my mother called out.

I nearly shrieked my frustration at that. She loved Ryan and loved it when he came over to our house. His parents were wealthy, old money, and that was enough to impress her.

"Yes, Mrs. Harmon," he responded, shrugging at me when I shot him a dirty look.

For the past three years Ryan and I had been a pretend couple, and it had been the most fun I'd ever had. We went to parties together and the movies, he came over to my house, and I went over to his house. His parents were very uptight about the company he kept, but somehow they approved of me, probably because of who my parents were. We never gave them a reason to question what we were doing in our bedrooms, not that there was anything for them to question. There's not much trouble a gay teen can get into with a straight teen when they're in a bedroom together, not sexually anyway.

"Call me Roxana!" my mother insisted, appearing at the threshold looking like her normally prim self. She was wearing an emerald dress that fit her like a glove. It had a low-cut bodice that enhanced her cleavage, and the material made her already shapely figure look more pronounced. Her face was radiant, her light caramel eyes bright and her dark brown loose waves piled up into a knotted bun. The gold heels she wore clinked against the marble floors as she strode toward us in the foyer of the house.

She leaned in and gave me a quick hug and kiss on the cheek before turning to Ryan and doing the same.

"You're coming to the party tonight?" she confirmed with Ryan.

"Yes, ma'am," Ryan said with a smile. His face always flushed when he spoke to adults, making his strawberry freckles blend in with his cheeks.

"Good," she said then turned to me. "Brooklyn, you're going to dye your hair one color for tonight, right?"

"Yes, Mother," I responded.

My hair was blonde at the time, which I could pull off because of my green eyes, but I had streaks of pink all throughout. She tried to get me to dye it back to just blonde or my natural chocolate brown as soon as she saw it, which was two weeks after I'd dyed it the shades of pink to begin with.

"Good, because it's embarrassing. I don't know how such a good looking kid like Ryan puts up with it," she said with a tsk.

I ground my teeth together, my eyes downcast.

Ryan put his hand over mine and threaded our fingers together, squeezing. "I actually really dig the pink, it's cute."

"For Halloween maybe," my mother retorted.

"It doesn't matter. I'm dying it back by tonight," I said with finality.

"Okay. I'll send your dress up for you in a couple of hours. Ryan, you remember it's a white party, right?" she said as she took down the pins that were holding her hair up.

"Yep. I'll be here in all white," Ryan said.

My mother nodded at us, seemingly happy enough with our conversation and pivoted to leave, swaying her hips and her arms like the true model that she was.

When Ryan and I were in my room I went to my en-suite bathroom and took out the box of hair dye I had under my sink, deciding I should do that first.

"Your mom is a bitch, but she's still better than mine," Ryan commented, knowing I was still brewing over our encounter with her.

I let out a loud breath. "I know. What the hell did we do to deserve them as parents?"

Ryan shrugged. "Be born, I guess."

I walked up to the bed where he sat shaking my old Bambi snow globe. I lay my head on his shoulder.

"It sucks," I said.

"Yep," he agreed.

He helped me dye my hair as we danced to Britney Spears. Ryan loved Britney. When Nina, who was staying with our Uncle Roy in San Francisco for the weekend, got to my house, Ryan went home to get dressed.

"Such a shame," Nina commented. "The cute ones are all gay. You should see how many hot guys there are in San Fran. Do you think they even look at me?" she asked in dismay.

I laughed, knowing it was true. I'd gone to visit my uncle and his boyfriend a couple of times and noticed the same thing. It was just funnier when Nina said it because she thought everybody was supposed to admire her beauty.

"Did Uncle Roy come with you?" I asked distractedly as I dried my hair.

"Duh. How would I have gotten here? Oh my god, and if I had to hear one more old Spanish song I was gonna die. He says it reminds him of his mom, but holy shit, Bee, the music is like lullaby music putting me to sleep," Nina said, groaning.

"Maybe that's what he wanted, to shut you up so he could drive in peace," I said, laughing when she threw a pillow at me.

"Whatever. Uncle Chris really outdid himself this time," she commented.

I rolled my eyes at that. Everyone said that every time there was a White Party. My dad was known to host the best parties and he always "outdid himself" from the last one. I couldn't really disagree with them; each party was more lavish than the last. He really thought he was The Great Gatsby or something, and that's not even a joke. He would actually say, "This is going to be a Gatsby party."

I was wearing a robe, waiting for the dress my mother promised me, when there was a single knock on my door, followed by it opening.

"Hey, Nina," my mother greeted, "you look pretty."

"Thanks, Aunt Roxy," Nina said with a smile.

"Maybe you should let your cousin in on your little diet secret since she refuses to listen to me," my mother went on, handing me a dress bag without even looking at me.

I snatched it from her and walked into my closet, drowning out their conversation with my humming. I would rather not listen to the discussion about how I was so fat that size two jeans were starting to look snug on me. It wasn't my fault that my butt had a mind of its own when it came to developing. I let the robe pool at my feet as I stood in front of the mirror to look at myself. It's not like I had a fat stomach or anything. My boobs were smaller than I wished they were, but the combination of my flat stomach and thin waist made my butt look bigger than it actually was.

I opened the garment bag and took out the dress, a short white dress that had embroidered detail at the top. I raised my eyebrows at the material, which was much like the green dress my mother had been wearing earlier that day, so I knew that meant that it would stick to me like glue. I wore it anyway, even though I felt overly exposed. My regular wardrobe consisted of loose ripped jeans and vintage band T-shirts, so anything that showed off my legs was going to feel like it was exposing me.

Nina's words to me were: "You look pale."

"I'm tan, Nina," I argued.

"Yeah, but your hair is blonde, almost white, and you're wearing a white dress. You look pale as fuck. Why didn't you dye your hair back to your normal color?" she asked.

I shrugged. "Didn't feel like dying it back yet."

She shook her head. Her dark hair was cut to her shoulders and styled straight, so when she shook her head that way it would swing into her eyes. "When are you going to stop dying your hair weird colors?"

She'd asked me the same question every time she'd seen me for the past six months. Each time I gave her a different answer, usually one that I knew would shut her up. I never told her the reason I thought it did it. In the beginning I did it because I wanted a change—I was bored of the same old hair. Gradually it became more, though. It meant I could escape and become someone else for a little while, and I liked that. Mainly because obviously the person I was wasn't good enough for anyone.

"When I figure out who I should be, I guess," I responded nonchalantly with a shrug.

Nina, who had never been one to pay attention to detail when you spoke to her, stopped applying her makeup and looked at me, eyes wide. "What's wrong with who you are now?"

"Everything, apparently," I mumbled under my breath. "Nothing," I said louder, shooting a reassuring smile at her.

She looked at me for a second longer before going back to her eyeliner.

The party was the same as they always were: loud and cheerful. There were actors, musicians, rock stars, movie directors, producers, DJs, Hollywood agents, models. Anybody with a known name was there.

"Who's that?" Nina asked, tugging my hand just as Ryan joined us.

"Who's who?" Ryan chimed in.

"That," Nina said, pointing at a guy, about our age. He was dressed in a white T-shirt and dark washed jeans. His hair was dark brown and ruffled. He was thin and shorter than Ryan, but Ryan was tall for his age. It wasn't his looks that made him attractive, though, it was just *him*. The way he was smiling at the pretty model he was talking to. The way his eyes lit up at his own jokes. He just had that fire in him that made you want to get to know him, and when he looked at me, I did.

"I dunno," I mused and was about to say something dumb, like, "but I want to." I didn't get to finish my sentence because my mother glided up to us. She walked like she owned the world, which was something I tried to practice, but never got down.

The thing was, I realized later, that my mother really did think she owned the world and everybody that walked it. Everyone was a puppet to her and she was pulling all the strings.

"Brooklyn," my mother said cheerfully, wrapping her arm around my shoulder and pulling me into a hug. I remember wishing I could go to a party every day so that she would hug me. "Let me introduce you to a couple of people. Excuse us, Ryan ... Nina," she said, giving them each a pointed look.

I walked off with her, catching their baffled looks when I shot them my own confused glance over my shoulder. My mother handed me the drink she had in her hand, I figured for me to hold.

"Drink it," she insisted. "You're at home, might as well enjoy the party properly."

It's not like I hadn't drank alcohol before. I was sixteen years old, living in Beverly Hills. I'd gotten drunk a handful of times. Hanging out with child actors at adult parties will do that to a kid. Still, I'd never been given permission from my own mother to drink. I took it and brought it to my mouth, wondering where she was going with this whole thing. I smelled it first; it smelled fruity, much like the drinks I'd had before, so I took a cautious sip. As fruity as it smelled, it went down heavily, burning my esophagus, but I liked it.

"What is it?" I asked curiously, watching her delighted face from the corner of my eye.

She stopped walking and turned to me, fake smile still plastered on her face. "Liquid courage," she said. "Just drink the damn thing and don't eat any of the fried food." Her eyes did a swift take of my body. "The dress looks perfect on you. Much better than I thought it would. Don't mess it up," she snapped, smile still in place, but her light brown eyes were drilling into me.

I nodded, taking a bigger sip of her liquid courage. "Yeah, God forbid I don't look good enough to be your daughter."

"Exactly," she remarked. She either missed my sarcastic tone or chose to ignore it. Probably the latter. "Mind your posture, walk with your head held high, not looking at the floor. If it's below you, it's not worth looking at."

I rolled my eyes inwardly and let her lead me through the crowds of people, introducing me as we went.

"Oh, she's beautiful," some said in reference to me. My mother especially liked the "She's as beautiful as her mother" comments. My favorite was, "You've raised her well." That made my empty stomach turn.

We circled our way around until we reached the "cute guy" Nina pointed out earlier. He was speaking to my father, who looked at me, his big green eyes smiling warmly when he caught sight of me walking with my mother.

"Hey, baby girl," he greeted.

"Hey, Dad," I responded, leaning into his arms for a moment. My mother was now holding my hand and pulled me away from him quickly.

"Chris, I was just about to introduce Brooklyn to Shea," my mother explained.

My father narrowed his eyes for a quick moment before nodding. "Shea, this is my daughter, Brooklyn," he said, turning toward the guy who was indeed a little taller than me in my heels.

His messy hair fell into his eyes when he tilted his head to appraise me and I was done for. One tilted head, charming smile, twinkling eyes look was all it took for my platonic crush on Shea to set.

Then he opened his mouth and spoke. "So good to meet you, Brooklyn," he said, his voice velvety and silky. I just wanted to bathe in it for days. His greenish-brownish eyes were set on mine. They were the oddest color, like green grass with patches of mud on it. Muddy green, I would later call them. "Chris, if you would've told me you had such a pretty daughter, I would've gotten here sooner."

Done. For. It. That's what I was.

You can't really blame a girl, though. I was sixteen years old with hormones spurring out of control. I got no attention from anybody in my house, the only people I could count on were: my brother who was never there, my cousin who lived in New York, and my gay best friend who was battling his own demons at home. I thrived for attention the only way I knew, which was by going to parties and being the party girl. The "it" girl everybody wanted to be friends with, but not real friends, just friends on the weekend. They didn't give a shit that I was hurting; they didn't give a shit about my life. All they cared about was getting invited to parties, getting drunk, and being able to say they knew Chris and Roxy's daughter.

"Brooklyn," my mother cooed, facing me to her and holding me at arms' length so she could look at me. "You know what would be great? If you could show Shea our studio. Why don't you introduce him to your friends?" She pulled me close to her again and placed my face on top of her chest. I was shorter than her, so that's where my head landed anyway. But it was such an intimate gesture, the way she held me there and ran her fingers through my hair the way she did when I was a child. I remember thinking in that moment that I would do anything for her. Anything to have her hold me like that. Anything to have that smile on her face when she looked at me and her approval when she touched me. So when she asked me to be nice to Shea, listen to his music and to please report back to my father about anything he said to me, I agreed.

I often wondered if she knew the destructive path I was already treading at that point, and whether or not she would have ignited the gallop, had she sensed how serious it was. I wondered if she knew what Shea's friends were most likely carrying around in their pockets when she handed me to the wolves that night. I wondered if she even cared.

Ryan and I walked to the studio hand in hand, Nina following not far behind, already talking to one of Shea's friends. He was shady, that friend of his, his name was Drew. I'll never forget the way his dark eyes looked at you like you were already dead. It was an odd look he had, a dazed one.

"So, this is the studio," I said, flipping on the light switch and letting everyone walk in before me.

"Nice digs," Drew commented. He sounded like Shaggy from Scooby Doo. He kind of looked like him too.

I nodded my agreement. "Yep. There's only one booth, but the system is the best of the best."

After a while of standing around awkwardly, everyone took a seat. Ryan and I were on one of the black couches, Nina and Drew on another, and Shea sat on the seat directly in front of me. We made small talk about normal things like school. Drew and Shea both went to a local public school I was familiar with, mainly because I'd heard horrible things about the fights there. Anytime I'd been around kids that went to worse schools than mine, I felt weird talking about my own sheltered upbringing. I knew *sheltered* wasn't the way most people described my crazy life. They threw around *poor little rich girl*, whenever I complained about my parents never being home or having time to talk to me. Poor little rich girl was right, though. I wasn't blind to everything I had at my fingertips. I had everything a newly sixteen-year-old girl could possibly want, and everything I didn't need.

The only thing that kept me from being completely reckless was my own conscience, which Nina hated. "Where'd you learn to be so responsible, anyway?" she'd ask when she was pissed that I didn't go along with her getting drunk and sneaking out of the house schemes. She always wanted to sneak out of her house, which I hated. She had a good mother, an attentive one, one that set rules and boundaries for her. I didn't have to sneak out of my house. I could walk out the front door at two in the morning and nobody would stop me or care to ask me where I was going. Maybe my dad or Hendrix would if they were home, but they weren't. So again, poor little rich girl with a closet full of purses and shoes and nobody to give a shit about what she does with her life.

Shea took out a little bowl and started packing it with marijuana. I'd seen every drug in the drug pyramid by that time, so I knew what it was even though I'd never tried it. Ryan was into that kind of stuff, he would smoke with some other friends, but he never wanted me around it. His hand squeezed mine when he saw where it was going. He knew Shea would offer it to me, and he knew I was already caught up in impressing him so I would take it and try it. I shrugged and let go of his hand, taking the bowl in my hand when Shea handed it to me.

"You sure you wanna do that?" Ryan asked.

I looked over at him, his green eyes worried, and I shrugged. "Why not? You do it all the time. How bad can it be?"

Ryan shrugged back. "It's not like drinking though."

I didn't care. The only reason I got drunk was to escape my own mind for a while. This was just another form of escape. I put it up to my lips and smiled at Shea, waiting for him to light it for me.

"First time, huh?" Shea asked playfully. His muddy green eyes were looking at me with so much interest, I wanted to take the bowl away from my lips and just kiss him.

"Yep," I said coyly.

"Oh, hurry up, Bee, puff-puff pass already," Nina whined.

I rolled my eyes and Shea laughed, shaking his head at her as he lit up the green grass for me and signaled for me to inhale. And I did. I inhaled and reveled in the burn it left in my throat. I let out the air, going into a coughing fit because I clearly took too much in. I had no clue what I was doing and it wasn't properly explained to me. I passed the bowl. It came around two more times before I started to finally feel the effects of it. My eyes began to feel heavy, and my smile was a little wider on my face now. I was laughing at every single stupid thing anybody said. Even Drew was hilarious to me at that point.

As the night went on, somebody suggested we go into the house and watch *Dumb & Dumber* in our built-in movie theatre, so we did. I numbly led the way into the house, clutching on to Shea's arm along the way so I could take off my shoes. He steadied me with his firm hold. He wasn't strong looking with defined muscles, but I could tell he wasn't a vegetable either. Later that night he told me he surfed sometimes, like a good California boy. I loved that he did. I made him promise he would take me surfing one day.

I'd seen *Dumb & Dumber* once before, it was one of Hendrix's favorite movies. I hated it the first time I saw it. Hated it. But that time, with Shea's arm around me and my head feeling so light—like a balloon, like a kite—I thought *Dumb & Dumber* was a classic. I'm pretty sure I even went as far as saying it should've been nominated for an Oscar. Really.

When the high was wearing down, Drew took out yet another little packet. This one was white powder. And again, something I had seen before but never touched. Neither Ryan nor Nina had done it either, so we were all curious enough about it. I decided that day that I would try everything once. In hindsight, I wish I hadn't tried any of it. I wish I could press the rewind button and go back to the moment where my mother hugged me and I felt whole.

We became fast friends and somewhere along the way he finally ditched Drew. Then it was Shea, Ryan and me. We were together more than we weren't. We went to the studio with Shea every day while he recorded his first album. We went to his first show and cheered him on from the side of the stage. He would take me on to the stage and proclaim his love for me every chance he got and then take me to his dressing room and screw me senseless before we got high.

On days that I'm really feeling sorry for myself, I wish I would have never met Shea at all, and then I'm glad I did because we both fucked each other over that first summer. He introduced me to the drugs that would consume me and my best friend's lives for the next two years, but I made him sign that contract with Harmon Records. So in the end, I don't know who was worse: my mother for handing me over to the wolves that night, or me for constantly feeding the talent I found to the sharks in the music industry. Wolves may be ruthless, but at least they showed their loyalty by traveling in packs and sharing their prey. Sharks are blind and scout out the weak, attacking anything that's already bleeding. I found myself getting lost in all of it sometimes, wondering which I was—the shark or the prey? Was it possible to be a bleeding shark? And if so, how long before I got torn into?

CHAPTER TWELVE

Present

I woke up at the crack of dawn to sort things out and make sure I packed everything in time for my one o'clock flight. I'll only be gone for a week, which isn't too bad, but it's long enough to have me second guessing my wardrobe and what to take. Shea has concerts and a media tour going on at the same time to promote his single and upcoming CD release, so I'll have to find things to keep me entertained while he's busy. It's insane the amount of things he has to cram into just a couple of days at each city. Our first stop is San Francisco, which I'm both scared and excited for. A part of me dreads going back there, but the other part of me knows it's time to face the music-it's been long enough.

My phone starts ringing just as I reach the door of Harmon, so I walk off the side to sort through my bag in search for it. As I do, my fingers touch something round, which I pull out in confusion. I smile when I see that they're some of Melody's gold play coins and shove them back in, finally finding my phone.

Shea's name is bright on my screen, no doubt to make sure I'm still going on the trip.

"Hello?" I respond as I begin walking back to the elevator.

"Hey, you're still coming, right?" he asks.

I stall for a moment, letting the anxiety coursing through me settle before I respond. "Yes. I told you I'd be there."

"Okay. Can you do me a huge favor? Stop by the studio on your way up to work or down, whatever, and ask Gia for a bag of mine that she has," he says.

"Okay," I respond slowly, surprised by this. "Isn't she supposed to be touring with you?"

"Yeah, but she won't be over there till tomorrow morning. She's in the studio laying down a verse for one of my tracks, though, so I asked her to take my bag," he explains.

"'Kay, I'll get it. Anything else?" I ask, tapping my fingernail against the backside of my phone as I wait for the elevator. I swear that out of all of the elevators in Manhattan, this is the one that takes the longest.

"Nope. See you soon," he says before hanging up the phone.

Butterflies swarm my stomach as I ride up to the forty-fourth floor, knowing that I'll see Nick shortly. The last time I felt butterflies when I was going to see a guy was when I was sixteen years old and had just met Shea, which is ironic considering the situation I find myself in now. As I walk toward Studio 10, I wonder how Shea would feel if anything ever did happen between Nick and me. I can't imagine he would be upset or actually jealous, but men act like cats—territorial and possessive over you one day and discarding you the next, so you never know which way their crazy minds will go.

I pull the door open, ready to say hi, but stop short when I find Nick sitting down, his back facing me, and Gia draped over him with her arms wrapped around his neck. The blood rushes out of my head quickly and I feel myself go completely cold before it fuses back just as fast, boiling in its return.

"Gia, get the fuck off me," Nick growls, shifting his body from under hers.

"Aw, come on, Nick," she coos. "Cassidy told me how fun you can be."

He swivels in his seat, effectively throwing her off of him, and she stands back with her arms crossed in front of her chest. The navy blue romper she's wearing covers close to nothing, leaving her long legs on display and her breasts practically spilling out from the top.

"Cassidy needs to learn to keep her mouth shut," Nick responds in a deadly quiet tone, his blue eyes narrowed at her. Both of them are so upset that they haven't even noticed that I'm standing here. "When I'm working, I'm working," he continues as I backtrack my steps to step outside. "You're with Shea and he's my boy. Show some fucking respect." That's the last thing I hear before tiptoeing out, still walking backwards, and shutting the door quietly.

I wish I had stayed longer to hear her response or to see if she tried anything further, even though with the look Nick gave her, I doubt she would. I'm still holding the doorknob in my hand when it's pulled open from the other side, and I yelp.

"Oh, sorry," Gia mutters, her eyes wide when she sees me.

"Hey, no big deal. Shea told me to come by and get his bag," I say, hoping my voice sounds as steady as I'm trying to keep my facial features.

She has the decency to flush at the sound of Shea's name and she nods her understanding. "I'm going to take a quick break, the bag is by the bathroom. Enter at your own risk, you may want to stay quiet because Shadow is working," she says the word *working* with an attitude and an eye roll. "And he's a total dick when he's in the zone."

I let out a laugh. If I hadn't just witnessed what I did I would think Gia was crazy, but being that I did, I just nod. "Got it. See you tomorrow."

She waves and says goodbye before storming off.

Walking in again, I shut the door quietly behind me and walk toward the bathrooms. I have to pass by Nick to get there, so I stand behind him for a moment, studying the way his defined arms move along the soundboard and the back of his downcast head bobs along to whatever is pouring out of his earphones. His back is wide and strong and I wish I had the balls to throw my arms around him like I saw Gia do earlier. I wonder if he'd tell me off like he did her.

I contemplate two things:

1. How ridiculous would it be for me to do it?

2. How awkward would it be if I did it and he chewed me out for it?

I turn toward the chairs beside the bathroom, noticing there are two bags, a pink one and a black one. The black one has Shea's signature "S" on it, so I pick it up, swinging it over my shoulders and take one last look at the back of Nick's head and back before turning to leave.

"You're not even gonna say hi?" Nick says behind me, startling me. I place a hand over my quickening heartbeat and turn around slowly.

"I was told you didn't want interruptions," I explain quietly.

Nick pushes himself back in his seat, stretching out his legs and crossing his arms over his chest. The gray V-neck shirt he's wearing is clinging to his hard body, and I can see the ripples that etch his toned torso. He tilts his head and looks at me with those knowing blue eyes of his as he purses his lips.

"Really?" he asks. "Who told you that?"

"I caught Gia on her way out," I explain. "She looked ... upset."

He raises an eyebrow. "Good. So she told you not to interrupt me?"

I shake my head with a smile. "Not exactly. She told me you were working and that you don't like to be interrupted when you're working," I say with a shrug. "I only came by to pick this up for Shea."

Nick nods and scratches his chin. "Cool. I could've taken it to him."

"I had to come in anyway. I have stuff to do before I-" I stop short, frowning. "Wait a minute, you're going too?"

He tilts his head to the other side, his eyes dancing in amusement as a slow smile spreads over his face. "I am."

"Hmm." I nod, not trusting myself to say anything else. "Well, I'll see you later then."

"See you later," he says, looking at me as if he's on the verge of laughing at my expense, surely from the mix of emotions painted all over my face.

I turn around and walk to the door, feeling his eyes on me as I do.

"Hey, Brooklyn," he calls out again, and I swear he's enjoying the whole watching me go thing that guys do.

"Yes?" I ask, unwilling to turn around because my heart is pounding at my throat.

"You have permission to interrupt me," he says.

I turn around, stunned, because I have to—how can I not?

"Okay," I say.

"Okay," he agrees with a sense of finality before he turns around and gets back to work.

Shaking my head, I turn around and take the elevator up to my office. I stick my head in Stacey's office on the way to mine and ask her if my brother's in yet. She's on the phone, so she nods with a smile and signals me to go into his office. I knock once before I let myself in, finding him standing, facing the window as he talks on the phone.

"I'll be there on the weekend," he says quietly. "I know we need to talk. I have to go. Okay. Bye."

Hendrix's face is clouded as he turns to face me, and I can tell he's still mulling over the conversation he had.

"Who was that?" I ask with a frown as I walk toward him and give him a kiss on the cheek. I haven't seen him in a couple of days. It seems like when I'm home, he's not and vice versa.

"Sarah," he says with a sigh, running his hand through his curly blond hair.

"Oh. How is she?"

"Fine. She wants to talk." The way he says the words, as if he's not sure he wants to talk to her, makes me think there's a lot more to the story, so I do what every good sister would and take a seat.

"Talk. What's going on?" I ask; glancing at my gold boyfriend watch quickly to make sure I have time to be nosey.

Hendrix sighs loudly and takes a seat in his huge cherry leather chair. He places his elbows on the desk and buries his face between his hands. "How did things get so fucked up?" he asks, seemingly talking to himself. "One minute we were in love, crazy about each other, married. The next we were thrilled to be having a baby together, and then it seemed like we couldn't even bear to look at each other. I just don't get it. What the fuck went wrong?" His voice is soft and cracking and it breaks my heart along with it.

"I'm sorry," I offer in a whisper. I'm not good with comforting others. Hell, I can't even comfort myself most of the time. Growing up we weren't really shown empathy, and I think that's one of those things that you kind of have to be shown in order to give.

He shakes his head, still in his hands. "I just … I love her so much, but I don't think we can work this out anymore. She's there and I'm here and I'd *rather* be here … but I can't bear the thought of completely losing her."

I purse my lips, nodding as if I understand what he's going through, even though I don't. It's easy to dish out advice when you're not the one in the situation, though, so I do.

"I think if you really feel that strongly about the whole thing, you should fight for your girls," I suggest.

He nods in agreement. "I think you're right and I will."

"Good. I'll be back in next week but I'm having Stace email me whatever she has for me. I'll listen on the road," I say, ruffling his hair as I lean down to place a kiss on his forehead.

"See ya. Please be careful, Bee. PLEASE," he pleads, frowning his sad brown eyes at me.

"I will," I promise. "Stop worrying, Mother Hen. Geez," I joke, making him smile.

A nagging thought strikes me as I'm walking out of his office, so I turn around and face him. "Hey, Henny … why do you want to fight for her now? After all this time? What changed?"

He looks surprised by my question and averts his eyes from me. "Some guy in that band she's producing asked her out," he grumbles.

My mouth falls open. "So a guy asking out your ex-wife is what made you realize that you might lose her? Jesus Christ, men are fucking stupid," I mutter under my breath, turning back around and walking out.

"We are! Remember that for future reference!" Hendrix screams behind me, making me laugh.

On my way back downstairs, my elevator stops at the

forty-fourth floor and Nick gets in with a couple of guys and one older lady. I scoot further back in the elevator to make room for them and anybody else that will get on as we descend floors. Nick pins me with his gaze, causing butterflies to re-awaken in my core, and he scoots beside me.

"Did Gia finish recording her part of the song?" I ask, tilting my head to look up at him.

He nods, his eyes locked on the elevator door. "Yep. She's usually pretty good once she stops fucking around."

I nod and turn my face forward to look at the metal door as well. "Cool."

"You headed straight to the airport?" he asks, scooting closer to me when more people step into the elevator and go completely still when his bare arm touches mine. It's so dumb, really. I'm not in the fifth grade, surely I can handle a man's arm touching mine, but holy crap his arm touching mine makes my insides mush. I decide in this moment that this is the most ridiculous crush I've ever had in my life. So what if he looks like a God himself sauntered down here and sprinkled gold all over him. So what if he smells like one of those little ads that come in Esquire magazine for men to sniff the next perfume of their choice? He could totally model for one of those ads too. It doesn't matter, though—I've seen plenty of hot guys. I've been with some too. The difference between them and Nick, however, is that he is a man, not a guy. He. Is. *Man.* If you look up the definition of *hot man*, you'll find Nick. No joke.

He nudges me, snapping me out of my crazy thoughts. "Huh?" I say, confused, looking up at him.

He grins and I feel my knees go a little weak. "Are you going to the airport now?"

"Ohh ... well, I have to get my bags and then I'm going." I frown. "Are you?"

He nods. "Responsible." He points at himself.

"So am I," I counter, a little offended at his suggestion.

Nick laughs loudly as we step out of the elevator. "Hey, I don't know."

I push his shoulder playfully with my hand, making him laugh louder as he takes my hand and squeezes. "I am responsible! I just need to get my suitcase and that's it!" I say with a laugh.

"Sure. You don't need to pack your hair products?" he jokes, grabbing a lock of my hair and shaking it in his hand.

I slap his hand away. "Stop it," I fume jokingly. "I do need to pack my hair iron," I mutter under my breath, making us both laugh.

"Figures," he says, his sea-green-blue eyes twinkling.

"You know your eyes change colors?" I ask randomly.

Nick slows down his pace until we both stop walking. We're standing in the entrance of the building and people are walking past us on either side, but neither one of us move. We just stand there; holding each other's stares until I feel dizzied from the way the look in his eyes makes me feel.

He steps in, just an inch closer to me, close enough for my breath to catch at the proximity. Close enough that I have to crane my head to look at him. Close enough for the amazing smell of fresh smelling man that radiates from him to wrap around me. His gaze dances over my face and falls onto my mouth, lingering there as he licks his own lips slowly, making a new kind of warmth curl in my stomach. When he looks back into my eyes, the side of his mouth tilts up, as if he can hear my thoughts ringing loudly in his head. I'm sure what I want is written all over my face. I've never been good at hiding my emotions.

"They do change colors—my eyes," he says quietly, as if I

might've forgotten what we were talking about. "And I love the way you look at them. Like you get lost in them, like you can't help yourself."

My eyes widen, but I'm too stunned to move or reply to that. What would I say, anyway? Yes? I swallow loudly instead and bite down on my lip, looking toward the door for a distraction.

Nick's finger tipping my chin brings my attention back to him. "See you later, Brooklyn," he says, dropping his hand and tugging a lock of my hair before walking off.

CHAPTER THIRTEEN

By the time I climb the stairs of the jet, Shea and Nick are already sitting in there playing the Xbox that's connected to the big screen television toward the back. Shea nods his head at me in greeting, not taking his eyes off of the screen as he continues to shoot his opponent. Nick turns his head to me and smiles, tipping his fingers in a salute.

"Dude! You're gonna get me killed!" Shea shouts.

Nick laughs and looks back to the TV. I shake my head and walk toward them, plopping down behind them.

"Is anybody else coming?" I ask, propping my head on my hand and laying my body sideways across the couch so that I can still look at the game they're playing. I don't think I'll ever understand the excitement of these Call of Duty games, but Shea loves them.

"I'm surprised you're a gamer," I say in reference to Nick. "I wouldn't have pegged you for one."

Nick chuckles and turns his head, his brows raising slightly as he does a slow sweep of my entire body that leaves me shivering. When his eyes reach my face again, my stomach feels like it's zip lining from the look he's giving me. He looks like he wants to devour me and between the way my heart is beating against my chest and the rest of my body is coiling, I wish he would.

"I'm a man of many talents," Nick says, his voice dropping into what I can only describe as a sensual timbre that makes me bite down on the inside of my cheek.

"Nick! You're gonna fucking die!" Shea screams, visibly upset over the game.

Nick completely ignores Shea's plea to get back in the game and lets his gaze continue to rock through me, making me feel unnerved, bare, as if I'm under a microscope. I'm not one to back down from a challenge, but I know that the only reason people look at each other like that is because they either want to kill each other or fuck each other to death. Because I know we're both aiming for the latter of the two and I don't know if I would survive that with him, I find myself shuffling to my feet quickly and excusing myself to go to the bathroom. Shutting the door behind me, I sag against it and let out a breath, closing my eyes until my heart goes back to normal speed.

There's a knock on my door shortly after, followed by the flight attendant telling me they're ready for departure. I open the door and peek out, noticing that the bathroom light is on and only Nick is in the cabin. I take a breath and push my shoulders back, walking toward the couch again to buckle my seat belt. We don't have to do this, people rarely actually put their seatbelts on during private flights, but I like to be safe and not rolling all over the cabin. It happened to me once before and I learned my lesson.

Nick is on his computer with his earphones on, his head bobbing, and hasn't acknowledged my arrival. If he knows I'm here, he shows no sign of it. Shea steps out of the bathroom, stretching his arms up, his white T-shirt riding up and the top of his underwear showing. It's the same underwear I saw him in an advertisement for.

"Do they give you free underwear now?" I ask curiously.

Shea grins his shit-eating grin that he throws around when he catches girls checking him out and I have to laugh because he's that ridiculous. He sits down beside me and throws his arm over my shoulder, tucking his face into the side of my face. Normally I would laugh at his antics, but for some reason the only thing I can think about is Nick and the fact that he's sitting right in front of us. The entire thing makes me feel weird for some reason, though I don't know why.

"You wanna see them?" Shea whispers into my ear, causing me to shiver, but it's more on the disgusted side than turned on side. It's not that I'm disgusted by Shea, but the idea of being with him in that way only clouds me with bad memories, horrible memories even, ones I don't care to explore more than I'm doing by going to San Francisco with him. Even that's pushing my luck, I realize, but at least I can rationalize my visit by thinking I'll get some closure.

I move my face further away from him and catch Nick's eyes bounce from the computer screen directly into mine. Shea's oblivious to my discomfort. Oblivious to the fact that I'm more tuned into what the guy across from us is doing, the guy who hasn't even touched me, yet ignites tiny fireworks in my veins with just one look. Shea doesn't feel that my body isn't responding to him but leaning away instead, the way it has been for years. He doesn't get it though, he just keeps leaning in, trying to drain me of whatever I have left, even though it's not his. Not anymore.

Nick, however, notices. He sees it all and he doesn't look pleased with any of it. Why does this thrill me? What is it about him looking at me like he wants to possess me that makes me giddy inside? Maybe it's the fact that I've never felt as wanted as he makes me feel with just one glance, just one phrase. Maybe it's because stupidly, I want to believe that he'll prove me wrong and show me that not everybody is selfish.

When he doesn't take a hint, I push Shea off, not taking my eyes off of Nick's. "Stop clowning around. I was just wondering," I joke, watching Nick's eyes and the way they watch my mouth move when I speak, even though I'm talking to Shea.

"Sure," Shea says. "You know I'd drop Gia if you said you wanted to be with me again, right?"

My eyes widen at his words. The way Nick's face darkens doesn't go unnoticed, and I realize that he can hear our conversation despite the earphones covering his ears.

"Shea, you wanna listen to this?" Nick asks, shooting daggers at Shea, who's scooting even closer to me.

Shea snaps his head in Nick's direction and moves away from me but leaves his arm over my shoulder. "Sure. I'll listen to it in a little while," he responds to Nick. He looks back at me. I can feel his eyes on me, but I'm scared to turn my face to his because how close we are. "Bee," Shea says.

Casting my eyes down so that I don't see Nick's probing eyes on me anymore, I exhale. "What?"

"You never answered me."

"About what?" I whisper, not wanting to have such a personal conversation in front of somebody. Shea may think Nick's not paying attention, but I know better. And the kicker is that I actually care.

"About Gia," he says, his words short as if he's annoyed that he has to clarify.

"Can we not talking about that?" I ask, shrugging his arm off of me.

Shea exhales deeply. "Sure."

When we're in the air, Shea moves away from me and sits beside Nick. They go back and forth over music and songs that he can record for his album. After listening to them go over the same things a couple of times, I plug my own earphones in and tune them out. I have at least ninety demos I hope to get through during the flight, but by the tenth, I find myself falling asleep. I'm not sure when it finally happens, but at some point I do end up completely asleep because the next time I open my eyes, I'm laying down in the bed with Shea sleeping beside me.

Rubbing my hands over my eyes, I sit up in a stretch, admiring the sleeves of tattoos that adorn his arms and remembering the first one he got. It seems like ions ago, and in a sense it was, even though sometimes it feels like it was just yesterday.

I cover him with as much of the covers as I can and get out of bed quietly, careful not to disturb his slumber. Grabbing my bag, I close the door behind me and tiptoe into the bathroom beside the bedroom. Gazing in the mirror, I run my hands over my flushed face and take out my toothbrush. My eyes are still glazed over from my nap and my hair is a mess. After looking for my hairbrush for a while, I decide to finger comb it as best I can as I open the door, jumping back when I find Nick standing right outside of the bathroom. At the sight of him, my heart instantly picks up speed, warning the lightning bugs in my core to wake up in the process.

"Did you have a good nap?" he murmurs, stepping into my personal space, making me feel like there's not enough oxygen in the entire airplane for the two of us as his eyes wash over me.

"Yeah," I whisper. I'm wearing flats, which means I'm at eye level with his chest. I take in a breath, inhaling him as I look at his face and decide that his smell is my favorite of all the amazing smells I've ever smelled.

His gaze softens as he looks at me and exhales. He straightens out and looks away for a moment, running both hands through his short faux hawk as if mulling something over, and I notice his last name scripted in his inner bicep as he does it. I've never understood why people get their own names scripted on themselves, as if they're going to forget it or something, but Nick's tattoo totally does it for me, just like everything else about him that I've seen so far.

He lowers his arms, looking at me again and walks forward a step, forcing me to walk back one. I can see the question in his eyes and I don't even think twice about the response, there's nothing for me to think about. I step back into the small bathroom allowing him to come in as well. The way he keeps dropping his gaze to my lips, I know he wants to kiss me. I also know I wouldn't stop him if he did. When he cups my face in both his hands and draws circles over my cheeks with his thumbs, still staring into my eyes, I automatically part my lips, welcoming him, pleading him to place his mouth over mine.

Nick dips his head slowly, his eyes never wavering from mine, still asking. I wrap my hands over the backs of his muscled biceps and stand on the balls of my feet, begging him to get closer. He dips his head slightly so that our breaths are mingling together, but not close enough that our faces touch.

"I really, really want to kiss you, Brooklyn," he murmurs, his voice raspy and soft and filled with need. "I really, really want to."

"So do it," I whisper against his lips.

He shakes his head, rubbing the tip of his nose against mine. "I don't want to share you."

"I'm not yours to share," I breathe.

"That's why I'm not going to kiss you," he whispers against me, so close I can practically taste his tongue on mine.

My breaths are coming in short spurts; that's the kind of need I feel for him. I *need* him to kiss me. I need it so much more than the damn oxygen I'm lacking in my lungs right now. I need it more than I need this plane to land. That's how his warm touch on my face makes me feel. I feel like I'll die if he doesn't kiss me, but at the same time my heart might explode if he does.

He leans in closer, nudging my legs apart slightly with his own and presses his hard body against mine. When he dips his head, I open my mouth automatically for his, but he doesn't kiss me. He sucks on my bottom lip, slowly, savoring it, moaning as he does it, making me feel like it's the best thing he's ever tasted in his life. Once he's finished with it, he moves to my top lip, and then to the side of my mouth before slowly sucking his way along my mouth from one corner to the other. I can't breathe as he does this, the only thing I can do to keep me from sagging to the floor is hold on to his arms. My head is spinning at the feel of his mouth on mine and the calculated way he devours me without letting me kiss him back. He pulls away slowly and places his forehead against mine, closing his eyes as if to level his thoughts. I'm still breathing heavily when his eyes flutter open and he looks at me again, the heat in his eyes never wavering. As I look into his blue eyes, my heart and stomach still pounding away, I realize that never in my twenty-five years of life have I experienced anything more erotic than this. The longer we stand here, the thicker the air grows between us. I feel like if my heart beats any faster, it'll end up inside his chest, which seems like a likely place for it at the moment. I move just a little closer to him, my pelvis hitting the hardness in his and he elicits a low groan that resonates through me, making me tighten my grip on him when my knees buck beneath me.

"There's nothing I want more right now," he says in a

strained whisper, answering an unvoiced question as the tips of his fingers dance along my face.

The mesmerizing way he looks at me makes me want to tell him to take it all right now, and I open my mouth to do just that when the bed creaks in the room beside us. Nick's eyes dart in that direction as he backs away from me, letting go of my face and holding my arms to steady me. He looks into my eyes one last time, his eyes swimming with desire as he runs the pad of his thumb over my cheek, and exhales before he turns to walk out. As soon as the door clicks shut behind him, I lurch forward to lock it right before sitting down on the floor beside the toilet. I sit here feeling dazed, stunned, running my hands over my lips until I've willed my heart and my breath to even and decide to go back out. Unwilling to look at Nick in the eyes, I walk back to the bedroom and close the door behind me, glad that Shea is no longer in here.

I throw myself on the bed, burying my head into the pillow as I play the kiss but non-kiss over and over in my head. I don't know whether to laugh at how it made me feel or cry because I want it to happen again so bad. Why didn't I just tell him I would be his, dammit? I hate those moments that you wish you could press rewind and have a do-over. The worst part is the thought that he may not try to kiss me again. The second worst part is that I have to see him for the next week and I don't know how to act normal around him without thinking about him sucking my lips. This is going to be the longest week ever. I already know it.

I'm not sure how long I'm in here before Shea knocks on the door and asks me to go back to the sitting area so I can listen to one of his songs. I get up hesitantly and brush past him. He closes the door behind us and grabs my arm to stop me when we step into the sitting area where Nick is sitting typing on his computer. He looks up, our eyes locking for a moment before his gaze drifts to where Shea is holding my arm.

"You feeling okay?" Shea asks, turning me to face him, his voice is full of concern. I nod, even though my stomach is tying up in knots of discomfort.

"Yeah," I assure him. "Perfect."

He frowns, searching my face and pulls me into a hug. I wrap my arms around his waist and turn my face, placing it over his chest. My eyes find Nick's as I lay my head there, listening to Shea's beating heart under my ear. Rather than tearing my eyes away from his intense stare, I drop my hands from Shea's middle and begin to walk to my seat.

I sit down across from Nick, beside Shea, and cross my legs Indian style on the seat to get comfortable. Shea scoots close to me and places an arm over one of my legs, the way we always sit when we're together. I notice that my heart doesn't sputter in my chest the way it used to once upon a time when he touched me or was near me. I realize that I'm just comforted by him, the way I have been for the past seven years. Nick isn't looking at us anymore; he's consumed by whatever he's doing on his computer, so I tilt my head and look at Shea. His messy hair is getting longer and he needs a shave badly. He's beginning to look like a slob, despite his expensive clothes and jewelry.

"You need a haircut," I tell him, ruffling his hair softly.

He closes his eyes. "I know," he says with a slight moan. "Can I lay my head on your lap so you can do that to me?"

I smile, knowing how much he likes it when I play with his soft curls. "Sure."

He scoots his body away, laying his head on my lap. "That feels so good. I'm so tired, Bee. So tired," he whispers.

Looking down at his face, I can tell that he is. He looks terrible and I hate it. "Go to sleep for a while." I grab his arm and look at the time on his watch. "We still have an hour."

He nods, closing his eyes. "I wasn't kidding about Gia," he murmurs, his words drifting off.

I let out a laugh. "I know you weren't. You weren't kidding about Tonya either," I say playfully, reminding him of one of the many, many reasons we couldn't work the first time.

His eyes snap open. "I'm a fuck-up," he says regretfully.

I shake my head slowly, still smiling. "You're not a fuck-up, sweetie," I say quietly, knowing he needs to hear this from somebody, very much like I do sometimes. Shea and I were both neglected growing up and continuously reminded about what fuck-ups we were. "You just love the ladies," I joke.

Shea chuckles quietly, his eyes looking on the greener side. "Nope, I love you … I just like to mess around with the ladies."

I smack his arm. "Well, thank you for the reminder."

He laughs for a second before his face turns serious as he looks up at me. "But one day I'll be ready, you know?"

I avert my eyes from the sadness in his, but find myself looking at Nick, who's looking directly at me. "Then one day you'll make one girl a very lucky lady," I say, still looking at Nick, who's now staring at my mouth, reading my lips.

Nick purses his lips to stifle a smile, but I can tell it's there. I can see it in his eyes. Shea lets out a breath and shifts on my legs.

"Keep playing with my hair," he says sleepily. So I do.

CHAPTER FOURTEEN

A dreadful feeling begins to slowly consume me at the sight of the Golden Gate bridge outside of my window. Suddenly, I'm second-guessing my decision to come here. It's been eight years. Eight freaking years. Isn't time supposed to heal all wounds? Who the fuck said that anyway? Clearly a genius. Long buried sorrow begins to creep up inside me, rattling my heart, making my breath come in more rapidly. I don't know if I can hide the amount of emotions that are slowly flooding me. Shea has been asleep on my lap for the past hour, so he's oblivious to the fact that we're here. If he doesn't wake up on his own soon, I'm sure the nervous bouncing of my leg will do the trick.

"You okay?" Nick asks, tearing his earphones from his head. His eyes are darting between my eyes and the fingernail I'm relentlessly chewing on.

Dropping my hand from my mouth, I shake my head vigorously as I feel the panic building inside of me. Years ago I would've lied. I would have said I was perfectly fine. I would have hidden from my panic, run away from the pain, and fallen into an oblivion of narcotics. I can't do that now, though. I won't. So I cave and admit to the last person that I want to see me crumble, that I'm not okay. I see no other choice other than waking up Shea, and he's already saved me enough times from the same nightmare. And although this time I want to save myself, I realize I may need some help through this moment to get there.

Nick doesn't ask anything else. He unbuckles his seatbelt, puts his computer to the side and crosses over to sit beside me.

"Do you think you can move him off of your lap without waking him?" Nick whispers, nodding toward Shea's sleeping form.

The flight attendant steps out of the pilot's cabin and looks at us, but doesn't say anything, she just smiles making sure we're fine.

"He may want to sit up, we're landing soon," she suggests before going back into the cabin.

I pick up Shea's head and scoot from under him, moving closer to Nick as I place Shea's head on the seat. He doesn't even flinch, just stays dead asleep, the way I expect him to. He's never been a light sleeper. The moment I take my hands out from under his face, I start to shake uncontrollably. I've only done this twice before.

"Hey," Nick says, his voice concerned, but I refuse to look at him. When he wraps his arms around me, squeezing me into him so that I'm swaddled into him. "Breathe, baby. I've got you," he whispers against my hair.

I make an attempt to nod as I breathe him in and let his scent bathe over my frenzy, immediately feeling a sense of calm wash over me. Despite feeling lighter, old memories begin to play out in my head and I begin to sob quietly against his chest. It's been eight years, but I can still feel the wind on my face when I close my eyes.

It was chilly that day, more so than usual. I shivered, wrapping my arms tightly around my middle and held on the metal railing. Closing my eyes as a gust of wind hit my face, my hair swooshed wildly as my heart continued to beat erratically against my chest. When my eyes were closed, I could feel the world spinning around me, and the floor giving out beneath me. I just wanted to curl up into a ball and die. I wished I never existed, just like she did.

I blinked my eyes open, sniffling back tears as my chest began to heave in broken, whimpered sobs. Tilting my head, I looked at the sign beside me. I hadn't seen it there before, it must have moved. I squinted my eyes, my head feeling heavy and lazy as I tried to read the hazy letters before me.

There is hope.

Hope.

The word lingered in my mind for a moment, so foreign and out of place there that I couldn't help the loud laugh that escaped my lips. Tearing my gaze from it, I looked back out, focusing on the city, on the buildings that seemed so small from where I was standing. The world looked endless from the larger than life bridge, making me feel even smaller and more worthless than I had before I came here. I started to cry again, thinking of him, wishing we could trade places.

At the sound of blaring horns, I clumsily let go of the rail and ducked behind a large column. The ocean was a dark shade of blue, mirroring the gloomy sky above it. I reached out in front of me, making slow waves with my hands, scissoring the fog that was clouding my vision.

I shuffled my feet forward again, leaning into the rail and taking a deep shaky breath. More drops of tears escaped my eyes, quickly followed by an entire dam as I thought of my brother, the only person who would miss me. The only one who would care that I was gone, but even that would pass. A sense of guilt flowed through me as I thought of the way he took care of me when we were young. The way he held my hand when our parents had arguments at the dinner table, and the way he assured me that I was fine just the way I was.

Bending forward, I placed my weight on my forearms and buried my face in my hands as sobs raked through me. A myriad of memories played in my head, none of them good, none of them giving me hope for a brighter tomorrow. They all led to the same conclusion: I would never be good enough for anyone.

Something cupped my shoulder, jolting me out of my thoughts and I jerked up, turning my body. My eyes felt heavy as I wiped them with the sleeve of the oversized hooded sweater I was wearing. I looked at him then, saw his dark eyes and had to blink twice more to clear my vision. My chest was rising and falling rapidly, my mind running a mile a minute even though I felt like my head was submerged under water.

"What?" I tried to ask, but the ocean waves and cars around us swallowed my question.

His mouth moved, formulating a response I couldn't make out.

We stood there staring at each other, him trying to figure me out and me trying to convince myself that he wasn't real, that he wasn't there. I had taken an obscene amount of drugs, mixing them together and creating the perfect concoction to numb myself with.

"What are you doing?" he asked, his voice somewhat snapping me out of my reverie.

"*You're real?*" *I breathed in a half question, half statement that he didn't reply.*

He tilted his head to examine me, making some of his hair fall into his eyes. He brushed it back with his hand and hid it under the beanie that covered his head. My eyes squinted as they searched his face, trying to catalog every inch of it. My mind wandered again to the breaking point that brought me here to begin with and my shoulders slumped, the reminder stabbing at my heart.

"*What are you doing?*" *he asked, repeating his question. His voice sounded anxious, alarmed and my mouth parted in wonder. Did he care?*

I swallowed back my sadness and took a shaky breath. "*What are you doing?*" *I countered quietly, though my voice sounded like a shriek in my ears, making me cringe.*

His eyebrows knit as he looked at me, his eyes reaching into me, trying to take something, everything. But there was nothing left to take. There was nothing left of me. He muttered something under his breath that sounded like, "*Looking for you.*" *That's what I wanted him to say, anyway. Either way, the sound of those three words, imaginary or not, made hope ignite within me.*

"*Jogging,*" *he said, moving closer to me.*

My eyes fell over his body and I noticed he was dressed in sweats and a thin black sweater. He took another step closer, making my head swim in the mix of his sweet yet musky scent.

"*Wanna talk about it?*" *he asked.*

I tried to keep my eyes open, tried to widen them, tried to really look at him as he spoke.

"*Huh?*" *I asked dumbly.*

"*Talk about it,*" *he repeated, my eyes followed his hand that signaled at the bridge, the ocean, the city of San Francisco below us.*

My breath hitched and I shook my head rapidly in response, suddenly feeling horrified. I felt a strong pain in my stomach that made me clutch on to it and my breathing became faster than normal, my heart beating more rapidly, making me feel like I was swallowing it. My eyes widened, really widened and I looked at him, pleading something. I don't know what I wanted him to do, leave me there to die or get me help, but it was the last thing I remember before I started seizing.

"Hey," Nick whispers, rubbing my arms as if he's trying to ignite warmth in my body.

I gulp once, twice, then a third time before opening my mouth to take a deep breath. "I can't go back there. I can't go back there." My whisper trembles along with my body as he rocks me in his arms.

"What is it?" he asks, concerned, looking over my shoulder and out the window. "The bridge?"

My teeth clatter as I try to form a response but before I can say anything, Nick scoops me up in his arms and tucks my face into the crook of his neck as he strides over to the bedroom. He shuts the door behind us, not bothering to explain himself to the flight attendant that suggested we take a seat. He sits down on the bed, bringing me down with him, and lays down sideways so that we're facing each other. I keep my eyes closed while he pushes my hair away from my tear-streaked face before running his fingertips over my tears and wiping them away.

"Brooklyn" he says, his raspy voice sounding like a plea that I can't deny. I open my eyes to look at him and see the sad look in his eyes. "What happened on that bridge?"

I close my eyes again as new tears form. "I can't," I whisper.

The speaker in the room scratches and I blink my eyes open.

The pilot speaks, interrupting us, "*I have to fly around for twenty more minutes, but please take a seat shortly. It can get bumpy.*"

Nick's worried eyes are still probing me. "Please," he says.

I shake my head, begging him not to make me talk about it, but I know that if he insists I will. "Please," I counter, brokenly.

He nods and I can see the pain in his eyes. "Come home with me," he whispers.

I frown, wiping my face and the bridge of my nose. "What do you mean?"

"When we land, don't stay in the hotel, come home with me," he says, pushing himself up into a sitting position and bringing me up with him. He makes me feel like a rag doll, the way he carries me around and pulls me up like I weigh nothing.

"Where do you live?" I ask, following him back into the sitting area.

He chuckles, turning around suddenly and making me walk into his chest. I apologize dumbly, but he just looks down at me and gives me a lopsided smile. "I live out of a suitcase, but I have a place here. I have a guest room you can stay in," he says, playfully tugging my hair.

I breathe in and close my eyes at his scent hitting my nostrils. "Okay," I say. "I'll go. But Shea's going to be pissed," I warn with a raised eyebrow.

He raises one back at me, no longer looking amused. "Does Shea have ownership over you?"

I scoff. "No! This isn't the medieval times, you know?"

Nick nods and pulls me into a hug, dipping his head to my ear. "I like the medieval times, though."

A smile tugs at my mouth, despite trying to be a hard ass.

"Whatever," I mutter. Nick laughs and grabs my arm to steady me when the plane goes into a cloud, causing friction.

"Let's sit down," he suggests, holding on to my arm as he leads me to the seat.

"So, San Francisco … you have to have a house in freaking San Francisco, of all places," I joke.

He tilts his head to look at me as he puts on his seat belt and tugs on the longer part of his hair. "I grew up here," he says.

"Oh," I respond, nodding. "Cool."

"Does that make me less cool, Valley Girl?" he jokes, poking me in the ribs, making me laugh.

"No, not really."

"I'm going to wake Shea up and then I'm going to tell him you're going home with me. Unless you want to tell him something else?" he asks.

It's merely a suggestion, but I know he's testing me, and even though I'm nervous to tell Shea, I don't want to *not* go home with Nick.

"Why can't you just stay at the hotel?" I ask, trying to figure out a way around this, even though it's childish and Shea is not my father.

Nick shakes his head in dismay and lets out a breath as he looks away. When he looks at me again, he doesn't look very pleased. "Do you want me to?" he asks, despite the look on his face.

I chew on my lip. "I think it would be better. I mean, everyone will be there," I add with a shrug.

"Yeah," he says, raising his eyebrows as if that's exactly what he wants to get away from. "I'll stay there if you want, even though my house is literally ten minutes away."

I purse my lips, trying to contain my happiness. "You would do that? Stay ten minutes from your house for me?"

Nick's eyes bounce all over my face and when he looks into my eyes, his blue eyes are tranquil and soft. "I would if you want me to."

"Thanks," I say, reaching for his hand and squeezing it, thanking him for so much more than that.

He flips his hand over and threads our fingers together, making my heart flop around in my chest. I shoot him a surprised look, and notice that he's looking at our joined hands. "You're welcome," he responds, his voice barely a whisper.

CHAPTER FIFTEEN

"**H**ow'd you end up over there?" Shea croaks, groggily wiping his hands over his face.

I smile, untangling my hand from Nick's. "You looked comfortable. Didn't want to wake you."

Shea blinks a couple of times, focusing his eyes on me "What *happened*?" He gets up from his seat and crouches down in front of me. "You were crying. What happened?" He narrows his eyes at Nick for a moment before leaning up and wrapping his arms around me. "Let's go," he says, straightening up and standing me up with him. The doors of the jet have been open for a couple of minutes, but we're waiting for the luggage and our car to drive up.

"I'm fine," I respond, shrugging out of his hold, though he doesn't let me go completely. "I'm good now." I inch a little further away, feeling self-conscious about the attention he's paying me and needing to put space between us.

Shea's eyes move from my face to Nick's in a glare. "What the fuck happened?"

"Not my place to say, bro," Nick responds quietly.

Sighing, I back away from Shea completely and pick up my things. "I freaked out when the city came into view," I offer, adjusting my purse on my shoulder.

"Fuck," Shea mutters behind me. "I'm so sorry, Bee." He wraps his arms around me from behind and tucks his face into my neck. "You should've woken me up." His voice is remorseful, but the thing about remorse is that it's one of those feelings that you can only selfishly welcome when you need it, and I don't need it now.

"It's fine. Nick helped me not go into full-on panic mode," I say with a nonchalant chuckle, feeling Shea's arms stiffen around me.

"Hmm," Shea says against me, dropping his arms. "Thanks, man," he says to Nick.

Nick doesn't say anything, but his loud exhale brings my attention to him. When I turn around with a frown, I see that he's watching me as if he wants to say something. I raise an eyebrow at him, but he just shakes his head dejectedly and grabs his bag and walks out of the plane.

"What was that about?" Shea asks, suddenly all perceptive and shit. It makes me want to slap him.

"I dunno," I respond, shrugging as I switch my phone on.

We walk down the steps, grab our bags and head to the tinted black SUV that's picking us up. One of Shea's usual bodyguards, Darius, is waiting for us beside it.

"Brooklyn!" Darius greets with a wide smile. Darius is about six feet five inches tall and two hundred and something pounds of hamburgers. I would love to say muscle, but I've never seen any on him. He's on the heavier side and has an intimidating look with his bald head and his black wraparound glasses. He looks like Laurence Fishburne in The Matrix, but fat.

"Hey, Darius," I respond, walking up to him to bump his fist with mine.

"How's life been treating you? Still no Boogie Downs?" he jokes, making me laugh. Darius has this running joke that when I have a kid I should name him Bronx. He's a real comedian, this one. He has this whole, "And then you can call him Boogie Down as a nickname" spiel that further proves my "this guy thinks he's a comedian" point.

"No, not yet," I answer with a fake chuckle. I shoot Shea a look that tells him to please say something so Darius won't keep talking.

"You ready, D?" Shea asks, catching my drift.

"Sure, boss," Darius responds, turning back to the car and holding the door open for us.

Nick stands aside, letting me slide in first.

"I'm not riding in the middle," Shea says, shaking his head before opening the passenger door and climbing in the front.

"You're such a child," I say with a laugh as Nick slides in beside me.

"Whatever, I got claustrophobia," Shea comments.

"Sure," I reply, still laughing and rolling my eyes.

Nick scoots over so that our legs are touching, making me hyperaware of his presence. Tilting my head at him, I smile. He nudges me with his arm playfully in response and I smile brighter. I can't remember the last time I felt this comfortable with somebody, if ever. Even with Shea it was just easy in the beginning. Our relationship kind of jumped from friends to lovers. Thinking back on it now, I'm not sure we were ever really even friends to begin with. We definitely became friends afterwards, but before, I'm not so sure. It probably had a lot to do with the fact that we were never sober when we were together as a couple. Not once. Our relationship revolved around drugs

and alcohol, and that in itself should have been a red flag for
the both of us, but we were too busy trying to numb ourselves
to care.

With Nick I just feel free, like I can be myself, but at the
same time terrified of the depth of this feeling. The way butterflies swarm the pit of my stomach at the mere thought of him
scares me. I'm scared of the feeling going away, I'm scared of it
staying and him going away. I don't have any experience with
this and it freaks me out. I can't even recall when Nick slipped
through the barriers around me, but as I sit here looking deep
into his eyes, I know I never stood a chance at keeping him out.
When he looks at me I feel like nothing else matters.

My phone vibrates inside of my purse, snapping me out of
the moment. I dish it out quickly to busy myself.

Nina: You there?

Me: Just got here.

Nina: You okay?

Me: Yeah

Nina: No breakdowns I should know about?

I roll my eyes but respond: **Just one**

The phone rings instantly and I let out a breath, knowing
I have to answer.

"Hello?" I respond quietly just as Shea gets on his phone
in the front seat.

"What do you mean just one?" Nina asks.

"On the plane. I can't talk right now," I respond, hoping she lets me off the hook for now.

"You with Shea?" she asks.

"Yeah."

"Did that dirty bastard try anything on the plane?" she asks, her voice deadly quiet.

I laugh. "Nope."

"Humph," she says. "Did anyone else go with you?"

"Yeah," I say quietly, not wanting to say any more. As it is, I'm almost positive Nick can hear her loud ass voice since he's sitting so close to me.

"Who? Gia the whore bag?" Nina asks.

Nick laughs, confirming that he can hear her, and I turn my face to look at him, my eyes wide in shock. He shrugs and throws his hands up in defense, still chuckling softly.

"No. Not her. I gotta go," I say quickly, still looking at Nick.

"Who's that? Shea? Let me talk to him," she says.

"No. Shea's on the phone. I'll call you later, Nina."

"Who is that? The Hen didn't go with you, did he?" she asks, unwilling to let it go.

I groan. "It's Nick. Hendrix is in New York. I gotta go," I repeat.

"Nick ... the hot guy from the club?" Nina asks, gasping.

Nick's loud laughter fills the SUV now.

"Bye," I say and hang up on her without waiting for her to respond.

Nick taps my foot with his, but I turn my face to look out the window to hide my flushed cheeks. Damn Nina and her loud voice. She never fails to do something to embarrass me.

I feel the seat dip beside me, so I know he's close. "You're so cute when you blush," Nick whispers in my ear, making me shiver. I hate that he has this effect on me and I really hate that he knows it. I push him back with my shoulders and glance at Shea, who's turned slightly in his seat looking at us curiously.

"Shut it," I mumble. "My cousin is crazy."

Nick scoots away from me with a laugh. "The cat lady sounds like a smart girl," he comments.

"Clearly, you don't know Nina," I respond.

"Clearly," Shea agrees, shaking his head and facing forward again.

When we get to the hotel, we find Shea's fans swarming the entrance, which isn't surprising but can make it difficult.

"Oh fuck," Shea mutters.

"Do we have more security?" I ask, suddenly worried for Shea. The last time I was with him and people found out where he was staying, his shirt was ripped off and he had scratch marks all over him. I was unharmed because I never walk in with him, but I felt terrible for him. Not to say that Shea doesn't love the attention, because he lives for it, but I'm sure he doesn't want to be all scratched up.

"Yeah, I'm driving to the back entrance, that's where Carlos is meeting us. Don't worry, BK, I gotchu," Darius says.

"I'm not worried about myself," I retort, my eyes bouncing to Shea, who's turned sideways in his seat.

"I'll be fine, Bee," he says, giving me a reassuring smile, but it doesn't calm my nerves in the least.

Nick's hand reaches out for mine. "Hey, it'll be okay, we'll create a fort around pretty boy so he doesn't get mauled by his adoring fans," he jokes, making me smile.

"But then they'll go for you," I say, smiling even though the idea bothers me even more than the one of them attacking Shea. I don't know what I would do if one of these groupies ripped a shirt off of Nick's back. I haven't even ripped a shirt off his back, dammit!

Nick raises an eyebrow at me, amusement dancing in his eyes. "Would that bother you?" he asks, his lips twitching. I try to mask the emotion on my face by pursing my lips and rolling my eyes, but I know it would bother me. I'm sure he knows it would, and from the look on Shea's pissed off face, I'm assuming he knows it as well. I don't worry about Shea when it comes to me dating other guys. He's been there for me while I was in "relationships". He's even gone as far as inviting them to go to shows with me. The look Shea is giving me now, though, confuses me. He turns around huffing as Darius parks in the back of the hotel, and I know this will be a topic of conversation later.

Nick pulls my hand toward him when Darius walks around the car to open the door for us. "Come on and whatever you do, don't let go of my hand," he says, helping me hop out of the truck. I nod in understanding and do as I'm told. There are fans on this side of the hotel as well, but they're limited because of the barriers the hotel put up, creating a walkway from our car to the door. Shea pulls a Dodgers cap over his head and covers his eyes with his Aviator sunglasses, looking at me to make sure I'm fine and walking ahead of me when I nod.

Ducking my head, I press the side of my face into Nick's hard back as we barrel through the flashing cameras and hoots and hollers from both fans and paparazzi. The three of us are standing in line to check-in when Shea turns to me and asks me if I want my own room or a room in his two-bedroom suite.

"Isn't Gia coming tomorrow?" I ask, my brows crinkling.

Shea nods. "Yeah but she'll have her own room."

My lips twist as I mull over my options: stay with him and listen to them having sex, which they will have. Or get my own room and relax. It's pretty much a no brainer for me, so I shake my head vigorously. "I'll get my own. Thanks."

Shea shrugs. "'Kay, I'm sure Hendrix booked you a suite anyway. I just wanted to share one for old times' sake," he says, his voice nonchalant and his face showing no signs that there may be a double meaning behind that, but I know better. I see the way the front of his teeth grind against each other slightly. It's his tell, what he does when he wants to say something cheeky but knows he might get slapped. Thankfully, he doesn't say anything else as he turns to face the counter.

While he sorts out his room situation, I text message Hendrix to see if by chance he got Stacey to book me a room. My brother is thoughtful enough to do that. More like *controlling* enough and because he knows I'm already in an uncomfortable place and he can't be here to save the day, he may have done it.

Exhaling while I wait for his response, I turn to Nick. "Are you sure you want to stay here?" I ask quietly. The more I think about it, the dumber the idea seems to me.

Nick chuckles, shaking his head slightly. "No, but I want to be here for you. You don't want to go home with me so ..." He shrugs, letting the words simmer in my head.

I consider offering him to stay with me, but I think that could be awkward. My phone vibrates in my hand and it's Hendrix saying that he booked me a suite. He says he tried to get me the penthouse but Shea's assistant had already booked it, so he couldn't.

I laugh out loud at my brother's attempt to out-do Shea's rock star lifestyle for me, then exhale and turn my body to face Nick. "Stay in my room," I say finally. "I'll have an extra bed anyway."

Nick raises an eyebrow, approval swimming in his blue eyes. "You sure?"

I smile, nodding my head once. "A favor for a favor," I respond.

Nick's mouth slowly forms into a smile and just as he opens his mouth, Shea turns around, cutting him off. "What's the difference between sharing a room with him and me?" he asks, completely baffled.

I shrug. "You have Gia coming in tomorrow morning, I wouldn't want to interrupt."

Shea begins to shake his head slowly, confusion clouding his face before he blinks it away and narrows his eyes at Nick. "Isn't Steph going to think it's weird that you're not going home?"

I physically feel my heart plummet into my stomach, but I try hard to keep my face as passive as possible, looking away and walking up to the check-in counter before I hear anything else. I'm not sure I'll be able to keep my emotions under control if either one of them gives me any more information right now. I check-in quickly and walk away, moving toward the elevators. I can hear footsteps following closely behind me, but I ignore them, I know it's Nick. I don't need to turn around to confirm it. I can feel the energy radiating off of him as if it were my own. I don't know if I have the right to feel mad or jealous or deceived, but all three of those things stream through me as I wait for the elevator.

As soon as the elevator doors slide open, I step inside, muttering my apologies to the woman stepping out with a suitcase. I take a deep breath and exhale it slowly, clearing out my flustered emotions, and when I turn around to press the number to my floor, I look down at Nick's white sneakers. Refusing to look into his eyes, I let my hair curtain my face as I reach my hand out and press number thirty-five.

"She's having a moment," Nick says softly to the girls trying to step in. I don't look up at their faces, but I can see the matching pink Toms on their feet and assume they're teenagers.

"Okay …" one of them says, stepping back.

If it weren't for the fact that I don't know what to say—at all—I would have told him off for that, but I can't even open my mouth to speak. When the doors close in front of us, Nick steps forward, crowding me into the nook in front of the panel of buttons.

"Talk to me, Brooklyn," he whispers into my hair.

His chest is on my back and I have to fight myself not to lean against him. I have to fight the draw that pulls me, that makes me want to fall into him. I have to fight the urge to turn around and look into his ocean eyes because I know that if I do all I'll feel is disappointment. What bothers me the most is that all I do is hound Nina about always being the other woman, about always selling herself short when it comes to men and letting them have her as the girl on the side. Yet here I am, second to everyone. Always. And this time, I didn't even see that as a possibility, that's how blind I am.

"Nothing to talk about," I say, smiling, even though he can't see me. I close my eyes and coach myself into being neutral: he was never yours, he never said he was single, you never said you weren't taken, you guys are friends, you didn't even kiss him. When I feel I can do it, I push back with my body, forcing him to take a step back, and turn around to face him.

Smiling, I look into his eyes, and for a fleeting moment I think I may cry at the loss of them even though I never had them. This is unchartered water to me, no big deal. "I didn't realize you and Stephanie were serious. When I saw you at the airport that time I didn't get that impression. And since you never talk about her when we're together …" I shrug. "Had I known, I wouldn't have offered you to stay with me."

I don't even know what the fuck I'm apologizing for if he's the one that leads me on every time we talk. Yes, we're friends, but he flirts with me and acts like he wants more and … what a motherfucker. Thankfully, before I can get mad, the elevator opens behind me and I turn around to walk out, thinking that he's going to stop me, but he doesn't. At this point, I don't know if I want him to take the elevator right back down or follow me to the room. I don't know if I want to punch him in the throat for omitting his relationship or make out with him and tell him to get the hell away from me forever. It's so sad that I've never been this confused. It's sadder that the first time I feel this way, I'm a quarter into my life. It's saddest that he doesn't feel the same way about me that I do about him.

In short: I'm experiencing a case of sadness overload.

I walk as nonchalantly as possible to my door, which fortunately isn't that far away from the elevator, and slide my card in. Letting out a breath, I push the door open and swallow the stupid knot that refuses to clear my throat. I step in, my eyes quickly scanning the large living room area, and toss my purse aside. When the door clicks shut, I finally turn around and see Nick standing beside it, pulling on the tip of his faux hawk.

I exhale, placing my hands on my hips and tilting my head to look at the high ceilings. "You can go," I say.

Nick lets out a laugh. "Do you want me to leave or explain myself?"

I narrow my eyes at him, crossing my arms over my chest and shrug. "I already told you we have nothing to talk about."

He nods, narrowing his eyes back at me. "I beg to differ."

"I'm sure you do," I mutter then exhale. "Nick, it really,

really doesn't matter. You have nothing to explain to me. I'm your friend, at least I thought I was, so I'm just shocked that you have a live-in girlfriend and you acted like she was nothing," I shrug.

He frowns. "That's not-" he starts, but I put my hands up to stop him.

"It's fine," I interrupt. "I just don't understand why you would lead me on for no reason." He tries to speak again, but I keep going. "And then you invite me to your house like it's all good. What were you going to do? 'Hey, Stephanie, remember Brooklyn? She's staying here for the next couple of days,'" I say, mimicking his deep voice.

"Dammit, woman," he growls, striding over to me so quickly that I don't have time to move away. Dipping his head so that we're at eye level, he grabs the nape of my neck and pulls me to him, pinning me with his blue eyes, daring me to protest, and slams his lips over mine.

I wish I could intricately describe every single emotion his mouth makes me feel, but there are so many, I think I might burst. Tiny fireworks soar between us when his tongue parts my lips and begins to dance wildly with mine. His hands travel down my body in a frenzy, pulling me to him as if I can't be close enough, and that's exactly the way I feel as I pull on his hair and scrape the back of his neck. I would let him pull me inside of him if he could. I've been kissed a million times, yet none at all. That's how this kiss makes me feel. Like I'm freefalling, like I'm dying, like I'm breathing for the first time. Like I'm high on ecstasy and a million expert hands are massaging me. This kiss is my life. And when we break apart, completely breathless, both of our chests heaving, I slap him. Hard.

"Get out," I whisper, I can barely make out the words. As amazing as that kiss was, as incredible as Nick makes me feel,

I can't be just another notch on somebody's bedpost, especially not his.

"You're kidding, right?" he asks, his eyes seething into mine as he grinds his teeth together and places his hand over the spot on his cheek where I slapped him.

I look at him for a moment longer before turning my back to him. Thankfully the suite's doorbell rings and Nick attends to the bellman at the door. I run into the bathroom and lock myself in, switching on the water so that it'll drown out my sobs when they finally pour out of me. I cry because I can't believe I slapped him. I cry for that kiss that'll forever be engraved in my heart. I cry because I fucking hate him for lying to me. I cry because somehow, without my knowledge or permission, he snuck himself into my heart and I don't know how to push him back out. I know that I'm letting my bottled up emotions get the best of me, but I can't help it. At the feel of water crashing between my fingers, I get up and turn off the running faucet. Standing in front of it, I dip my hand in the pool of water, dejectedly looking at the way it seeps through my fingers.

CHAPTER SIXTEEN

After taking a long, hot shower, I explore the empty suite. It's not lavish like others I've stayed in, but it's spacious and has a wonderful view of the bay. Rounding the kitchen counter, I notice the hotel left a chilled bottle of champagne, two glasses, and a cup of strawberries with a note that says they hope I enjoy my stay. I decide that I will enjoy my stay courtesy of their bottle of champagne, which I quickly open. I'm on my third glass when I sit down on a barstool and notice that there's a note written on the little pad of paper on the corner of the counter.

Putting my glass down, I slide it over to me and read.

Say it, just say it. I contemplate it for all of two seconds before hopping off the stool, picking up my glass and the bottle, and walking to the floor to ceiling window. Plopping down on the couch behind me, I kick up my feet on the coffee table and take a sip on the bubbly drink. My phone begins to ring in my purse, and I'm thankful I tossed it on the couch beside me so I don't have to get up and walk to get it. I put my glass down and scramble the things in my purse in search of it, seeing Nina's face looking at me when I finally find it.

"Hey," I answer.

"Hey, how's everything?" she asks, her voice cautious for once.

"Fine. Just hanging out at the hotel, drinking some champagne. You know, the good life," I mutter.

She sighs loudly. "I should've gone with you. Why are you drinking? You never drink anymore." Her voice is small and helpless, matching my feelings. I don't laugh because if I do, I think I'll end up crying again.

"I'm good, I just needed to relax," I respond, finding that it's true. I actually don't feel terrible right now.

"So you don't need me to pack my bags and fly my ass over there?" Nina asks.

I laugh. "Nope. I think I'm good."

"Where's the hottie? Is his room near yours?" she asks.

"Funny story ... he was supposed to stay with me. Hendrix booked a two-room suite, but we sort of made out and then I slapped him and told him to leave."

Silence. Shocking silence.

"What?" Nina asks quietly, clearly taken aback.

I explain everything that happened, from the airplane to the car, to the hotel lobby and elevator to the kiss.

"Wow. I mean ... I can see why you're pissed, but wow ... I can't believe you slapped him," she says and falls into a fit of giggles. "That's my girl!"

I can't keep the laughter from escaping my lips. Of course Nina would be happy about something like that. She makes me promise that I won't finish the bottle of champagne by myself.

"As much as I want you to loosen up and live a little, I'm scared of you doing that without me there to watch you," she says.

Her words make me feel loved, wanted, and because of that, I promise her that I won't get drunk and that I won't let anybody lure me into doing any drugs. I've come too far to let myself relapse.

There's a knock on my door shortly after I hang up with Nina, and I look through the peephole to see who it is. I find myself staring at a mop of unruly brown hair until Shea lifts his face, showing me his annoyance for having to wait for me to open the door. I swing the door open and move out of the way so he can come in.

"About time," he says, brushing past me and looking around the suite. He shrugs. "Mine's nicer."

I roll my eyes, even though he can't see me, and let the door shut behind me as I follow him into the living room. "That's because you got the penthouse suite."

"You could've stayed with me, but noooo you wanted to stay with Shadow," he says mockingly. "Where is he?"

I shrug. "He left. I'm sure he'll be back later." I don't want to get into what happened between Nick and me, not with Shea. We may be good friends, but I don't like to bore him with my sorry excuse for relationships.

"Hmm," Shea says, plopping down on the sofa and turning on the television. "You drinking this?" he asks, tapping the bottle of champagne with the tip of his sneaker.

"Yeah. You want?" I offer.

He tips his head up to look at my face. He looks amused by the question, as if it's a given that he would want it, and I know it is, but if I'm going to be honest, I didn't want him to stroll in here and start drinking with me. Who knows what he's going to pull out of his pockets after his second glass of alcohol? I know he wouldn't offer me anything that he takes, he knows better than that and he's really made an effort not to include me in his illicit behaviors, but it doesn't change the fact that it makes me uneasy. Especially when we're alone. For the past couple of years, anytime Shea and I have hung out by ourselves it's been because we've gone out to a restaurant or a bar to hang out. I don't think we've been alone in a hotel room with a bottle of alcohol in over five years.

I guess life has made sure that this trip should test me in every way imaginable. Since he doesn't reply with words, I pick up the extra flute and pour a drink for him, handing it to him as I pick up my own. I sit down on the couch beside him, but make sure to leave room between us. When he takes a sip and flips the channel, I let out a breath, realizing that I'm totally overanalyzing the situation.

"Let's go out tonight," he says after a moment.

"Where?" I ask, doing a mental catalog of the clothes in my suitcase.

Shea shrugs, his eyes darting from the TV to me. "Anywhere. Out. They're throwing a little party in the lounge downstairs, but we can ditch it and go wherever you want."

"Who's hosting the party?" I ask, furrowing my eyebrows.

"Some promoters," he replies flippantly.

My eyes widen. "Did they pay you already?"

His eyes shoot heavenward. "BK, they always pay me, doesn't mean I have to stay the entire night."

This is the kind of shit that gets celebrities in trouble, the careless way they seem to think that the world caters to them, and they can do whatever the hell they want even if they are being paid and expected to do whatever they agreed upon.

"How many hours are you supposed to be there?" I ask, unwilling to let it go. I know that if Shea starts causing trouble before his tour even starts, the label is going to have a mess to clean up afterward.

"Two hours. God, I hate that you're the boss's daughter," he mutters under his breath, looking back at the TV.

"And I hate that you're so unprofessional sometimes, but you don't see me complaining," I retort.

He shifts his body to face me, folding his left leg on the seat between us. "Do you wanna go to that shit? Or do you want me to ditch it and take you somewhere else? I want to make you feel comfortable since I dragged you over here to begin with. Excuse me for trying to be a good friend over here," he says seriously, emphasizing the word *friend* in a way that makes me clamp my teeth together. The thing about Shea is that the last time we hooked up wasn't that long ago, even if it was a mistake on my part. He has a way of making you feel like you're not just a pastime to him, like you're more, and because we're friends and we talk, sometimes the lines blur. Maybe it's true what they say: men and women can't just be friends. I really want to prove that theory wrong, though. I heard somewhere, probably on Elvis Duran or something, since that's my source of useful information, that men and women can be friends successfully if they are each in a stable relationship. Since I wouldn't know what a stable relationship was if it hit me in the face and Shea wouldn't know how to keep his dick in his pants long enough to even learn the definition of the word relationship, I think we're pretty doomed.

Still, I refuse to get caught up in his little games. I know the smile spreading on his face is his weapon of choice against my libido, and I refuse to let myself sink enough to acknowledge it. I've also had a lot of time to reflect on the kind of friendship we have, and I know it wasn't good for me then, and it's probably worse for me now, but I'll be damned if I leave him behind. The truth is, I tried for a little while not to speak to him and it worked, but then I kept running into him everywhere.

The business isn't that big. Everybody knows somebody that knows somebody, so when I realized that we were bound to continue to run into each other, I gave up trying to push him away. And the thing is, he's a good friend when he's not trying to hook up with me. Thankfully he hasn't tried again after our last hurrah when I made it clear that it couldn't happen again. He's hazardous to me, the things he's into can make me crumble—we both know that—so he's accepted his place in my life. It doesn't change the fact that he's a guy that usually gets what he wants and sometimes he looks at me like I'm exactly that.

Standing up, I grab the notepad with Nick's number on it and take my empty glass to the sink. "Let's just go to the party in the lounge," I say over my shoulder. "I'll be ready at nine."

Shea stands, leaving his empty glass on the coffee table. "You wanna go to the store with me so I can get new shoes?"

I look into his eyes for a moment and see the sincerity of a true friend and the loneliness of a lost boy. I don't hesitate anymore. I grab my large purse and place it on my forearm before following him out. We spend a couple of hours shopping because Shea can't just buy one thing, he has to buy the shoes and matching belt and sunglasses that look good with the shoes and matching belt. I'm not one to talk, since I left the store with a new purse. But only because I didn't have that style and I really, really liked it.

"You talked to the Wicked Witch lately?" Shea asks as we stroll down Fillmore Street. There are three bodyguards around us now, blocking us from the views of most of the cameras that follow. It's times like these that I'm glad Shea isn't tall, because he can sort of hide out within the fort of the bodyguards.

"Nope," I reply, not needing to elaborate the many reasons I haven't spoken to my mother. Shea knows better than anybody how much I've struggled with her in the past. "You talk to yours?" Our mothers are one and the same. His is nicer to him than mine is, but nicer means that instead of pointing out certain things she doesn't like about him, she ignores him entirely. Unless she wants to go to an event or she needs a new car, then Maria is all over her son. It's sickening to witness.

"Eh … a couple of weeks ago," he says, scratching his head in thought.

We eat lunch in a little Asian restaurant and head back to the hotel so that he can drop me off.

"I have interviews with two radio stations, then I'll be back. I'll pick you up at nine," Shea says as I exit the car in the back of the hotel. I get my bags and wave him off, promising that I'll be ready. When I get back to my room, I'm a little disheartened to find that it's still empty. Even though I didn't call Nick, a part of me hoped he would come back. The stupid, wrong, forever dreamer part of me, that is.

I'm sitting in the living room, waiting for Shea, noticing that the clock on the wall says it's 9:28. I figured he would be late because he's never on time, not that I usually am, but I'm never usually this bored either. I've already listened to thirty demos, changed my clothes three times, and checked my hair and makeup seven times—this will be the eighth time I get up and go to the bathroom to look at myself. I'm wearing a short black dress and killer black wedges that I had to practice walking in a couple of times before tonight. They have a very Lady Gaga look to them, with the heel curved inward, which I love. My hair is down, as usual, because I never really know what to do with it, and my makeup looks flawless, which is good because if I hadn't learned anything after the countless makeup classes my mother paid for me to go to, she would have a coronary. She always calls when she sees photos of me in magazines and we "discuss my makeup, hair, and outfit" and "where

I went wrong" or "what I did right." It's a favorite pastime of hers, discussing the way I look.

At ten o'clock, I get tired of waiting and call Shea's cell phone. He answers on the fourth ring.

"BK, I'm going up there now. Fuck. I completely forgot to pick you up! Shit!" he curses loudly, speaking quickly into the line.

I breathe, not letting disappointment consume me. I try not to remind myself that this is the same guy who offered not to go to this party but to take me somewhere else to cater to me. I try not to remind myself of the countless times he's let me down.

"It's fine. I'll meet you down there," I say, instead.

"You sure?" he asks.

I bite my tongue. "Positive," I say, smiling so that he can hear it. I hope he hears the fakeness of it through the line.

"Awesome. See you here. You're my date," he says.

I laugh because I can't stand it, and I hang up the phone as I head out of my room. I figure that Leo and Fern will be down there, so I'll have them to talk to anyway, and I don't want to stay holed in my room the entire night. I spot Darius when I get to the lounge, and he ushers me in, taking me to where Shea is sitting with two girls on either side of him. He's wearing a black button down shirt and jeans, his hair a crazy mess as usual. He's talking to one of the girls, the blonde one wearing a red dress, when he spots me and his eyes bulge out of their sockets for a second. I internally pat myself on the back and let myself smile, though it's not a smug smile, it's the fake one I reserve for Shea when I catch him off guard.

"Damn, BK," Shea says, standing up and giving me his hand, which I don't take.

"Thanks," I say, cutting off his compliments. I don't want

him to tell me that I look hot or fine or whatever other compliment he wants to throw at me right now. I'm not in the mood for it. "Where's Leo?" I ask, looking around.

Shea stands beside me and puts his arm around my shoulder. The wedges I'm wearing make us stand at the same height. I may even be a drop taller than him. "I'm so sorry I forgot to get you. They kept calling me, so I came down thinking I would have enough time to go back up, but then I got caught up," he explains, his voice soft and cajoling.

I nod in understanding, knowing exactly what he got caught up in. "It's totally fine," I say. "I'm going to get a drink and see if I spot Leo," I respond, shrugging away from his hold.

"All right, I'll be here," he says, walking back to his groupies. They're faceless to me. I stopped looking at the girls around him a long time ago. They always have the same "He's taking me home tonight" look in their eyes regardless of the state they're in.

Making my way down the steps, I walk to the bar, which is lit up with a nice blue glow around it. I squeeze between two empty stools and ask for a rum and coke when I get the attention of the bartender. I smell Nick standing beside me before I turn to acknowledge him. It doesn't even cross my mind that it could be another man wearing his cologne because the pounding of my heart tells me it's him.

"Rum and coke, huh?" he asks before I figure out what to say to him. He leans in closer, his chest brushing against the back of my arm and I close my eyes.

"I'm sorry," I spit out while I still have the courage to apologize, hoping he accepts it without me having to turn around and look into his eyes as I do it.

His hand wraps around my forearm and he pivots my body so that we're facing each other. My senses are hyperaware of him, of his smell, of the tension that's radiating off of him as he stares at me … while I stare at nothing under my eyelids.

"Why are you sorry?" he asks, his voice low and in my ear now. I intake as much breath as I can without feeling light-headed, which is pointless because the only thing I breathe in is Nick and he makes me feel breathless.

Slowly, I open my eyes and find his for a second before quickly dropping my gaze. Instead of looking at his face, my eyes trail down his body and back up. He's wearing jeans and a striped button down shirt that he has rolled up to expose his strong forearms. His hair is styled into his signature faux hawk and I can see a shadow of stubble over his jaw that makes me want to extend my hand and trace it. His eyes look amazing under the glowing blue light of the bar, almost matching the color. The way he's looking at me so intently, I almost don't hear the bartender tell me my drink is beside me.

"I'm sorry I slapped you," I say looking into Nick's eyes, and surprisingly, I feel lighter after saying the words this way.

He nods, accepting my apology. "You here with Shea?" he asks, his words coming out tense.

I let out a laugh. "Does it look like I'm here with Shea?" I ask, raising an eyebrow and knowing that Nick, who towers over me even in these heels, can see what Shea is up to behind me. He glances over me, probably confirming what I'm saying before pinning me with his gaze again.

"So you're here alone?" Nick asks, seemingly needing a confirmation.

"Nick, did you get my drink already?" a female voice to my left asks. I'm still looking at Nick, whose face shows no signs of anything at the question. I tell myself that it's because he has nothing to hide, he's with Stephanie—I know this. When I look at the girl beside him, I notice that she's a redhead, not the

Stephanie girl I saw him with before. He did say that she wasn't his girlfriend, but goodness, this is like Shea all over again. Because I am really trying not to be that girl—the one that's always second place to everybody—I pick up my drink and put a bill down on the bar before walking away. Nick doesn't come after me, which tells me everything I need to know, and I don't turn around to see what he's doing because I don't need to see him with another woman. Actually, I would rather rip my eyes out than have to see him with another woman.

My heart is still beating out of my chest when I reach Shea's table. He's narrowed down his two groupies to one, it seems, because only the girl in the red dress remains.

"What'd you get?" he asks as I take a seat beside him.

"Rum and coke," I respond, noticing the way his bottle of vodka is almost out already.

"I would've offered to get you a bottle, but I know how you get about sharing drinks," he says.

Again, I bite my tongue. I wonder if he remembers the time they slipped something in our drinks at a club and had us hallucinating well into the next night. After that experience, I decided that if I ever stepped foot in a club or lounge again, I would buy my own drinks. This night is proving to be grating my every last nerve. I decide that I'm going to have this drink and call it a night. Nick walks up the stairs soon after, the redhead trailing closely behind him. I wish I could fight the way my heart soars around him. I wish I could tell him to stop looking at me with those eyes that tell me he wants me, especially when he's with somebody. And more than anything, I wish I could just forget about him and his lying ways.

I stiffen when Nick takes a seat directly across from me. Because of the way the couches are set up, our legs brush against each other's when he extends his legs to get comfortable. He locks eyes with mine and takes a sip of his amber drink; I take a sip of mine. The redhead sits in the seat beside him and my stomach turns when she leans in to whisper something in his ear. They continue their conversation, as Shea's conversation with the lady in red has progressed to him sticking his tongue down her throat, and I just sit here, alternating between staring at my drink, taking large sips and sorting through my clutch purse.

When Shea leans in to me and asks if I want to dance, my eyes dart to Nick, who's explaining something to the girl he's with. She looks completely enthralled by the conversation and he looks just as into it, using his hands to emphasize his every word. I catch random words of it and notice they're talking about producing, which is better than sexual positions, but it still makes me crazy.

"Oh, you decided to come up for air," I say to Shea, who laughs, throwing both arms around me and squeezing.

"Jealous?" he asks playfully.

"Fuck no," I respond, and it's the truth. I'm more disgusted at him than jealous of him, and knowing that the entire universe thinks he's exclusively dating Gia and he's in here making out with some nobody is even more of a turn-off. "What would Gia say if she walked in the door right now and saw you?" I ask curiously. It's not like Gia is a saint either.

Shea drops his arms and shrugs, scrunching his nose the way he does when he thinks. "I dunno, never really thought about it ... she'd either be pissed or want to join us."

I make a face. "Gross."

Shea laughs. "So you wanna dance?"

Throwing back the rest of my drink, I look at Nick, whose eyes are now on me, even though the redhead has now moved so close to him that she's almost sitting on his lap. I smile at him, showing no teeth because I'm grinding them together, and stand up, adjusting my dress as I do. Nick's eyes travel slowly from my feet all the way up my legs, taking in every inch of skin I'm showing. He doesn't stop until he reaches my eyes, and when he does, his are filled with the kind of desire that makes it hard for me to breathe.

Memories of what we shared in the bathroom of the airplane and in the hotel room come flooding into me, making my stomach clench. I know that we're totally eye fucking each other, I can feel that we are and it crosses my mind that we're being rude, but I can't find it in me to care. Shea pulls my hand suddenly, breaking the spell Nick has cast on me, and drags me to the dance floor. I feel Nick's eyes boring into me as I walk away from him. I'm not sure if I should relish the fact that he's looking or let the feeling of uneasiness that is tingling through me win. In the end, the music squashes the uneasiness, and I find myself dancing to a hip hop song with Shea.

I think one of the things I always liked about dancing with Shea when we went out was the way people made room for us, even at a crowded club. This lounge isn't crowded, but the dance floor opens for us just the same, giving us room to move around, not that we need it with the way we dance. Shea and I have the art of seductive dancing down to a science, even though we make it look more like a dirty sonnet. We've done it so many times and have heard so many cheers, and we both know the right moves that will get us that praise. And we do it tonight, just like we always do.

He puts his arm around me and grinds against me in a sensual motion that drives women all around the world crazy, gaining us hoots and hollers. When he spins me to face the crowd, I notice that Nick is standing, watching us intently. I almost expect him to grab his date and leave, but he doesn't, he just stays there, his eyes transfixed on mine, daring me to look away from him—so I don't. I watch him the entire time my body moves against Shea's. I see the way his eyes blaze when Shea takes his hand and places it flat over my stomach, and the way his jaw clenches when Shea dips me toward him. Thankfully the song switches to another one, and even though we get a request for an encore, I hear Shea turn it down. I don't even pay attention to the cheers coming from the crowd; I don't bask in them the way I normally would because the person whose praise I want is looking at me like he just experienced his own death before his eyes. It's not an upset look; it's more of a tortured look, one that makes my heart feel hollow.

Shea kisses me on the cheek and tells me he's going to get laid before walking back to the girl in the red dress, leaving me standing there torn on what to do. Nick's eyes stay on mine as he makes his way over to me. A guy with a thick black beard has now started to move beside me, probably thinking he's going to get that show and maybe more out of me, but I don't look at him. I can't look at him, not with the way Nick is striding over to me like a cat trying to catch a mouse, even though the feral look in his eyes tells me he knows I won't run.

When he reaches me, he cups one side of my face with one of his hands, his eyes boring into mine, and begins to walk me backwards. To everybody else we may look like we're dancing, or moving to dance in another area, and maybe we are. I don't know what he has planned; I just know I want to be part of it. I jump when my back hits a wall, my eyes widening as I look at him. The air, which started out as little clouds of desire, is now fogging around us, making it impossible to acknowledge anything but one another. Nick lowers his head slightly, close enough to kiss me, but doesn't. It's driving me crazy that he's only touching my face.

"You never got a chance to tell me who you were here with," he says, the rasp in his voice potent near my ear.

I swallow loudly, trying to unclog the haze in my ears that my ricocheting heart is causing. "I'm not with anybody," I respond, surprised at how steady my voice is.

He pulls back, narrowing his eyes as he drops his hand from my face. "Fair enough. Who are you leaving with?" he asks.

Looking at him I can only think of one reply, so I answer before I chicken out. "You," I say, mouthed, not spoken.

Nick closes his blazing eyes and takes a breath before opening them again. "Are you staying with me tonight?"

"Are you staying with me?" I retort.

He dips his head, his teeth clamping down on my lower lip before he sucks it into his mouth, and just when I think he's going to stop, his lips begin to move against mine, his tongue slipping into my mouth and exploring it in a way that takes my breath away completely. I wrap my hands around his neck, squeezing it with my fingernails, moaning into his mouth at the sound he makes when I do that. Nick breaks the kiss and looks at me, both of us are panting, our eyes wild on each other's.

"I'll stay wherever the hell you want. Let's get out of here," he says, pulling me toward the exit and to the elevators of the hotel.

CHAPTER SEVENTEEN

O ur elevator ride up to the room is quiet, but when Nick
takes my hand in his, I don't feel the need for extra talking.
"Why didn't you call me?" he asks, swinging our hands
in a playful motion that makes me relax despite his question.

"I wasn't sure what to say if I did," I respond truthfully.

He takes the room key out of my hand and I stand beside
the door waiting for him to unlock it, looking up at him when
he doesn't. He turns me so that my back is on the door and he's
hovering over me. Once again, I find myself getting lost in his
scent, in his molten eyes and the way he looks at me, and when
he dips his head and brushes his nose tenderly against the side
of my face, I feel my resolve crack a little more.

"I want to take you into this room and lose myself inside of
you," he whispers roughly, voicing my sentiments.

I bite the inside of my cheek and nod. "Okay," I whisper in
response.

I watch the bop of his Adam's apple as he backs away and
swallows, staring at me with intent eyes. "Okay?" he asks quietly, dragging his thumb over my cheek, making me lean into it,

savoring his touch.

"Yes," I respond while I still have enough air to get it out.

Nick looks at me for a moment longer before his lips crash against mine as he opens the suite door, grabbing my clutch purse and tossing it along with the key before lifting me up and wrapping my legs around his waist. His lips never sway from mine. We're frantic, me tugging on his shirt, trying to take it off. Him pulling my face closer to his, making our teeth clash against each other's as our tongues dance together wildly. I've never felt this exhilarated when it comes to having sex with somebody, I've never felt this needed, this desire to possess and be possessed.

"Which room?" he asks, breathing heavily against me as we break our kiss.

"Whichever is closest," I respond, making him chuckle darkly before he takes my lips again.

Nick throws me down on the bed, making me yelp, and crouches down. He begins to unstrap my shoes, kissing along the top of my feet as he does it. When they're both off, he runs his lips up my calves, kissing, nipping, and sucking as he goes. My chest is heaving by the time he stops, just below the hem of my skirt, which is now bunched up to the top of my thighs.

"You have the sexiest legs," he murmurs as he sucks on my thighs in a way that has me throwing my head back and gasping. "The things I want to do to you," he whispers, so quietly that I almost don't catch it. His words ignite a fury within my core that makes me bite down on my lip and intake a breath when I feel his fingers inching the edge of my underwear.

"Look at me, Brooklyn," he says. I lift my head up and notice he's still fully dressed, the fire in his eyes burning into mine. "I need to taste you," he says, biting down on his lip when I moan and writhe at his words. "All of you."

He stands, pulling me up with him, and peels my dress slowly over my head. I'm not wearing a bra since my back is exposed, and I feel the urge to cover myself up. I don't though, because I don't want to seem inexperienced, even if I am. Even though I've had sex with three guys, I've never been fully naked in front of any of them, not even Shea. Things have always been quick—in tour buses, bathrooms, in dressing rooms, the back of limos or cars, never like this. Never on a bed. Never with somebody that devours me with his eyes alone and makes me feel beautiful, wanted. He tugs his lip between his teeth as he trails over my mostly naked body with his hooded eyes and then he's on me again, his mouth hot on mine as I stumble with the buttons of his dress shirt, trying to claw it off as fast as I can. By the time I manage to take most of it off with his help, it's missing a couple of buttons and ends up in a heap with his shoes, socks, jeans, and my dress.

I let myself fall back on the bed when Nick walks me to it, and I admire him as he strides to his jeans, taking a condom out of his pocket. His body is perfection; it's everything I've never touched before. The guys I've been with pale in comparison to Nick. While Nick belongs on Men's Health, they belong on the cover of Teen Bop. His arms are well defined, curving in and out at every muscle, but not overly done that he looks like a juicehead. I can read the scripted tattoo of his family name, Wilde, on his inner bicep and look at the nice musical notes over the side of his ribs. His stomach is in perfect shape but not overly cut, though I can tell he definitely works hard on maintaining it. His legs are strong and thick. When my eyes move to his again, I catch him doing his own trail of my body, and I feel a little more self-conscious now that I'm lying before him. He looks like perfection, whereas I look like a regular girl with a butt and thighs that I doubt he's used to. The women I've seen around him are all thin and tall and I'm just me, somebody who does Pilates four days a week and watches what I eat. I'll never look like any of those women, but for some reason he's not with one of them, he's here with me.

When Nick looks into my eyes again, all of my insecurities take the backseat, because the only thing I see in them is blazing desire. He's setting me on fire from the inside out. My breathing instantly turns ragged when he strides to the bed, the large erection very apparent in his boxers as he nudges my legs apart with his knees. He moves forward, placing both hands on either side of me and hovers over my mouth.

"I forgot to tell you how beautiful you looked in your dress, but you look downright gorgeous right now," he says in a husky whisper before placing a kiss on my lips. "Any questions before I have my way with you?" he asks, the tip of his nose trailing over my face.

"No live-in girlfriend?" I ask just to make sure.

Nick chuckles. "No, ma'am," he responds, sucking my earlobe into his mouth, making me moan.

"No girlfriends or women at all?" I ask, again, just to make sure we're on the same page. Just to make sure I don't get burned.

Nick backs away from me so that I can look into his eyes. "Nobody. You're the only one I want."

I swallow, allowing myself to let that sink in before wrapping my arms around his neck and bringing him back into me. "Then have me," I say against his lips.

He growls and delves his tongue into my mouth in response, his hands skimming my body as mine do the same to his, reveling in the way his muscles clench beneath my wandering fingertips. His mouth leaves mine and traces kisses along my collarbone and to the valley of my breasts. He takes his time exploring before finally pulling a nipple into his mouth, moaning loudly as he does and making my body bow off the bed.

"Oh God, Nick," I pant, pulling at his hair. He does the same to the other and moves down to my stomach, nipping, sucking, kissing, as he pulls down the black lace thong I'm wearing. Raining kisses along the insides of my thighs, he spreads them, licking and sucking close enough to my lips that my hips begin to buck in anticipation. He chuckles when the hold I have on his hair tightens, and finally he begins to lick, up and down the center of my folds, turning his head sideways to suck. He does this, teasing me, making me pant out his name once, twice, three times, before giving my clit his full attention, moaning when he pulls it into his mouth.

"I could have this all day," he says, his tongue diving inside of me, his words taking me on a natural high I've never experienced. His mouth suddenly clamps over my clit and he sucks, making my insides feel like they're on fire, hot and cold, tingling and dizzying. My insides are fireworks as my body convulses.

He's kissing my stomach, making his way back to my breasts as I come down from my high and gather up everything in me to flutter my eyes open again. My vision traces his moving arm and I catch the muscles of his stomach flexing as he pleasures himself, looking down at me through half-mast eyes as he bites down on his lip. He dips his head and kisses me, a slow, sensual, languid kiss as he positions himself between me, his thick tip sliding in but not enough. I arch my back and plant my heels on the bed, aiming him inside of me, but Nick backs away, breaking the kiss to look at me.

"You're sure," he says, more than asks.

"Positive," I respond without hesitation.

His eyes search my face again, dropping to my bare chest

and to the spot where we're united but not.

"Please fuck me," I whisper, arching myself against him again. His nostrils flair as his eyes dart to mine again, blazing, and he dips his face to mine, biting down on my lip. Hard. I close my eyes as reveling in the way he makes me feel.

"Open your eyes and say that again, Brooklyn," he says, his voice strained.

I want to keep my eyes closed, afraid of looking at him, afraid of him seeing me in this moment, a moment I've never shared with anybody before him. I've never made eye contact during sex; it's always been weird to me, which I know sounds weird to most. They say the eyes are the doors to your soul and I've never wanted to let anybody in that deep when they're inside me physically. Besides, I'm used to seeing the faraway look guys have when they're high and inside me. I'm not used to seeing the awed look Nick is giving me when I look into his, as if I might disappear if he looks away.

He waits, pushing in slightly, but not enough.

"Take me," I whimper, squirming for him.

He closes his eyes as if to savor the moment and opens them back quickly, letting me know the yearning he has for me as he pushes himself slowly inside of me, letting out a guttural moan as he rocks himself deeper. My breath falls away from me, eyes fluttering closed at the feel of him, at the completeness I feel with him in there.

"I want you to look at me," he says quietly. "I want to remember the look on your face when I make you come again." He rocks his hips into me. "I want you to remember the look on mine when I come inside of you for the first time."

Opening my eyes, I shudder at his words and can't bring myself to look away again. This time, as I lay below him, with him thrusting into me at a leisurely pace, I let myself drown in those eyes of his.

"The most beautiful woman I've ever seen," he says, his voice barely a whisper. His eyes bore into mine, letting me know he speaks the truth, daring me to question his statement, and I find that I can't, because when Nick looks at me that's exactly how I feel.

My head is in the clouds as I lay in Nick's arms as he traces over the bee tattoo on my hip. I don't know what to do with my hands, I've never lain in somebody's arms after sex, so I awkwardly place my arm over the side of his body, letting my hand hang over his back.

"What are the notes for?" I ask quietly, bringing my fingers to trace over them.

Nick shifts beneath me so that I can get a better look. "It's a song I composed a while back," he explains, tucking my hair behind my ear and touching my face lightly.

The way he looks at me makes me feel whole, which scares and confuses me. I've never been one of those women that walks around looking for her other half, but the way he looks at me makes me wonder if that other half talk is real.

"Sing it for me," I say, smiling and scooting closer to him.

When he chuckles, I scoot closer, closing my eyes so that I can remember that sound and replay it when I'm having a gloomy day. "I only composed it, babe, I don't have words for it."

Opening my eyes, I give him a confused look. "What will you do with it?"

He smiles. "I don't know. Maybe sell it. We'll see."

"Will you play it for me?" I ask, hopefully, not knowing if

sex will make things weird for us now.

He leans in and places a kiss on my forehead. "Of course I will, beautiful."

"What instruments do you play?" I ask.

"Guitar, piano, violin, bass, drums," he says, laughing when I gape at him.

"That's ... wow ..." I comment, at a loss for words. I knew he played some, from my experience, most producers do, but I didn't consider that Nick would be a band geek. I laugh at the thought.

"What?" he asks, looking amused at my amusement.

"I was just thinking that I didn't peg you for a band geek," I joke.

His blue eyes twinkle. "Band geek, huh?" he asks, faking offense. "I'll show you band geek," he says, running his finger-tips down the side of my body, making me shiver, and stopping at my clit, which is sensitive and swollen, yet throbs in antici-pation welcoming his hand. He dips his face and kisses me pas-sionately as he continues to tease me. "Band geeks are probably good with their fingers," he muses, dipping one inside of me, making me gasp. "And the ones that play wind instruments are probably good with their mouths," he says as his tongue swirls around my pebbled nipple. Nick continues to show me every-thing band geeks are probably good at, and when he's finished, he tells me he was never part of his school band, but wishes he would've been.

At some point during the night, we get up to shower be-fore getting back into bed and snuggling close together as we watch a rerun of Curb Your Enthusiasm and laugh our asses off at Larry David's antics. I wake up to the sun kissing my face and groan, covering my head with the comforter. When I feel the bed shift beside me, I peel my eyes open, noticing Nick is awake and sitting on the bed watching me. I rub my eyes and tuck my hands under my pillow.

"What time is it?" I ask groggily.

"Ten," he replies, lying beside me and tucking his face into the crook of my neck. I breathe him in, as he does me, and sigh at the clean smell that radiates off of him.

"Ten in the morning on a weekend and you're already showered?" I ask, my hands tracing the curves of his muscled arms and over his chest, down his torso. I smile when he sucks his stomach in.

"Yes," he says, gripping my fingers in his hand and bringing it to his mouth. "Get up, so I can feed you and take you somewhere." He doesn't give me a chance to argue, just drops my hand and places a hard kiss on my mouth before getting up and walking out of the room.

Once I'm dressed and ready to go, I make my way over to the living room and find Nick fully dressed. He's wearing earphones and bobbing his head as he takes sips from the mug in his hand. I walk up behind him and wrap my arms around his middle, placing my face on his hard back and closing my eyes, allowing myself to feel content.

"Ready to go?" he asks, taking the earphones off and closing his laptop.

"Yeah," I sigh against him.

He laughs softly and I squeeze him tighter, unwilling to let go.

"Let's feed you and then we'll go," Nick says, turning his body so that I'm standing between his legs, my arms still around his body. He kisses the top of my head and rests his chin on it. "Mine," he whispers, making me smile.

Nick sits with me, working, as I eat my breakfast and catch up on emails. I sent Allie a design a couple of days ago and still haven't heard her thoughts on it. Once he's done on his computer again, I show him my design and he asks me how I come up with them, which I explain to him. He tells me that he wants the first custom headphones Fab makes so that he can wear them proudly.

"If you're lucky, I'll actually use them," he says.

I laugh. "What would you want them for if not to use?"

He raises an eyebrow. "Baby, if I wear those things around my neck people will be all, 'damn, look at that guy with those awesome headphones, where did he get those?' I'm taking one for the team here, modeling them for free," he jokes, winking at me.

I roll my eyes but laugh. "My own personal model, how fun," I deadpan.

He slaps my butt as we walk out the door and leans in to nip my ear. "Yours," he whispers, causing a shiver to run through me.

"Maybe I should tell Shea I'm leaving so he won't freak out if he tries to find me later," I say.

He usually sleeps until way past noon, but I know he's awake because he has a list of places to go for his promotional tour.

Nick makes a face but doesn't argue as he trails behind me. I notice that he has his duffel bag in his hand, which makes my stomach sink a little.

"Yo, BK!" Shea shouts behind me. When I turn around, I see him standing shirtless in the threshold of his door with Darius standing beside it. Shaking my head, I walk over and step into his room, Nick following behind me.

"Where you guys going?" Shea asks, his eyes flickering between the duffel in Nick's hand and my face.

I shrug. "Probably to eat and stuff."

"I have to go home and then I'm going to show Brooklyn some stuff," Nick says flippantly.

"Huh," Shea comments, his eyes narrowing a bit. "You'll be back for my show, right?" he asks, looking at me.

"Of course! I wouldn't miss a show at The Fillmore," I say, smiling.

Shea shakes his head and chuckles. "No, of course not. Your favorite place in the world," he jokes, wrapping me into a hug. He smells like one of those Axe things he uses, so I know he just showered.

"What do you have to do now?" I ask, stepping away from him.

He shrugs. "A lot of shit. Danielle is coming over here now with a huge list of things to go over. I gotta go to some stations then pass by the venue to sound check. I'll probably come back here after that and check out the tour bus they're bringing. Change, chill and shit and then head over for the show."

I exhale, knowing that's the short version of his list.

"Don't forget to eat," I say.

Shea has had problems in the past because he skips meals when he gets caught up in things. He's the only guy I've ever met that can go hours without eating. Hendrix is always scarfing something down and Ryan was the same. Shea, on the other hand, needs to practically be handfed, it seems.

"Yes, ma'am," Shea says, smiling at me. "Okay. Well, I guess I'll see you later." He looks back at Nick, who's standing behind me. "You gonna have those tracks ready for me tonight?"

"They've been ready. I think we have to re-do one, though, your voice sounds off."

"Fuck. Which one?" Shea asks, exhaling and crumpling his messy hair.

"Toxic Love," Nick says.

"Where are Fern and Leo?" I ask, suddenly remembering that I haven't seen them anywhere. Shea doesn't need a band for what he does, but Fern and Leo have always performed with him, and even though he doesn't sing rock, it works. They even play while he raps. It gives his performances and his music a different feel to it, which I love.

"They're around. They're all wifed up so I don't wanna bug them too much," Shea explains. I nod, imagining how uncomfortable it must feel to be the odd one out when it comes to relationships. When he and I were doing whatever we were doing, we acted like a couple when we were together. I think it was mainly because his friends were already in serious relationships. As soon as I left town and went back home was a different story—that's when Shea would have his flings with anybody that walked and had a vagina. I can't blame him, though. I know what it's like to be young and rich. If you add famous to the mix you have a recipe for relationship disaster.

"We'll work on it tomorrow then," Nick says. "Good luck on your show tonight, bro."

"You're not coming?" Shea asks, his eyes wide.

I wonder why he'd never mentioned Nick to me, or maybe he had and he just called him Shadow and I never noticed it because I was to busy working on my microphone line. Who knows, but it seems like he values Nick's opinion of things.

"Yeah, I'll be there. Wouldn't miss it," Nick says, bumping fists with him.

"Good luck in the interviews and stuff," I say, giving him a kiss on the cheek before walking away.

"Thanks. Be careful," he calls out behind me. His voice sounds hesitant and I know why, but I refuse to acknowledge it as I leave him behind.

CHAPTER EIGHTEEN

Nick holds the lobby door open for me and gives his ticket to the valet, who runs off to get the car. As we stand there, Nick wraps his arms around me from behind and places his head on mine. We're both quiet, enjoying each other's company while we wait for his car. I've decided I'll try and guess what he has. Ryan and I used to play this game, picking out people's cars based on the way they look. My mom, for example, always drove a Mercedes, which we decided was a perfect stuffy car. My dad drove, or was driven around in, a Bentley, which matched him well. Hendrix has driven an array of cars, but has mainly stuck with Range Rovers. My first car was a two-door Cadillac, but I quickly realized it didn't match me. I ended up getting a two-door BMW, which also didn't match me, so I got an Audi A5. That was the best fit for me. Ryan drove an Aston Martin, because you can't go wrong with that car regardless of who you are.

As I stand here, thinking about Nick's car, I can honestly say I can't figure him out. It could be an old collector's car like a badass Shelby, or a BMW. It hasn't even occurred to me how much money he makes. I know a producer like him, working with an artist like Shea, is getting paid a pretty penny. And from the people he's worked with in the past (Google has become my best friend), I know he's doing well. I don't pay attention to things like watches or cars in order to define how well off they are because I've known many people who have beautiful cars and amazing watches and live paycheck to paycheck. Still, everything about Nick Wilde intrigues me, even to the car he drives.

"There it is," he murmurs when a beat up Honda Civic pulls up to us. My mouth falls open and I'm so glad he's standing behind me because I definitely did not picture him in this tiny beat up red car. I bite my lip to keep from laughing, mainly at myself for being the presumptuous douchebag I always told myself I wouldn't become, and take a step forward when the car comes to a full stop. My eyebrows knit together when a young kid, not the valet, steps out of the car, taking a pizza box out of the backseat.

Turning around to look at Nick, my mouth agape, I find him laughing, his eyes twinkling in amusement. "You're so stupid," I comment, shaking my head and turning back around at the feeling of embarrassment that I refuse to show him.

He wraps his arms around me again, kissing my cheek loudly. "I love that you were going to get in it regardless," he says, turning me so that I can look at him. His eyes are still playful, but his tone is serious.

"I'm not a gold digger," I say with a shrug, fighting a smile. It's a ridiculous statement, and I know he knows it, but it makes me wonder if he deals with them as much as I have in the past.

"I know you're not. You run your own successful business and work for a good company doing something you're great at," he says, his lips brushing against mine. I smile against him, loving that he doesn't mention my father's money or my mother's fame. Loving that he treats me like I'm my own person and doesn't throw my last name in my face.

"I would get on the back of a bike with you," I say, truthfully, looking up at his gleaming eyes that have become possessive over my own. His mouth meets mine again, giving me a long, hard kiss. "I meant a regular bike, not a motorcycle," I add bashfully, feeling the need to correct myself.

Nick laughs. "I know what you meant."

A sleek charcoal grey two-door Jaguar drives into the carport of the hotel and Nick pulls my hand, signaling that this is his. A smile takes over my face at a couple of things: this car is sexy as hell, just like its owner, and I find that I was completely serious when I told him I would get on the back of a bicycle with him. And I don't think I've ever even ridden a bicycle.

The ride to his house is fun. I sort through all of Nick's music and find that the last song he was playing was The Door's "Touch Me", which Nick serenades. I won't tell him, because he looks way too sure of himself, but he does a hell of a Jim Morrison impersonation. My stomach drops slightly at the view of the Golden Gate Bridge outside of my window, but I don't pay much attention to it otherwise because Nick is doing a great job of keeping my eyes on him.

"We're here," he says as we pull up to a tall glass building. He lowers his window and presses a card into a monitor that opens a gate and drives in, backing the car up into a space. He holds my hand on the seatbelt and gives me a look that confuses me, but I take as a warning not to get out, before he walks to the other side of the car and opens my door.

"Chivalry isn't dead," I muse, leaning up to kiss him as a thank you.

"Not when I'm around," he responds with a twinkle in his

eye as he grabs a handful of my ass and squeezes it, which makes me laugh because it totally cancels out my previous statement.

"You left that girl alone last night," I point out as I follow him to the door of his building.

"What girl?" he asks, playing dumb.

"The redhead that was all over you—the one you bought a drink for," I say, raising an eyebrow as he opens the big glass door for me and lets me step in.

"The girl that wasn't you?" he asks. I look up at him and notice he's trying to stifle a smile.

"Obviously she's not me," I respond, failing to see the point.

He shrugs. "There's your answer. Only one girl was leaving with me last night and that was you."

I cock my head at him as we step into the elevator and he slides his key in the slot. "What if I had been with Shea or somebody else?" I ask curiously.

Nick presses his body into mine, pushing me against the cold elevator wall behind me. "I would've had to get into a hell of a fight and lose a hell of a client then," he murmurs, dipping his head into the crook of my neck and sucking. I throw my head back, enjoying the feel of his lips on me.

"But Shea's your friend," I remind him breathily. "You don't want to lose your friendship over some girl."

He pulls his head back and looks down on me, his blue eyes intense as he speaks, "First of all, you're not just some girl. Second of all, he's my friend, and I value that, which is why I didn't try anything before. But seeing his hands all over you … fuck," he says, placing my hand over his heart. "I hated that, Brooklyn, and if going after you makes me the ultimate asshole, then so be it, but I want you."

The fast pounding of his heart beneath my hand makes his words easier to believe, to swoon over, even. And I don't swoon. Not ever. I've known enough guys to see through their bullshit sweet talk, but Nick's talk isn't sweet, it's transparent.

"I want you too," I offer quietly.

"I know," he murmurs, brushing his lips against mine, making my heart skip a beat as the elevator doors open. Nick backs away from me and takes my hand, pulling me into the hallway. There's only one door, so I know the floor is his, just like Hendrix's place and my parents' place in New York.

He drops my hand to sort through his keys until he locates the one he's looking for and unlocks the door. "I hope you like dogs," he says as he opens the door.

Before I have time to react, there's a black horse galloping toward me. "Whoa," I say, putting my hands up to guard my face with a laugh. Thank God I love dogs because if I didn't this one would have given me a heart attack.

"Scooby! Down!" Nick says firmly, effectively stopping the dog from jumping on me, which is good because he could completely knock me down.

"Scooby?" I ask as I pet the Great Dane. "Not Marmaduke?"

Nick scoffs and rolls his eyes, but his eyes are smiling. "Please. Scooby is way cooler."

"What if I had been terrified of dogs or something?" I ask as I pull on Scooby's ears. I've always loved these dogs; they have the most amazing bark in the world. Growing up, Ryan had three of them, so I'm very familiar with them. I kept his favorite one, Rascal for a while before I had to give it to his mom because the pain it caused me to see him every day.

Nick frowns. "I don't know, I guess I wouldn't be able to keep you around," he says with a shrug as if it's no big deal to him either way. I laugh when I notice his lips twitch as he turns around and walks toward the living room. "To be honest, I'm more worried about you freaking out over this," he says, signaling at the view of the Golden Gate Bridge his floor to ceiling windows provide. My breath gets caught in my throat, mainly at the beauty of it.

"Wow," I breathe. "This is nice."

My parents' homes and offices always have the most spectacular view of each city they're in, but no view ever gets old to me. I've always had a fascination with nature and with man-made things. That bridge for example, holds memories for me that I wish I could forget, but people made it with their hands. Men labored on it for years and years and built it so that people can get from one canyon to the next without having to rely on a boat. It's a marvelous thing, really, despite the lives lost on it yearly by accident or otherwise.

"No freak outs?" Nick asks quietly from behind me, wrapping his arms around me and breathing me in as he nuzzles his face into my neck.

"No freak outs," I promise in a whisper. And I mean it. In this moment, I feel completely at ease with being here.

He loosens his grip on me when he feels me turning around. I want to really see where he lives, really see what Nick likes and to know every little thing about him, so I tell him that. He laughs but agrees to show me everything. We start in the kitchen, as most people do, and he offers me something to drink and eat.

"I have someone come every day when I'm gone. Scooby goes to a doggy daycare, he's a spoiled brat."

I laugh, trying to hold in the water spilling from the corner of my mouth with the back of my hand. "Doggy daycare? Interesting."

"Don't judge. You don't want a Great Dane stuck inside a house for too many hours, that's when you come home and start discovering holes all over your walls," Nick says in a serious tone that tells me it's happened.

"Why do you have him here though? I mean, why not buy a house with a yard?" I ask.

He places his forearms on the counter across from me and leans in. I love the way his shoulders move up when he's in that position. And the way his neck extends … and the way his lips part slightly, making his full mouth look fuller.

"I will someday," he says.

I roll my eyes and exhale. "Let me guess, when you're ready to start a family."

His lips tilt up slowly. "Exactly."

"So predictable," I say, shaking my head.

Nick circles the counter and pulls my hand so that I hop off the barstool. When I turn to walk toward the bedrooms he slaps my butt and I yelp at the unexpected sting, though it wasn't hard.

"Nick!" I reprimand.

"I never claimed to be unpredictable," he says, growling into my ear and placing a rough kiss on my neck before squeezing me into a hug.

"This is my favorite room," he says, turning the knob to what looks like a recording studio with no closed off booth. There are musical instruments laid out across the room, leaning on the wall and sitting on chairs.

"Hmm. Not the awesome living room?" I ask, surprised that the massive living room with the stunning view and large sectional wouldn't be his favorite place.

"Nah, I love it, but it's not my favorite," he says. "This is where the magic happens."

I laugh. "Isn't that supposed to be your bedroom?"

Nick shakes his head and looks at me like I'm a moron. "That's so played out."

"So you make music here?" I ask, stepping into the dark room with black padded walls.

"Magic," he repeats, making me smile.

"Okay, so show me the magic," I say, giving in to his little game.

"Sit," he orders, pulling out a big leather chair that looks like it belongs in a living room more than a regular room.

When I sink into it, I realize why it's here to begin with. I could fall asleep on it, and I'm assuming Nick often does. He sits in the one beside me and hands me some earphones, putting on a pair himself before he starts touching the controls on the soundboard. I get lost watching the way his hands move over it, and before I know it, there's music playing in my ears. The song is slow yet fast, it's sensual yet trendy. It's difficult to explain, even for me, who listens to music all day. There's a bit of that Houston chop and screw vibe to it, yet it has a little Marvin Gaye too. It's absolutely brilliant, really, the way it's mixed in there.

Closing my eyes, I let the music sink in, and as I try to sort out the types of music in it, I hear Nick's voice, singing a verse. It surprises me so much, my eyes snap open and I gasp. He smiles at me, knowing I can hear him, and I notice it's something he previously recorded. He pushes down on a button and talks into his microphone.

"It's for Shea. He's going to kill this beat, right?" he asks, his voice sure like he knows this song is a sure hit. I can't argue there, I can totally picture it being played everywhere. I take my earphones off and he does the same.

"You sound really good," I say.

He shrugs off the compliment but smiles. "I try."

He's not as good as Shea, but he's definitely better than a lot of singers on the radio nowadays.

"How did you get into producing anyway?" I ask. "Did you want to be a singer?"

Nick laughs as he stands and takes our earphones and sets them down on the board. He takes my hand and pulls me out of my seat, stepping out of the room with our hands joined together.

"As flattered as I am, singing isn't my thing. I can compose a song, play it on different instruments, but not really sing it … not good anyway. Producing comes easy to me. I've always made songs, worked out beats. I guess it's in my blood," he explains with a shrug.

I mull his words over for a moment as he pulls open the door to what I'm assuming is his bedroom. It's a vast space: the walls are all dark gray and the dark wood king sized bed in the middle of the room is low to the ground. His bed has a big fluffy comforter like the feather goose ones that hotels have, which I love. I notice that his walls are plain and everything is pretty simple. He has a leather couch that's pushed off to one side of the room and a massive television on the wall in front of his bed. Why is that not surprising?

"Nice," I comment, walking around his room. I stop short when I take a closer look behind the couch. At first glance it looks like he has a regular bookshelf beside it, but looking at it closer I notice that they're not books, they're vinyl records. Holy smokes. The man is my ultimate weakness. It has been confirmed. I walk up to it, not even trying to hide my excitement, and hear Nick laugh behind me.

"Aha, I have something you like," he says.

"Shh," I respond, running my fingertips along the edges and taking a deep breath to smell that old lovely scent that means the world to me. I begin to pull some out but stop short when I find a specific one that makes my jaw drop.

"Oh. My. How'd you get this?" I ask, holding up a *Please Please Me* LP by The Beatles that says: Promotional. Not For Sale on the cover. I feel weird touching it, even if I'm only holding it by my fingertips. I lay it down on the couch and stare at it in complete awe. "How. Did. You. Get. This?" I ask in shock.

Nick throws his head back in a laugh, and as adorable as I find his carefree laugh usually, I can't bring myself to pick up my jaw from the floor. "Am I still predictable?" he asks amused.

I shake my head, my mouth still agape. "No, but for real, how?"

Nick just smiles and shrugs. "Ah ... one of the many unsolved mysteries of Nick Wilde," he muses like an idiot.

"You're not going to tell me?" I press.

"Maybe someday. I can't give you all my secrets in one day, then you'll get bored of me and leave me high and dry," he says as he disappears into his closet.

"I can't even touch that record to put it away now that I've seen what it is," I say. He laughs. "I'm serious."

"Brooklyn, it's just a record," he says from his closet.

My eyes widen. He can't see me, but I'm just shocked right now. I've seen a lot of stuff in my day. I've met a lot of important people, been to more exclusive events than I can count. Hell, I've even met Sir Paul McCartney himself. You would think seeing this record would pale in comparison, but it doesn't. Not one bit. Maybe because it's one of my favorite bands, maybe because I wasn't expecting to see it, maybe because my own father doesn't have an exclusive vinyl like this one, or maybe because I wouldn't in a million years expect Mr. Cocky Music Producer to have one.

"How did you say you got into the music business?" I ask, knowing he hadn't said anything about it at all.

"I love music," he answers.

I exhale, unwilling to let myself get frustrated. I'll find out sooner or later, even if I have to call Hendrix or Sarah for the real scoop. "Whatever," I mutter, taking a seat on the edge of his bed, which is super soft and comfortable. I just feel like crawling in it, but I hold back. It's weird how a place I've never been before can make me feel so comfortable, so at home. I'm not sure if I like that I feel this way in his house. Everything I feel around Nick Wilde is new, unsettling and scary.

"You wanna go somewhere with me?" he asks as he steps out of his closet again, this time wearing a black polo shirt.

"I thought I already did that," I answer as my eyes do a quick sweep of his body.

Nick pulls on his hair as if to style it and drops his hand suddenly when he sees me sitting on his bed. He walks toward me slowly, tilting his head as he appraises me with an unmasked desire in his eyes that blazes right through me. He sits down on the bed beside me and leans into me, placing a kiss on my jaw that makes me squirm. "I really love you on my bed," he says in a low voice. "Maybe I should tie you up and keep you here," he suggests, running the tip of his nose along my cheek up to my earlobe and inhaling a breath as he moves over my face. "Maybe I should give your body a thorough inspection and tease you until you beg me to keep you here with me," he says exhaling, his raspy voice over my ear now. I bite down on my lip when he licks the outer shell of my ear. "Would you like that, Brooklyn?"

I nod my head because I know how thorough his explorations are and how amazing they make me feel.

He bites my earlobe. "Hmmm," he says, moving in front of me so that I lay back on the bed and he's positioned in between my legs. "Every time I breathe you in, I want to taste you," he whispers huskily. "Would you like for me to taste you?"

"Yes," I say, my voice strained as he teases me with butterfly kisses down my neck.

"Yes what, Brooklyn?" he asks. A pleasured moan escapes my lips at the way he says my name against my skin. He enunciates it slowly, like he's having sex with it and enjoying every goddamn second. His lips stop moving against me and I know he's waiting for my answer.

My mind is in a haze; he had me when he said something about tying me up. "I don't know! What was the question? Just tie me up and fuck me already," I say, breathing erratically.

I feel him smile against my neck right before he begins to chuckle, making me throw my head back wantonly because his laugh courses through me, making me vibrate from the inside out. He continues sucking on my neck, traveling up to my face and stopping over my mouth. He sucks both of my lips into his mouth before parting them with his tongue and slowly exploring my mouth. As soon as I put my hands on his head, he breaks the kiss, leaving us both panting for air, needing more of each other.

"Oh, I will," he says, his voice gruff. I whimper at that, moving my hips off the bed, pushing myself onto him. "Just not right now. Right now, we need to get out of here," he whispers, adjusting his very obvious hard-on as he stands and pulls me from the bed.

"What?" I all but yell, my heart beating erratically.

He caresses my face softly as he looks at me, desire swimming in his eyes. "If we don't get out of here, I really am going to tie you to my bed and fuck you until you can't breathe," he explains.

Putting my arms around his neck, I fix his collar before dragging my hands over his sculpted chest. I stop on his belt buckle, making him groan.

"Maybe I want that," I counter, looking into his hooded eyes that match my own.

"Brooklyn," he says, my name sounding like a hiss.

"What?" I ask, trying on my best good girl voice.

He closes his eyes as he swallows and grabs my wrists so that I don't move my hands. "I want to take you places and if we start this, we won't stop."

"Okay," I agree, knowing he's right and wondering about his plans.

When we get back to his car, he opens my door and waits until I'm seated properly before closing it and walking to his side.

"Do you always use your chivalry to impress the ladies?" I ask playfully.

He shrugs, smiling. "Let's just say I was trained well."

I smile despite the pang in my chest. I can't help but wonder who trained him. Was it Stephanie? Was it another girlfriend? I groan internally and look out the window. Seemingly sensing my discomfort, Nick grabs my hand and places it on his lap, locking our fingers together and drawing circles with his thumb over mine.

"You're so easy to read," he comments, chuckling as he pulls into the narrow street.

"I know," I agree. I've always hated that. No matter how hard I try to school my emotions, they always show. He squeezes my hand when I try to pull it out of his hold.

"I have an amazing woman in my life who's taught me everything I know about how to treat a lady," he explains and I hate the way my stomach clenches at the thought of it. I hate the way my blood runs cold thinking about the women he's had in his life. It's a stupid feeling, this jealousy, but it's one I can't help or erase. "I'm talking about my mother, Brooklyn."

"That's nice," I comment flippantly, focusing my eyes outside of the passenger window, unwilling to look at him or acknowledge the feeling in the pit of my stomach.

"What's wrong?" he asks.

I swallow, looking up at the larger-than-life bridge and watching the waves of the ocean below as they crash against its columns.

"Nothing," I respond, smiling for his sake. "How many girlfriends have you had?" I ask because I'm morbidly curious. Emphasis on the morbid, because that's how whatever answer he gives me will feel.

"Define girlfriend," Nick says, his tone light.

I look at him and roll my eyes. "Answer the question."

He laughs. "Two. One in high school, one in college."

I look away again, hating those two nameless, faceless girls. "How long were you with them?"

He exhales loudly. "High school, I was with Tiffany for two years. College I was with Amber for a little less than one," he says.

I cringe because now they have names and that makes them real and makes me hate them more. I decide that the previous relationship discussion is the worst idea I've ever had and draw the line right here. I don't know why I was expecting him to say he'd never had one.

"So … you and Shea," he says quietly.

Letting out a breath of my own, I rest my head on the headrest and tilt my face to him.

"Yup," I say, not knowing what else to add to that.

"How long were you together?" he asks.

I tuck a strand of hair behind my ear and bite down on my lip, trying to figure out how to answer. Nick lets go of my hand when we reach a red light and leans over the center console to tug on my hair and pushes it back out of my ear, making me smile.

"I love this," he murmurs, his eyes darting from the strand of hair back to the street.

"We've known each other forever. We dated for a little while, then broke up, then ... sort of dated again," I say. How do you explain a fuck buddy? Are you supposed to say "he was my fuck buddy" or is there another more socially acceptable term that you use when describing a former fuck buddy to a potential boyfriend? This whole thing is a little bit of a pain in the ass.

"Sort of dated again when?" he presses.

"On and off for about five years," I murmur under my breath, looking away from him again.

"Five *years*!" he says loudly. "Five?" he asks again, sounding disturbed.

"Yep," I say, feeling my face getting hot as I look out the window.

Nick pulls over suddenly into what looks like a dog park, and he throws the gear in park. "Five years you were his—what? Fuck buddy?" he asks.

Cringing, I close my eyes. It sounds so much dirtier when you actually voice it. More judgmental. "Yep," I repeat, quieter this time.

"Brooklyn, look at me," he says. "Please."

My shoulders slump and I turn at his plea. Apparently I can't say no to someone with good manners. "What?" I whisper, still unwilling to look him in the eye, so I zone into his collarbone, hoping he won't notice.

He brings his hand to my chin and tilts my face. "Why'd you put up with that?" he asks.

I don't know what I was expecting or where I thought this conversation was going, but it wasn't that question at all.

"What do you mean?" I ask, frowning.

"Why would you let him use you like that?" he asks, frowning back at me.

"He didn't use me," I argue, shooting him a confused look. "It was just what we did. It worked for us."

Nick looks at me for a long moment and I see sympathy in his eyes. It occurs to me that he knows Shea well, and he sees the way he treats the women around him. He searches my face for a moment longer and finally drops his hand from my chin. "When did it stop? I'm assuming you ended it?"

"About a year ago?" I say, not meaning to make it sound like a question, but it does. We weren't actively together until then; a year ago was a slip up on my part. In the past I've needed drugs. A year ago, hanging out with Shea, I was tempted being around a lot of drugs and ended up choosing my best option for the night—which was him.

Nick nods rapidly as if he's trying to process all of this, and then suddenly hits his steering wheel. "Fuck," he mutters, shaking his head.

"What?" I ask, confused and taken aback.

He exhales, looking at me again. "So many things, Brooklyn. So many fucking things, one being that I didn't realize you hooked up with him that recently, I thought it was a teenage relationship, I don't know. I swear life has a way of taking a shit on your parade just when you think you have it all figured out. No more Shea," he says, a demand.

"He's a good friend," I say, secretly reveling in the way my insides flip flop at his tone and his words.

"You're not going to fall in his bed again?" he asks, his jaw clenching at the words.

"Never," I say quickly, knowing that's over for good.

"Good," Nick replies. "I hated seeing his hands all over

you last night. I swear I don't know what I'd do if I had to go through that again. He's my boy and all but … I just … no more Shea, Brooklyn."

"Yes sir," I reply with a smile, loving that he actually cares enough to be territorial over me. Nina would totally hate this, but I love it, I've never felt this wanted.

Nick chuckles when he sees my face and leans over the console again, this time to grab my face and kiss me. "You're adorable," he says against my lips.

When he starts driving again, Nick sorts through his music using the steering wheel until he finds the Beatles' *Please Please Me* CD.

"Where are we going?" I ask, leaning my head back on the headrest and turning my head toward him.

He looks at me and grins. "My parents' house."

CHAPTER NINETEEN

"**W**hat?" I shriek, wide eyed. "I can't go to your parents' house!" I look down at my wardrobe, completely horrified by this news. Nobody has ever taken me to meet their parents. Why would anybody want me to meet their parents? Oh my God, I think I'm breaking out in hives. This is so not funny.

Nick laughs, aware of my discomfort, and squeezes my hand in his. "Relax. They'll love you," he says, shooting me a quick glance.

My shoulders relax a little. "Shouldn't you tell them you're bringing company? Have you even spoken to them? What are their names? Are they nice? Is your mom super skinny? Is she going to look at me like I'm trash because I'm wearing ripped up jeans and flats and a loose T-shirt with a skull on it? Oh my God, I think I'm going to be sick, Nick. Just drop me off at the hotel and meet up with me later," I say, my words spilling out of me all at once. Nick is quiet throughout my rant and I can't even bring myself to look at him when I finish.

"Whoa. You lost me at 'is your mom skinny'," he says,

chuckling and letting go of my hand. He tugs on the end of one of my curls. "Look at me."

I do, and I try to remain calm despite the cluster of fucks running through my brain.

He's frowning as he searches my face. "I'll call them now, but what the hell is up with the skinny question? Are you competing? And why would she think you're trash just because of what you're wearing? You look beautiful, Brooklyn. You always do. Don't I tell you that every time I see you?" he asks, his voice soft and slightly concerned.

I let out a breath, slumping into the seat behind me. "My mom's a bitch," I explain, hating that he cringes when I say those truthful words. "If I had to see her right now, all I would hear is how much fatter I've gotten since the last time she saw me and how I need to watch what I eat and that I need a new wardrobe and that ladies don't wear flats. I dunno. Sorry," I mutter, feeling like a moron, but Shea's mom is similar to mine, as is Ryan's, and those are the only mothers outside of my family I've ever dealt with. Mothers are scary as hell, especially when they know you're interested in their son.

Nick shakes his head, his face disgusted. "Your mom is obviously a nut job and may need her eyes checked."

I smile, but insist that he calls his family to give them a heads up, so he does. I watch him as he holds the phone to his ear, waiting for them to answer. When his face breaks out into a huge smile, lighting his eyes up, I can't help but smile too. It must be nice to feel that sense of happiness when calling your parents. I've never felt that, but I don't get all woe is me about it. I just always figured that's how it was for most people. I think it is.

Once in a while I come in contact with somebody that has a great relationship with their family. It always makes me feel happy and jealous at the same time when I hear them talk about their fabulous family lives. On one hand I feel like I can experience a different life through them, on another it makes me sad to realize that even though I have it all, I have nothing at all.

"Hey, Mima," Nick says into the phone, smiling his face off right before he goes off into an entire conversation in the most perfect Spanish ever. I think I lost count at the amount of times he's made my jaw drop, but this was something I wasn't expecting. I understand it, the conversation, even though my Spanish sucks. My mom is Cuban, but she never made it a point to speak to us in Spanish. Our nanny, on the other hand, was Mexican and only spoke to us in Spanish. When I was little I didn't like it, but now I appreciate that she did because the only time my mother speaks Spanish is when she's talking shit about Hendrix, my father or myself. Nick laughs, hanging up the phone and blows Mima a kiss. My mom used to call her mom Mima, so I wonder if they share the same name, my grandmother and whoever he's speaking to.

"What the fuck, Nick?" I say as soon as he hangs up, still looking at him completely stunned.

He laughs loudly, his blue eyes twinkling. "What the fuck what, beautiful?"

"How do you know Spanish?"

He laughs harder. "Still predictable?"

I roll my eyes and slap his shoulder. "Asshole."

He brings his arm around my shoulder and pulls me to his side, kissing the top of my head when I lean into him. "My family's Cuban, I thought you knew that?"

My mouth drops open. "How would I know that if you never told me?"

He shrugs. "I don't know, I thought maybe I did. I know

your mom's Cuban and your dad's American. I thought we talked about it, the Cuban thing."

I shake my head. "No …" I say; my eyebrows knit together as I try to recall that conversation.

"Oh," he says suddenly. "It was your brother. Sorry, baby, I thought it was you."

Tingles fill my nerves at his endearment. I know it's stupid, but I can't help the way everything that comes out of his mouth makes me feel at this point.

"Makes sense. Still, your Spanish is perfect," I say.

He shrugs. "Not perfect, but good enough that my grandmother doesn't kick my ass over it."

That makes me smile. "So you were talking to your grandmother?" I ask.

"Yeah, you'll love her," he says, smiling.

"I'm sure I will," I respond, my voice drifting off as I look back outside, feeling more excited to meet them than the original terror I had. I'm not worried about them not liking me anymore, I'm only worried about the way I'll feel when I lose him and them, because I will. I always do. It's like my mother says, I can't keep the good ones around, which is probably why I always go for the bad ones. Until Nick.

"How do you drive here? The waves of the streets would drive me crazy," I say suddenly, unwilling to let myself get down on something that hasn't even happened yet.

"Used to it, I guess. Don't you drive in the Hills?" he asks, referring to Beverly Hills.

I nod. "Yeah, I guess you have a point. Still, this is worse. Our actual streets aren't like this, only the hills."

"Well, we have over fifty hills. Most of our neighborhoods are named after them: Nob Hill, Potrero Hill, Russian Hill," he states, counting them with his fingers.

I laugh softly. "I'll be sure to note that and save it in my box of Random Facts of San Francisco."

Nick brings my hand up to his mouth and nips the tips of my fingers. "You never know when they'll come in handy," he counters, raising an eyebrow.

"I know. They may call me to do Who Wants to Be a Millionaire next week," I say, shrugging.

"Well, keep my number handy if they do, I'll be your lifeline," he says, smiling, though his eyes are serious.

I stare at his profile for a moment and all I can think is that I've never wanted anything more. Then I snap out of it and tell myself I don't need anybody to be my lifeline. But if I did, Nick would be my number one choice.

"We're here," he announces as we make a turn onto Cliff Road, which I would laugh at if it weren't for the fact that it terrifies me to know we're on a cliff. One thing I noticed after being sober for the better part of seven years is that I'm a total chicken when I'm not high as a kite.

Nick keeps driving, passing a couple of homes until he reaches the last one on the street; a stunning redwood home with windows and glass doors everywhere. It reminds me of the home my father is building in Calabasas right now. It has a modern feel to it, but the old cherry wood makes it feel cozy. The view of the San Francisco bay is stunning even from the front of the house. I can only imagine the back view. Nick goes around the car quickly and opens my door, pulling me out and walking me to the front door. He pauses in front of the door and unlocks it.

"Lucy, I'm home," he bellows as we walk in, and I laugh even though I am completely mortified that this will be the introduction. I'm on edge mainly because I still don't know what to expect, but then a very short and rather round older lady with completely white hair dressed in a flower nightgown and slippers walks over to us with open arms.

"Nicky," she says brightly with a heavy Hispanic accent.

"Mima," he greets, throwing his arms under hers and picking her up to hug as if she doesn't weigh a ton. He whispers something in her ear that makes her laugh a throaty laugh as he sets her down.

"You must be Brooklyn," she says, walking over to me and wrapping her arms around me. I hug her back, instantly feeling a sense of calm wash over me. She smells like fried food and seasonings, which makes my stomach rumble.

"Nice to meet you." I let the words hang because I'm not sure whether or not to call her Mima too, since it's a nickname.

"Evelyn," she says. "But you can call me Mima, Eve, whatever you feel comfortable with."

I smile gratefully at her. Her eyes are the same aqua ocean blue as Nick's. Unlike Nick's mischievous look, hers are welcoming and warm.

"Nicky!" another woman's voice sings out from another room in the house.

"Ven," Mima says in Spanish, so we follow behind her. "Your mom is in the kitchen. Isaac and Damien went kayaking. They should be back soon."

The kitchen is a vast open floor plan, much like the rest of the house. It looks clean and simple; everything is a blend of cherry wood and off white. The light that bathes the house comes from the floor to ceiling windows that surround it.

"Hey, Mami," Nick says, wrapping his arms around the woman that's probably my height and has the same chocolate brown hair as me. Hers is completely curly, unlike mine that only curls on the ends. She has an hourglass figure that I can appreciate since it's a lot like my own, and I almost have to laugh at the similarities, even though I haven't seen her face yet. It makes me wonder for a second if the rumors that men marry their moms have any truth to them. Not that Nick wants to marry me, but still. God help me if he turns out to be anything like my father, because I will not be choosing him, that's for sure.

"Hey, baby," she coos, turning in his hold to wrap her arms around his middle. My stomach sinks at the sight. Everything is so happy in this house that it's borderline sickening. "Let me look at you," she says to him, extending her hands out. Now I can see her face, she has fair skin and hazel eyes. She looks like a modern day Snow White with her delicate features. "Will you be home for a while?" she asks, still not acknowledging my presence, but I don't care, I'm too busy watching their dynamic.

"I dunno, Ma," Nick says, turning around and extending his hand out to me. "This is Brooklyn, I called earlier to tell you I was bringing her over."

His mother's eyebrows shoot up, eyes widening as she gasps and sees me. "Oh, honey, I'm so sorry! I'm being so rude, I didn't know you brought company," she says, walking over to me. She does a sweep of me with her eyes, it's fast enough that it's not rude, so unlike my mother, before she gives me a kiss on the cheek.

"I'm Mirielle," she says, introducing herself. "Brooklyn, that's such a nice name. Different. And my God, your eyes are amazing," she says, looking in them.

I can't keep the smile off my face. "Nice to meet you, Mirielle. That's a pretty name too," I say, my stomach in knots even though everything is going well so far. Still, this is Nick's mom, whom he obviously has a great relationship with, and I'm in her house wearing the most casual clothes ever while she's dressed in a 50s style polka dot dress and heels.

Mirielle smiles at me; taking my face in again before she turns back to the stove. "Well, you better set an extra plate," she tells Nick.

"Yes ma'am," Nick says at the same time that Mima says, "Already done."

Nick takes my hand in his and walks me to the back of the house, telling his mom and grandmother that we're going to wait for his brothers out back. He told me once that he had two brothers, but we never discussed them.

"So this is when you introduce me to your brothers and I have to choose which one I like more?" I ask, recalling our conversation about them.

Nick stops walking right when we reach the doors that are open to the backyard. His head snaps toward me and he raises an eyebrow. "Over my dead body," he growls, pulling me close to him. "You're not sharable. Don't get any funny ideas. I'm not worried about Isaac, but I'll have to keep my eyes on Damien." His jaw clenches as he says this, as if he's really not looking forward to my interaction with his brother. I laugh it off, shaking my head. How could he possibly think he has anything to worry about?

Nick walks out, bringing me down the step with him and moves aside so I can take in the stunning view.

"Wow, this is better than your place," I whisper.

He chuckles, wrapping his arms around me from behind and tucking his face into my neck. "Way better," he agrees, taking a deep breath and nuzzling into me.

I close my eyes, wanting to capture the moment and save it for any day that I'm feeling down on myself, so that I can remember that one time I was at Nick's parents' house and he held me like I was the only thing that mattered. The wind is in synch with the sun above, making it the perfect day to be out on a boat or have a picnic. And the view from here is so gorgeous that it makes me wonder how often they eat outside and enjoy it. I can see Alcatraz and the bottom of the Golden Gate Bridge from here. It gives me a completely different view than from the top of Nick's condo.

Nick's arms leave me and he walks over to the dock, waving his hands at the red kayak that's nearing.

"Yo!" one of the guys yells. "Nicky's here."

I don't know why it makes me smile so wide when I hear everybody call him that, but it makes me picture him as a child, and for some reason it fills my heart with joy. We definitely had entirely different childhoods growing up.

"Hurry up, losers," Nick calls out. Both guys give him their middle fingers at the same time, making me laugh. They couldn't have coordinated it better if they tried.

"At least we didn't get stranded out there and call someone to come get us on the boat," one of them calls out, making the other laugh hysterically.

"That was one time, you asshole! I was drunk!" Nick calls out in defense and I laugh along at the thought.

Nick looks back at me, narrowing his eyes as his lips quirk up. "Oh, you think that's funny?" he asks, stalking toward me and lifting me over his shoulders, making me shriek loudly.

"Put me down!" I say, laughing as I hold onto his back. "You're going to drop me!"

Nick laughs, his chuckle reverberating through me as he slides me down the front of his body slowly. He holds on to my waist when we're at eye level and looks at me seriously. "I would never, ever drop you, Brooklyn."

I'm completely aware of the fact that we're in his parents' backyard, and for all I know, everyone is watching us. As it is, his brothers can see us clearly as they pull up to the dock beside us. Nick is either oblivious or doesn't give a crap because he presses his lips against mine, giving me a quick but thorough kiss and leaving me breathless as my feet land on the ground.

"Nick, we're at your mom's house," I whisper, feeling my face flush at the sound of clapping and hooting from his brothers.

"If you don't want me to kiss you, stop being so damn sexy all the time," he responds with a shrug.

I smile because what else can I do?

Two tall guys, one a little shorter than the other, walk toward us. The slightly shorter one is thin and reminds me of my brother in a way. His straight hair is dark and falls to his shoulders. He has a goofy kind of skip in his step that makes me feel immediately comfortable with him. His skin is golden and his eyes are the bluest of blues, much like Nick's. They practically pop out of his face when he sees me up close. I wonder if he knows me as Chris Harmon's daughter, the drug addict, or if he's surprised I'm not what I'm assuming is Nick's normal type, like Stephanie.

The other guy, the taller one, is blond and built more like Nick. His skin is fair like their mother's and his eyes are brown. He is completely checking me out, despite the fact that Nick is standing beside me holding my hand, and I assume he must be Damien. He looks like he could be the perfect Prince Charming, the way his smile spreads over his face, showcasing the dimples on each of his cheeks.

"What's up, D?" Nick says, giving him a hug first. "Damien, Brooklyn, Brooklyn, Damien."

We shake hands and Damien leans in to kiss my cheek, making me smile. "Nice to meet you, Damien."

"Likewise," he says, turning to Nick. "Friend?"

"Don't even fucking think about it," Nick warns.

Damien laughs, throwing his head back. "Well, damn," he says, walking into the house.

The other guy, whom I'm guessing is Isaac, is standing in front of us just looking at me, which is a little unnerving, if I'm going to be honest. He's just staring. He looks at Nick with a face that I can't understand, and Nick shakes his head in response. I know they're having a sibling conversation, the kind I can only have with Hendrix or Nina. The ones you can have with people that really know you without having to hear any words coming from your mouth.

"I'm Isaac," he says, standing closer to me.

The funny thing about Isaac is that he's not traditionally good looking, but he's sort of my type. I almost have to laugh at Nick warning me off about Damien but not Isaac. As if it's assumed that everyone will be more interested in the muscular, mischievous guy. Little does Nick know that he's not my usual type; he's the complete opposite of any guy I've ever been with. He's the guy I stay away from the most, not because I don't think they're good looking, but because I either don't think they'd ever be interested in me or they just turn out to be complete douchebags. I have a theory about guys that spend a ridiculous amount of time working on their muscles, and it doesn't work in their favor. Nick has proved it wrong, though, but it could be because there's a lot more to him than being fit.

So the way Isaac looks at me, and the way he makes me feel when he shakes my hand, makes me stomach drop. I don't know why. Despite him being my type, the attraction isn't there, so it's not that. It's something more. And I can't pinpoint it, until he does a sweep of his hair and tilts his head and then it all comes rushing back to me all at once.

"What are you doing here?" I countered.

"Looking for you," I heard him mutter.

My mouth drops at the memory, my heart racing at the mix of it and the bridge behind him, is in my direct line of vision. His face blurs as I look at the bridge, then the bridge blurs as I look back at him.

"Oh. My. God," I whisper. "Oh. My. God."

"You may want to hold her a little tighter," Isaac suggests to Nick. "I think she remembers."

That's the last thing I hear as the rest of my vision blurs, and the little polka dots around me become the only thing I see before I don't see anything at all.

CHAPTER TWENTY

F un fact about the brain: it blocks out memories you don't
even know you don't want to remember. I guess sometimes
that's what saves us from ourselves, our self-selective an-
esthesia. I remember everything about that day. Everything
except what happened after I got to that bridge. Everything except the important things like who found me, who saved me,
who was in the hospital for me when my family was absent.
I guess a part of me expected that. A part of me knew they
wouldn't come for me, but a bigger part was delusional enough
to hope they did. I was filled with enough dread to not care
either way. Cloaked with enough darkness that I would have
been fine with not being helped. By that point, I didn't want to
be saved.

Yet here I am: healthy, as happy as I can make myself, and
stronger than I was that day. I'm also sitting in front of the man
who helped me get here. If it weren't for Isaac, I wouldn't have
made it to the hospital back then. Nick and Isaac hover over
me for a moment making sure I'm okay. When Damien comes
outside to tell us the food is ready, I stand up slowly, holding on

to Nick's hand for balance.

I sit down beside Nick as Mirielle serves our food and calls out for Michael, Nick's dad, to join us. I squeeze my hands on my lap. Tilting my head, I steal a look at Isaac, who happens to turn his face toward me at the same time. My eyes widen in surprise, and he gives me a comforting smile that kicks the air back into my lungs.

"Are you okay?" Nick asks quietly, for the third time since we sat down. I nod in response, but don't look at him to confirm it because I'm not sure that I really am.

"You okay?" Isaac whispers. He's sitting to my left, and even though I don't want to make eye contact with anybody right now, I find myself tearing my gaze from the gold brimmed plate in front of me to look at him He looks younger than me, which makes me feel even worse.

"How old are you?" I whisper back.

"Twenty-three," he answers.

His response makes my heart sink to its knees as I quickly do the math in my head. It's been eight years. I was seventeen, almost eighteen at the time, and he was just fifteen. Not that age matters here. All I want to do is apologize a trillion times to this poor kid who had no clue what he was getting into when he went for his run that morning. Tears prick my eyes the longer I look at him, feeling like a complete selfish bitch—not for wanting to take my own life, but for not stopping to think about others when I went there. I didn't care what my family thought, and looking back at that time I *still* don't care what they thought. But this poor kid shouldn't have had to deal with that.

"I'm so sorry," I say, my voice wavering as my chin begins to tremble.

Isaac places his hand over mine under the table and

squeezes. "I'm glad you're okay. I'm also glad Nick was there to help me help you. Shit happens, right?"

A small laugh escapes me, despite the fact that I feel like bawling my eyes out for this guy. "Shit happens," I repeat quietly. "Where's your bathroom?"

"Let me show you," Isaac says, placing his napkin on his plate.

"I'll take her," Nick says, standing up beside me and waiting for me to do the same.

"Thank you," I whisper to Isaac, who offers me a small smile before turning to Damien, who is animatedly talking into his cell phone.

Nick walks me down the hallway, massaging my shoulders gently. "Are you sure you're okay?" he asks, his voice a whisper against my cheek.

I shiver but nod. "Yeah, I just need a minute," I reply, walking in to the bathroom and shooting a look over my shoulder to let him know I'm okay. Once the door is closed I sit on the toilet and bury my face in my hands. My shoulders begin to shake as I sob into them, asking for forgiveness,—whose, I don't know. I've never been taught to pray, but that's the only thing I can think of doing right now. It's either pray or call my sponsor because I can feel a part of me beginning to itch for the easy way out. The easy numb that I know I can get if I go back to the hotel right now and walk into Shea's room. He may not be into the hard stuff anymore, but anything will do right now. Anything. But I can't. And I won't. So instead, I silently pray to whoever or whatever may be listening to me. I ask for forgiveness over and over and when I feel a little bit lighter, I wipe my face and get up.

I wipe under my eyes as best as I can so I don't look like I've been crying and then I step back out into the hallway. I hear Nick having a conversation with somebody in the other direction, so naturally I walk that way. I don't want to eavesdrop, but the open floor plan of the house makes it pretty impossible not to.

"So you're only recording for Shea right now?" a man's voice asks. He has a deep voice, one of those voices you hear on one of the corny radio stations with "power love hours" and "slow jams." That type. It's sexy low, but it reminds me of corny nineties R&B singers.

"Yes, Pop, I already told you this," Nick responds, sounding irritated.

"You keep selling yourself short, you're never gonna make it anywhere," his father responds.

"I already made it, didn't I?" Nick retorts.

His father scoffs. "How much are you getting paid per track right now?" he asks.

"Enough. Are you gonna eat with us or should I tell Mom you're busy?" Nick asks, clearly irritated.

"I'll be right there. I heard you brought a friend home," his dad comments.

"Yeah … and?" Nick asks, his voice getting quiet.

"Your mom seems to like her. Is she someone I know? Singer?" his dad asks.

"No. I'll tell Mom you're coming," Nick responds and I hear him close a door.

Stepping back, I walk closer to the dining room, standing off to one side so I can wait for him. I watch him as he walks toward me, pulling on the dark blond hair in the middle of his head. The hallway is so massive that I feel like I get lost in it. Somehow Nick makes the tables look small beside him and the walls look like they're opening up wider for him. His eyes look troubled when he notices me, but quickly calm when I smile at him. Walking straight to me, he wraps his arms around me, placing his chin on top of my head and letting out a deep breath. I instantly sag against him and wrap my arms around his middle, pressing my cheek to his chest and breathing him in. I close my eyes and squeeze him harder, smiling when he does the same.

"Isaac said you were there to help me," I whisper against his chest, hating the way he stiffens. I want to know why he never told me, but more than anything I'm ashamed and hurt that they were there to witness all of that.

"We'll talk about it later, baby," he says, kissing the top of my head and dropping his arms. He tilts my head up to look at him. "I hope you're hungry," he says as the side of his lip curls into a smile.

"Always."

He chuckles and places a chaste kiss on my lips. "That's my girl."

Mirielle beams at us when we walk back in and take a seat. Damien is talking to Isaac, leaning over the table to emphasize whatever point he's making. I realize that he's very expressive, like my brother, and the thought makes me smile. A tall man walks into the room as Damien is explaining to me the difference between two film cameras. He's an independent film director and has already told me about two scripts he's currently reading. The man looks identical to Nick. There is absolutely no room to question that he's his father. He has the same body build: tall with very defined muscles. The same deep golden skin, the same aqua blue eyes and the same dark blond hair, the exception is his is long and gelled back. Upon looking at him I decide that Nick's dad is a DILF. For real. He smiles at me, the same gorgeous panty-dropping smile that Nick gives me and I almost gasp as I shake his hand.

"Michael," he introduces.

"Brooklyn," I respond.

Nick nudges me under the table with his leg and I shrug at him, widening my eyes.

"Uncanny, right?" Mirielle says with a laugh.

I blink rapidly a couple of times. "I've never seen two people look more alike," I respond.

She laughs. "I always used to joke that if Michael ever left me, he was going to have to take Nicky with him because I couldn't deal with seeing him every day."

"I don't blame you," I agree with a laugh.

We start eating the best food I've had in a very long time: white rice, black beans, and breaded chicken. It's so good that I want to ask for a doggy bag and pretend that I'm giving it to Scooby when we get back to Nick's place. I don't, of course, because that would make me sound pathetic. And fat.

"So, Brooklyn," Michael starts as he takes a sip of red wine. "You're in the music business?"

I open my mouth, snap it shut, and open it again. Fuck, I hate this question. I sigh, conceding that he's going to find out at some point. "Yes." Michael raises an eyebrow and signals me to elaborate, so I do. "I'm a talent director for Harmon Records."

Michael's eyebrows shoot up as he puts down his glass. "Nice," he says, nodding in approval. "How'd you get into that?"

Nick's hand finds mine under the table. I think he can sense how uncomfortable I am talking about this. As he draws circles around my thumb, I find it in me to continue my explanation. I don't even mind explaining it. I don't mind saying who my family is. What bothers me is what comes after that—the assumption that I am what I am because of them. I hate that assumption, but it's one I've learned to accept a little better.

"Chris Harmon is my father," I say, making Damien drop his fork onto his plate loudly, but my eyes stay glued to Michael's. His eyebrows knit slightly and he smiles. I can hear his thoughts. He doesn't have to voice the typical "that makes sense" for me to know that's what he's thinking. He surprises me by not saying that, though.

"I knew you looked familiar," Michael says, sounding like if he's having an "aha" moment. "We'll all have to get together for dinner one day. We used to go over to your house a lot, many moons ago," he says, looking at Mirielle, who smiles back at him adoringly. "I'm sure your dad has calmed down a lot since then," he says laughing. "I haven't been to one of his parties in ages, but they used to get wild."

"Tell me about it," I mutter under my breath.

"Nicky finally picked a good one," Michael says quietly, still looking at me. His words make me cringe inwardly. They're the same words Shea's mom used when we started dating. "You picked a keeper, Shea. Don't let this one go," she'd say. Her gold digging self thought Shea couldn't make it by himself and needed to cling on to me to become anybody, but she was okay with him never becoming famous as long as he married into my family. I'm used to this.

Michael laughs suddenly. "I don't mean it in a bad way, Brooklyn," he says, I guess reading my expression. He signals around his house. "Trust me, we're doing quite well. I just mean, he didn't bring home another one of his gold diggers."

For some reason, his words don't make me feel any better, and the death grip Nick has on my hand lets me know that it makes two of us.

I shrug. "It's fine. I can see how that would be a concern," I respond, because it's true. I'm hesitant to trust people because in the past I've been burned. Being Chris Harmon's daughter means attracting a lot of the wrong kind of guys. Other than Shea, my other exes have also been musicians and most of our conversations have revolved around the business. I let out a relieved breath when Michael changes the subject to talk to Damien about his film company, and smile at Nick reassuringly. There are still a million questions running through my mind, but I'm not sure I'll ask him any. I think more than anything, I'm scared that if I ask him something and he gives me the wrong answer, I'll shut him away.

We eat the rest of our meal in peace and say our goodbyes. Michael and Mirielle both welcome me to come over again and send their regards to my parents. Isaac and Damien both give me a hug, followed by Mima, whose hug lasts longest. When I sit in the car, I can smell the fried food and spices on both Nick and me and it makes me smile.

"You're a lucky guy," I say, as we drive away from his parent's house.

Nick smiles and takes my hand, bringing it up to his mouth and caressing it with his soft lips. "I am."

His words zip-line to my heart, making it skip a beat. I turn away, hiding a smile as I look out into the bay, my eyes lingering on the bridge.

"When did you know?" I ask quietly, still looking at the bridge. I know I look different. I refuse to look at photos of myself back then. I looked anorexic with barely any meat on my bones, and my hair was bleached blond, much to my mother's dismay, which is why I did it.

"You mean after I saw you again?" he asks, just as quietly.

I nod, hoping he's looking at me.

Nick lets out a long loud exhale. "Will you look at me?" he asks. I can tell by the tone of his voice that he's expecting me to say no. "Please," he adds, and it's a plea I can't deny, so I do, even though there's a sadness in his eyes that I wish I could erase. "I think I always knew ... but I knew for sure the second time I saw you. You look so different. So different. But those eyes ... God, I've dreamt about your eyes so many times, I don't think I could ever forget them."

My heart stops when he says that, and I close my eyes for a moment, not wanting to forget those words and the way they sound coming out of his mouth. I wish I could walk around recording him and the things he says to me.

"Can I ask you something?" he asks suddenly.

My eyes blink open. "Sure."

"Why were you there? Why were you doing it?" he asks.

I bite my lip and lower my eyes. Even though it's been years, the pain is still so raw to me, which is why I try not to think about it. "I had a million reasons," I say when I can bring myself to look at him again.

He nods as he switches lanes. "How many reasons did you have not to?" he asks.

"One," I say automatically, not even having to think about it.

"Which was?" he asks, his voice wavering as if he's unsure he wants to hear it.

"Isaac."

We're stopped at a red light now and I can see Nick's eyes glistening. He blinks a couple of times and clears his throat. "Do you know how hard it is for me to hear that?" he asks, his voice a raw whisper.

"It's not like you didn't help me," I mutter. "Thank you for that, by the way."

He shakes his head and looks at me, pinning me with his eyes. He looks pissed off. "You're thanking me for helping you?" He closes his eyes and takes a breath before opening them back up. "Brooklyn, do you realize you were within an inch of your life by the time we got you there? Do you know how scared we were? Do you know how fucking scary it is to wake up in the morning, thinking you're going to help your brother train for a fucking marathon and have him call you on the verge of tears when you're on the other side of a bridge timing his run? I had to make him drive halfway there so I could hold you as you shook uncontrollably in the backseat of my car. Your mouth was fucking foaming. Fuck. That was the single scariest thing that has ever happened to me. I waited for two days in that fucking hospital until you woke up from that coma. Two days without sleeping or eating because I was that freaked out. Then your uncle Robert comes and thanks me, and your fucking mom demands that I leave. Demands it because you were awake already." Nick is seething by the end of his statement, completely ignoring the cars honking behind us, telling us that the light is green.

Tears begin running freely down my face. "I'm so sorry," I whisper, remembering my mother giving me hell over the whole thing. She was so sure that whoever helped me get to the hospital was going to go sell their story to the first gossip magazine they found, but they didn't. There was no news about me ever being on that bridge or in that hospital. The only news they reported was when I entered rehab. Then it was "Chris and Roxy Harmon's daughter, torn up about breakup with Shea Roberts, turns to drugs. Seeks help" everywhere for about a week until everybody forgot about me again.

When he pulls into the parking spot in his building, he puts the gear in park, unbuckles my seatbelt and pulls me into his arms, cradling me, letting me sob freely into his shirt.

"You don't get to apologize. You don't get to thank me for doing the right thing, and you don't get to apologize to me for making me go through it. I would have done that for anybody. It just fucking kills me that it was you—the most gorgeous woman on earth with the most beautiful smile and the best sense of humor. I hate that you ever considered ending your life. I hate that nobody was there to make you want to fight for it, and I hate that it took me so long to find you again."

Wiping my tears with my hands, I bring my face to his, grab his head and kiss him deeply, thanking him for that day and for every time he's ever looked at me and made me feel like everything. He carries me to the elevator, not letting go of me as he unlocks his door and stalks straight to his room, lying me down on his bed. I let out a breath as my body sinks into the softness of his comforter and prop myself up on my elbows to watch him kick off his shoes.

"Can I take a shower?" I ask, feeling rundown from the long day and knowing I still have a lot ahead of me to get through.

He tilts his head and smiles at me. "We can do anything you want to do," he responds.

"Anything?" I ask, raising an eyebrow.

His smile widens and he stalks toward me, pulling his shirt over his head on the way. My eyes trail from the Wilde tattoo on his inner arm to the music notes over his ribs. Once again, his body takes my breath away, but the look in his eyes, the one that tells me he wants to devour me in one sitting, that's what makes me stop breathing all together.

"Do you have wine?" I ask, almost panting and he hasn't even kissed me yet.

Nick chuckles as he pulls me to stand. "Yes, but you can't have any."

My eyebrows shoot up to my hairline. "What?"

"You heard me," he murmurs, kissing my neck, making my head loll to the other side on its own accord. "No drinking. I want you sober."

It's almost as if he can read my damn thoughts and I hate it. Except I don't. I am worried about how this is going to happen, though. Thankfully his blinds are shielding the light that the setting sun is bathing the bedroom in.

"Can we shower together?" I ask, my voice small. I feel like a coward suddenly. I feel like I've been stripped bare for him, and even though I'm still fully dressed, I've never felt so naked in my life.

"You sure?" he asks quietly, sweeping my hair from my eyes to look at me. I respond by leaning up on the balls of my feet and wrapping my arms around his neck and kissing him deeply. He moans when my tongue touches his and lifts me up, holding my bottom as he carries me into the bathroom.

Without letting me go or breaking our kiss, he switches on the shower. The fleeting thought that he must have done this a million times before crosses my mind, but I don't let it sit there, I push it right out. When he sets me on my feet and releases me, looking at me as if I'm a pond of water in the desert, I pull my shirt over my head and toss it to the side, my bra quickly following. His eyes stay on my face, searching, and then trail down to my breasts. He throws his head back with a groan before looking at me and kissing me again.

This isn't a sweet kiss like the one before; it's a possessive kiss that leaves my head swimming in desire. His lips graze down my jaw, my neck, the valley of my breasts, until he finally pulls a nipple into his mouth. My body begins to shiver at the sensation. It feels so good that I have to hold on to his head with both hands, losing myself in the power of his tongue as it swirls around each one. He falls to his knees suddenly and continues his exploration with his mouth until he reaches the top of my jeans, which he unbuttons and peels off along with my boy short underwear.

Grabbing my hips, he presses his face to me, his tongue traveling over the inside of my legs, from one thigh to the other. He takes his time, gently teasing me, taking me to the edge without doing much other than massaging my ass in his hands and sucking every inch of skin between my thighs. He pushes me up to the counter and spreads my legs wide, placing a hand on the inside of each thigh, and runs his tongue up and down my folds at a slow, torturous pace. I throw my head back and moan deeply, trying to keep my hands on his head, tugging his hair, begging for more, but I can't even form words. The feel of his tongue on me is too much as it is, so when he tweaks my nipples with his fingers, the way he tweaks the buttons on the soundboards, I fall over the edge, the orgasm hitting so hard that all I can do is scream his name.

Nick stands up, shedding his jeans and briefs as he does it, but I don't have time to admire any of it because my eyes are still half closed. I bring my gaze up to his face and admire the way he looks at me through hooded eyes, making me feel desired, sexy; everything I've ever wanted to feel is bottled up in the look he's giving me right now. His chest is rising and falling heavily as he scoops me up and takes me into the shower, walking under the water that sprays over us. He backs me against the wall, placing his lips against mine. He doesn't give me a warning; he just squeezes my bottom and groans loudly as he pushes into me with a hard thrust that makes me gasp for air as I throw my head back on the wall behind me.

"Oh my God," I scream, my fingernails digging into his flesh, making him pound into me harder. This is completely unlike the last time we had sex. This is rough, possessive; this is primal. His moans and dirty words make me feel like I'm about to go over the edge, and just when I gasp, feeling a bolt of electricity coursing through me, he slows down the pace and looks at me, his eyes wild with hunger, need.

"So fucking beautiful," he says, his voice raspy and guttural, and that's all it takes for me to fall.

CHAPTER TWENTY-ONE

"**A**t what time are those people you're supposed to watch going to perform?" Nick asks as we lay on his bed facing each other.

I groan at the reminder of all of the things I have to do. "They'll be there at nine," I mumble, pouting my lip at the thought of not having more alone time with Nick.

He bites my pout and sucks it into his mouth. "God, you're sexy," he growls before letting go of me to get out of bed. Wrapping the comforter around my body, I sit up to watch him pull his jeans over his briefs and loop his belt on. He stops at the belt buckle, glimpsing up at me with a smirk when he catches me watching him.

"You're not going to get dressed?" he asks, raising an eyebrow.

I fight a smile. "Soon. I'm just enjoying the show."

He laughs, shaking his head as he pulls a soft grey T-shirt over his head. He pulls on his hair to style it in the middle, stops mid-finger comb, and yanks my exposed feet, making me yelp. Sitting on the edge of the bed, he raises my feet to his mouth and presses a kiss on each of the tiny anchors I have on the insides of my ankles.

"What's the story behind these?" he asks. "You into pirates?"

My laughter comes out sounding more like a "pffft" as I look at him in amusement. "No. They keep me grounded."

His brows raise as if that wasn't the answer he was expecting, and he nods in appreciation. "They're cute," he comments, his face looking unsure about something.

"What?" I ask, sitting up.

He shrugs and brings his eyes to mine. "They sink ... anchors," he says quietly.

I smile slightly, bringing my hands to cup his worried face. "They also keep the vessel from moving into dangerous waters in the ocean. It depends how you look at it," I reply with a shrug. Nick's worried look begins to dissipate as he looks into my eyes, and a slow smile begins to form on his lips. He leans into my hands, pushing towards me until his nose is touching mine.

"I like that answer," he whispers, his lips meeting mine in a slow sweet kiss that doesn't fail to leave me breathless. He backs away from me slowly, his eyes intently on mine as if he's searing this moment in his head, and I do the same. Watching him walk to the bathroom, I wonder if his lips will always feel that good against mine, if his kisses will always be that pure. After pondering that for a moment, I stand up and dress as quickly as I can, tying my hair back into a ponytail with the elastic I have in the back pocket of my jeans.

He reappears and leans on the threshold of the bathroom door, crossing his muscular arms over his chest as he looks at me. "That was fast," he says, pushing off of the door and walking toward me. It doesn't matter that we just had sex, not for the first time, and that I've seen him more times than I can count with both of my hands, the way he makes me feel when he looks at me as he walks towards me takes my breath away every time.

When he reaches me, he curls his arm around me to tug my ponytail. "Will you stay here with me?" he asks.

I want to say yes so bad, especially with the hopeful look in his eyes. I look at the ruffled sheets beside us and smile. I wonder what all of this feels like for him. I wonder if it's even remotely close to the way it makes me feel, like it's everything. I wonder if he'll shower when I'm not here and think of me and what we shared in there, or if he's done it so many times that it'll just be a distant memory to him. I want to ask him what all of this means to him. I want to ask him if he's as caught up in me as I am in him, but I can't. I know I'll sound like a stage five clinger and I don't want him to think I'm some crazy person who's planned out our entire future together based on amazing sex. The idea that it may have been just sex to him makes me want to cry. I realize as I look at him that I really do drown in him. I really have given him everything I have left of myself.

I shake my head slowly, lowering my eyes. "I don't think that's a good idea," I whisper.

He cups my chin to look at him. "Why not?" he asks, frowning.

Because I'm scared that I'll fall in love with you … because I don't want to attach myself to someone who's going to realize I'm not all that and leave me high and dry. I don't say any of these things, of course. I just let them consume my thoughts.

"Didn't you say you would stay at the hotel?" I ask with a small smile.

He exhales. "I thought maybe I would've changed your mind, but I'll stay over there."

I lean in and kiss him. "Thank you," I say against his lips.

"For the record, we're sharing a bed," he says, raising an eyebrow as if daring me to argue with him.

I just laugh and bite down on my lip again, unwilling to tell him that I wouldn't have it any other way. Nick is too full of himself to need the constant reminders of how good looking he is or how he'll probably always get his way. The ride back to the hotel is different. I feel more at peace with myself, with everything. Nick lowers the music and points out a park, slowing down as we near it, and tells me he used to play little league there. He points out the different places he used to hang out growing up, and it feels like a double-edged sword. It warms my heart that he's sharing his experiences with me, but it makes me sad that my only good experiences were with Ryan and even that went wrong in my life. I went through a phase where I shut everybody out, and ended up with less than a handful of people because of it. I don't feel like I experienced my youth to the fullest. I love that I can live vicariously through somebody like Nick, though.

"Can I ask you about your time in rehab?" Nick asks quietly when we stop at a red light.

I take a breath and let it out quickly, turning my body to face him. "Sure, what do you wanna know?"

His face looks relieved when I answer. "I saw that you went right after the hospital," he says slowly, taking a breath before continuing. "That was the last I heard or saw about you after I left the hospital that day ..."

I swallow back the sadness marinating within me, reminding myself that the important thing is that he's beside me now, even though I'm not sure what that means for this, for us. "They kept me in the hospital for a couple of days after I woke up to monitor me, then forty-eight more hours to make sure I wasn't going to try to kill myself again," I roll my eyes at the memory. "Then my parents decided I needed to go to rehab. My dad was scared because his mom was an addict so he thought it ran in our blood, I dunno. My mom just wanted to lock me up somewhere so that people wouldn't point fingers at her and tell her what a disgrace of a mother she was," I scoff.

"Long story short, I went for a month and loved it. I didn't feel like I needed it to keep me off drugs. I knew what I had to do to stay off of those, I needed to get rid of the people I was hanging around. When I was in there less than a handful of people came to visit me, so when I got out, I started shedding friends like layers of winter clothing and found that even if I got cold, I would rather build my own damn fire. I was better off without them." I shrug, letting him know that's all there was to it.

He brings my hand to his face and brushes the back of it against his lips. "You're a brave woman, Brooklyn."

His words make me smile.

"I'm just a woman. I think being brave comes with the territory; it's just taking me a while to fully uncover it."

He steals a glance at me. "You haven't used since you got out though, right?" he asks.

"Do drugs bother you?" I counter before I give him my response.

Shrugging, he drops my hand and places it on his lap so that he can switch gears. "Not really. I'm around them enough that they don't, but I wouldn't want the woman I'm with to be into them."

I nod, trying not to read too much into the meaning of his words, even though my heart can't stop from skipping a beat. "I haven't done any since I got out of rehab. I've come close, usually when I've been drunk, so I try not to let myself drink too much, just in case. I really never want to be that girl again, you know? The one that depends on something that only tears her down," I say in a whisper, surprised at how candidly I'm speaking about it. I haven't been able to talk to many people about this. Hendrix loves me but is too judgmental since he's never been in the situation. Nina doesn't care for drugs either; drinking is her thing. Allie doesn't get it because I don't think the girl has ever been upset in her life. She's always been the star daughter, exceptional student, good friend and has never found a reason to try anything—she doesn't even drink much. Shea practically lives with a joint over his mouth, so he's not the best person to speak to about it. And Ryan was into them, as well as the rest of the friends I forced myself to shy away from. Nick is the first person that's made me feel comfortable enough to talk about it, other than my sponsor, and Nancy doesn't count because she deals with real addicts every day.

We pull into the front of the hotel and Nick puts the car in park. "Good enough for me, baby," he says, leaning into me and placing his lips softly on mine.

After leaving the car with the valet, we ride up the elevator quickly and go to our room. Once I change into a pair of skinny jeans, a shirt and my favorite ivory scarf, opting for boots instead of heels, and throw on a bunch of chunky bracelets, I'm ready to go. Chunky bracelets or a nice necklace are my answer to all wardrobe disasters. If you look like a bum, throw on chunky bracelets and a nice necklace. If you're hair is a mess, put it up, put on chunky bracelets and big earrings. It works for me, and from the sound of Nick's whistle, I know he approves.

He walks up to me with heated eyes and lets out a breath as if he's looking at the book with the answers to every solved mystery on earth. "So beautiful," he murmurs as he pulls me into him, his lips instantly molding around mine. "So fucking beautiful," he whispers against me, breaking the kiss and brushing the tip of his nose against mine softly.

I smile. "Thank you," I respond quietly. I've never really been good at accepting compliments from anybody, but the way he tells me I'm beautiful makes me not question it.

"You have a lot of these, huh? What does this say?" he asks, tugging at my scarf. I love that he pays attention to detail. Nobody else has ever noticed so many things about me, not the way Nick does.

"It's *The Raven*," I say. "Poe," I continue when he gives me a confused look.

He tightens his grip so that I stop walking and holds it in his hands to read it. Once he reads a few lines and decides it's cool, we continue to make our way to Shea's door before we head downstairs to see how he's doing.

"Waddup?" Darius says, opening the door for us.

"BK!" Leo bellows from the balcony when he sees me walk in. As usual, he runs toward me and practically mauls me, and Nick has to let go of my hand so it won't break.

"Leo," I greet with a muffled laugh against his chest. Everything about Leo is bear like, which is why I love his hugs so much.

"You look damn near edible," Leo says when he backs away from me. I slap him on the chest playfully and roll my eyes. Leo loves to say shit that he knows makes me uncomfortable. He laughs when I give him what he wants and shift from foot to foot, my lips pursing to contain my scowl.

Nick is beside me in a heartbeat, his arm draping my shoulders. "Leo," he says, his voice clipped, his body rigid beside mine. I almost want to laugh. I know if I look up at him, he's wearing a full scowl on his face and his eyes are narrowed at Leo. I don't even have to look at him, I just know it, and Leo's deep laugh confirms it.

"Aw shit. Does Shea know about this?" Leo asks, completely amused.

I love Leo like a brother. I love him more because ever
since Shea started working with him and Fern, his drug abuse
yielded. I'm not stupid. I know he still uses, but not like before.
Not like we used to.

I let out a breath, my heart beginning to pound a little
louder, a little faster. I don't want to hide anything from Shea,
but I'm scared of his reaction. Not because he's interested in
being with me, because I know he's not, but I know how his
mind works. I know that he sees me being with other guys as
yet another person bailing on him. I understand him, despite
his stupid reasoning, since I felt the same way about him for a
long time.

When I look at my life, I see it as a series of songs. I've
classified Shea and my relationship as a terribly sung version of
"Ex-Factor" by Lauren Hill. Mainly that one line: *you said you'd
die for me, why won't you live for me?* Every time things went
south in our relationship, whether it was the first or the fifth
time, I always clung on to that song and that line. And just like
it, I can't do it anymore. I can't be on hold forever and I don't
want to be. I love him so much, and he loves me so much, but
we need to let go of the idea that we're it for each other. We're
not. God forbid we were actually IN love, which I don't think
we ever really were.

A relationship based on sex, drugs, and the wrong kind of
love isn't much of a relationship at all.

"We're built on friendship," Shea used to argue anytime he
wanted me to get back together with him, or more importantly,
back in his bed.

"We're built on heroin and cocaine," I used to counter, right before letting him have his way with me in a bathroom stall.

As if hearing what's going on, Shea walks out of his room, pulling a shirt over his head. The redhead that was all over Nick the night before is trailing behind Shea, with lipstick still smeared on her face. My stomach curls when her eyes widen as she sees Nick standing here. I wish it wouldn't bother me and that I could say that the question of whether or not they've been together in the past doesn't cross my mind, but unfortunately it does. I steal a glance at Nick and see him shaking his head at Shea in amusement, and that makes me feel slightly better, even if it doesn't mean anything.

Shea's face isn't amused when I look back at him. His eyes are glued to Nick's arm around me and he gives me a questioning look as he walks up to us. I answer it, tilting my head a little. There is so much communication in unspoken words sometimes that you don't even have to voice anything at all. He raises his brows as if impressed, but doesn't say anything at all. Nick drops his arm and says hi to Shea with a sideways hug, and then I say hi to him with a kiss on the cheek. He puts his arm around my shoulder, the same way Nick had it, and it feels foreign there. The smell of marijuana reeks off of him, but it doesn't bother me. I just take a deep breath and let it out, as if I'm taking a hit of him, glad to see my friend is in one piece after a night of partying.

"You ready for the show?" Shea asks.

"Yup. Let's do it," I reply, beaming at him.

He smiles back and begins to lead me out the door, but I stop halfway there so that I can wait for Nick. My hand feels bare without his in it and that scares me. Shea notices my pause and frowns at me, then looks at Nick and shrugs as if he gets it. He drops his arm from my shoulder and walks out in front of me.

"I'll listen to what you sent when we get back," Shea tells Nick over his shoulder. "Maybe we can work on those tonight."

"You wanna go to the studio after the show? Is the bus here yet? I know Hendrix said there would be a small booth in it. That's all we need," Nick responds. He falls in step beside me and threads our fingers together, squeezing my hand slightly. I tilt my head up to look at him and smile at the boyish grin he gives me: my smile. It makes me want to kiss him to death and take a detour back to our room, but I restrain myself, only squeezing back with reassurance.

Shea shakes his head and turns toward us, opening his mouth to respond to Nick's question, but his eyes zone onto our hands and he stops mid-answer. I internally kick myself for not telling him about Nick and me. I should've hinted at it at least, but something tells me he knew. I can read him well enough to think he saw this coming and I want to ask him that as well, but now I'll have to wait.

Shea clears his throat, bringing his eyes to mine and he looks more hurt than pissed. "The bus isn't here yet. It'll be here tomorrow night and they didn't book a studio. You think your pops will let us go to one of his?" he asks Nick.

Nick lets go of my hand and runs his through his hair, letting out a breath. "Will he? Yes. Do I want to ask him? Hell no. You wanna go to my house?" Nick suggests. My heartbeat slows down and I can hear it pulsing slowly in my burning ears.

"Yeah, we can." Shea shrugs. "Brooklyn, would you mind that?" he asks, staring into my eyes. The spots of mud are more visible in his eyes now, and I can tell he's testing me with his hot-headed attitude. Shea's always been a bit of a spitfire; thankfully he uses that energy on stage or when he writes his raps. He saves his melancholy and broken heart for his ballads. You can say he's a mix of J Cole and Bruno Mars, which is pretty eclectic for one artist and exactly what I love about his performances.

"I'll go." I say, narrowing my eyes slightly at him, daring him to say something stupid.

Nick's posture has changed now too. Noticing the tension, his thumbs are tucked into the pockets of his jeans and his fists are balled up a little. Leo and Fern are either completely oblivious to it all or are just ignoring us with their cell phones. For all I know they're texting each other about this. Darius is just looking straight at the elevator door. Thankfully the ride is short and we reach the ground level before anybody says anything else. Shea's assistant meets us there, an older woman the same age as our mothers. She's another reason he's kind of been in check for a couple of years now. He's more scared of letting her down than anybody else, I think.

The show starts off with a woman named Tracey performing alone: just her and her piano. Her voice wavers as she sings the way only a handful of people can, and it's beautiful. After her set, I pull her to the side and take a demo and her information, talking to her for a little bit about signing and what she's looking for. Of course, as usual, at the sound of the name Harmon Records, she's all ears and wants to know everything I have to offer. Others perform but I only speak to one besides Tracey—the rapper Shea told me about. The man is on another level. His raps are poetic and on point, and he has a look that I know will sell.

Talking to him, I find out about his background: single mother, six siblings, grew up in a bad neighborhood. The amount of untold stories and undiscovered talent there is out there never ceases to amaze me. It's also one of the things I love about what I do. I give them a chance to be heard, to get out of their struggles, even if that often means falling into a bigger heap of them. Notorious BIG said it best: more money, more problems. I've had money my entire life and even I know that to be true. By the time I'm finished talking to everyone, I'm completely exhausted, I would never leave without watching Shea perform, though. As I head backstage to his dressing room where everybody is hanging out, the poignant smell of marijuana hits my lungs. I visibly take a step back when I turn the corner and Darius laughs at my surprise.

"You not used to it anymore?" he asks with a hearty laugh that makes him cough.

I shake my head. "Please." I am so not used to it anymore. Not that I mind it. I'm fine with that smell and having people around me smoke it, for some reason it doesn't give me the urge to do it. It's one of those drugs that I can take up and put down whenever I want. Not that I do it anymore. Unlike the heavier things, there's no temptation in weed for me.

When I pull the door open, the smoke instantly swirls around me. Shea is lounging on the couch, playing Xbox with Nick. There are at least eight people, including four women I've never seen before. This life has to get old. How many different cities, girls, and drugs can you possibly do every night? For Shea, I know the answer is: unlimited. He'd rather be doing this than anything else. I know he does it for the thrill he gets when he's onstage, but this extra shit is just too much.

"Shea, you're on," an older man with a headset says from the door as he waves the smoke away from his face.

"Boom, motherfucker!" Shea shouts, getting up from the couch and tossing his controller.

"That's fucked up," Nick says with a chuckle. "Damn."

Shea grabs both sides of my face and kisses my forehead as

he brushes past me. "Stand by the stage," he says.

I nod. "'Kay, break a leg."

"Yeah, yeah," he says, smiling back as he walks away.

The women in the room begin to follow him out, but Darius stops them by putting his hands up. "Go to your seats. Maybe I'll let you back in later."

They don't even respond to that as they walk away. At least they're not disgusting and trashy looking, like some I've seen before.

Nick grabs my hand and pulls me out of the room, walking toward the stage to a couple of chairs set off to the side. Nick sits down in one, not caring whether or not they're for us, and extends his legs before pulling me into his lap. Smiling, I position myself sideways so that my face is in his neck. He begins to brush strands of hair out of my face, tickling the side of my arm as he does it.

While the host is talking and getting people riled up to welcome Shea, I look around the venue. It's intimate and dark with all black walls and huge glass chandeliers that drop over the stage and the crowd. I love The Fillmore, it's actually one of the best sounding places in San Francisco. I used to frequent it often when I visited. Because of this place and the bands they host, I've been able to get a lot of great artists to sign under Harmon Records, so in a sense I feel like this is my music mecca. I've never seen Shea perform here before, which makes tonight that much more exciting and a little nerve-wracking. He left the room before us but he's taking a long time to get up here. I have half a mind to go see what he's up to. Anytime Shea takes too long to get onstage, he's up to no good.

"So you're coming home with me," Nick murmurs against my head, distracting me from my thoughts.

I smile. "I guess so."

I can feel him twirling the curl at the end of my hair. It makes me sigh and move my face further into his neck, burying my nose in it. I love the way he smells, like a beautiful concoction of nature and cologne.

"I should be happy about that," he says, his flat voice making me frown against him. "But it took another man asking you to convince you."

I almost roll my eyes at that. Almost. Until I put myself in his shoes and realize what he must think. Instead of arguing or explaining myself, I go another route, the only one that matters. "But you're the one that I'll be sleeping with."

Nick leans away from me, making me lift my face to look at him. His eyes are blazing with intensity. "Damn right," he growls before taking my mouth in his and kissing me senseless, leaving no space in my mouth unexplored with his tongue. He breaks the kiss as suddenly as he started it and looks at me again, chest heaving against mine. Shaking his head he lets out a breath that mingles with my own. Our mouths are so close to one another, both slightly parted.

"I won't share you, Brooklyn," he says, his voice sounding almost pained as he shimmies beneath me and readjusts himself.

I don't have time to ask him what that means because I get distracted when Shea walks past us, not acknowledging either of us. My stomach sinks, knowing he must have seen us kissing. Knowing he saw me sitting on Nick with our arms wrapped around each other. Shea is the type of friend that is happy for me regardless of what I do, even if he doesn't agree with it, as long as he *knows* what I'm doing. He's always been what Ryan used to call "childish" in that sense, but it's not childish. Shea obviously knows what I'm doing, but the fact that I'm sitting on top of his friend/producer's lap and I never told him about Nick and I makes me feel horrible. I'm a fucking idiot. Maybe I should have Hendrix get me that on a travel mug for Christmas.

"Why do you only work with Shea?" I ask Nick as I watch Shea turning his neck side to side in a stretch.

"What do you mean?" Nick asks, bouncing me on his leg. I get the feeling he's getting tired of carrying me so I make to stand, but he holds my hips so I can't move.

I look at him. "I heard you tell your dad you're only working with Shea. Why is that?"

Nick purses his lips in disapproval, I'm assuming for his father. "My dad's an asshole, in case you didn't notice." He sighs. "He was … is … a good producer. He's won a lot of Grammys and to him this is a 'show me who you work with and I'll tell you what you are' sort of thing. Me working with Shea doesn't bode well with him because he thinks Shea's music is garbage. My dad's more into jazz and classical. He worked with a lot of famous musicians, mainly Hispanic, back in the day. Anyway, he's only heard Shea rap, so he doesn't approve. He doesn't understand the quality of music we're recording." Nick shrugs as if that's all.

"So that's where the name Shadow comes in," I say, my voice drifting off in wonderment.

"Exactly," Nick responds, kissing me on the tip of my nose. "We pretty much live our lives trying to outdo each other now. It's stupid, really, since he has me beat by a long shot."

I shrug. "Who cares? Besides, you have a long career ahead of you," I say with a smile.

Nick smiles back and opens his mouth to say something, but we're cut off by the cheering of the crowd. I stand up, clapping along with them and smiling at Shea when he looks at me over his shoulder and smirks at me. He turns back around as the lights turn off completely and the tempo of one of his songs starts. Shea runs onto the stage and stands in the middle right when a purple spotlight shines on him. He begins to sing, his voice wrapping around every note perfectly. This song is a slow ballad about heartache and the one that got away. It's one of my favorites from his last CD, and I sing along with him as if I was the one performing.

As I stand there, swaying my hips slowly to the beat and singing, Nick stands beside me with his arms crossed in front of his chest, nodding his head along. Shea performs another song right after and then takes a break, taking a swig of the Hennessy bottle they placed in an ice bucket onstage. I cringe at the sight; I've never understood how he could do that. His white T-shirt is already clinging to him from his sweat, but I know he won't take it off. He'd rather come to the side of the stage and change into another one than take it off. His old manager used to encourage him to take off his shirt. Shea always turned that down, saying he wanted to be taken seriously as a musician and not seen only as a sex symbol. Now he has both, so sometimes he concedes and takes off the damn shirt when he's hot. That's probably the women's favorite part of the show. It's so stupid, really. The man puts on a hell of a show with his clothes on, so it makes me mad when I hear young girls or women discussing how the best part of the show was when he took his shirt off.

"Hello, San Francisco!" Shea yells into the microphone, making everybody scream. He smiles. "How you all doing out here tonight?" He pauses, letting them cheer. "This is a special city for me, one that brings a lot of memories. Some good, some bad, but no matter what's happened here, I'm always glad to be back with you all!"

There are hoots and hollers and women screaming they

love him. He eats it all up. Nick chuckles beside me, knowing Shea is enjoying the hell out of all of it. I roll my eyes but laugh along as I watch the spectacle. I keep enjoying myself until Shea turns and looks right at me. Even with the blinding lights illuminating over him, he finds me, the way he does when he wants to prove a point. This knowledge makes my heart stop beating.

"This next song ... isn't mine ..." he starts and chuckles when someone shouts for him to perform a specific song of his. "But I keep listening to it. It reminds me of someone in my life that I keep striking out with."

He turns his body then and looks straight into my eyes as the familiar beat of Drake's song, Connect, starts playing in the background. The bass builds up slowly with the tempo of the song, dropping in perfect synch with the hi-hat of the drums Leo is playing. Shea does a little sensual dance along with it, moving his pelvis slowly. He doesn't even acknowledge the catcalls of the women in the audience; he's completely in the zone watching me. He begins to rap the first verse, smirking as he does it, and I can feel is the adrenaline beginning to bubble through my body. The only thing I can hear is my heart pounding loudly in my ears as heat creeps up in my face, and I'm thankful for the darkness in the building.

I don't have to turn my head to look at Nick's pissed off face. I can see his jaw clenching and his fists balling from my peripheral vision as he glares at Shea. I feel jealousy swirling in the air, wrapping its little claws around each one of our necks and gripping, taking each of our breaths slowly away from us. The crowd is oblivious to it all. And the worst part is, there's not much I can do to ease the palpable tension. I feel like I'm rooted to the ground, unable to move from here.

"Oh the idea is fun," Shea sings. I find my lips moving,

singing along, even though I'm glaring at him, hot tears forming in the back of my eyes. "Oh the idea is so fun every time,
at least we try for homerun every time. Swinging. Eyes closed
just swinging …"

He continues to sing, turning to the audience with a bop in
his step and waving his arms in a dance as the tempo switches,
and then turns back to face me. He walks over to me slowly
until he's standing directly in front of me, his eyes narrowing as
he sings, "She just wanna run around the city and make memories that she can barely remember. And I allow her. Talk about
pussy power. She just wanna run over my feelings like she's
drinking and driving in an eighteen wheeler. And I'd allow her.
Talk about pussy power …"

Tears begin to trickle down my face as Shea continues to
sing to me, planting little bombs inside my chest with each look
and detonating them with each word. When he sings that he's
just trying to connect with something, he turns around and
keeps dancing, performing for the crowd now, getting them
riled up. I continue to watch him in a daze. When he finishes
the song, he looks at me again, his mouth curling into a wicked
smile that makes me want to run up to the stage and slap it off.
Blinking away my tears in disbelief, not understanding how he
could be so downright mean to me, how he could see that he's
hurting me and smile at it, I turn around and begin to run toward the dressing room.

The more steps I pound into the ground, the harder my
heart pounds in my chest, matching the steps chasing me from
behind. Wiping my face, I make sure that there are no tears left
on it, even though I refuse to look back now. I know he's running toward me but I can't look at him. I just want to get away,
but he doesn't let me. Nick's arms wrap around me and he lifts
me up, carrying me like a baby as he cradles me to his chest and

continues to walk me outside of the building. The wind hits us as we step into the alley. Nick tells one of the drivers to take us back to the hotel, carrying me into the car and leaving me on his lap as we drive. I don't cry. I don't lose it like I expected to when I'm comforted. I hold everything in, unwilling to let myself crumble in front of him over this, even though I feel hurt. I shake my head against Nick's chest out of confusion, unable to understand why Shea would do that to me.

Deep down I understand why he did it and I think that bothers me more. He's been there for me to see me through things I didn't think I could survive, and he wants it to stay that way. He doesn't know how to accept that I can't wait until he decides that he can give me what I need, and what's worse is that I don't want him anymore. I don't want him to fill the void I thought I needed him to fill all those years ago. I want to be happy in my life the way I see fit, but I want Shea to be part of it. I'm scared to let go of him because he's the only thing I have left of my old self, and I'm not willing to let that girl go completely. No matter how tortured she was, she's still part of me.

The drive back to the hotel is quiet. Nick doesn't say a word to me; he just runs his fingers through my hair and down my back soothingly with his lips pressed against my forehead. I'm grateful for the peace he gives me when he's near. More than anything, I'm thankful that he doesn't question me or act like he's angry with me for being hurt. That's what Shea would do: get angry with me for letting other people's actions get to me. When we pull up to the front of the hotel, Nick shifts me to the seat and hops out of the SUV before helping me out, holding my hand all the way up to our room.

Stepping in, I let out a shaky breath and close my eyes.

"I can't believe he did that," I whisper at nobody in particular. Nick, who's standing behind me, lets out a breath of his own.

"I can," he says.

I nod, blinking my eyes rapidly, the tears now leaking from my eyes. I walk toward the bathroom so that I can get myself together, and thankfully Nick gives me space. When I come back out, feeling much better and composed, he's sitting on the couch with earphones on, working on Shea's music, I'm sure. Nick takes off the earphones when he sees me and lays the computer down on the table in front of him, standing up and striding over to me with a sympathetic look in his eyes. I've heard Nina say in the past that she hates when people look at her with sympathy when she's down, but as Nick walks toward me, I can't imagine why. I've never had anyone look at me like this. People usually kick me when I'm already down, either expecting me to get right back up or not caring if I walk at all.

Nick cups my face in his hands, his thumbs caressing my cheeks softly as he looks at me with the most caring expression on his face. I have to swallow hard to dislodge the lump forming in my throat. His eyes question me, asking if I'm okay. I nod, beginning to feel overwhelmed with emotion. Before I get a chance to blink my tears away again, his lips are desperately moving against mine. I can't tell who's taking and who's giving as our tongues twirl around the other in harmony. The way he kisses me, like he needs me more than he wants me, takes my breath away every time. He runs his hands down my body, palming my butt before lifting me up and circling my legs around his waist. His mouth leaves mine and trails down my neck, kissing and sucking as I grab on to his shoulders and throw my head back, letting him bathe me with his lips.

He backs away suddenly and looks at me, pinning me with his gaze.

"I don't want to share you, Brooklyn," he says, his voice

strained with desire.

"I'm not yours to share," I whisper, telling him the same thing I told him on the airplane, which betrays the way my heart feels in this moment, but I want to hear him disagree with me. I need him to.

He weaves his hands into my hair, threading them together at the back of my head and places a kiss between my jaw and my ear. "I want you to be mine. Only mine," he says, his voice as soft as his dizzying kisses.

"Why? Why me?" I ask quietly. Nobody has ever cared if I belonged to them; in fact, I think they preferred that I didn't. Nick can have Stephanie or the slutty redhead or even Gia for that matter, so I need to know what makes me different to him. I need to know that I'm not just some conquest that he'll leave high and dry.

His lips freeze over my chin and he pulls away to look at me, his face confused when he does. "Because I think if I ever see another man touching you and dancing with you the way Shea was, I will cut his arms off. Because I need to know you won't go back to him just because he sang you a little song out of jealousy. Because the thought of you kissing anybody else the way you kiss me is enough to drive me crazy. Because I want to be the one that owns this," he says, placing his hand over my heart. "And this." He brushes his fingers over my lips. "And this." He trails the tips of his fingers over my head, making me smile. "And this," he says, placing soft kisses over my neck and down to my chest. "And this," he says, cupping me between my legs before dropping his hand and looking at me again. "And most of all, because I'm selfish and I don't want you to make anybody feel the way you make me feel. Because I want those big green eyes to only light up when you look at me. Because. I. Need. You." He says the last four words slowly, letting them sink in as my breath leaves me. What is it about need that makes us want to step up to the challenge?

"What about you?" I ask breathily, even though I'm sold.

"What about me?" he counters, raising an eyebrow.

"What if I don't want to share you?" I ask quietly, realizing how much I don't want to and how that's never been an option in my past "relationships".

Nick smiles, a slow caring smile that makes my insides curl. "I don't want to be shared," he says, lifting my hand to his lips and kissing the tips of my fingers. "I want to be yours."

"Okay," I whisper as my heart thunders against my chest, standing up so that I can place my lips chastely on his.

"Okay?" he asks, searching my eyes once more before he walks us to the bedroom and leans into the bed, placing me on the edge and peeling off my shirt as he stands upright. He undresses me, quickly pulling off my boots, socks and jeans in fluid movements, as if he can't have me naked soon enough. I begin to unbuckle his belt, but he steps away and undresses himself as well, tossing everything into the heap of clothing in the corner of the room. My breath accelerates as I lay back on my elbows, admiring his naked form and wanting to run my fingers through every ripple on his chest, but the way Nick is looking at me with his jaw set and his eyes blazing don't let me move from the bed. He plants his knee in between my legs and moves me up on the bed, placing me at the center of it while he kisses me deeply and palms my breasts with his large hands. A groan of complaint escapes my lips when his hands leave my chest. He places one on the bed beside me while the other grasps my hip, squeezing it slightly before he moves it to my ass, grabbing it harder and pulling it from the bed.

He breaks our kiss, both of us panting, and looks at me. His eyes are narrowed and full of desire. "I can't, Brooklyn," he says, his voice raspy. "I can't share you."

I shake my head, my lips parting slightly. "No," I moan out when he presses against me.

"Say it," he growls as he positions his cock in between my folds. "Say it," he repeats, circling his hips so that I feel him so close, yet so far.

"You're not sharing me," I whimper, arching my back hoping to push him in, but his grip tightens on my ass so that I don't try it.

He lowers his head to mine and licks the seam of my lips. I tighten my hold around his neck, tears threatening to fall over my face because of the amount of need I feel for him. I've never felt this kind of indescribable desire for somebody, the kind that makes my heart feel like it's about to completely combust if he doesn't take me right this second.

"Tell me you're mine, baby. Tell me," he says in a guttural voice, positioning himself closer, his tip inside me making me quiver around him as I toss my head back in a moan.

"Please," I whisper. "Please, please, please." I plant my heels on the bed behind him and swing my body to his, but he backs away, taking himself out completely. I screw my eyes shut and bite down on my lip so that I don't bring myself to beg him again, but then he lowers his head and closes his mouth around my nipple, flicking in a tantalizing pace as he thrusts into me just enough that he's at my lips but not inside of me.

"Give me what I want and I'll give you everything," he says, his voice husky and low.

My eyes flutter open and I look at him wide-eyed. "You already have what you want," I say breathily.

Nick shakes his head, a slow grin spreading over his face, his eyes twinkling despite the obvious need in them. He bites down on his lower lip and moans deeply when I move again, closer to him, letting him feel how wet I am.

"I know I do. I wanna hear you say it," he responds, dipping his head and taking my lips in his and kissing me slowly. "Tell me you're mine," he says, his voice a strained whisper. "Tell me that this-," he says, fully sliding his cock into me, the fullness it provides making my legs shake uncontrollably. "Is mine," he says as he thrusts deeply in and out before pulling out again and leaving me empty. I can't take it anymore. I begin to cry.

"Please," I whimper. "Please, Nick. I'm yours!" I say, my voice trembling.

He lets go of my ass and places both of his hands beside my head, hovering over me, his ocean eyes searching mine before he finally gives in, bringing his mouth down to mine at the same moment that his cock fills me. His thrusts are rigorous and I feel my insides burn as he brings me to the brink within seconds, clenching around him and crying out as my climax washes over me.

"That's right, baby," he whispers, his breath hot against my ear. "Mine."

He grabs my bottom again and positions me off of the bed as he continues to wildly drive into me, groaning with each thrust. I scratch his back, begging him for more, and he moves faster, deeper, harder, crying out my name as he spills pieces of himself inside of me.

CHAPTER TWENTY-TWO

The feel of feather light kisses over my shoulder awake me and I smile knowing whose lips are placing them there.

"Good morning, beautiful," Nick murmurs against my skin.

"Good morning," I respond, my voice raspy with sleep.

"Do you want to do something fun and touristy today?" he asks.

Turning my body to face him, I hook my leg around his hip and look up at him, smiling. It should be illegal for somebody to look this good when they first wake up in the morning. I bury my face in the crook of his neck and breathe him in. He even smells fresh, despite how sweaty we got last night. He chuckles when I snuggle my face deeper against him, and I smile at the sound of it.

"You even laugh sexy," I comment, my voice sounding muffled against his neck.

He runs his fingers along the curve of my body, slowly downward and back up, repeating the movement languidly. "Is that a yes, Nick, I'll do touristy things with you? A no way,

Nick, I just want to stay here and let you fuck me senseless all day. Or a yes, Nick, I'll do anything you want me to," he says, his hand traveling down the valley of my waist and parting my legs. He glides his fingers between my thighs and begins to tease me, making me moan. "Hmmm … I think I'll take that as a 'yes, Nick, I'll do anything you want me to' then," he mutters.

There's a question in his voice that makes me swallow and nod slightly.

"Should I do anything I want with you?" he teases, inserting his fingers inside me and pulling them out, repeating the action slowly and making me bite down on my lip. My eyes flutter open when he stops suddenly, and I find his face hovering over mine, his eyes blazing. "Should I?" he asks, repeating his previous question.

"Yes, please," I breathe, my body bowing off of the bed at the feel of his fingers back inside of me as his lips tease my nipples.

After Nick makes good on his word, we shower together and get dressed. He keeps telling me we should do touristy things, but I don't know what I want to do. I don't really want to go on the Alcatraz Tour. As much as I've wanted to do that I don't think I'm ready for it. If I'm going to do it with anybody, I definitely want it to be with Nick, though.

"Let's take a cable car," he suggests, so we do. I've actually been on them before, so it's not a new experience, but it feels brand new being on one with Nick. We hold onto the bars and make out as he hangs from it as if he's going to let go and fall into the street. We go up to the Coit Tower and get a view of the city from the top of it, which is spectacular. And then go grocery shopping when Nick suggests a picnic in Golden Gate Park. It's nothing major, the picnic. We get sandwiches and wine and sit outside, enjoying the sun and nice breeze outside.

"We could've gone to a good seafood restaurant," Nick says, lying back on the cheap striped towel we bought in the pharmacy on our walk over.

As I take the last sip of my wine, I tilt my head to look at him, my eyes wide with shock. "Are you kidding? This is the most fun I've had …" I frown, thinking about the answer to that, even though there's not much to think about. This is the most fun I've had—ever.

Nick smiles sheepishly, grabbing my arm and pulling me down to lay with him. "I didn't think you usually do things like this," he says, his lips on my forehead as he tugs on the ends of my hair lightly.

"I don't," I respond, closing my eyes to bask in this feeling of satisfaction. I've never felt this content with anybody in my life, other than Ryan, and even that was different.

"Have any of your boyfriends ever taken you on a picnic?" Nick asks, even though I pretty much just said I've never done this.

I scoff. "You're joking, right?" I ask. Shifting my body to look at his face, I place my palm on his chest and lean up.

"Is this your first picnic?" he asks, his eyes twinkling with contentment.

I twist my lips, trying not to smile. "Maybe."

"Maybe?" he asks playfully, sitting up to tickle me. I squirm away from him, laughing.

"It is," I say, laughing and blocking his hands from my ribs.

"Hmm," he comments, his body covering mine. His arms are on either side of my head now and he's looking down on me with those intense eyes.

"Sea foam green," I blurt out quietly.

He frowns.

"Your eyes, they're sea foam green today," I explain.

Nick shakes his head with a chuckle and dips his mouth to mine, running his tongue along the seam of my lips for me to part, and I do, welcoming him. He breaks the kiss but continues sucking alongside my mouth and lips, making me feel like my heart is going to detonate in my chest at any moment.

"You're so adorable," he says, smiling when he's finished devouring my mouth. He lies back down beside me, propping his head on his hand. "So no boyfriend picnics, that's good. I'm glad I can give you something you've never had with anyone before. Especially here."

I smile, grateful he knows how much it means to me to make nice memories in a city that's felt haunted for me. "Thank you," I say, leaning in to kiss his bicep where he has his Wilde tattoo scripted. I want to tell him he's given me a lot of things I've never had before already, but I lean into him with a smile instead.

Nick stands and helps me up and we start picking up the things we brought. He puts his arm around my shoulder and holds my hand there. The way he always holds my hands makes me smile, as if he doesn't want me to get away from him or he can't get enough of touching me. I love it.

I'm pointing at the Coit Tower, telling him how different it looks from down here and frown when he doesn't answer me. When I look over at him, he's staring at my lips as if he hasn't heard a word I've said. I'm about to reprimand him for not paying attention, but he cups his hand behind my neck and pulls my mouth to his, kissing me until I can't see straight. All I can think about is how fast my heart is beating and how my stomach feels like I have exploding pop rocks in it. The way he makes me feel scares me. The way I think I would feel without him scares me more.

"How old did you say Melody was?" Nick asks when I stop

in front of an American Girl store.

"Four," I say, smiling proudly.

He smiles back. "That's a cute age."

"It is."

"My friend has a son that's five, he's cute. I don't see him often but when I do it's always a fun time," he says.

"When was the last time you saw him?"

Nick shrugs. "Couple of months ago when I went to his birthday party."

"Cute," I say with a smile, trying to picture Nick at a kids' birthday party.

"What was the theme?"

"Pirates," he says, his eyes twinkling as he looks down toward my feet.

I laugh and fish through my purse until I find one of the coins Melody gave me. I take one out proudly to show him, as if it was a lost treasure that I found. He frowns and laughs when he realizes what it is.

"Those were at the party," he says.

"Of course they were," I say, matter of fact. "Golden Doubloons. You can't have a pirate party without them."

Nick drops my hand and turns his body to mine and I mimic his movement.

"What?" I ask curiously.

"Do you want kids?" he asks.

I raise an eyebrow. "Isn't it a little too soon for you to ask me that?" I joke.

Nick raises an eyebrow back at me as he walks forward, moving me until my back is on the glass of the store. "You think so?" he asks, his voice low as his eyes flicker between my eyes and my lips, effectively making my stomach coil. When he does that I just want to pull him to me and beg him to kiss me.

I nod my head slowly, breathing heavily now. "Yes," I whisper.

"Let's go over the things you think it's too soon to talk about then," he suggests, his mouth dangerously close to mine. "Kids?" I nod. "Moving in together?" I nod. "Marriage?" My stomach flops in excitement when he says that, and I nod. A smile tugs his lips. "Hmm ... so I assume you're on the pill," he says, making me frown and my eyes widen in realization.

"Yes," I whisper, wondering why he didn't ask me this before.

"It doesn't matter to me," he says, his voice a whisper against my lips, so close yet so far.

"Why not?" I ask, my heart strumming loudly against my chest.

He smiles against me. "We can't talk about that," he says.

I close my eyes and bite down on my lip. He totally got me. When I flick my tongue out to wet my lips, it hits Nick's and he groans, grabbing my face and finally kissing me. When he's made sure that we're both breathing heavily and can't take the lack of oxygen, he lets me go and we continue walking.

"Charlotte," I murmur, looking at one of the dolls on the storefront. "That's a nice name."

I always notice names. I think because mine is uncommon, I've always been slightly intrigued by the more "normal" names. Not that it matters, I'm sure I'll end up naming my kids weird names anyway when the day comes.

Nick tilts his head and smiles. "What other names do you like?"

"Hmmm ... for a boy I like Jorel," I say.

Nick stops walking and makes a face that makes me laugh.

"What? You don't like it?" I ask, laughing.

"It sounds like a cleaning product," he comments.

"It does not!" I say, slapping his shoulder playfully. "I bet Isaac would like it."

Isaac is into comic books, much like Hendrix, and I know for a fact that Superman's dad's name is Jorel.

Nick scoffs. "Isaac's a nerd. And yeah, it does sound like a cleaning product." He adds, mimicking a female voice, "You have a stain on your shirt? Oh, spray some Jorel on that, it'll take it right off."

I laugh at his impersonation and the face he makes as he says it then put my hand in his again as we continue walking.

It does sound like a cleaning product. Damn him.

I've had so much fun with Nick that I haven't given much thought about Shea's performance last night, but when I do, my heart breaks a little.

CHAPTER TWENTY-THREE

'm stirred awake from our nap by pounding on our door, followed by shouts from Shea calling out my name. Nick stirs beneath me, muttering for him to shut the fuck up, and pulls me into his chest again, cradling my head on him as if he were carrying a baby. Placing a kiss over his heart, I untangle myself from him and sit up.

"Don't go," Nick groans sleepily.

"I have to," I respond, brushing my lips against his. "I'll be back soon."

He turns over in the bed as I get up to look for something to wear. I pull on a pair of sweats that I brought just in case I decided to work out and a loose T-shirt over my head. Pulling my hair up into a ponytail, I make my way toward the door.

"Brooklyn, please open the door," Shea says as he pounds on it once more.

Rolling my eyes, I open it and stand beside it as he walks in. He's wearing a black T-shirt, camouflage cargo shorts and Jordan flip-flops. He walks to the couch and plops down on it, ruffling his hair nervously without looking at me. Assuming he's not going to leave any time soon, I let the door shut close and make my way over to him, crossing my legs as I sit on the couch across from him.

He lets out a breath, wiping his face roughly with both of his hands and looks at me, his muddy green eyes no longer glazed over with intoxication. "I'm so fucking sorry, Bee," he says, swallowing loudly.

I shake my head, biting the inside of my cheek to contain the emotion that's threatening to come back. "That was an asshole thing to do," I whisper brokenly. "And you know what, Shea? I don't even fucking care that you hurt me like that. But what about Nick? Did you ever care to stop and think about what he might have been feeling? He's your friend too."

Shea narrows his eyes at me. "Fuck him. He should've told me what was going on. YOU should have told me what was going on. I'm not fucking blind, Brooklyn. I see the way you guys look at each other. I hear the way you talk to each other. How long have you known him?"

I gape at him. "You introduced me to him!" I remind him. I'm not about to tell him about the bridge and about Nick's brother. I don't even remember Nick being there to begin with so I can't count that as the first time we met.

Shea laughs, though it's with little amusement, and then stops and furrows his eyebrows when he sees I'm serious. "You're not kidding."

I shake my head. "Why would I be?"

He shrugs. "I dunno. I just figured the way you act together ..."

"Whatever. Even if I'd known him for years, which I haven't, that doesn't excuse what you did."

Shea agrees, nodding his head. "I fucked up."

"You did," I say softly, beginning to forgive him for the

little show he put on.

He moves over to the couch I'm sitting on and takes me into his arms. I lay my head on his shoulder when he squeezes me tight. "What about us?" he asks, his voice quiet.

"What about us?" I whisper.

Shea exhales, burying his face into my neck. "I don't wanna lose you, Brooklyn. I can't," he says, his voice wavering.

"You won't, Shea. Never," I reply, picking my head up to look at him.

He nods, searching my eyes. "You promise?" he whispers.

"I swear it," I whisper back, feeling my chest tighten as tears form in my eyes. I hate that I have to reassure him of this. I hate that he feels so alone in his life that he needs me, of all people, another lonely soul, to cling to. I hate that we couldn't make it work because we were both too miserable to bring true happiness to each other.

Straightening out in my seat, I cup his face so that he'll look into my eyes. "You're my best friend, Shea. You can't get rid of me. Haven't you learned that by now?" I ask quietly.

His eyes glisten. "You're more than my best friend, Brooklyn," he whispers. "You're family," Shea continues, breaking the dam that was holding in my tears.

I lean in, hugging him tightly, unwilling to let him go. "I love you, Shea."

"I love you more, BK," he responds. "I'm sorry I can't be more to you."

My throat closes in at his words, making it impossible for me to speak, so I nod instead. Sniffling back tears, I let go of him and wipe my face quickly. "You weren't meant to be more to me," I say, my voice wavering. "But that doesn't mean you haven't been enough."

He blinks rapidly, his lashes now wet as he smiles. "You

always know the right thing to say."

I smile back and tap his toes with mine. "I'm cool like that," I joke, smiling brighter when I make him laugh.

"Well, you kind of have to be cool to hang out with me," he counters.

"Stupid," I mumble, shaking my head with a laugh, feeling lighter than I have all day.

Shea props his feet up on the table, crossing them at his ankles. "You missed my best fucking song," he says. "It's a new one. I just recorded it last week."

"Oh yeah? How does it go?" I ask, laying my head on his shoulder and closing my eyes when he starts humming the beat of it. I drift off with a smile on my face as he croons to me about life, love, and forgiveness.

The next time I wake up, I'm balled up on the couch, and Nick and Shea are talking in the kitchen behind me. I stay still as I listen to them discuss songs they still have to record and smile, grateful that there's no bad blood between them. Sitting up and stretching my arms over my head, I hear my phone ringing and get up to get it from my room. I shoot a glance over at Nick who smiles and winks at me, running his fingers through his ruffled hair. I let my eyes trail over his naked chest one time before blinking them away and heading into the room.

We decide to go out for pizza, just the three of us. Well, the three of us and two huge bodyguards, but still. After the initial awkwardness of the three of us being together and Nick claiming me by holding my hand the entire time, we end up having a good time talking about music and people they've worked with that I know. Shea tells me about the next part of the trip. The bus got in last night and will be leaving after the show tomorrow night, taking us to Berkeley for his next show. Nick will be touring with him until the record is finished, which he says should be soon, as long as they're able to get three more solid songs. I agree to stay until they head to LA on Wednesday. I've wanted to see Allie anyway and check up on some things in regards to Fab, so it'll be perfect.

The following morning I wake up in Nick's arms again, breathing him in deeply as I cuddle into him. Picking up my head, I notice that it's only eight o'clock in the morning and the bus isn't leaving until this afternoon. I stand up carefully and walk to the bathroom, deciding that I should head to the gym today. I normally don't work out when I'm on vacation, but I've been eating way too many good things and feel a little bit guilty over it. Standing sideways in front of the mirror, my gaze drops to my plump butt and I decide that I definitely need to do squats today. Once I'm dressed in my workout clothes and sneakers, I grab my purse, stuffing it with clothes so I can hit the showers in the spa when I'm finished and head out. I doubt Nick will be up early today. He and Shea stayed up way past the time I went to bed working on the album. I find my phone on top of the kitchen counter where I left it, frowning when I see a little note from Nick, which I'm assuming he left when he got back from the studio last night.

Brooklyn,

Say it, Just Say It— The Mowgli's

—Nick

Smiling, I unravel my earphones from my phone and put them in my ears, and ignore the missed calls I have as I search for the song, which I've never heard, as I walk toward the elevators. The smile on my face is huge by the time I get on the treadmill for my warm up, and as much as I would love to listen to the song again, I begrudgingly begin to sort through my gym playlist, trying to find a good song to start off to. Once I have one, I sort through my missed calls noticing they're mostly from Nina and Hendrix, but there are some from my mom, dad, and Sarah, which instantly fills me with an uneasy feeling in the pit of my stomach. I begin to panic slightly, walking off the treadmill and heading toward the lady's locker room, because when that many people call you in the early hours of the morning, it can't be good news.

I call Nina first, knowing she'll tell me what happened before she even says hello to me. Nina knows no bounds when it comes to formality, and I appreciate that, especially if she's going to tell me somebody died.

"Brooklyn!" Nina says shrilly.

"Oh my God. What happened? Just tell me what happened!" I say, my words piling into one another as I'm close to hysterics. It didn't go unnoticed that Uncle Robert was the only person that didn't call me and he's usually the first one there. If anything happened to him I would die.

"Have you talked to Allie?" Nina asks, still sounding uneasy.

I feel my stomach plummet as my chest struggles for air. "No. Oh my God, what happened to her? Is she okay?" I know I sound frantic, but I don't do well with death or accidents or anything of the sort.

"What?" Nina shrieks. "Brooklyn, calm the fuck down! Shut up and listen to me! You're eating my sandwich."

When she says that, I calm down slightly. We use that phrase to refer to when we're finishing each other's sentences wrong. There was a commercial about it at one point, and we started making a bigger joke of it when it aired.

"What happened?" I ask. "Why is my mom calling me?" I say quieter.

"Fuck," Nina mutters under her breath. "Well, if you read any gossip magazines, you would be informed. It's being reported that Allie is suing you for half of Fab Enterprises."

I frown, my mouth drops, I gasp, and blink rapidly all at once before I plop down on a bench behind me. Thankfully I'm in a little private room where nobody can see me. "What?" I ask dumbly, needing her to repeat that for me.

"You may want to call her, Bee, because your microphones are all over the place and everything says she's suing you."

"That's impossible," I say under my breath. "Allie wouldn't ... I have to call you back," I say, hanging up quickly to call my friend. Allie's phone rings and rings until it reaches her voicemail.

"Hey, Al, call me back. I've been trying to reach you for a couple of days and Nina just called to tell me something ridiculous ... so yeah, call me back," I say before hanging up.

My phone vibrates instantly, and I look at it expecting Allie, but see Hendrix's name instead.

"Where the hell have you been?" Hendrix says as soon as I place the phone to my ear.

I exhale a breath. "Hen, please don't bitch at me. I'm sure you can imagine the kind of morning I'll be having."

"Damn it, Brooklyn," he mutters. "You need to get to LA, as in *yesterday*. The plane is on standby waiting for you, you leave in an hour. I swear to God, I feel like I'm your fucking assistant sometimes. Maybe I should take over for your brain so shit like this doesn't happen."

"Wait. What? Back up. What do you mean LA? Why is the plane standing by? I'm waiting for Allie to call me back. Are you seriously buying into the rumors? You, of all people?" I ask incredulously. You would think that with the amount of rumors reported about our family they would know that more than half of the things they say aren't true. He can't be serious.

Hendrix lets out a laugh. "Well, when Drew calls telling me he has papers for a lawsuit in his hand, I stop listening to gossip magazines, Brooklyn. Allie or someone she knows must've contacted the magazines as soon as those papers left her because Drew got them last night. It started getting reported right after."

My mouth falls open. "But why would she sue me?" I whisper, not entirely believing what he's telling me. She's my friend. I was the maid of honor at her wedding. I paid for her honeymoon. How could she just sue me over half of a company that I started and brought her on board for? Is that even legal? I make the designs; she's more of an assistant than a contributor.

"I know it's a lot to take in, Bee, but the faster you let it sink in, the better. Your best friend fucked you over and is suing you for half of the company that you created with your own hands. If you want to stop all of this, you need to get to LA as soon as possible. Chin up, sis. Chin up," Hendrix says, sounding like a little league coach.

"Yeah, chin up," I mumble dejectedly as I hang up the phone.

I change my clothes numbly, my hands moving of their own accord as I mull over everything Hendrix told me. I think about Allie and my last conversation with her, studying every word said, every tone it was said in, and finding nothing out of place. I take a seat again, burying my face in my hands, taking

deep shuddering breaths to calm down. I hear the doors to the
locker room open and shut, the room filling with the laughter of women, and am thankful this hotel has these individual
rooms so that I can have my moment by myself.

"So you just got here?" one of them asks, her loud voice
and the sound of the faucet drowning out my heavy breathing.

"Yep. Just landed. My show is tonight," the other, whom I
know is Gia responds. "I can't fucking wait to get this leg of the
trip over with," she says with an exaggerated sigh.

They both walk into the stall beside me and I consider
leaving until I hear Gia speak again.

"You're still hooking up with Nick?" she asks.

"I haven't seen him yet," the other says. "But it's what we
do, so I'm sure I will," she says with a laugh.

My blood boils at her words, even though I feel like she's
punched me in the stomach.

"I heard he's dating Brooklyn Harmon now," Gia says before I hear her sniffle loudly. She coughs right away. I don't have
to look over the stall to know what they're doing. "Did you see
that her friend is suing her for those microphones?"

The other girl scoffs. "I saw that. I'm not worried about
Nick, he'll get bored of her soon enough. Besides, if she's not
here ..." she says, letting her words drift.

I feel like screaming that I am, but I'm motionless; I have
no words.

"Maybe," Gia says, not sounding interested.

"And if she's Chris Harmon's daughter, I know exactly what
he wants," the girl continues, sniffling. "He's starting his own
label, he probably wants her to get him people or something.
Who knows? Nick is smart. Very calculated," she says.

I didn't think I had it in me to be shocked after just hearing
about Allie, but her statement did it again. Adrenaline begins

to shoot laser beams within me. Placing one hand over my rapidly beating heart, I massage it, as if that will help ease it. As if
anything could. I take out my phone and Google *Nick Wilde*
but find nothing about a record label, just photos of him at different events. I try again: *Nick Wilde, record label.* A couple of
gossip sites claim that there's a rumor to it, but I find one that
catches my attention.

*Michael Wilde tries to outdo Chris Harmon with label.
Fails.* Surprised, I click that one open and browse through it.
It pretty much says that Nick's dad was trying to steal artists
from my dad in 1986, but somehow they both ended up on
friendly terms. As I scroll down the article, I see Nick's name
mentioned, saying that he has a couple of artists that he's been
seen scouting to sign.

My mouth still agape, I open the stall and leave the girls
gossiping, heading up the elevator and back to the room. When
I step back in the room, he's still sleeping, so I pack my bag
quickly and take it to the kitchen. I'm sorting around the living room, trying to see if I've left anything, when Nick startles me by walking out of the bedroom wearing a pair of khaki
shorts and no shirt. His light brown hair is wet and his bare
chest is glistening so I know he just showered. I wonder how I
didn't hear it, I wonder how long he's been awake, but it doesn't
matter, between my phone call with the attorney and trying
to sort things out, I wouldn't have noticed it either way. Nick
looks at me and gives me a smile that would probably leave me
breathless at any other time, but not right now when the emotions inside me are stirring. So many things are going through
my head that I don't even know where to start. He looks at my
packed bag sitting on the kitchen counter and frowns, his smile
disappearing.

"Why'd you pack?" he asks.

I turn my eyes from his because I can't take it; my chest physically aches at the idea of not looking into those eyes again depending on what he tells me. "I have to go to LA," I say slowly.

He begins to walk toward me, looking concerned, and I back away, putting space between us, which makes him frown again.

"What's wrong?" he asks. "Are you okay?"

"No, I'm not, but I will be. I always am," I reply quietly.

He walks toward me again, crossing his arms over his chest when he notices me back away, again.

"Can I ask you something?" I say, my voice quiet and calm.

He tilts his head to appraise me. "Of course," he says, his voice tensing.

"Are you trying to start your own label?" I'm trying to keep my face as passive as possible, trying not to show the hurt in my eyes when his jaw slacks right before he catches himself and closes it.

I find myself closing my eyes and taking a deep breath. I just want him to tell me it's not true. I want him to look at me the way he always looks at me, with desire and care laced in his eyes, not the regret that's there now. I want him to tell me that he's with me for me, not who he could be because of my name.

"I'm working on one, yes," Nick says, putting his hands in his pockets. "But it has nothing to do with you."

"Why didn't you tell me?" I ask in a whisper.

He shrugs, taking his hands out of his pockets and waving them around as he speaks, "What was I going to say, Brooklyn? 'Hey, by the way, I'm starting a label and I would love it if you would ditch your father and come work with me instead.'"

I blink a couple of times, half expecting to wake up from a nightmare. Hoping that he's not saying what I think he's saying to me. I grind my teeth, trying to collect myself even though the adrenaline that's running through me feels like it's peaking instead of slowing.

"So you've been using me? You've been trying to get under my skin—for what? So I could stop working for Harmon and go work for you?" I spit out.

He shakes his head. "No," he exhales, his face crumbling. "That's not what I meant. I didn't want you to think that and it never came up."

"It never came up?" I scoff. "It never came up?" I ask louder. "It never came up because you didn't want it to! Am I supposed to guess? I've asked you about your work. I've asked you a million questions because I want to know everything about you, but it never came up? Just like the fact that you found me on that bridge and took me to the hospital never came up until I saw your brother?" I ask in a shout. "Let me guess, if I wouldn't have remembered, you wouldn't have told me that anyway because it never came up?" I ask, air quoting. I grab my bag from the counter and turn around to storm out, but Nick grabs my arm to stop me.

I yank my arm out of his grasp, but not before he turns me around to face him again, his jaw clenched as he looks at me through narrowed eyes. Those eyes that I love to swim in, sail in, drown in, but will now remind me of betrayal. Our chests are both rising and falling heavily as we stand here, staring at each other. The only thing I can think about is the fact that he's been using me just like everybody else.

"Oh, you're Chris Harmon's daughter? Cool ... wanna hear my demo?"

"You're Roxy's daughter? Cool. I model on the side."

"I sing."

"I'm a video dancer."

Those are the reasons I cut back on the hundreds of friends

I had before. They're the reasons I deleted my Facebook and twitter account and said "fuck it, I don't need friends." I'd rather have 3 friends I can trust than be dragged along and lied to for months, investing my time on blooming a friendship, or worse, end up falling hard for somebody, only to find out they're starting a music label. And to hear it from coked out sluts in the bathroom. And to have them confirm my worst fears: he may be using me for my name. It just fucking sucks. Especially since I just got blindsided by a lawsuit from somebody I thought was truly my friend.

"Where does this leave us?"

I let out a laugh in disbelief. "Are you serious?" I ask.

His eyes narrow more. "I wasn't using you, Brooklyn. I would never use you, you have to know that!"

"No, I don't have to know that, Nick," I respond, grinding my teeth together at the remembrance of the conversation his fuck buddy and Gia were having in the spa. Closing my eyes, I take a deep breath. *I will not cry. I will not allow him to see that I'm hurt by any of this.*

He lets out a dry laugh. "So that's it? You want to walk out of here as if none of this happened?" he asks, waving his hands around the suite in disbelief, his eyes beginning to spark blazes.

"I don't know," I say, my voice wavering, showing some of my pain. "I don't know anything right now, Nick."

He stares at me for a long moment, studying my face before speaking again. I see the moment his gaze flickers from disbelief to painful before setting on angry. His beautiful eyes dimming, taking me from the shallow to the deep end, showing me their depth as he speaks. "I can't believe you can just walk out of here as if what we have is nothing … You know why you've never had a real relationship before, Brooklyn?" he starts, his jaw is set and he looks livid. "Because of this," he says, pointing at me. "Your flippant attitude about the whole thing. That's why men treat you like you're disposable. They're not doing it because you're not worth their time or they don't like you enough, they're just returning the favor," he spits.

His words shred me. Burn me. Make me feel like I've been slapped and kicked at the same time. My chest constricts as I blink at him in disbelief with my mouth hanging open. Finally, I let out a surprised scoff, shaking my head.

"You know … I wanted you to be different. I wanted you to assure me that you weren't with me because you have a hidden agenda and need me in order to fulfill it. But more than anything, Nick, I just want the man that I've developed these feelings for, these stupid fucking feelings, to feel something back. I just wanted you to be real," I say, on the verge of breaking down. My chest feels tight from the tears I'm trying to hold back. "I want all of the bad memories you've replaced in this city to be real memories with real laughter and real fucking passion, not calculated or made up ones! But thank you. Thank you for returning the fucking favor," I say, my eyes burning with angry tears. "Good bye, Nick," I whisper, turning around and stalking to the door, letting it slam behind me. Sadness envelops my heart with each step I take, and I welcome it. Sadness is my home, I belong in it, it belongs in me; we are one and the same.

I send a text message to Shea explaining to him, in short, what happened with Allie and letting him know I'll text him again when I land in LA and know what's going on. I sit on the airplane in the same seat that I sat in on my way to San Francisco. The same seat that Nick comforted me in when I freaked out over seeing the Golden Gate Bridge. Turning my head, I look out the window and look at the bridge and the blue water under it, and I don't feel a thing.

Once upon a time I would've killed to feel numb, like I

do now. I would've reveled in the abyss of emptiness that fills my heart. The fear of the unknown would've made me want to kill myself. Again. But now I feel nothing. I've been stripped of everything that matters and I'm left with nothing. So much of nothing that I don't want to end my life in some dramatic, painful way because I'd rather let myself marinate in the bleakness for a little while longer. When I'm ready I'll begin to feel again, and I'll feel much more suffering than I would if I just ended it all right now.

And I want that.

I want to become that pain.

CHAPTER TWENTY-FOUR

Past

I remember that day like it was yesterday. It still makes me want to vomit when I think about it, so I don't unless I want to feed into my depression. Ryan picked me up on Thursday night to head to San Francisco for the weekend. The foggy city had become our stomping ground over the past year. We felt free of judgment there. He could make out with as many guys as he wanted, and I could wear my hair in fifty million shades of blue and nobody would even look at me twice. We loved it. The perk was that Uncle Robert would let us stay at his house on the weekends, and we loved being with him and his boyfriend, Victor. That weekend in particular, Rob and Vic were out of town and were letting us stay there, but Ryan and I passed up on their offer and decided to stay in a hotel closer to the bars. I was seventeen; he was eighteen. Neither of us could get into any bar legally, but legal doesn't matter when you have endless money and the right last name.

I made a couple of calls and got in contact with friends

of friends that I'd met at the parties I frequented and was able to get us into a couple of good clubs that Friday. We did our usual lines of cocaine in the back of the car on our way to the club. Cocaine and cough syrup, that's what we were about at the time. Periodically we would add heroin to the mix, but that was only when one of us was hitting rock bottom. Heroin was a rock bottom drug for us, the one we went to when we were feeing extra depressed. Shea loved it when we were on our heroin trips—that was his drug of choice, so when he'd hang out with us he brought it. He'd been to San Fran with us a couple of times but was busy that weekend. At that point he was still playing smaller shows in shopping malls and radio stations. He hadn't hit it big yet, and our relationship was on the rocks, quite literally. The last time I'd seen him had been over cocaine.

The thing about cocaine was that it was awesome the first handful of times. We felt like we were energized and on top of the world. After that, we started to become jittery after our first hit. That's where the cough syrup came in to calm our nerves. We could've died, we knew that; we were playing with fire, we knew that too. We cared very little though. When you're seventeen, you think you're invincible as it is. When you're seventeen and have nobody to show you that they genuinely care about you, or everybody that you want love from is too busy for you, you act out. That's what we were doing: acting out, begging for attention from our parents. We realized at some point that we weren't going to get their attention, but by then we were in too deep.

We went to the club and danced our asses off that Thursday. On Friday we slept past noon, woke up, had breakfast again, sunbathed, got ready for another club and it was a repeat. Ryan's parents were being more annoying than usual, blowing up his phone every hour. I never heard what they told him, but I saw the way his face crumbled every time he got off the phone. I saw the way he reached for our little Ziploc of coke the second he hung up on his screaming mother or berating father.

That night, we went to a different club. Ryan disappeared with one guy, while I danced with a couple of others—it was our usual thing. When Ryan came back, he had a beaming smile on his face, his eyes glassy, and his red hair was slick with sweat. I asked him where he went and he told me he went to the bathroom with that guy. After they did whatever they did (Ryan and I never talked about specifics when it came to those things), he shot him up with heroin.

"Best. High. Ever," Ryan said.

I pursed my lips in disbelief. "Yeah, right."

"Watch," he said, calling the guy over and telling him I wanted some too.

We ended up going back to our hotel. We had a two-bedroom suite with a huge living room and a gorgeous view of the city, so it made sense. Because my high was practically non-existent by that point, I wanted to get straight to business. The guy, a skinny blond with shaggy hair and a grin that was way too big for his face—he kind of looked like The Joker. He was just as creepy, too. He wrapped my arm with a band and I balled my fist so he could get my vein. This guy, a nurse practitioner, he said he was, claimed he was the best vein finder. I don't know if he was right or not, I didn't care. I let him do it anyway. He inserted the needle and pulled the plunger until I could see my blood rush into it, then slowly pushed the plunger, pulled it back, then squeezed. Tingles instantly started rushing up my arm and I let out a sigh of relief as I felt them before throwing my head back in ecstasy when the high hit me. It was magical, beautiful; it was unicorns, painted ponies, rainbows, kisses, tight hugs, acceptance and unconditional love all wrapped up in one beautiful medley.

Ryan was right, it was the most amazing high I'd had on it yet. I tried to stay away from heroin, only doing it when Shea came to town and wanted to do it. I never understood why he wanted to do it with me. Heroin wasn't like ecstasy where we would do it and have sex for hours. He could barely get it up when he was high on heroin, but the feel of the drug running through his veins was more important than him being inside of me. I tried to limit myself from it by not keeping in contact with the people I knew could get it for me. I even banned Ryan from telling me who his suppliers were. I really didn't want it to be my downfall, and I knew it could be because none of my heroin highs ever topped the first one. Looking for that first high, that irrevocable one where I felt like I was having a conversation with God and his angels, would kill me. I knew it even then. And I didn't want to die at seventeen; I just wanted the attention that would come with almost dying. I wanted to play with death through the fence; I didn't want her to invite me in for tea and crumpets.

We partied all night that Friday. All. Night. And when I woke up the next morning and stumbled to Ryan's room, I shook him awake and he laughed with me at the craziness of the night before. Then his phone started ringing and I knew it was his mom calling again, so I stepped out. When I stepped back in again, he was brewing. I always knew to leave him alone when he got that way because he was like me, he didn't want people to see him cry.

"I'll be back, Rye, I have to buy a dress for tonight anyway," I said.

"Cool. See you later then," he said.

I spent the afternoon shopping, and when I got back, Ryan was ready for dinner. He was his usual smiling self, and I was glad he wasn't letting his parents ruin the weekend for us.

"I don't understand what their deal is," he said over dinner.

We went to Akikos that night, his favorite Sushi joint in San Fran.

"Why do they keep harassing you?" I asked.

He tilted his head as he looked at me with a look, telling me not to be dumb. "Because I'm gay, Bee, and they don't want their socialite friends to find out about it."

My shoulders slumped. I felt so bad for my best friend. He was a straight-A student, graduated Summa Cum Laude, and got accepted to Georgetown University. What more could they possibly ask of him? Ryan had been gifted an Aston Martin for his seventeenth birthday and had never even gotten a speeding ticket. I even got a speeding ticket driving the damn car, but not Ryan. Other than his frequent drug use, which stemmed from the hatred he got at home for being something he couldn't change, he was a straight-laced kid.

"I don't get it," I muttered. "What does that have to do with anything?"

Ryan shrugged, letting out a breath. "I think they're just embarrassed since I'm going to Georgetown and that's where they went. I dunno."

My brows furrowed. "What does that have to do with anything? They were the ones that made you decline Yale and Harvard. How stupid can they be?"

"Very," he said, laughing.

I laughed along in agreement.

"Don't you have that thing tonight?" Ryan asked.

"Shit," I said, looking at the time. "My mom's gonna kill me. I'm supposed to be there at nine."

My mom had signed me up to attend some type of party for a popular magazine since she couldn't make it. I agreed because I knew if I didn't, she would try to cancel my trip with Ryan by canceling my credit cards. When my mom asked me to do something, I did it, not because I wanted to be a good daughter, but because there was a stringent catch attached to it.

"What are you going to do?" I asked, feeling bad that I couldn't take him as my date. Mom had already set up for me to go with some guy I didn't know. He was supposed to be picking me up at my hotel half an hour before the event.

"Eh, I dunno, I'll find something," he said, shrugging.

We went back to the hotel and hung out there for a while, talking crap and flipping through magazines, making fun of the men and women's faces. The front desk called when my date was downstairs waiting, and I groaned at having to go.

"I'll be back soon," I said with a pout, throwing my arms around him and kissing him soundly on the cheek.

"Yeah, yeah, have fun," he joked. "Love you, Bumble Bee."

I rolled my eyes, laughing. "Love you too, Rye face."

Sprinting to the elevator, I cursed when I realized I forgot my phone and went back to the room. When I opened the door, I saw Ryan stretched out on the couch, watching TV, typing away on his phone.

"Forgot my phone," I said in response to his questioning look.

He nodded and went back to his phone. I went downstairs, smiling at my date when I saw him. He was wearing a suit and a pair of Chucks, which I thought was cool. He had long black hair that tucked behind his ears, pale skin, and black eyeliner around his blue eyes. I instantly liked him and hated myself for it because that was one of the things my mother had said to me.

"You're going to love him, he looks all rocker and gross like those guys you like," she'd said.

His named was Bryant and he was the drummer for a band

that had been signed with a rival record label. My mother, once again, feeding me to the fish and knowing that I was the shark to catch them, took the opportunity and paired us together for that event. By the end of the night, I had Bryant and the rest of his band members dying to sign, not because I did much pitching, but because I got drunk and high with them and they thought I was the "coolest chick they'd met in a while."

Bryant and I ended up hooking up in the limo on our way back to my hotel, which I informed Shea of on my way up to my room. Shea's words were, "Why would you do that to me? Why would you hook up with another artist knowing I'll have to see him at parties? What the fuck, Brooklyn?" Shea never called me Brooklyn, only when he was beyond mad at me. "Don't call me again," he'd said and hung up the phone. The funny part was that the reason I called Shea to tell him was because I wanted him to get jealous. I wanted him to care that I hooked up with somebody else and leave all the groupies he was hooking up with. I wanted him to look around and decide that I was worth more than them. I was an idiot for thinking he would.

I went up to the room and noticed Ryan wasn't in the living room anymore. His room wasn't completely closed, so I knocked a little and peeked in.

"Hey, Rye," I said.

"Hey, Bee. How'd it go?" he asked, sounding sleepy.

The room was dark so I couldn't see him clearly, but I heard him ruffling in the sheets and I knew he was in bed.

"It was good. Met a guy," I said.

"Yeah? Cute?" he asked.

"Very."

"Your usual grungy type?" he asked with a laugh. Ryan hated my usual type of guy. He was always saying I needed to hook up with a nicer looking guy, a preppy guy that would treat me right. I promised him that maybe one day I would stop hooking up with musicians and actually give the nicer looking guys a chance. He would laugh and say that I was going to marry a heavily tattooed guy with piercings and my mother was going to really disown me then.

I laughed. "Yeah, black eyeliner and everything," I said.

"Nice," he responded.

I yawned. "'K, I'll see you tomorrow. Maybe we can actually do touristy shit."

"Yeah, that sounds good. I've always wanted to actually walk that damn bridge," he said. "I'm sure you can see Alcatraz from there. Maybe we can go on one of those boat tours to Alcatraz," he suggested.

"That would be cool!" I agreed. "Goodnight, Rye-Face. I love you."

"I love you too, Bumble Bee."

I went to my room and threw myself on the bed, not bothering to take off my makeup. I remember smiling about that and picturing my mom flipping the hell out over me going to sleep with an unwashed face. I went to sleep peacefully that night, despite my fight with Shea. I knew he'd come around, he always did.

Stretching my arms over my head, I rolled my neck and looked over the covers, catching a glimpse of the sun peeking in through the drapes. I groaned and pushed my head back into the pillow, wondering if Ryan was still sleeping. Ryan loved to sleep late, so I assumed he was, even though I wasn't sure what time it was. With a sigh, I decided to get out of bed and groggily made my way to the bathroom. My limbs were sore from last night and the night before; the mix of drugs, dancing and sex catching up to me. After I showered, I noticed it was noon and decided to wake up Ryan. I stepped out of my room and noticed his door was still half-open. I looked inside and smiled when I saw him sitting up.

"Rye, I thought you would be sleeping," I said, walking over to the window and opening the top layer of his curtains. I glanced at him over my shoulders and felt not as if my heart fell through my chest, but everything in my body just plummeted all at once at the sight of him.

"Ryan?" I shrieked, running to him with wide eyes that were already welling up with tears.

He looked gray. Lifeless. He was sitting up in bed but looked more like a stone sculpture than himself. I knew. I just knew. A majestic blue band was wrapped tightly around his bicep and his arms were laying over his crossed legs, his face hanging down over his chest, the needle in his right hand.

My heart went from still to sixty as wildfire spread through my body, my chest heaving out of control in sobs and breaths that would overtake me at any moment. Lurching forward, I wrapped my arms around him, trying to keep him warm because his body looked like it was freezing. He was so cold, so, so cold under my touch, so dead, so lifeless. My sobs started spilling out.

"Ryan, noooo," I kept saying. "Please, no!"

I grabbed his phone from the nightstand and called 911. The operator picked up on the second ring.

"911 Emergency, how may I help you?" she said.

"My friend. I think he overdosed. Oh my God," I said before losing my ability to speak. "Please, please help him," I cried into the phone.

"Calm down, ma'am. What drugs did he take?" she asked soothingly, but I couldn't calm down. I couldn't talk, I couldn't think. All I could do was hold my friend in my arms. My best fucking friend. The only person who was there for me at all hours, any hour of the day to listen to me, to hold me, to kiss my tears away, to put up with my endless rants about my unloving parents. The only person that I could turn to with anything and know I wouldn't be judged. And he was gone. I knew he was gone. I knew nothing I did, nothing the operator told me to do, nothing the paramedics would do when they arrived would save him.

"Where are you?" she asked, rushed. "I'll have someone there shortly."

I told her the number of our suite at the Fairmont Hotel and let the phone drop from my hands, unwilling to stay on the phone with her. I couldn't bear to hold it up as I held the only positive thing in my life in my hands, knowing he had withered away from me without me being able to help him. I should've slept with him last night. We should've gotten a one-bedroom suite, like we usually did. Why had we gotten two rooms? What did we need all of that for? Those were all things I sobbed against him as I rocked him in my arms, refusing to let him go. Letting him go would be watching the light at the end of the tunnel disappear, and the worst part was knowing that it should have been me that was gone, not him.

He was the one with the bright future ahead of him. I was just Chris and Roxy Harmon's fuck up socialite daughter, the one that didn't have anything in her life worth raving about. I was nobody and I would be nothing without Ryan. I cried until I had nothing left in me. When the paramedics pounded on the door, I zombie-walked over to it, opening it and letting them in, not even bothering to look at their faces as they rushed over to Ryan. I stepped out of the way as they checked him and confirmed that he was gone. They asked me a million questions that I couldn't make out through the hollowed sounds in my ears.

"He was fine last night," was all I could offer between cries. "I just saw him last night." My knees buckled and I fell on the floor as I thought about it. The more I thought about it the more fucked up this all was. "We were supposed to go to Alcatraz today. He always wanted to go to Alcatraz. He always wanted to walk the bridge," I sobbed. "He always wanted to see the world." I'd never felt such heartache and I never would again. Not like that. Nothing could ever hurt me as much as losing him did.

I rode with him in the ambulance and went to the hospital where they would perform unneeded tests. I knew how he died. They knew how he died. The one question everybody kept asking me was, "Did he have a reason to commit suicide?" The only question I could give them was, "Don't we all?" It didn't mean he did, though. It didn't mean he purposely took his life. He wouldn't. As fucked up as his parents were and as much as they bullied him for being gay, he wouldn't have taken his own life. He was almost out of his house. He was supposed to leave for DC a couple of months later. He was waiting to celebrate my eighteenth birthday with me and then he would be gone. He was waiting for me. The way he always was. And he died because of it. He died because of me and everybody would constantly remind me of that.

Ryan's mother blamed me and my "crazy rock star lifestyle." My own mother blamed me for it, saying I always took things "too far."

"You're probably the reason he was gay," my mother said a couple of days after his death. "You're probably the reason he can't bear to be with a woman."

I had no response for that. What could I say? My mother didn't even fully accept the fact that her own brother was gay and living with a man. You would think she at least had a reason, like religious beliefs that made her be that judgmental. She was weirded out about it. The funny thing is that Hollywood is very much like a small high school: everybody talks, everybody has gossip on everybody's parents, and one of the many rumors I had heard was that my mom had been with one of my classmate's mother back in the eighties.

I never found out if it was true or not, but rumor had it that they had a real relationship, not just a sexual one. My mother and another woman was something that didn't bother me, as weird as it was, but it was something that I wanted to bring up every time she talked bad about my uncle or my best friend being gay. I never did, though. I never said anything to her because even though I wasn't raised not to be disrespectful, I had set my own boundaries about it, and deep down I knew it would be wrong to bring up.

I fell into a deep depression after losing Ryan. I didn't want to step foot outside of my room. I didn't want to see or talk to anybody. I didn't want to take Shea's phone calls or know how he was doing. I shut down from the world for a couple of weeks. The only person who really cared was Uncle Robert, but he was busy working most of the time. My brother had gone off to Europe with his girlfriend Sarah because my father was opening up a Harmon Records branch over there. Hendrix would call me every other day to see how I was doing, but it wasn't the same. My cousin Nina was living in New York and had just gotten kicked out of her mom's house for God knows what. She came to visit me one weekend, which helped. She left thinking I was fine after she took me shopping and did a whole makeover on me. I loved Nina, but she should have known better than anyone that hiding your pain under your makeup and nice clothes was the easy part.

One afternoon, while I was lying in bed as usual, my mother barged into my room. She'd just come home from a trip to

Belize where she was doing a photo shoot for her new skin care line.

"Oh, Brooklyn," she said, running her fingers through my hair as I lay my head on her lap. I was happy for a moment, with her showing me attention the way she used to when I was a child. Despite all the hurtful things she'd said and done to me, I still wanted her. I still needed her. And she was supposed to want and need me too. She was my mother, dammit. She was supposed to care. She was supposed to show me love.

"I want to see a therapist, Mama," I said, wiping tears from my eyes. I hadn't said that to anybody at that point. Not even to my brother who'd asked me countless times. I didn't want to admit the extent of my dark state, and I knew saying I needed a therapist would be doing just that.

My mother's hands stilled in my hair. "Why would you need a therapist?" she asked, confusion clear in her voice.

She couldn't possibly be that fucking blind. She couldn't possibly not see that I was a mess. The only thing that kept me stable enough was my drug use, and even that was becoming unbearable to me, which was saying a lot. It felt like I couldn't take enough to mask the pain, but I was too scared to take too much. I was scared of becoming a stone statue. I didn't want to be gray. My mother would hate me if I was gray.

"I think I'm depressed," I whispered into her pencil skirt. "You have nothing to be depressed about," she countered.

She was so wrong. So very wrong, but I wasn't about to list the endless reasons I had for my depression.

"I didn't realize depression needed a reason," I said, my voice hoarse.

She exhaled and twirled my hair. "Why can't you pick one color and stick to it?" she asked, changing the subject. "Your hair is going to fall out if you keep dying it."

I picked myself up, wiping my tears with my back to her so she wouldn't know I was crying, and headed to my bathroom. Maybe I should have let her see me crying. Maybe I should have slit myself and let my hurt pour out in front of her.

"Nothing I do is good enough for you," I said, taking a steadying breath as I held the bathroom door open.

"You're right," she answered. "Maybe if you actually did something with your life, I wouldn't feel that way."

"I'm seventeen, Mom," I said, gritting my teeth. "Surely you remember being seventeen."

She raised a perfect thin brown eyebrow. "Of course I do," she said, smiling slightly. "And I was the best at everything I did. Even at seventeen."

"Well, congratu-fucking-lations for being such a fucking winner," I muttered as I stepped into the bathroom, slamming the door behind me. I switched on the shower but never made it in. I slid my body down against the door and buried my face in my hands before I started to cry.

When I got up from the floor, I turned off the water, changed my clothes, and called the car service that Ryan and I used sometimes to come get me. I didn't trust that I would make it to San Francisco by myself. I had never actually driven there, Ryan always did. Just the thought of him made my heart ache, but I felt like I needed to go. I needed to be closer to him. I called my father on my drive, ready to tell him that I needed to see a therapist.

"What do you want, Brooklyn?" he growled into the phone. "I'm busy."

Tears pricked my eyes. "Nothing," I whispered. "I'll talk to you later."

He let out a loud sigh. "Sorry. But yeah. Later." Then he hung up the phone.

I'd never felt so alone. I'd never felt so broken, so lost, so worthless. And the only person that could help me was gone. I sobbed, swallowing a couple of pain killers that I'd taken from my dad's bathroom cabinet and washing them back with the vodka I'd filled my water bottle with. When I knew we were closer to San Francisco, I told the driver that he could drop me off at the Golden Gate Bridge. He furrowed his bushy black eyebrows in the mirror and asked if I was sure. I said yes with my bitchy attitude and he didn't bother talking to me again. I took out one little blue pill that had a star drawn on it. My favorite drug, ecstasy—my Shea drug, I called it.

I waited for it to hit, but I knew it wouldn't for another ten minutes. When the car pulled up to the bridge, I threw a handful of hundreds his way, not bothering to wait for change and jumped out. I staggered my way up the walkway, moving out of the way for runners and tourists. I smiled at some kids that fathers carried over their shoulders and blew kisses at the tweens that walked by and checked me out. I was wearing an oversized sweater so there was nothing to check out, but boys always look at blondes. It was one of the reasons I liked when my hair was that color.

Shakily holding onto the cold railing, I made it to the middle of the bridge with tear-filled eyes. My head lolled every which way from the amount of things in my system, but I felt happy. I felt free, I felt tingly. Every time the wind touched my face, I smiled.

Until I remembered.

And then I didn't smile anymore. My chest shook as sobs exploded through it at the memory of my lost friend, at my father's cold voice when I called, and my mother's indifference. Once I stopped crying, I looked around, trying to spot the cameras. I had heard they put cameras on the bridge to record the jumpers. I read somewhere that there were actually survivors. I hoped I wouldn't be one of those. I hoped I wouldn't be "Chris and Roxy Harmon's drug addicted daughter who killed her best friend and attempted but failed to jump to her death." I could already hear the jokes that would be made about how I couldn't even kill myself right, about what a complete failure I was, just like they'd reminded me of countless times over the years.

I could already feel the pain shooting through me at my mom's berating voice. I thought of my brother, my uncle and my cousin, the only people that would care. But for some reason the thought of my brother was the only one that scared me. He'd been absent a lot over the years, but never ignored me. I felt bad, but not bad enough. The pain had consumed so much of me that I wouldn't let anything stop me. When I saw Alcatraz, I began to cry again, thinking of Ryan. I screamed, not caring who would hear me. I sobbed loudly, not caring what passersby thought of it.

And then he found me. And he told me he was looking for me. And I believed him. And then I blanked out. I went into a beautiful, shaky state of oblivion. I wondered if I would find Ryan there. I wondered if he would be waiting for me with his cherry colored cheeks and dazzling smile. I wondered if his wavy red hair would be waving in the wind. I wondered if he was happy and at peace. I wondered if he would forgive me and tell me he still loved me.

The next time I woke up, I was in a hospital bed looking into the exhausted brown eyes of Uncle Robert. He cried hysterically when he saw that I was awake. His cries stabbed my heart. They made me feel guilty and sad.

"Where's the guy?" I asked.

"What guy?" my uncle asked, rubbing my hand in his.

"The one that gave me hope," I said.

My uncle cried again, louder, shaking the bed with his sobs. "Oh, Brooklyn," he repeated through his tears. "I'm so sorry I wasn't there."

I blinked my tears away and ran my fingers through his soft hair. "It's okay, Uncle Rob, you're here now." I wanted to soothe him somehow. I felt bad for making him feel that hurt. I didn't want his pain to match mine.

He sniffled, wiping his tears with the backs of his hands. "I'm sorry, baby girl. I'm sorry you're hurting."

Tears fell down my face. "I need help," I whispered, praying he would take me seriously.

"Of course. Of course," he said, his voice hoarse as wrapped his arms around me. "We'll get you help."

I felt myself breathe for the first time in years, as if in his arms I found the peace I was so desperately waiting for. My mother came by to visit me. She acted heartbroken by the whole thing and I believed that she was. Her eyes were hurt as she looked from me to my uncle. She stayed for one day and promised that she would put me in the best rehab facility she could find. She made good on her word and sent me to a good facility in Newport.

I spent my eighteenth birthday there, cutting a cake with the rest of the patients. I'd learned to appreciate having them there, holding my hand through all of it. We had a lot of days where we wanted to sign out, and we could have. But we didn't. We held on to each other, all of us did, and together with our sponsors, we survived our time there.

Shea visited me a couple of times. The first time was on my birthday. He looked miserable as he walked the halls to get to me. The last time I'd seen him was Ryan's funeral, and we barely talked there. We couldn't quite process that we were burying our best friend. When Shea saw me in rehab that first time, he fell to his knees in front of me and wrapped his hands around my waist.

"I'm so sorry," he cried. "I'm so sorry I wasn't there for you when you're always there for me."

"You're here now," I whispered. "And that's all that matters."

And it was. We hugged each other and spent the rest of the day together talking like we never had before, because that time we were both sober. That time, we couldn't hide behind our masks. I think that was the first and maybe the last time we ever spent a day like that. Shea promised me he would never do heroin or ecstasy or any heavy drugs again. He said he couldn't give up marijuana. I was okay with that. I was just happy knowing he would give up the rest. I knew he wouldn't break his promise to me. Shea and I never broke our promises to each other.

"I love you, BK," he said on his way out. "You mean so much to me."

So much wasn't everything, but it was enough for me.

CHAPTER TWENTY-FIVE

Present

I take a deep breath when I step out of the airplane in LA, closing my eyes against the beating sun. I have a feeling this one breath will have to give me the strength I need to get through this trip. Turning my phone on, I see a voicemail from Shea to add to the four I have from my family. I scroll away from that screen, not wanting to talk to anyone unless I absolutely have to and groaning when my phone lights up with an incoming call from Hendrix. I answer it and he tells me that the driver is waiting to take me to the lawyer's office.

Sure enough, when I tug my suitcase out of the building, a tall young man dressed in a black suit sprints over to me and introduces himself as Carson. I say hello to him and quickly climb into the back of the SUV, while he places my suitcase in the trunk. Clutching my phone, I look at it for a long moment, contemplating whether or not to call Allie again. I decide to wait, hoping she'll call me before I speak to the lawyer. As we drive down the Pacific Coast, the urge to call her becomes unbearable, so I do, and again my call goes directly to voice-mail. I don't leave a message this time, though, but I do send her a text message that says to please call me back.

Sighing, I connect my earphones to my phone and sort through my playlist, choosing a song by Sleeping At Last. I close my eyes and think of my times with Allie, reminiscing on our college days and the parties we went to together. The look on her cherub face when the date I set her up on with her now husband went well.

When I get to the attorney's office, I check in with the receptionist and am soon greeted by the lawyer's secretary. Drew, my brother's lawyer, is actually an old friend of his and I'm glad to see it's him I'll be dealing with and not one of my parents' old fart attorneys that think they know everything. Drew sits down on the other side of the desk and slides me a stack of papers. I grasp them, running my fingers over my name, Allie's name, the name of my brand, to convince myself that this is real. My best friend is really suing me.

Tears threaten to fall, but I won't cave to them. I won't let them win, not here. Not in front of Drew.

"I just don't understand," I whisper.

Drew takes my words as an opportunity to explain to me, in layman's terms everything the lawsuit says. Allie is basically suing me for not holding up my side of the bargain and wants half of the company's earnings and anything that it will earn in the next ten years. I laugh because there is no bargain, it's my company; it's my baby. It's something I built up from nothing but my imagination. Fab represents my love of music and is my way of trying to fit in with my successful family. It's what I made to show them that I, too, can be somebody.

We only have about ten clients right now, and that's not including the contracts with recording studios that I was working on. Quite frankly, as much as this situation makes my stomach turn, I'm flattered that Allie would want half of my earnings for the next ten years. At least it shows that she believes in me and in my brand enough to think that it'll still be around then. I swallow loudly, hoping to rid myself of the emotion that's bubbling.

"Well, the kicker is she has already supplied some microphones to some studios in Long Beach," Drew informs me.

My mouth drops open. "No, she didn't," I say, gasping in disbelief.

Drew's blond eyebrow rises. "Yes, she did." He hands over some pictures of the microphones with dates and names of studios they're in.

"Where's the money for this?" I ask quietly, scrolling through my phone to pull up my bank account as I rack my brain over the recent invoices I've seen. I would remember studio microphones though, so I know these weren't in any of the papers I've seen.

Drew smiles and it makes him look like a shark. It reminds me of everyone I've ever worked with, including myself. An odd sense of calm passes over me. I don't even want to know what that says about me.

"That's the best part. She didn't put it in your business account. All the money for this went directly into hers. Because she's been keeping this from you, she's pretty much fucking herself over before she has the chance to see any money from her suit."

As much as it hurts me that Allie is doing this to me, I just want it all to go away, so I ask if there's any other way that we can solve this without going to court. Drew tells me that the only way would be to get her to drop it, which he says probably won't happen.

"This can get ugly, Brooklyn. I need to make sure you know that," he says and I know he's pretty much preparing me for a shit storm.

Because my mother is lawyer happy, suing people left and right if they even look at her the wrong way, I'm familiar with things getting ugly. My father has been sued in the past as well, but his cases are usually much cleaner than my mother's.

I shrug. "She asked for it." I'm trying to sound as nonchalant as I want to feel.

It kills me that the reason I let Fab take the backseat when I started working at Harmon was because I thought I could trust Allie to be my right hand girl and work with me on all of this. Letting out a breath, I stand to shake his hand before I start walking out of his office.

"Hey, Drew," I say, glancing over my shoulder. He looks up from his desk. "What if she calls me and apologizes and drops the entire thing before you draft the papers?" My voice is low, almost a breath, but I know he hears me. His mouth turns up slightly.

"I doubt she'll back down. That would be best case, but don't hold your breath. I'm sorry. I know it's hard to get screwed over by someone you trust."

I nod. "I'm used to being screwed over." I'm amazed at how steady I manage to keep my voice as I say the words.

When I get out of there I call Hendrix and tell him everything. He agrees that I did the right thing. Next I call my father, who actually stands by my decision and seems understanding about the whole thing. My father can be a huge asshole, but he knew the right thing to say this time. He also tells me that he spoke to Michael Wilde, who told him I had been to his house. I give him the short version of the story and tell him that Nick and I are friends. I don't have the kind of relationship with my parents where we talk about things like dating, so I know my answer is enough for him. I speak to Nina on my way to my favorite hotel on Sunset Boulevard. And when I hang up with her and feel that I have just enough energy to make one more phone call, I call my mother.

"Hello?" I say into the receiver when I hear a lot of shuffling going on. Just my luck, I finally call her and she picks up by mistake.

"Brooklyn. Hold on," she sings.

I look around, watching the people walking by and on bicycles; the big city tourist buses that go by the hotel and snap photos make me smile. People are so easily amused.

"Are you there?" she asks.

"Yes. How are you?" I ask cordially.

"Better than you, I'm sure," she responds, but her voice sounds light, not malicious, so her words roll off of me.

"Yep, I've had better days."

She pauses for a moment. "It'll blow over, you know? This whole thing will blow over and people will forget about it. You have a good thing with those microphones."

My mouth falls open. My mother has never paid me a compliment before. The only time she has is when there are people around to hear her. I don't know who she's in front of right now, so maybe she's saying it for the sake of her guests, but something tells me she's not. I think she's honestly praising my work. I don't know if I'm too shocked to react and let happiness sink in, or if I'm just hesitant to believe her. I don't say anything for a long time.

"Thank you," I say quietly, still in disbelief.

"I was sued by a friend once," she continues. "It was the most hurtful thing that happened to me when I was young. But shit happens, people change, and you learn. Don't let it get you down, Brooklyn."

My throat begins to close in and I blink unshed tears as the driver parks in front of the Chateau Marmont.

"Thank you, Mom," I whisper.

"Are you going to the White Party this year?" she asks, changing the subject.

"Where will it be?" I ask, hoping it's in their Beverly Hills home so I have a reason not to go since I plan on heading back to New York as soon as I can.

"The house in The Hamptons," she says airily. "It's this weekend. Shea will be there, his assistant just confirmed. Maybe you can come with him."

"Maybe."

"All right, doll, I'll see you next Saturday then. You're welcome to stay at the house all weekend, if you'd like," she says before blowing me a kiss and hanging up on me.

I roll my eyes as I hop out of the car. She's such a bitch. I note that down as yet another thing I would never say to my daughter. I'm going to be such a different mom if I ever have kids. I'm never going to invite them to stay in my house because they'll know that anything that's mine is theirs too. Once I check-in to the hotel and run into a couple of people I've met in the past, I go out to my cabana. I love staying at the cabanas here. Not for the pool because I rarely even use it. Sometimes I lay out but most of the time I just stay in bed and listen to the people laughing and having fun outside. I like to pretend that one day that'll be me.

Lying back on the bed, I close my eyes and ignore the persistence of my ringing phone. I just want to be left alone for a while. Finally, I slide my finger on the screen and seeing another missed call from Shea, I decide to call him. I can't ignore him, of all people.

"BK, what the fuck is going on? Allie's really doing that shit to you?" He sounds pissed, with good reason. He's known Allie a long time too, but his loyalties are with me just the same as mine are with him. If anybody betrays him, I would feel betrayed too.

"Yeah, I guess she is. She won't even answer my calls, Shea," I say quietly.

"Pussy," he mutters as he lets out a breath. "What happened with Shadow?"

Even the sound of his nickname makes my heart feel like somebody is squeezing it. "Nothing."

"He's pissed, you know?" Shea continues, clearly not caring that I'm dealing with enough right now.

"Yeah? Well, so am I. You can tell him I said that too. You can tell him to fuck off and go to hell, for all I care." As I say the words, hot tears spill down my face, and I'm glad for them. At least my tear ducts aren't broken.

"You're just saying that because you're angry right now," Shea says.

"When the fuck did you become Mr. Peacemaker?" I ask. I know I'm taking my anger out on him and he doesn't deserve it, but I also know that he understands this.

"When the fuck did you become cynical?" he spits back.

"Fuck you," I spit, my voice breaking.

"No, fuck you! I'm just trying to be there for you," he responds angrily and finally, I start crying freely. All of the hurt I've tried to contain in one box finally spills over and travels through me at once. Shea is silent until I'm calm enough to speak again. I feel much better after letting it all out.

"I'm sorry," Shea says quietly once I've calmed down.

"I'm sorry too," I whisper. "Can we start over?"

Shea laughs. "Don't we always?"

That almost brings a smile to my face. "I can't believe she's suing me," I whisper.

"She's a piece of shit," he says.

"I guess she is," I agree, a laugh escaping me.

"So you really through with Nick then?" Shea asks.

I screw my eyes shut, the name causing the hole in my heart to grow bigger. "He was using me for my name, Shea," I say quietly.

"You really believe that, BK? He has his own name. If he really wanted to he could use it," he says.

"In the producing world, maybe, but starting up a label?" I retort stubbornly.

Shea exhales harshly. "He wasn't using you, Brooklyn. Open up your goddamn eyes."

"Why are you defending him all of a sudden?" I ask.

"Because he's my friend and he's a good guy. And I can see how much he cares about you. And because I'm a fucking asshole for trying to come between you when I know you deserve someone like him," Shea offers quietly. "Seriously, just give him a chance to explain."

I shake my head, wiping my face as new tears fall. "He hasn't even tried calling me, so clearly, there's nothing for him to explain."

Shea has no response to that, but I hear him exhaling again and cough immediately after, so I know he's smoking.

"Did Gia make it up to your room?" I ask.

The sun is already setting and I've been gone all day so I know she did, but I want to hear him say it.

"Yeah," Shea says, his response sounding like a question, probably wondering why I care.

"Who was she with? I heard her and a girl talking in the spa locker room."

"This girl, Steph—she does her makeup and shit some-times. I think she's going with us to a couple of shows," he says nonchalantly, without realizing that his words are twisting the knife in my heart.

"Oh," I whisper. "Do you guys share a tour bus?" I ask, internally begging for him to say no.

"Nah, she has her own, but you know how it is. Gia wants to come on mine tonight, but Shadow and I are supposed to work, so I dunno ..."

My chin begins to tremble at the thought of Nick hook-ing up with Stephanie ... with anybody. I never knew that something aside from the death of a loved one could hurt this much. That's exactly how I feel, too, like somebody died. I just keep thinking about him fucking her out of anger toward me. I picture his eyes and the murderous look they had when I left the room, and I feel like dying. It hasn't even been twenty-four hours since I left, and twenty-four hours isn't enough time for wounds to heal, but that's when we do our worst—when our wounds are raw.

"Has he seen Stephanie?" I ask quietly, pressing my finger-nail into the palm of my hand.

Shea exhales. "Huh. So you know about them."

I face the mouthpiece of my phone up so that he doesn't hear me crying again.

"Yeah, they saw each other," he says, his words slow and careful.

"Did they hook up?" I whisper, needing to know.

"Why are you asking me that?" he asks. "Why would you even want to know that?"

I take the fact that he doesn't give me an answer as the confirmation I need.

"Brooklyn, you're doing this to hurt yourself," he warns

after I don't respond. "This is what you do before you start using."

I close my eyes at his words. "Thanks for the reminder," I whisper sarcastically.

"Call your sponsor."

"Go get a sponsor," I counter.

"Okay, I see you wanna act like a child right now and pick another fight. Call me later. I got a show to put on soon," he says. "I love you, BK, don't forget that."

"Thanks. Break a leg," I say quietly.

The longer that I wallow in my own sadness, the more I wonder if Shea is right about calling my sponsor. The last time I was in this hotel, in a cabana similar to this one, was with Shea, Ryan, and a group of other wild teenagers. I push those memories out of my head. Even though I don't want to think about him, my mind drifts to Nick and what he may be doing right now. I wish I didn't have a clear picture of him putting his arm around Stephanie at the airport the first time I saw him, because my chest physically aches at the thought. I wish I didn't care about him. I wish I'd never spoken to him or become friends with him, but most of all, I wish we'd never had sex because I can't take the image of his eyes blazing into mine out of my head.

Swallowing my sadness, I flip on the television for the first time in what seems like ages, and start watching *Housewives of Atlanta*. At least reality shows should take my mind off of everything weighing down on me right now. I start checking my messages and deleting the voicemails. I let them play back to back in my ear and when I hear Nick's voice, my insides flip.

"Brooklyn, it's me. I'm an asshole. I shouldn't have said that to you, I was pissed off. I'm sorry … call me." His voice is raspy and deep and sounds exhausted.

I look for the time of the message but it shows the time I turned on my phone, so there's no telling. I wonder if he left it after he spoke to Shea or after he found out that him starting a label wasn't the reason I left. Not entirely anyway. A part of me wishes he would've told me but I realize that if he would have, I may have treaded more carefully around him. I love the way he made me feel free. I don't even know what to think anymore, but I know I'm not ready to call him yet.

I order room service and a bottle of wine and let myself drown in a couple of glasses instead. I figure that it's better than drugs. Three glasses later, I feel drowsy and decide to go to sleep. Tomorrow will be another day. Tomorrow will be better. Soon I'll head back to New York and leave this tainted state behind me again.

CHAPTER TWENTY-SIX

Depression is a cruel bitch. She starts by planting little seeds all over your mind, knowing that life's troubles will water it daily until it grows into a massive bonsai tree that crowds your thoughts and feelings, not leaving any room for leaves of hope to spur from it. Those are my thoughts as I lay in bed. I've lost count of how many days I've been in here, faking headaches and period pains so that my brother doesn't try to drag me out.

Turning to lay on my stomach, I swivel the volume tuner on my iPod so that I can get lost in music. The more melancholy I feel, the more depressing I want my music to be, so I've been listening to what my brother so aptly calls, my suicide playlist. Clearly, the no filter thing runs deep in my family. Nonetheless, it's a fact of life—when you're sad, you listen to sad music; when you're happy, you listen to party music. I wish I could stop. I wish I could press pause and put away the iPod, but I can't.

I see my door open, mainly because there's light in the room now, but I don't look up to acknowledge it. I just see my brother's shiny black shoes and Nina's equally as shiny black patent pumps before my earphones get tugged out of my ears.

"What the hell?" I mutter, sitting up on the bed.

"You're acting like a fucking bear," Nina scolds, pushing the button to open the drapes.

"Bee, you need to get out of this funk," Hendrix agrees. "Are you taking your anti-depressants?"

My eyes begin to water as my lower lip trembles. "I don't want to."

I really don't. I don't want to take any kind of drugs, not even ones I'm prescribed. I'm scared that I'll try to drown in them if I take one. It's easy to take two and then three and then drink. And I'm scared that I'll fall back into something I can't get out of. My sponsor says I'll be fine. She asks me to call her every day to update her on my progress, which I do even though there is none. I spoke to Allie's husband on the phone when I called her the other day and he screamed his head off at me. I still haven't had any communication with her and it's killing me. I know I shouldn't call her, but I hate that we haven't spoken. I hate just leaving our friendship hanging like that even if she did try to screw me over.

Apparently I'm that girl, the one that needs closure. The one that's unwilling to accept that sometimes people in your life vanish into thin air.

Nina sits down beside me and pulls me close to her, laying my head on her shoulder. "Okay, no drugs. What else can we do to help you?"

"Get me a new heart," I murmur.

"Oh my God," Hendrix says. "Stop being so melodramatic. You knew the guy for what? Two months?"

"I knew him long enough for him to make himself my life," I say quietly as new tears start.

Nina rolls her eyes and shakes her head, looking at me like

I'm a pathetic excuse for a woman. I swear if she starts spewing her women power bullshit right now, I will kick her.

"So fucking call him," Hendrix says. "If you feel this way, fucking call him or pick up the goddamn phone when he calls you! Why are women so fucking complicated?"

"Listen," Nina starts with an attitude, letting go of me and standing up to place her hands on her hips. "Men are fucking stupid. That's why they think women are complicated. Women want three things. Three simple things: Keep your dick in your pants. Be honest with us. Worship us. That's it. That's all. You motherfuckers can't do all three without getting your brain mixed up. She cannot call him because she is the woman and he should be groveling at her feet and kissing them while he's down there. Fuck him. Fuck you. Fuck all men. I'm taking an oath right now and writing all men off."

Hendrix starts laughing, throwing his head back and clutching on to his stomach. "Oh, that'll be the day, Nina. That'll be the day," he says, laughing.

"Go home to your ex-wife, you miserable, childish little man," Nina says, pivoting back to me while Hendrix laughs.

"She's not my ex-wife. We're still married," he says.

"By the grace of God," she mumbles, sitting beside me again.

"Look, the point is that if she's this miserable she needs to call him," Hendrix says.

"You're not bothered that he's been working on this Wildfire Label all along?" I ask.

Hendrix crouches down in front of me, looking at me with seriousness in his caramel eyes. "Bee, do you know how Dad started Harmon?"

I shake my head. I've heard a million stories of how, but I wouldn't know which one is true: the one where my dad fought off the bear that was around old records or the one where he started selling CDs out of his trunk.

"He was an intern for Donny, you know, from Mojo Records, and he started taking clients. Anybody that wanted to sign that Dad really liked, he spoke to on the side. That's how Harmon came to be. This is a shark business, Bee. If you're not ready to bite, you're gonna get eaten. You know this. So no, I'm not mad at Wilde. He has the right to do whatever he wants, and you know what? He's beating his dad at his own game. I respect him," Hen says with a shrug.

"His dad is an asshole," I mutter.

"Bigger than ours," Hendrix agrees, making me smile.

"Damn. I gotta meet this man," Nina says, making Hendrix and I shoot a warning glance her way. She puts her hands up in defense. "Just to see if he's really a bigger asshole than Uncle Chris! Geez ... oh ye of little faith and shit."

I laugh despite myself and bump her with my shoulder.

"Seriously, Brooklyn, it's been a week already, you need to get your shit together. You have other things going on," Hendrix reminds me.

One week. That's how long it's been. One week since I last saw him. One miserable week and I'm still not over him, not that I thought I would be. It's amazing how you can live without somebody your entire life and then you meet them, let them in, let them take over your every thought, and then the moment they're gone, you feel like you're fucking dying. My shoulders and head drop at the thought of it all. Just when things seemed to be going in the right direction for me, my comfortable rug gets pulled from beneath me. Nick called me the first couple of days and then stopped, I don't know if it was to give me space or because he finally decided to quit on me. I expected the latter to happen at some point, but I didn't know it would hurt this bad. I didn't know it would feel this painful.

"Do you have a dress for Saturday?" Nina asks, bumping me back with her shoulder.

I shake my head, not caring if I even go to that stupid party. Nothing good has ever come out of those damn White Parties anyway.

"Shea will be there," Hendrix says. "Maybe Nick will go."

"Yeah, with a date, I'm sure," I scoff, the thought making my stomach turn.

I get out of bed and shower, not because I feel like I have the energy to do it, but because my cousin and brother will kill me if I don't. Hendrix places a cup of coffee in my hand as Nina drags me out of the house, insisting that we go dress shopping. The White Party went from "dress in all white" to "tux and gown mandatory" throughout the years. My mother got sick of rockers showing up in jeans and a white T-shirt claiming that they were properly dressed for the party. Being that she was the only one in a custom floor-length dress, she changed the rules. My father laughed and argued that it would no longer be a white party if they changed the wardrobe, but he went along with it anyway.

After browsing a couple of stores, we end up in Oscar de la Renta on Madison Avenue, which is where I suggested we go to begin with, but Nina always has to get her way and fail before she goes along with anybody else's idea.

"What if I wear a short dress?" I ask, holding up a sleeveless black dress with a boat neck and a full skirt. It's not short, it would probably fall where my knees end, but it's not floorlength like my mother wants it to be either.

Nina scrunches her faces. "That looks like an old lady dress, Bee."

I purse my lips, examining the dress, which now that she

points it out, does kind of look like an old lady dress with the red flowers on it. "I don't really want to wear a gown though."

Nina takes the dress out of my hand and puts it back on the hanger before thanking the employee and pulling me out of the store, informing me that we're going to Barney's.

"I'll never hear the end of it if I end up wearing the same dress as somebody else," I groan as I browse the racks of long gowns there.

Nina agrees and we move on to Neiman Marcus. As we're getting to the designer dresses, I spot a one shoulder beaded bodice ball gown that makes my heart skip a beat. Because this is the first time I've even felt my heart beat in a week, I decide that's the dress I want. I try the Naeem Khan gown on and fall in love all over again.

"This is it," I breathe, swiveling in front of the mirror.

Nina nods in approval. "That is beautiful," she says, walking up to me and looking at the price tag. She shrugs. "Could be worse."

I laugh, looking at it and agreeing that it could be. Price aside, the dress is couture enough that I know most of the invitees won't wear it. I like to push the envelope when I dress for events like these. I never go for the plain dresses unless they have a classic look, like the de la Renta one I'd seen. Nina tries on a strapless floor length Monique Lhuillier gown with a whirlwind of green hues and a slit that shows off her thin long leg. As soon as she steps out of it, I grab it from her and start walking to the register, as she gets dressed.

"Don't try anything else on," I say over my shoulder. "You're wearing this."

She laughs but doesn't argue. We both decide on gold shoes: Nina's a peep toe Prada, I'm a strappy Jimmy Choo, and then we head over to Hell's Kitchen to eat with Uncle Rob and his husband Vic.

We leave everything in the car. Nina tells Marcus, the driver, not once, but twice, that he better be careful with our purchases. He laughs as if it's the funniest thing he's ever heard, but Nina is dead serious about her request. We got to a tiny little café called The Eatery.

Uncle Rob and Vic greet us and pull up chairs for us before ordering each of us a mimosa.

"I love coming here," Nina sings as she lets out a happy breath.

"Yeah, it's cute," I agree, tilting my head to look at the rainbow painted American Flag across the street.

"Have you noticed how many gays are hot as fuck?" Nina asks suddenly, blatantly checking out the gay couple walking by us.

My jaw drops, but I laugh when Uncle Rob and Vic start laughing.

"The things that come out of your mouth," Uncle Rob says, shaking his head.

"Seriously," I agree, looking at my menu.

"Whatever," Nina continues. "I work with a lot of them, but it seems like the really hot ones are out here. I mean, look at him," she says, pointing at a strong blond guy walking an English Bulldog.

"You do realize that he can hear you, right?" I ask, gripping the finger she's pointing. "And it's rude to point."

"I don't think he would think it's rude that I'm saying he's hot," she counters, glancing at her menu.

Vic laughs. "No, probably not. When's your next play?"

"I start one in two weeks. It's going to be huge, I just know it," Nina says, beaming.

I love watching her talk about her plays. She gets so excited about every single one of them. Even if she doesn't play a major role, she treats it like she's the main character. I love that about her.

My uncle places his hand on mine while Nina talks to Vic about her play. I look up and find his hazel eyes looking at me with concern. "You okay?"

I nod slightly and offer him a small smile. "I'm getting there."

He raises an eyebrow. "Have you gone to the therapist I sent you to?"

My shoulders slump and I shake my head. "No, not yet," I whisper.

"You know you don't have to wait until the last minute to seek help, right? You don't have to wait until you're drowning in your sorrows to go talk to somebody," he says, his voice quiet as he rubs my hand.

"I know," I agree. "I just … it's always the same thing, you know? I go and I tell them my whole life story and I feel stupid. I feel stupid for needing help. I feel stupid for feeling depressed. I'm crying out and feeling sad and here I am, sitting in a café in the middle of the day after I just spent twelve thousand dollars on clothes without a second thought. It just makes me feel petty. There are people starving, kids that need water, and here I am … feeling depressed over what? A friend that sued me, a guy that let me walk away from him, that may have tried to use me, a best friend that's always on tour and has issues of his own, a best friend that died because my interest in drugs led him to get stuck in it?" My throat closes in on me, not letting me continue my rant and I blink away tears, running the tips of my fingers under my eyes just in case.

My uncle stands up in the crowded space and rounds the table, crouching down beside me and pulling me into a hug.

"Depression has no reason, Brooklyn. It'll eat at you, showing no remorse, because it can. You don't have to let it. You can own the universe and still feel this way."

I know he's right, but just like depression has no reason, it also doesn't allow you to reason things.

"If I can't get myself out of it, I'll go see your lady," I promise, and I will.

He smiles and kisses the top of my head before returning to his seat. Our meal is filled with laughs and funny stories from both Nina and Vic, who can entertain a stand-up comedy audience with their obscene jokes. As we head back home, my heart begins to cry again. As great as it is to get out, it still doesn't erase what I feel when I go back home and am alone with my thoughts. I get my bags out of the car and kiss my cousin goodbye and when I get upstairs, I decide to FaceTime with Melody and Sarah. Sometimes the only thing that can truly cheer you up is the sound of a child's laughter, and Melody's giggles never let me down. I choose to listen to her tell me stories about what her day was like and what she's going to be for Halloween. Instead of suffocating myself in darkness, I choose light. For once.

CHAPTER TWENTY-SEVEN

I yawn, feeling exhausted from lack of sleep. Nick called me last night while I was in the shower. By the time I saw the missed call, it was too late to call back. The feeling of needing to see him has become unbearable. My phone vibrates beside me on the nightstand and I reach over, turning on the bed to look at the screen. My stomach does this crazy flip when I see his text message pop up on my screen.

Nick: I miss you

Ignite butterflies.

Me: Stop saying that

I hate that his words, written or voiced, have a direct line to the blood that flows to my heart, but more than anything I hate that I want to hear them so bad. I've spoken to Shea a couple of times for about a second each time. He says they've been working their asses off on the album and rarely have time to even eat, which makes me secretly happy because that means they don't have time to screw around either.

Nick: I can't help it.

I clutch my phone harder, but don't respond. What would I say? I've been spending so much time alone with my thoughts, that just as I made it to the point where I convinced myself he wasn't using me for his label, I backtrack and decide he may have been. I have to give myself a couple of days to clear my head completely so that I can talk to him in person. A couple days of no lawsuit drama, no heartache, and no pain relief, which is beginning to sound more and more like a vacation. After a moment, my phone chimes again.

Nick: I want you

Holy. Shit. I stare at the message for one second, two seconds, three seconds, four … all while my heart sputters in my chest. How is it that he makes me feel like I can't breathe even when he's far away from me? It's only a text message, but I can hear his raspy voice saying that into my ear and it makes my skin break out in goose bumps.

Me: Stop

Nick: I can't

My insides are no longer mine; they belong to the butterflies and every other creature with wings that are currently fluttering inside. When he doesn't text again, a tiny part of me is relieved, the bigger part of me wants to scream at the phone for him to send another, even though I don't want to respond again. Maybe I should just call him. Maybe I should just wait. I wrestle with the idea for a moment longer before I do what any normal woman with a beating heart does: I call Nina.

"Do not text him back again. And definitely no calling," she says firmly. "Make him sweat it out, that asshat."

I nod once, making up my mind to do just that. "Good. I needed to hear that."

When I hang up with her, I decide to go to a Pilates class that I'd signed up for eons ago and never went to. The rest of my day is spent pampering myself. I think whenever I get down on myself like that, this is what I need to do—make myself leave the house and pamper myself. It's easier said than done, obviously, but since this is the first time I'm actually doing it, I feel proud of myself. That night, Hendrix walks in with a box of pizza, completely fucking up the "I'm going to start leading a healthy lifestyle" mentality I practiced throughout the day.

"Bastard," I say to him as he puts down the box and greets me with a kiss.

He laughs. "What? Just because you did Pilates today you're a changed woman?"

"No," I grumble, my stomach growling. "Hey, you wanna go with me to get a tattoo?"

"Another one?" he asks, pulling out disposable plates and napkins.

"You act like I'm a tatted up shrine," I say, taking a bite of pizza.

He makes an annoyed face. "What will you get?"

"Breathe," I state simply.

He scratches his head and tilts his head at me. "Breathe? The word? Where?"

"Here," I say, tracing a line over my wrist with my finger.

He blinks his caramel eyes a couple of times. My brother is so not a tattoo kind of guy. He's so straight-laced it's disgusting. The real reason he hasn't gotten any is because he knows my mom hates them. I've gotten three: the bee on my hip and the anchors on my foot, because I know my mom hates them. And because they're meaningful, but my mom hating them definitely factored in to my reasoning when I got them.

"Because you need a reminder to breathe," he says sarcastically.

I nod. "Yeah, sometimes."

He looks at me again, gauging whether or not I'm serious. When he sees that I am he agrees to go with me. After we eat our pizza, we head out to Shea's favorite tattoo parlor in Soho. I tell the guy what I want and he squeezes me in with no appointment since it's so small and simple. My phone rings as he prepares the needle, and I ask Hendrix to pick it up since it's my mother. I listen to his conversation with her. He's smiling for the beginning part of it and then frowns and then cringes and then grimaces; his facial expressions match exactly what I feel as the needle hits my wrist and begins to move.

"She wants to talk to you," he says, holding the phone on his chest.

I shrug with my free arm. "Okay." He holds the phone to my ear. "Hey, Mom."

"Brooklyn Paige Harmon, tell me you are not getting another tattoo," she scolds.

I roll my eyes. "I am," I respond, smiling.

"So trashy," she says. "Anyway, I was calling to inform you that you have a date for the party on Saturday."

My jaw drops. "What?"

"Yeah. He's pretty popular, unsigned, he goes by the name Rapture ... is it Rapture?" she asks somebody in the background. "Yeah, it's Rapture."

For the sake of not arguing with her, I go along with it, like I always do. I'm not losing anything by going along with her. I stopped trying to make her proud years ago, but if I'm lucky, I'll gain a commission from this Rapture guy. "Okay. Whatever. It's not like I had a date anyway," I mutter under my breath, rolling my eyes again. When I speak to my mother, I might as well be in a state of permanent eye roll.

"Good girl," she says. I hate when she says that to me. "Talk soon," she says right before hanging up on me.

I shake my head and look at my brother. "Who the eff is Rapture?"

Hendrix laughs. "No fucking idea. He must suck if you don't know him."

Ain't that the truth. I'm a little worried about what I may find on YouTube when I get home and look him up.

The tattoo artist chuckles and cleans me up, smearing the ink on his cloth and letting me look at my new tattoo: **Breathe**

"I love it," I say, smiling. "Thank you."

The next couple of days fly by, and before I know it it's Friday and I'm headed for The Hamptons with my brother and Nina. A drive that usually takes us two hours is going on three today. It took us forever to get out of the city and on the road, but we finally make it to the gates of my parents' Water Mill mansion. I used to love coming here when I was a kid and laying out in the pool or going boating with the guests. The house looks as beautiful as ever, sitting on the luscious green lawn. It's so big—twenty-two thousand square feet of house—that when we were kids, it would take us hours to find each other when we played hide and seek. After the millionth time Hendrix forgot that we were playing and gave up on looking for us, Nina and I decided that we would only play if we set perimeters for the game. We were sick of being left alone in one hiding spot for hours. The house was built in the 1920s, but my parents remodeled it when they bought it and keep on updating it every couple of years. They've kept its original colonial style with a modern twist.

There are white event trucks cased out on the further end of the lawn, already setting up for tomorrow's party, and I actually begin to feel a little bit excited.

"We are going to paaarty," Nina sings, making Hendrix and I laugh. "Is Sarah coming up for the party?" she asks Hendrix.

"Nope," he says quietly. "She has work to do, and Mel is sick so she doesn't want to leave her or make her fly."

"Bummer," I say. "I always like partying with Sarah."

"You like partying with a tree, Brooklyn," Hendrix mutters.

"Liked," I correct. "I don't usually party anymore."

Nina scoffs. "Seriously, going out with her is like going out with a dead guy."

As soon as she says that, her eyes widen apologetically. Hendrix shakes his head in disbelief, but I smile at her.

"You know what I love about you, Nina? The way you can take the most tragic things and joke about them and not make me want to cry when you do it." I let out a breath, blowing my new side swept bangs out of my face. "Besides, you're right, partying with me is pretty much like partying with a dead guy." I bite the inside of my lip after I say it and train my vision to the sunny clear sky, blinking my eyes rapidly so that I won't shed any tears for the part of my heart that is gone but will never be forgotten. Eight years is a long time, but no time is long enough to heal the loss of a life.

We settle in, Hendrix in his room and Nina and I in mine. One of my mother's maids comes in and informs us that my mother wants us to join them for a dinner party they're having tonight.

"That Rapture guy will be here tonight too," Nina says when she walks back into my room after we've lounged by the pool and she's flipped through a dozen gossip magazines.

I've been getting ready for the past fifteen minutes and still don't know what I'm going to wear.

"Oh yeah? How do you know?" I ask, putting down my blush.

"Your mom just told me. Apparently he's one of those YouTube sensations," Nina explains.

"Yet we've never heard of him," I mumble as I apply my eyeliner.

Nina laughs. "True."

I decide on a short sequined silver dress and black wedged heels.

"Nice," Nina says when she sees me. "Very nice. I hope you don't have to bend over at any point."

I laugh, finger combing my hair to separate the big curls at the end. "No vagina shows from me. That's your job," I say, pointing at her short little black dress.

We bump into Hendrix on our way down the stairs and link arms with him, each of us on one side. We always do this and I think he must feel so cool when we do. I can picture him internally high fiving himself and thinking, "I'm a pimp" as he nods at other guys in the room.

When we enter the sitting room, my dad is talking to an older man with white hair, but catches my eye and stops talking to him, turning his body and opening his arms to embrace me as I walk up.

"Hey, baby girl," he coos into my hair, hugging me tight. "So glad you made it."

"Me too," I respond, kissing his cheek.

He's wearing a white button down shirt with the first button popped open, just like Hendrix. I notice they're both wearing black slacks too, like father like son. If they stood beside each other, they'd make a perfect whiskey commercial too, the way they're holding their drinks in their hands so casually.

"What a nightmare, huh?" my dad comments.

I raise my eyebrows and nod. "That's exactly what it's been."

He tips my chin and looks at me for a long moment, his wise green eyes assuring me that it'll be okay, and then walks away talking to somebody else.

I get a glass of wine with Nina and try to find out the dirt on who's coming tomorrow night, mainly because I want to know if Shea will be here, and in turn, maybe Nick. We're talking to my mom's friend and model, Giselle, about it; she usually knows things that are going on even when they're not in gossip magazines. The moment Giselle stops talking and gasps, looking up with admiration, I know my mother has entered the room. That's how people, mainly models, react to her: they stop and stare as if she's the light they live for. I've always thought it was ridiculous, but she's my mother, so maybe I don't appreciate her as much as everybody else does. Or maybe I just see her for who she is.

Either way, I pivot my body to watch her come in because whether you like her or not, Roxana Harmon is a sight to see when she walks in a room. She doesn't walk, she glides in with such grace that you can't help it—you have to be awed. She's wearing a form-fitting black dress with sleeves that purposely fall off her shoulders and a hem that reaches her knees. Her hair is made into a bun that looks like ribbons of brown hair and her golden skin is flawlessly made up with very light makeup. She looks like a wicked queen in black Louboutin heels and a smile plastered on her face. My mother doesn't have a genuine smile; her smiles are all for show, until she looks at my father and sometimes my brother.

When her eyes meet mine, she stops greeting people and strides over to me, fake smile intact. She doesn't even examine my body closely today, which is both surprising and relieving. The last thing I want to do is regret the pizza I had for dinner the other night and the lack of exercise I've had lately.

"Brooklyn," she says charmingly."You look nice. Let me introduce you to this Raptor guy," she says flippantly.

Biting down on my lip so that I won't laugh, I tilt my head to look at her. "Is it Rapture or Raptor?"

Her eyebrows scrunch up as she thinks, then stops walking and turns to me. "You know ... I can't remember ... why do these kids have to name themselves after dinosaurs? Jesus ..."

"Mom ... what is it that this guy does again?" I'm laughing a little, but now I'm nervous about who she's setting me up with.

She sighs. "Brooklyn, just have a drink and talk to the guy. I'm sure you can convince him how great the label is in ten minutes tops, especially with the dress you have on," she says.

My heart drops a little at the possibilities of what that statement could mean. Does that mean she thinks I have sex with everybody I've signed? Or is that her way of complimenting me? It's hard to tell.

"Here he is," she says cheerfully when a guy, probably around my age comes up to us. He's tall and thin, yet fit looking, he has nice dark brown eyes and dark brown hair that's cut short and a perfectly trimmed beard. I'm not into beards, but he makes it work. "This is my daughter, Brooklyn. Brooklyn this is ..." my mother lets the words hang so that he can introduce himself.

"Jayson," he says, offering me his hand to shake, which I take and smile when he brings it up to his lips. "Pleased to meet you, Brooklyn," he says, dropping my hand.

"Likewise," I say with a smile.

And I am glad. I'm instantly comfortable with him, and as we walk over to get a drink, I find that I love looking into his eyes. He has childlike eyes, full of awe and wonder. Things I don't remember mine ever having. The industry hasn't killed him yet, and I find his energy refreshing. I also find that I'm slightly jealous of it, of the amazement in his eyes as he looks at things. I wish we could trade places for a day and he could live this lavish lifestyle and I could live his normal everyday life. I can tell he's not lonely, I can tell he has people that care for him, and I decide that if he's good, I will sign him, regardless of whether or not he's "gotta have it" material. This will be the first time I'll sign somebody because I feel like they can handle this business and not because I know we'll make money off of them.

If he sucks, I'll have hell to pay, but I want to give this kid the opportunity to make a name for himself. I'm sick of selling poor lost souls to the devil. I'm sick of feeling like I need to wash my hands as soon as they sign on the dotted line. I think of Shea and I know he would be worse off if he hadn't signed, but still, where he is now scares me. The amount of stress he deals with and the little real support he has terrifies me for him.

"So, you rap, Jayson?" I ask, standing beside him as we look at the pool, letting the breeze of the night hit our faces.

"I do," he says. "Wanna hear?"

I smile. "Why not?"

He begins to freestyle, and obviously we have no music to go on, but he still impresses me. Jayson doesn't do the regular throwing his hands all over the place, trying the beatbox thing that I'm used to new guys doing. In fact, he doesn't even look like what I would expect him to, judging by the rappers I know. He's not wearing a chain, not a flashy one anyway. He is wearing a big watch, but it's not large enough to call attention.

When he finishes, he flashes a bashful smile at me and takes a sip of his drink.

"That was very, very good," I say. "Why haven't you signed again?" I ask with a small laugh. It's a rhetorical question since there are better unsigned talented people than signed. Sometimes I have to laugh at the quality of music we're putting out there nowadays, but then I remind myself that it's called commercial for a reason. If what the people want is shit, then we'll give them shit.

Jayson laughs and shrugs, taking another sip of his drink. The longer he stands there and looks at me, the more I wish we were in a group setting. His eyes keep flickering to my lips when I talk and I can tell what he's thinking. Not that he's being disrespectful at all, but we're going to have to attend the party together tomorrow night and I'm wondering if maybe I should make sure he knows it won't be that kind of date.

"Do you have a manager?" I ask.

"I'm talking to someone now."

This doesn't surprise me in the least. A YouTube sensation that's about to get himself a manager and a record deal. It's like Justin Bieber all over again. But better. Okay, maybe not better. Bieber started at the perfect age, where he could get tween fans to grow with him and their moms to think he was cute. Now they're kind of stuck with him regardless of his bratty ways because, well, Bieberfever doesn't have an antidote until a newer better version of him comes out.

I nod. "Are you going to make me guess who or are you going to tell me?" I ask, signaling him to follow me back in the house.

He chuckles. "How old are you?" he asks, changing the subject.

Old enough to know that your manager is going to try to fuck you over before you even sign on the dotted line. Old enough to know Harmon or whatever label you sign with is going to make you record an album, maybe three, and may hold on to whatever you record for months, years even, before they release it. If they even do.

I sigh, shooting him a glance over my shoulder and catch him staring at my ass but resist rolling my eyes. "Twenty-five," I answer. "You?"

He swallows hard, his dark eyes on mine. "Twenty-three."

I turn around and look forward again, my feelings conflicted even though I know this kid is going to sign with somebody and may end up getting screwed over regardless of who it is. "Get a manager. Get a lawyer," I suggest.

"Don't you have my best interest?" he asks, his voice is low and flirty now.

"Yes and no," I respond truthfully, glancing over my shoulder as we come to a stop in front of the doors of the dining room.

He nods in understanding. "I want to perform worldwide," he says, his eyes hopeful.

I smile at him. "We can make that happen for you."

He lets out a breath and my heart clenches for him. He really is just a kid, a kid with big dreams that he wants realized, a kid that wants to help his family out as best he can. Jayson carries his heart in his eyes and even though he's not much younger than me, he seems it and that makes me feel responsible for what will become of him.

"Jayson," I start, speaking lower so that only he can hear me. "How many friends do you have? Real friends? People you trust?"

He gives me a confused look and answers, "Six."

At the same time I shake my head. "Sleep on it and let me know tomorrow."

He's completely confused by my question and probably thinks I'm crazy, but I want to take this kid under my wing. It's the damn childlike eyes. Even over dinner he's looking at everything like it's his first time in Disneyland.

When Jayson, who asked me to call him Jay, goes to one of the guesthouses, I finally make my way upstairs and see a text message from Shea.

Shea: Yo, you still my date tomorrow?

Me: My mom asked me to go with some new guy :(

Shea: So cancel!

Me: Can't.

Shea: Trying to sign? Who is it?

Me: Name is Jay. Jayson. Raptor. Rapture. Idk about the last two. My mom confused the shit out of me with those.

Shea: LOL. YouTube guy right?

Me: That's what I hear

Shea: He's dope. K see you tomorrow. I get there in the afternoon but I'll be there.

I'm so glad he confirmed that he would be, but I don't ask about Nick. Just the thought of asking makes my stomach flop. We haven't spoken since the text messages the other day, which I've looked at close to a hundred times now. Nina thinks I'm insane, I think she almost suggested I call him the other day when she caught me looking at them, but shook her head instead and looked at me like I was crazy.

CHAPTER TWENTY-EIGHT

Turning over on my side, I open my eyes and notice that Nina's bed is empty. I blink my eyes to adjust to the light pouring in from outside and see that the clock reads ten o'clock. Yawning, I turn over in bed and close my eyes again. I know I have to get up because somebody will be knocking on my door shortly for one thing or another. My mom doesn't like to let me sleep in for too long when we have an event. She usually has nails, hair, waxes, and collagen appointments through the day and likes me to go along. Mainly to chastise me about whatever I desperately need to get done. I go anyway because Aunt Mireya and Nina always come with us and I like spending time with them.

"You're up," Nina says sleepily as she walks out of the bathroom.

I yawn again. "I'm so tired."

"Your mom sent the old lady to come wake us up," Nina says, walking over to her bed and plopping down on it again. She looks as tired as I feel, but at least she's showered and dressed.

I groan, throwing my head back into my pillow again. "Is your mom here yet?"

"Yeah, she got here early this morning. They went walking or running or something."

Stretching my arms over my head, I get up. "They're so friggin weird," I mutter, disappearing into the bathroom.

They really are. Half the time I don't know how Aunt Mireya can stand my mom, but then they get together and go running before they go Botox their saggy faces, and I get it. Botox on Wednesday, collagen treatment on Saturday, that's what my mother's reminders on her phone look like the week of events.

I shower, even though I have no will to today. If I could, I would stay in bed all day with the blinds shut, basking in an abyss of darkness, but I know Nina and Hendrix won't let me, so I don't even try it. Once I'm dressed, I step out of the bathroom and find Nina enthralled in her cell phone, typing away furiously with scrunched eyebrows. I don't ask questions, I'm not really in the mood to talk right now. I just hope this mood passes me by soon. Maybe after a cup of coffee I'll feel better, this is what I tell myself as Nina drags her eyes from her cell phone to my face and offers me a sad smile. These moments are totally uncharacteristic of her, so I know that whatever she sees etched on my face causes her concern.

Again, I don't ask and neither does she, I won't talk about it anyway so there's no use. There's no reason for my moods, no specific reason that I can pinpoint. Over time I've realized that it's just me. It's not only about the memory of losing a friend or a good friend suing me. It's not only about my parents thinking I'm not worthy of breathing their air or the guy that I want to be with more than anything turning out to be a complete asshole. It's not only about years and years of being treated as second to everything. It's about everything, it's about me, and because of this, I've come to terms with trying to make the best of things. It just takes time for my mind to process what that even means. Thankfully it doesn't take as long as it used to. I am the master of my own destiny. I repeat this mantra for a couple of breaths and get ready to start the day.

We head to the kitchen, taking the stairs closest to the guesthouse to see if we spot anybody else who might be staying here. We're both standing on our tiptoes looking through one of the tall windows at the end of the hall, when a door slams shut behind us, scaring the ever living shit out of us.

"Hendrix!" Nina and I both scold at the same time as we turn around with our hands over our hearts.

His shoulders shake with laughter. "Nobody told you to be so nosey."

Nina scoffs. I roll my eyes. Hendrix shrugs.

"Did you eat breakfast already?" I ask him.

"Nope," he says, tucking his hands inside the pockets of his jeans and frowning. "Oh shit. I totally forgot. Melody gave me these to give you when I saw her last week. She said it was so you could cheer up." He hands me three gold coins and even though the dark clouds have somewhat dissipated, I start to cry. Just like that. Three Golden Doubloons and I'm crying as if my dog died.

Nina and Hendrix don't make a move to console me; they just stand back and wait. They've learned that sometimes the best way to deal with my fucked up emotions is to take a step back and give me a moment.

"Golden Doubloons," I sniffle, wiping my face. I feel like a moron for crying, but I can't really help myself. Sometimes there are scattered showers before the storm inside me completely clears out of my system.

Hendrix smiles and tugs on my hair. That little gesture makes my eyes water again, but only because it reminds me of Nick. Closing my eyes, I take a deep breath and wonder if maybe I should skip out on this entire day. Maybe it would be best if I stay in my room for a while longer, at least until I get my emotions in check.

"Don't even think about it," Nina says quietly, holding my hand in hers. "You're going to be fine. This will pass. I promise."

I cry again, this time wrapped inside of Nina's arms. Hendrix hugs me by hugging Nina and putting his arms around me too. He's about as good with dealing with emotions as I am, so it almost makes me laugh that he's participating in this hug, but instead I cry harder, even though it's now turned into a happier cry. I'm sure this would make me sound like a complete crazy person to somebody else, and maybe I am. Maybe I'm okay with being a crazy person. I'd rather be crazy than perfect. There's no excitement in perfection.

"I'm fine. I'm fine," I say, wiping my eyes again and stepping out of their embraces. "I dunno what's wrong with me," I lie.

"Are you still against taking the medicine?" Hendrix asks quietly. His anxious eyes tell me that he's dying for me to take my antidepressants.

Slipping my fingers into my hair, I begin to massage my head with my eyes closed. "I don't know anymore. Maybe I'll start tomorrow," I respond in an exhale.

The thing about my depression is that it's up and down. Some days I'm perfectly fine, some days I'm not. Some days I laugh the entire day and cry during the nights. Some days I don't feel at all and those are the days I isolate myself most. For the most part, I'm fine though. It almost seems like it really hits me seasonally, like I'm one with nature, feeling as dull as the fall leaves and bright as the spring sun.

When I'm sure I won't break down again, I tuck the Golden Doubloons in the back pockets of my jeans and link my arms with Nina and Hendrix on either side. We eat our breakfast, saying hello to the guests that walk by us, most of them older men and their wives. My parents' homes have always served as a sort of hotel for their friends. Anytime one of them knows they'll be in a place where my dad has a house, they call and ask him to stay there. I've been greeted by a perfect stranger on more than one occasion when I've stayed in their Miami or New York homes in the past. That's the biggest reason I refused to stay in their empty New York penthouse. The other reason was that it would be just another thing they can hold over my head.

"Oh, you're going to LA to make some microphones? Maybe we should change the locks so that you can't get in when you decide New York is where you should be."

They've done things like that to me in the past. Getting home after a night out and realizing you're locked out of your own goddamn house because you didn't answer your mother's phone calls is not fun at all. I wouldn't bring that up, though. Water under the bridge, that's how my dad classifies anything having to do with my past.

When my mother and Aunt Mireya get home from their workout and *revamping their faces*, as they call it, they tell us that the hair and makeup people will be here at four.

"Isn't that too early?" Nina asks, looking at me with a frown.

She wanted to lay out by the pool again today, even though I told her that I refuse to wear a bathing suit in front of all of my dad's friends. They keep circling around us like we're bait and I don't appreciate it. What's worse is that they keep reminding me of how cute I used to be when I was a toddler.

It makes me want to shake their heads and shout, "YOU JUST SAID YOU KNEW ME WHEN I WAS A TODDLER! STOP STARING AT MY TITS, YOU SICK PERVERT!"

I don't, of course, I just smile awkwardly and avert my eyes.

"No, it'll be fine," Aunt Mireya says, waving her hand. "Did you bring the dress?"

Nina shoots me one of her "oh fuck" glances that I don't know whether to laugh or cry over.

"Ummm actually, Brooklyn and I went shopping the other day and I got one," Nina mutters under her breath, her voice barely audible. Barely.

"What?" Aunt Mireya shouts. "Nina Victoria Garcia! No lo puedo creer!"

I bite my lip to keep from laughing, even though it shouldn't be funny to me the way our mothers have the ability to scare us even at this age. It's absolutely ridiculous, really. What are they going to do? Spank us? The way my aunt is looking at Nina, I think she may just take her Chanel flip-flop off, not caring whether or not she ruins her just-polished toes, and spank her. Nina looks like she wants to run far, far away. Her bony shoulders are squeezed into her body and her brown eyes are as wide as saucers, completely fixed on my aunt's hands. I know the same image is playing inside her head and it almost makes me laugh out loud. Almost. Until Mireya shoots a death look my way.

"Why would you buy clothes knowing that I'm coming, Brooklyn?" she asks me, her voice calm but lethal.

I slump my shoulders. "Because I knew you were going to be so busy and you have so many clients, and well ... we just figured it would be much easier."

Aunt Mireya narrows her eyes and tilts her head to study

me. "Okay," she says, letting out a breath. "Who designed them? Let's go have a look."

Nina and I smile at each other quickly as we get up and head to our room. My aunt designs beautiful gowns, I absolutely love them, but every time I've ever worn one, my mom gets fully involved in the alterations and that's where it becomes a problem for me. Then I have to hear about how small my boobs are and how I should get them enhanced or how big my butt is and how it makes me "appear fatter than I am." I can't deal with that, not anymore, so I buy my own clothes somewhere else even if I would kill to wear one of Aunt Mireya's couture gowns. Nina has no excuse not to wear her mother's clothing, with the exception that Nina's an asshole.

I ask the hairdresser to style my hair half up, half down. That way it's out of my face, but still natural. My mother argues with me for fifteen minutes (I counted) that my hair has to be up because of how the dress I'm wearing is designed. After the umpteenth eye roll I direct at her, she finally shuts up and lets the hairdresser do what I told him to do. My makeup is also natural with barely anything on my lips and light gold eye shadow over my eyes, the only thing that pops is my black liquid eyeliner and dark mascara that makes my long lashes look fake. My mom reminds me a handful of times not to wash my face after they'd just applied makeup, as if I would. Sometimes I think she just likes to hear herself talk.

When the butler knocks on my door to tell me that my date is downstairs waiting for me, I start getting butterflies in my stomach. I don't know why, but I do. Smiling at my reflection in the mirror, I pick up my gold clutch and head out, telling

Nina I'll see her later since she's still sitting in bed texting. I pick up the silk turquoise skirt of my dress and carefully walk down the stairs, smiling when I see Jay standing at the bottom of the steps waiting for me. He's wearing a black tuxedo, which is what all the men will be wearing tonight, unless they want an earful from my mother, and he looks good. He's so not my type, though, and it almost makes me laugh the way he looks at me like maybe there's a chance. I don't know why anybody would ever want to mix business with pleasure anyway, especially before business is even sealed.

"You look … wow …" Jay says, his dark eyebrows rising and lowering.

"Thanks. You look good too," I respond with a smile.

I place my hand on his bicep when he holds it out for me to hold, and we begin to follow the sign that signals to the front of the house. I'm assuming there will be some sort of carpet laid out there, as usual.

"They're going to take pictures of us and ask you questions," I explain to Jay, assuming he's never been to an event like this.

My dad really knows how to sell everything to people. He invites them to stay over at his house, lets them borrow his cars, yachts, and jet. He sees it as an incentive to show these people that they too can live this way. It's complete bullshit, of course. They don't live like this, even if they say they do, and that's part of the problem. We're selling them all of these tangible things: the money, the cars, the clothes, the hoes, but we're not letting the consequences of it all sink in. As a matter of fact, I would bet money that even if I sat here and went through the cons of what this lifestyle holds, only one out of ten would turn it down. People want to own what they can grasp in their hands, what they can take photos of and show off. They don't stop and think about the loneliness that comes with it all, the backstabbing, and the lies. And they wouldn't care, even if they did.

"So, what should I say?" he asks, tilting his head at me.

I shrug. "Say you're my date. Say you're a rapper. Say you're the best. You can even rap out there, for all I care. I'm just warning you so it won't take you by surprise," I respond with a smile.

Jay laughs in amusement. "Got it," he says with a wink.

"All right. Let's do it," I say, walking out and welcoming the instant flashes that hit my face with a warm smile.

"Brooklyn! Brooklyn!" one of the photographers says. "We haven't seen you in a while! You look gorgeous."

"Thank you," I say, squeezing Jay's arm so that he can fall into step beside me.

"What's your name?" the photographer asks as another yells, "Hey, aren't you the YouTube guy?"

"Yeah, Rapture," Jay says. "Actually, that's my YouTube name. I think I'll just stick to Jay from now on. Makes life easier."

My smile widens at his words. I am so freaking glad he dropped that name. I'll have to ask him about that later.

"So you're with Harmon now?" a reporter asks, the video guy coming up closely behind her. Photos don't make me nervous. I've been around them for so long that all they do is annoy me at best. Videos on the other hand, scare me. Those are there forever and they can show your actions, your words and the way you say them. Photos may lie; videos rarely do. I hold my breath waiting for Jay to respond.

"I'm with Brooklyn. I think she can make things happen for me," Jay says, and I blink my eyes, turning my face away from the camera and focusing on the green grass behind them so I won't cry. They may be just words to him, but Jay just paid me the biggest compliment anybody has ever given me in my entire life. Twelve words. Those twelve words make me feel so whole, that I want to take a snapshot and put it on my bathroom mirror so I won't miss them every morning when I wake up.

"Who are you wearing, Brooklyn?" another reporter asks.

"Naeem Khan," I reply, smiling brightly as we walk by, pose for one last photo and continue walking to the tent in the backyard.

"Holy shit," Jay breathes. "That was intense."

I laugh. "Get used to it!"

He nods with a smile, his eyebrows high. "I was trying to remember that moment, you know, enjoy it and remember it forever so that even if it doesn't happen again, at least I can look back on it and say: I walked a red carpet once with the prettiest woman on my arm."

I chew on my bottom lip to keep my emotions in check, but not because I feel sadness. "You'll walk more red carpets and you'll have more beautiful women on your arm," I tell him, squeezing his forearm.

"Maybe, but you'll always be my first and I'll always remember this one," he replies with a bashful smile.

I'm afraid to say anything to him because I don't want him to take any of my compliments the wrong way, so I just smile back. "I appreciate what you said back there."

"About you making things happen for me?" he asks, his face confused.

"Yeah."

"Well, I believe in your belief in me."

"Geez, you're making it hard for me not to cry tonight," I mutter, fanning my eyes with my hands.

"Aw shit. I didn't mean to make you cry," Jay says, chuckling a little.

"I'm not crying," I insist.

"Sure. Want a drink?" he asks as one of the servers makes his way to us.

"Vodka. Anything with vodka."

He smiles. "Coming right up."

Thankfully, this is a business where anything goes and drinking is completely acceptable and as my mom says, encouraged.

Jay and I make our rounds as I introduce him to some people, we talk about his family and where he's from. He seems like an all-around good guy.

"I know why you asked me the thing about my friends," Jay says suddenly when we take a break and sit down on one of the white loveseats near the empty dance floor. "You think they're going to either use me or turn their backs on me."

I nod, agreeing, and let him continue.

"They're not. Not these people. I've been through way too many bad things with them for them to only want me when things are going up," he explains.

"I'm glad to hear it," I say with a smile, even though I'm skeptical of his statement.

"You're still being sued by your friend over those microphones?" he asks.

My heart stops beating for a second before it readjusts itself. I hate that everybody and their mother knows about Allie's lawsuit. I hate that everything my family does is scrutinized under a microscope.

"Yeah," I respond with a shrug.

"Sucks. I'm sorry," Jay says compassionately.

I shrug again, not wanting him to know how much the lawsuit really bothers me, and more than anything, wanting to relay the message I was trying to get through to him about his friends.

"Business is business. Shit happens."

The music starts on stage, startling us out of our

conversation, and I instantly smile. This is my favorite thing about my dad's parties. Most of the singers attend the event and are encouraged to sing, but the catch is that they can't sing their own song. They have to sing songs from another artist, preferably one at the party. It's my dad's way of making sure everybody feels accepted in a business that so often turns into who's better than who, or who makes more than who. Art is art, and that's what my dad tries to establish in the company. It doesn't matter who you think is better because it's all up for debate. Shea may sing better than Jay, but Jay could have better lyrics. And still, listeners feel their music differently.

A singer/songwriter I've heard before walks on stage and adjusts the microphone to his level as he sits on the chair. I stand, muttering that I'll be back, when I notice the microphone he's touching is one of mine. It's as if I'm walking on air on the way over there, extending my hands to touch it. It's one in my Rat Pack collection, round and wide with a black thin band around the middle. That particular collection is vintage and very dear to me since it's the one my dad saw and loved. Still, I never thought he would actually buy one. I trace the tiny bee with the crown over its head that sits over the black band and smile.

"One of yours, right?" Brent, the singer asks as he holsters his guitar around himself.

"Yes," I say proudly.

"I want to get a few. Do you do custom?"

I nod. "I do. Do you have ideas?"

He nods back and strums on his guitar. "A couple. Do you have a card or do I just call you at Harmon?"

"You can call me there," I say because I don't have a card with me at the moment.

"Cool," he replies with a smile.

"Break a leg," I say as I walk away.

"I'm not an actor," he says back, making me laugh.

My laughter cuts short when I see Shea walking into the party with Gia's hand in his. I can feel my body burning from the inside, starting from the tips of my toes to the top of my head as I look around to see if I spot Nick. When I don't, I close my eyes to hide my disappointment, but realize it feels more potent when I do this, so I open them again. Smiling, I walk over to Shea and greet him and Gia. I quickly introduce them to Jay and explain a little bit about him. Shea begins to tell him how much he loves his stuff and I feel relieved for Jay, whom I know must be a fan.

As they continue talking, Jay moves his hand around my waist. Shea notices this and makes a face at me but says nothing of it. I can tell he wants to say something, probably on his friend Shadow's behalf. I almost roll my eyes, until I see Nick appear on the other side of the tent with a glass in his hand. I try to take a breath, but my lungs feel like they're being clogged by my heart and possibly my kidneys, like there's no room for air right now: system overloaded.

Nick doesn't even look around; he doesn't look like he's looking for anybody. His aqua eyes spot me in less than a second and they stay on mine, unblinking. The way he looks in a tuxedo is too good for me to wrap my head around and his hair, normally brushed forward with a bit of a spike, is brushed completely back today. I really wish I could look away from him and pretend I'm not checking him out, pretend I don't want my hands over the lapels of his jacket taking it off behind the nearest bush, but I can't. I can't because he owns me, and he knows it. And I hate it.

As Nick walks forward, his eyes trail slowly down my body, stopping at my waist where Jay's hand is sitting. I know this from the way Nick's jaw tenses. He throws back the drink with one large gulp and puts it down when he nears a table, picking up the pace to get to me. A moment of fantasy plays in my mind where I shrug Jay off and Gia and Shea part so that I can run in slow motion between them as Nick does the same to me and I jump into his waiting arms. That moment passes in one second when Jay pulls me to him, laughing at some joke Shea makes and Nick practically runs full speed at us.

"Brooklyn," Nick says, grabbing the hand I have on my side, and pulling me to him. "May I speak to you for a moment?"

What am I supposed to say? No? I let the current that is my body take me to him, the way it always does, because there's no denying the pull he has on me.

"Hmm," I reply, looking into the pools of every blue-green color in the crayon box that paint his intense stare.

"I'm Jay," Jayson says as an introduction to Nick. "I'm a huge, huge fan of yours, Shadow," he states.

Nick's lips tilt into somewhat of a smile, but he doesn't let go of my hand. He nods. "Thanks, I've seen you on YouTube, good stuff," he says cordially.

I hear Jay's intake of breath behind me, as if he can't believe Shadow has heard of him. I would laugh if it weren't for the fact that my heart has now started beating at a ridiculously fast pace, and I think I may throw up the vodka tonic I drank. Nick pulls me away from them, telling them we'll be back and takes me to the dance floor, where there are now several people dancing to Brent's music. He's singing Bob Marley, which isn't technically breaking the rule since it's not his music, but I know my mom is going to send somebody to complain soon enough because the artist is not living nor in the room.

Without asking, Nick pulls me into his chest and begins to move, circling an arm behind my back and holding me so that all I can breathe is him. Closing my eyes, I lay my head on his chest and sway along with him.

"You look beautiful, baby," he whispers into my hair. "Most gorgeous woman here tonight."

My heart skips a beat, because it sucks and it doesn't understand that when it's broken it can't skip beats.

"I've missed you so much, Brooklyn," he continues as the song changes.

I recognize this one as "Trouble" by Ray LaMontagne, and I'm glad that I saw him in the crowd earlier, so I know it won't be interrupted.

I move my head further into his chest, making myself comfortable there as we continue to dance slowly.

"You said some really messed up things to me," I whisper, knowing he can hear me.

"I'm sorry," he says instantly.

I've never had somebody apologize so quickly for their fuck ups, usually it's like pulling teeth to get a half-assed apology from somebody, so I stop dancing and look up at him to see if he's serious. He smiles at me, that slow grin that makes the butterflies in my core act like it's a cracked-out field day.

"*I've been saaaved by a woman,*" Nick sings, still smiling. He repeats the words along with Brent, and then lowers his mouth to my ear. "*She won't let me go. She won't let me go, no,*" he croons, his raspy voice making the last bit of breath I had leave my body.

"You can't sing to me," I scold softly, not meaning it.

Nick laughs and brings his face close to mine, and I can almost taste his lips on me. Almost. His breath smells like whiskey and I don't normally drink that, but I want to get drunk in his kiss so bad, that I don't mind it. He sighs, backing away from me and turning me as the song comes to an end, but bringing me back to him when the new one starts. Brent plays his guitar a little faster now and his band mate joins him. For a moment I don't think I've heard the song, until Brent begins to sing the beginning and I know it's by Del Amitri. I really, really hope Nick doesn't sing this to me because I'm not sure I can hold back my tears if he does.

He holds me even closer than before, placing his mouth right below my ear. He kisses me there, and it's a whisper of a kiss, barely there, but enough to make my insides flame with want for him.

"Tell her not to cry, I just got scared, that's all. Tell her I'll be by her side, all she has to do is call," he says, singing below my ear, his breath tickling my neck, making me shiver as tears form in my eyes. He continues to sing the song to me in his raspy, sexy voice and when he reaches the last part, I completely forget anybody else exists but us. *"Tell her nothing if not this, all I want to do is kiss her,"* he sings and kisses my neck again, more obvious this time.

When the song is over and people are clapping for Brent, I wipe carefully under my eyes, hoping I didn't smudge any makeup.

"Can we talk?" Nick asks, his eyes intense and hopeful.

My thoughts wrestle with my feelings over this, even though I know I can't deny him when he's standing in front of me. Finally, I nod, but hear my name being called just as I agree.

"Brooklyn, I need you for five minutes," Hendrix says, his voice as apologetic as his eyes when he glances from me to Nick.

"I'm not going anywhere ... without you," Nick says, and I smile.

"I'll be right back," I whisper.

CHAPTER TWENTY-NINE

I don't think I've ever noticed just how much people talk at these parties, but as I stand here pretending that I'm paying attention to the man Hendrix introduced me to, I keep wondering when he'll shut up. Jay is beside me, with his hand on my waist again, and I swear I think he does it more out of nervousness than actually wanting to hold me there. His eyes are wide and attentive when people speak to him and he responds as soon as they ask him anything, which is how I know this. My mind, however, keeps drifting to Nick and what he wants to say to me. I've decided it doesn't matter anymore, none of it does. The moment I saw him step in the room today, I just knew, and I'm not going to keep punishing myself by keeping him out of my life if he's who I want to be with. It's stupid, really. Yes, I'm scared, but love is scary. There is nothing about realizing that you want to hand over your heart to somebody that's not scary.

Take my heart, you're free to do whatever you want with it, including break it, rip it, shred it, and dislodge it from yours, but I'm going to give it to you anyway because I think you'll take good care of it. I don't think anybody has ever said that to another person because if they did they would be a little weird, but that's pretty much what I'm going to say to Nick, just not in so many words. I didn't need time away from him to know that I loved him, I knew it the moment he argued with me about whether or not you're supposed to stop or gun it at a yellow light. I knew it the moment he let me eat the little chocolate they left for us at the hotel instead of asking me to share it with him. I knew it the day he took me to his parents' house and let me see the way real, close-knit families live. And I knew it when I saw the pain in his eyes as he was recalling the day he took me to the hospital when Isaac found me on that bridge. I love him, I know I do, and I think he loves me too. And if he's willing to massage my feet every night, I think I'll keep him. How many things happen in the course of a life? How many broken promises and happily ever afters can you be promised before you realize that you're supposed to take it upon yourself to find your own happiness?

"Brooklyn?" Hendrix says, snapping his fingers in front of my face.

I slap his hand away. "What?" I ask.

"You're not paying attention," he mutters. "I was saying that I'm going to take Jay to talk to Dad, so we'll see you later … unless you wanna come."

I shrug and make a face. "No, I'm fine. Have fun."

Jay shoots me a look as if he wants me to go with him.

"Do you want me to go?" I ask him, feeling just a little bit bad about ditching him.

"You think I'm good?" he asks, needing reassurance.

"I think you're better than good," I say with a smile.

Stepping out of the other side of the tent, I decide to look for the bathroom before I talk to Nick. I need to calm myself down and figure out what I want to tell him.

"Hey, Bee," Nina says, walking over to me in her green dress.

"Hey, you look beautiful. It fits perfectly," I comment.

She smiles. "You too. Nick is looking ... oh, forget it, he's by the bathroom. He was looking for you."

"Thanks."

"Sooo ..." she says.

I roll my eyes and laugh. "Are you going to tell me not to give him a chance?" I ask.

She looks at me like I'm crazy. "Have you fucking seen him in that tux?"

I can't help it, I laugh. "You've been all woman power, we don't need men. What happened?"

"Uh ... Nick in a tux happened," Nina states obviously, then laughs. "I saw you guys dancing ... I think I was wrong about him."

I arch an eyebrow. "You gathered that from one dance?"

Nina hugs me. "Oh, Brooklyn, I gathered that from the look you gave each other at the club that night. I gathered that from the way you danced with him back then and from the way you spoke to each other at the studio when I went with you. It's just ... you. I dunno, you guys have that thing," she says into my neck. "I want you to be happy. I'm just scared that if anything happens and you're not, you'll ... you know."

"Spiral down? Become a drug addict ... again?" I say lightheartedly.

"Yes," she replies sadly, squeezing my hand. "I still want to kick his ass for lying to you, but maybe he didn't. I dunno. Shea seems to think he didn't," she adds with a shrug.

I smile. "You spoke to Shea about it?"

Nina narrows her eyes at me slightly but smiles. "Don't judge me! Shea and Nick are together like twenty-four seven, and Shea is a shit liar so he was bound to spill the beans if there were any to spill. I really think Nick means well, Bee. Just be careful though."

"I'll be fine," I whisper, smiling at her. Thankful that she cares enough about me to be a little sleuth and check on things for me.

Her brown eyes search mine before she kisses my cheek. "Good."

I take a breath and walk toward the bathrooms—they're off to one side in the pool cabana. Nick is leaning against the wall watching me as I walk up, his eyes leaving no part of me uncovered. I cross my arms over my chest, rubbing my arms to keep from shivering, even though I'm not physically cold. Nick kicks himself off the wall and strides toward me as I stop in front of the bathroom door.

"I'm going to-" I point at the bathroom.

He nods, his eyes boring into mine, as he continues to walk toward me. I turn around and open the bathroom door, my heart wild against my chest when I feel his chest against my back. I gulp loudly as he pushes us both inside the bathroom and closes the door behind us. His lips land on the back of my neck, creating a flurry of heat in my core. In an instant my breath is coming in heavily, my lids lowering as I look at our reflection in the mirror: the top of his light brown hair slowly making its way from my neck to my shoulders. He presses the front of my body into the vanity and bites behind my neck.

"I swear on all that is holy that if that fucking kid touches your ass one more time, I'm going to cut his hand off," Nick says, his voice husky as he nips along my exposed shoulder.

"Nick, stop," I say breathily, knowing that the sound of his voice and the words coming out of it will be my undoing if I let him continue. "We haven't talked about what happened."

"We'll talk soon," he says, his voice strained.

I want to leave it at that, but the thought that he's put those lips, MY lips, on another woman is driving me insane.

"Did you sleep with her?" I ask, hoping I don't need to specify. His mouth stills on my shoulder and he brings his eyes up to the mirror so they bore into mine.

He shakes his head, narrowing his eyes. "The fact that you can even think to ask me that tells me that you don't know how crazy I am about you."

I let out a relieved breath and nod, breathing heavily again when he places his lips on me, a little rougher this time. Smiling, I throw my head back so that he can kiss back up my neck.

"You are ... the most beautiful fucking woman I've ever seen, you know that?" he asks quietly as his hands pull up the silk skirt of my dress. He moves his hands up the back of my legs and palms my ass, rubbing slowly and biting my earlobe at the same time. "So beautiful," he whispers, moving his hand to my front and sliding it into my thong. He slips a finger inside me and begins to draw circles over my clit, my knees buckling at the feel of it.

"I want you out of this dress," he says, his ocean eyes connecting with mine in the mirror. I can see the depth of his desire in them and it makes me bite my lip and move against his fingers, wanting it as much as he does. "So hot," he groans as his eyes flutter closed and he bites down on his lip as his fingers find my spot, rubbing until he makes me come. He licks his fingers and turns my body around kissing me deeply, his tongue traveling along my mouth as I wrap my arms and legs around him, gripping the top of his hair and pulling his face closer to me, as if it were possible for him to ever be close enough. He sets me down on the sink and shrugs his jacket off, throwing it on the floor beside us before untying his black bow tie and unbuttoning his top button, breathing harshly as if he can't get enough air but looking at me like I'm more important.

He unbuckles his belt, dropping his pants and boxers to his knees and rips my thong off without second thought, making me squirm on the vanity. He chuckles at the surprise on my face and dips his head to devour my mouth again, inserting his fingers inside me as he does it.

"Why is he here with you, Brooklyn? Why is he touching you?" Nick asks, not able to let go of the fact that my date had his hand on my waist. His lips whisper soft kisses over my chest and he pulls down the shoulder-less part of my dress with his teeth, his tongue instantly swirling around my bare nipple.

"Oh, Nick," I breathe, throwing my head back when he thumbs over my clit again.

"Why, Brooklyn? Did you forget you were mine?" he asks, pulling my nipple into his mouth. "Do you need a reminder?"

I nod frantically, begging for a reminder from him, and he chuckles darkly, his eyes burning into mine. He drops his hand and swiftly replaces the loss of his fingers with his hard cock, making me gasp loudly at the feel oh him. He holds onto my hips as he drives into me.

"You're mine, Brooklyn," he says, his voice strained.

"Yes," I yelp when he begins to thrust harder, deeper.

"Tell me, baby," he demands in a whisper.

"I'm yours, Nick. Yours," I say, my voice hoarse as we look into each other's eyes.

He fucks me like he can't let me forget that he's the one inside of me. I wish I could tell him that he's erased the memory of anyone else ever being inside me before him.

He brings his lips to mine again, kissing me sweetly and slowing his pace to languid thrusts that don't let me breathe because of how good it feels.

"I don't want to live without you anymore," he says against my lips.

"Okay," I agree.

"Am I forgiven?" he asks, pulling all the way out of me.

"Yes," I whisper, but in my mind I'm screaming it.

He pushes all the way back in, making me arch my back and moan. "Awesome."

And that's how it feels when he takes me to ecstasy again.

We clean ourselves up and get dressed again. Nick shoves my underwear in his pocket and zips up his pants. I help him do his tie when he's done buttoning up.

"How did you learn how to do this?" he asks, his face perplexed as he watches me through the mirror.

"I lost a bet with Hendrix once," I respond as I finish the last loop and adjust his tie.

Nick chuckles. "Smart move on his part." He sighs when I lean up to place a small kiss on his throat, then pulls me to him and holds me tight.

"Why didn't you tell me about your label?" I ask in a whisper against his chest.

He drops his arms and steps away fro me, running a hand through his hair. His eyes stay on mine. "I wanted to, I just didn't know when or how. It's not even official yet, it's just something I'm working on and hope to have in the future."

Nodding, I bring my hands down from around his neck and grab both sides of the lapels of his jacket. "Please don't keep anything from me again," I ask. I know it's far-fetched. I know we'll never know every single crevice of each other's minds, and I don't want to, but I'd like to think we can get close to it.

"I promise you, Brooklyn. I will never keep anything from you again," Nick says, running the pad of his thumb over my cheek. "I promise you that I'll do anything in my power to make you smile every day, at least once a day."

That makes me smile. "Thank you," I say. "I promise the same."

"You already do," he says with a small smile, twirling the ends of my hair in his hand.

"Your eyes match my dress," I comment, smiling as I look into his eyes. They look more teal than aqua right now.

He raises an eyebrow, tilting his head toward me as we walk out of the bathroom. "Isn't that why you bought it?"

Laughing, I roll my eyes. "No."

"Sure," he says, not believing me, as he grabs my hand in his.

"I'm serious," I respond with a laugh.

"Of course you are," he replies cheekily.

"Brooklyn!" the shrill of my mother's voice interrupts us. I almost let go of Nick's hand out of habit, so she won't have any crap to talk about, but he squeezes it.

"Hi, Mom," I say, my voice monotone.

"I've been looking for you, there's someone I want you to meet," she says, looking at me, then Nick with curiosity in her eyes. She doesn't make a face, so I know she approves of him. I'm sure she's trying to figure out what I'm doing with him since he doesn't have the grungy look going and what he's doing with me since obviously he's much more good looking than I am. These are the things I decipher from the one surprised look she gives him.

"This is Nick Wilde, Mom. Nick, this is my mom, Roxana," I say as introduction.

My mother's eyebrows lift quickly. "Wilde. Michael and Mirielle's son?"

"Si," Nick responds.

My mom looks surprised again and I'm really beginning to

enjoy the way her eyebrows move, but the rest of her face stays unfazed due to the Botox. Then, she smiles, not one of her fake smiles, but a real smile. "Pleased to meet you," she says, extending her hand out, which Nick shakes.

"Likewise."

"Let me introduce you to my niece, Nina. Have you met her?" my mother asks, never fucking failing to make my stomach plummet one way or the other.

"Yes, I've met her a couple of times," Nick says.

"Oh," my mother says, curiosity in her voice.

I'm sure if she had enough nerves awake on her face she would be frowning at that. Clearly she doesn't understand why he would be interested in me, her own daughter, and not Nina the runway model lookalike that she wishes was her daughter.

Nick squeezes my hand again and runs his thumb over it soothingly. "I was just telling Brooklyn to get her things so that she could go home with me."

"Oh?" my mother comments, giving me a once over with a surprised look on her face.

"Yeah, forever," Nick says, his voice causing me to turn and look up at him. He's looking at me as he speaks. "She seems to think that running off and leaving me heartbroken is a good idea, so I decided that I'm going to take her home with me every single day to remind her that my heart beats only for her. That my day starts with her running through my mind and ends with her sleeping in my arms."

I have no idea why he is telling my mother this, but instead of feeling embarrassed about it, it makes me smile wider than I ever have before.

"Oh yeah?" I ask, completely forgetting that my mom is watching us.

"Definitely," he says, our bodies completely facing each

other now, not giving the air around us room to flow inside our bubble.

"What happens if I don't agree to go home with you every day?" I ask, unable to wipe the smile off my face.

"Then I guess you'll have to start taking me home with you," he says with a casual shrug.

"No running," I say.

"Not unless you want me to keep catching you," he murmurs, dipping his head to brush his lips against mine.

CHAPTER THIRTY

One month later ...

Allie decided to drop the lawsuit against me after Drew went after her with evidence that she violated our contract by selling my microphones to studios without my consent. The lovely thing about Fab Enterprises is that I had everything copyrighted in the beginning, so in doing that she pretty much screwed herself. I'm glad to put it behind me now. I had to end up paying her for a couple of things, but nothing like what she was asking for. And what I did pay her, I did just because I wanted to be nice, despite her trying to steal something I created and included her in years later.

Nick's hand closes over mine as he drives down the hills of San Francisco. We're on our way to his parents' house for lunch today. Michael took it upon himself to invite my parents over and invited us as well. I wouldn't have even known they were in town if it weren't for Nick telling me about the whole thing. Then again, I'm supposed to be in New York right now. I only flew in for the weekend because Nick and I hadn't seen each other since last week. Between Harmon and my microphones and Nick flying around to finish up Shea's album, which he's only putting finishing touches on, it's been impossible to be in the same city.

Nick holds my hand the entire time on the car ride over to his parents' house, even as we argue because he wants to listen to The Doors and I want to listen to John Mayer. He wants to ride with the windows down to enjoy the windy day; I wanted the windows up so that my hair didn't frizz. He wanted the air conditioning turned all the way up; I wanted it lowered from non-glacial temperatures. Through all of this, he holds my hand, and I wear a smile on my face, because I haven't had this much fun arguing with somebody in my life.

"We need to pick a city and stay there," Nick says, squeezing my hand. "No more of this not seeing each other for a week thing."

"What? You can't live without our bickering in your life?" I joke.

Nick's eyebrows rise as a grin spreads over his face. "Your bickering is one of the things I love most about you."

"Too bad that's a one way street," I say, laughing.

"Oh, really?" he counters, letting go of my hand and pinching my side, which makes me scoot toward the door with a yelp.

"Stop it!" I say, laughing. "At least we've been busy," I say, going back to his previous statement when he holds my hand again.

He lets go of my hand and tips my chin to look at him when we stop at a red light. "I'm never too busy for you, babe. Never."

The serious look on his face leaves no room for argument. I'm still coming to terms with the fact that he's so available to me, so there. Anytime I need to talk to him about anything, he picks up my calls. If he's busy in the studio, he sends me a text message asking me how I'm doing. Every morning, whoever wakes up first calls the other and every night we fall asleep with each other on the phone. It's something that I cherish since I've never gotten all of this attention—ever. Sometimes I don't know what to do with it. Not that I would ever complain.

"I know," I respond, trying to sound sure of it.

"I'm serious, Brooklyn. I'll never disappoint you."

His words fill my heart up with joy, and despite the fact that I'm a pro at dealing with loved ones disappointing me, I really hope Nick is right and I never feel that from him. His thumb grazes my lips and the side of my face before he drops his hand and continues driving.

"This is different than the last time you were here," he says after minutes of silence.

The last time I was here was when I left him for LA so I could deal with the lawsuit issue. I left with a broken heart; we both did, so I have to agree that it's very different. This time I know neither one of us will leave this or any city heartbroken.

"Very," I say with a relieved sigh.

This place will always hold dark memories for me, but Nick somehow manages to brighten them for me.

As soon as we pull up at his parents' house and step out of the car, we're greeted by an enthusiastic Mima. Her chubby arms wrap around Nick's waist as he hugs and picks her up slightly, making her squeal in contentment. When they're finished greeting each other, she moves over to me and hugs me tightly before kissing my cheek.

"I knew you'd be back," she says in a thick Spanish accent.

I laugh. "It was the rice and beans," I tell her jokingly, which makes her throw her head back in laughter.

"Wait until you try my Congrí," she states proudly.

Nick makes a sound that can only be described as blissful when he hears that, and it makes me smile wide. I make a mental note to ask Mima how to make that so that one day I can surprise him with it.

When we walk into the formal living room, I spot Mirielle, Michael, and my parents all talking animatedly. It's funny to see my mother beside Nick's. They don't really look that different in the way they're dressed, wearing linen pants and nice shirts, but their facial expressions as they greet us are night and day. Mirielle's smile is bright and contagious. She's genuinely happy to see me here with her son. My mother's, on the other hand, is fake. I wish I had the guts to point that out in front of people, but she's my mother and I would never do that. We say hello to them and my father stays hugging me to his side as we walk over to the dining room.

"I think you did the right thing with Allie," my father comments quietly as we reach the table.

I smile my appreciation and he nods back, giving me a kiss on the forehead as he takes his place next to the Ice Queen.

Throughout the meal, we all speak about different things, my dad questions Nick about producing and how he feels about the turnout of Shea's album, which Nick insists is a Grammy winner.

Michael visibly rolls his eyes at the statement and says, "We'll see. Nicky may never catch up to me."

"Or he'll surpass you," I say with a shrug as I take a sip of my wine.

I can handle being bashed because that's all I know from my parents, but Nick doesn't deserve it. I'm coming to terms with the fact that I don't either. Nick is really helping me see that I am a great person and deserve as much as everybody else that works their butt off.

I can see the smile on Nick's face from the corner of my eye, but my eyes are on his father's shocked face. Michael raises an eyebrow at my retort.

"Maybe he will." His eyes stay on me as he speaks. "So, Chris, what are you going to do if Brooklyn leaves Harmon to go help Nicky with his label?"

Nick's hands grip his utensils tightly and his chewing slows down. I can tell he's uncomfortable with the question, and I'm not sure why, but I'm not. Nick and I have spoken about it but not in any serious way. He asks me all the time to quit my job and go work for him so that we can be together all the time, but I laugh it off. I don't doubt that he would want me to work with him, but he's cautious in the way he says it, probably because of what just happened to me with Allie. Or maybe because he's scared that if he pushes me too quickly, I would bolt.

My dad lifts an eyebrow, but smiles as he looks at me. He opens his mouth to say something, but my mother cuts him off.

"Why would she do that? She's successful at Harmon, it has her last name and she has her own company. If she wanted she could start her own label—she wouldn't have to partner with Nick or anybody else," she says, her voice determined.

She's looking directly into her wine glass as she speaks and takes a gulp of it when she's finished. I'm stunned that she stood up for me and complimented me all in one sentence. A part of me wonders how painful it must have been for her to throw me a bone, but mostly I'm just shocked that she said anything positive about me at all, even if it was to one-up our hosts.

"You're completely right," Mirielle chimes in. "Brooklyn is a very talented woman in her own right."

"I never said she wasn't," Michael argues. "It was just a question."

My dad puts his hand over my mother's on the table and

smiles at me. "I agree with Roxy. Brooklyn doesn't have to do that, but if she decided she wanted to, I would wish her nothing but the best. Nick's a smart kid and he has that drive … reminds me of myself at his age."

The compliment doesn't sit well in my stomach. I love my father, but I don't want to marry my father. Not that I'm going to marry Nick, but I know I want him in my life for the long run, that's not a question. So I hope he doesn't turn out to be a workaholic that ignores his children and just throws money their way, thinking it'll make all their problems disappear.

"Nonsense, Chris, you were much cockier than Nick," my mother adds, winking at me.

Winking at me. And then she smiles, a genuine smile, the one she uses on my father and brother at times. For a moment I swear I'm seeing things, but when I blink, it's still on her face and I see a glint of pride in her eyes. The sixteen-year-old me wants to shed tears of happiness at the moment. My twenty-five-year-old self takes it for what it is and is glad she's somewhat proud of me today. I'm sure tomorrow she'll find something new to bitch about. But for today, I'll take the pride and the smile. I smile back, just as genuinely.

The rest of the visit goes as well as it can. Michael tones down his condescending-ness a notch and talks about how proud he is of Nick, despite "being a hard ass to him." Nick and I step outside and share a swinging wooden bench that lets us enjoy the cool breeze as we look at the foggy bay. Placing my head on Nick's chest, I take a thankful, cleansing breath, closing my eyes and letting myself enjoy the moment.

"What's up, guys?" Isaac's voice booms.

I open my eyes and smile at him. "Hey, Isaac."

"Hey. I didn't know you were coming," Nick says. "Good thing we didn't leave right after dinner."

"Well, if you would check your phone you would see I texted you back," Isaac counters.

"Well, as you can see, I'm kind of enjoying my life right now. I don't have time for cellphones," Nick responds back, making me shake my head with a smile. "Is Damien in town?" he asks. Damien hasn't been around today, but I know he lives in LA. Nick's question makes me wonder how often they come visit their parents.

Isaac shrugs. "Doubt it. He's working on a movie. You know how he gets when he works."

Nick nods. "Yeah, he doesn't know how to take a break."

Isaac scoffs. "Unless it's for a woman."

Nick laughs in agreement.

"You guys gonna be in town for a while?" Isaac asks as he takes a seat on one of the big rocks in front of us.

"Nah, Brooklyn has to leave soon, so I'm going with her," Nick says.

"You doing good?" Isaac asks, his blue eyes looking directly into mine, searching.

"Better than good," I respond with a smile.

Isaac smiles and runs his fingers through his long black hair, throwing it back out of his eyes. "Good," he says, nodding slowly and looking around before bringing his attention back to us. "So ... you guys wanna go to a comic book convention while you're here? I have tickets ..."

Nick and I both laugh at Isaac's awkwardness and turn down his offer, though we do humor him in discussing some super heroes, or rather letting him discuss the super heroes.

By the time Nick and I leave, we're ready for a nap, so we head back to his place and take one: Nick, Scooby, and me.

"What will you do with Scoobs if you move to New York?" I ask, testing the waters on that subject.

Nick smiles, leaning down and pressing his lips against mine. "When I move to New York," he corrects. "I guess I'll take him. Unless Isaac wants to keep him for a while; Damien is way too busy for a dog."

I nod against him, adjusting myself closer into the side of his body, letting out a sigh of content at the feel of his warmth against me.

"Mmm … I never want to let you out of my arms," he murmurs against me, breathing me in.

"Then don't," I reply, and I mean it.

CHAPTER THIRTY-ONE

I'm rushing, bouncing down the hall on one foot, trying to walk and put my other heel on at the same time as I try to hurry in Nick's Manhattan apartment, which I'm now sharing with him.

"Babe, you're going to hurt yourself," Nick says, tearing off his headphones and looking at me over his cup of coffee.

"Jay's manager is calling me in twenty minutes and I want to be sitting at my desk when he does," I say, leaning on the kitchen counter and finally putting the shoe on correctly.

Nick puts his cup down and cocks his head to one side as he watches me, his eyes scanning my body slowly. "Is that a new dress?" he asks.

I frown, looking down at my fitted plum dress. "No."

"Why haven't you worn it before?" he asks, rounding the counter to stand in front of me.

I make to move past him so that I can pour my coffee, but he blocks me and runs the tips of his fingers along my cleavage, causing me to shiver.

"Nick," I protest, but there's a moan in my voice as I speak his name.

"Brooklyn," he mimics in a breath, his voice caressing my name as he whispers soft kisses from my neck to my collarbone.

I throw my head back, my breathing coming in ragged. "I have to go."

"Hmm," he murmurs against me as he continues to place openmouthed kisses over my chest and the small hills of my cleavage.

My phone rings suddenly, making us both groan in protest, but Nick straightens and walks over to the living room, his bare feet padding on the hardwood. He plops down on the couch as I answer the phone, thankful that it's only Hendrix.

"Hey, I'm going over there now," I say, before he can bitch me out and walk to the living room, picking up my cup of coffee on the way over.

"Brooklyn," Hendrix says, his voice eerily quiet, the sound of it making an uneasy rattle shake over me.

"Wha-" I start, but the gossip channel on the television stops me short.

Breaking News: Shea Roberts' body found unresponsive due to apparent overdose.

I stare at the television in disbelief. My brother's frantic voice is in my ear, but I can't understand him. I register Nick's body moving from the couch. I hear him scream in horror, but I can't tear my eyes away from the TV. The words are screaming at me, bleeding through the screen for me. Flashbacks of Ryan sitting up on the bed with the needle sticking out of his arm circulate my memory. The grayness of his lifeless body, the distant look in his eyes, his cold, cold skin. Empty sobs threaten as I open my mouth, gasping as my hands begin to shake uncontrollably before they go numb and I drop the phone and coffee mug. I watch it fall, shattering and splotching coffee everywhere. It all happens in slow motion. I see it but I'm not there to take it all in.

"No, no, no, no, no, no, no, no, nooooo," I finally manage in an animalistic voice that isn't mine. "Please no!" I gasp out, painfully pulling on my hair as my chest heaves and I shiver uncontrollably. Nick's arms wrap around me, clutching me so tight that I can barely breathe.

"No!" I shout again, pleading with him, with anybody, needing somebody to assure me that this isn't real. Refusing to believe that Shea ... refusing to accept what the reports are saying because they're not true. They can't be.

"Baby," Nick says, squeezing me harder, his own voice hoarse and laced in pain. "Let's find out what's going on, let me call Darius, come with me so we can call Darius." He's pleading, his own body beginning to shake slightly, and I know he's trying to keep it together maybe for me, maybe for himself, but that ounce of hurt, of disbelief in his voice is my downfall. His obvious pain is what makes mine pour out of me, raking out of me in gasping, panting sobs.

Nick takes out his cellphone with one shaky hand as the other continues to hold my body against his, and dials Darius's number. It rings. Rings. Rings. Rings and Nick shouts a string of curses when it goes to voicemail. My mind drifts to Ryan again, to his lifeless body, and I picture Shea. I picture myself walking into Shea's room and finding him sitting up the way I found Ryan, with a needle sticking out of his arm, mute to my questions and my pleading. Somehow, even with Nick's grip on me, my shaking body manages to slip out of his hold and down to the floor.

Nick holds my arm to stand me up, but I jerk away from

his touch and crawl to the barstool where my purse is, pulling on the strap so that all its contents spill all over the floor. I pick up my phone, the screen blurry through my eyes, and see the missed calls I have from Shea's phone. I look at my two new voice messages, also from Shea, the time stamp on them tell me they're from last night.

"Brooklyn," Nick says, crouching down beside me.

I can't bring myself to look at him as I press the playback button and hold my trembling hand to my ear.

"Hey, Bee, it's me, come out with me today," Shea's voice says into my ear, his deep velvety voice.

My eyes are fresh with new tears when I bring myself to look at Nick's ashen face. "Is it?" he asks brokenly, unable to form the question.

I nod and continue playing the messages as my chest painfully constricts within me.

"I miss you, Bee. Come out with me. It's lonely for a playa out here," Shea says, sounding drowsy. *"Bring Shadow, I miss my brother."*

My mouth falls open as tears cascade down my cheeks as I hear Shea's pleads and watch the pain stab Nick's eyes as he listens on.

"He called," I whisper. "And I wasn't there for him." I failed him, I want to say. I failed another friend, I want to scream, but don't. Nick opens his mouth, his eyes filling with tears as he leans forward and pulls my head onto his shoulder, both of us shaking, holding onto each other, as we commiserate over our heartache.

Nick's phone rings between us and we both pull away quickly, desperate for an answer. "Darius," Nick says in greeting, swiping the escaped tears under his lids with his thumb. "We just heard," he says, his blue eyes never wavering from mine as he speaks. He reaches for my hand and squeezes it. I squeeze back, holding my breath.

"She's here," Nick says, his thumb rubbing over my gripped hand. Nick's eyes widen. "We're heading over now," he says, hanging up the phone and taking off my heels as he stands us up. "Shea's in Lenox Hill," he says, cupping my face tightly so that I look at him.

"I can't," I say, my voice breaking. "I can't see him like that," I finish in a hoarse whisper. "I can't see him dead." I shake my head in refusal. I can't see the only friend I have left. I can't bear to acknowledge that I'm the only person in our trio that's left. I can't bring myself to accept that Shea won't call me to bother me about a new musician he found or about a song he wrote. I can't.

"Baby, listen to me," Nick says, blinking away the tears that threaten to spill out of his own eyes. "Shea is in a coma, which is better than what we thought and he's at Lenox, you have to see him. When you were in rehab, who went to see you?"

I shake my head slowly, clamping my mouth closed as tears fall down my cheeks again. "Mmmmm," I voice, still shaking my head.

"You're my best friend, Shea. You can't get rid of me. Haven't you learned that by now?" I ask quietly.

His eyes glisten. "You're more than my best friend, Brooklyn," he whispers. "You're family," Shea continues ...

"I can't, Nick!" I shout as he holds me in a tight hug. "I can't do it. I can't do it!" I squirm to get out of his hold.

"Brooklyn, listen to me," Nick demands in a whisper against my hair. "We're going to go because if we don't and something bad happens, we're going to regret it for the rest of our lives," he says, letting go of me and holding me at arms' length. "Do you want to live your life with regrets?" he asks, swallowing.

"I already do," I respond. "I already fucking do!" I shout in a sob.

I've come to accept that Ryan's death happened and there's nothing I can do about it, you can either break or move on from something so impactful. I chose to rise. I chose to move on even though it haunts me, but moving on doesn't mean letting go and it doesn't mean living life with no regrets. I'll regret not getting back earlier, not looking into his room sooner, not sleeping beside him, not talking him out of drugs that night. That burden is mine to live with, mine to carry, and even though it's become lighter over the years, it's still there. It always will be.

"Ryan wasn't your fault!" Nick shouts back. "It wasn't your fault!" he repeats, holding me close again. "Stop blaming yourself, Brooklyn."

"Shea called last night," I whisper. "He fucking called me and I was too busy to acknowledge his goddamn phone call, Nick," I cry.

He inhales deeply, his breath tickling my ear when he lets it out. "Baby, your friend is in the hospital. My friend is in the hospital. He needs us," he says, his strong voice wavering, and I know he's right. I know I have to go even if what we find scares me, but at least I'll have Nick with me.

"Okay, let's go," I agree. He scoops me up in his arms and takes me to our room, putting me down on our bed and disappearing into the closet. I watch as he comes back out carrying a pair of flats. He crouches down in front of me and wordlessly puts them on my feet before carrying me out of the apartment and to the car.

The ride to the hospital is quiet. Nick nervously chews on his fingernails as he drives, and I alternate between staring out the window, wondering how such horrible news can be delivered on such a pretty day. As we drive by the park, I watch the orange autumn leaves fall from the trees, the horses that walk around us carrying laughing families and happy couples, all of them oblivious to the palpable pain in our car; all of them unmoved, their lives unchanged by the news that our friend is hooked up to monitors. The mental image makes me shiver as tears fill my eyes yet again.

When we pull up to the hospital, Nick hands the keys over to the valet and drags me out of the car, away from the reporters standing outside, and pulls me into the automatic doors, into the building that hold answers I'm not ready for. Once we check in and get our guest passes, we take the elevators to the ICU and see a flurry of big bodyguards swarm past us. I catch sight of a somber Gia in the middle of them and attempt to call out her name, but fail. My voice gets clogged in my throat along with every other intestine that has managed to lodge itself there.

"Gia," Nick says, making her turn around. She looks numb, scared as she shakes her head.

"I can't," she mouths before turning around to walk away, her slim body getting lost in the protective front the men have built around her. My heart picks up the pace, assuming the worst—he died. Shea died.

"Oh my God," I say to Nick in a panic, looking around the white halls that threaten to close in on me.

Don't break down.

Don't break down.

Don't break down.

Don't break down.

"Rye, I thought you would be sleeping," I said, walking over to the window and opening the top layer of his curtains. I glanced at him over my shoulders and felt not as if my heart fell through

my chest, but everything in my body just plummeted all at once at the sight of him.

"Ryan?" I shrieked, running to him with wide eyes that were already welling up with tears. He looked gray. Lifeless. He was sitting up in bed but looked more like a stone sculpture than himself. I knew. I just knew. A majestic blue band was wrapped tightly around his bicep and his arms were laying over his crossed legs, his face hanging down over his chest, the needle in his right hand ...

My heart feels like it's being pounded on with a knife repeatedly. "I can't," I say to Nick, yanking my hand from his. Nick grabs by hand again, but I plant my legs to the ground, bending my knees and pulling the opposite way. "I can't," I shout. "I can't. I can't," I repeat it over and over as sobs begin to rake through me and water spills out of my eyes without my consent.

I hear Nick sigh loudly as he wraps his arms around me, holding me tight and moving me out of the hall into a dark nook by the stairwell.

"Look at me, Brooklyn," Nick says, his voice firm but quiet.

I shake my head defiantly.

"Look at me," he demands. "We're going to find out what's going on, okay? If we can see him, I'll go in before you or we can go together," he says.

I blink. Blink. And wipe my eyes as I take a deep breath. "Okay," I croak.

"He needs you to be strong for him," Nick says, his voice wavering. He pinches my chin with his fingers so that I look at him. His eyes are etched with pain, full of quiet turmoil as he consoles me. "I need you to be strong for me," he emphasizes gravely.

That makes me cry harder. Nick pulls me into him, letting

me bury my face in his chest as he wraps his strong arms around me, offering me whatever strength he has. When I feel like I can breathe again, I nod my head and step away.

"Okay. Okay. I can do this," I say in a chant as Nick takes a hold of my face, wiping my tears with his thumbs. When he drops his hands, I close my eyes and begin inhaling deep breaths. *God, please, please, please, help my friend. Please help him. I promise I'll do whatever I need to do, just please help him. Please don't take him from me. I'll give you whatever you want. Just please help him. Please save him. Please let him be okay.*

A sense of calm envelops me and I peel my eyes open and look at Nick, who has both arms over his head and his own eyes closed, his lips slightly parted. He remains unmoving as I wrap my arms around the middle of his body and lay my head on his chest.

"I love you," I murmur quickly against him. I don't care that he hasn't said it. I don't care if he doesn't say it now, but I realize that life is so precious, so fragile, and being in this situation cements that further for me.

He lets out a breath and wraps his arms around me tightly. "I love you too, baby. So much," he murmurs, kissing the top of my head. "Are you ready?"

I sniffle, dropping my arms from him and taking a step back. "Are you?" I ask quietly.

He looks at me for a long moment, searching my eyes, taking something from me and replacing it with something of his own. He runs the pads of his thumbs over my cheeks. "If you're with me, yes."

"Always."

Nick gives me a small smile and pulls me back to the hallway, walking us to Shea's room. Despite feeling ready, I take another deep breath when we reach the door and are told we can walk in because Shea's mother stepped out. I walk in, my eyes filling with new tears when I see him lying in the middle of the room with an IV hooked up to his arm. My first thought is: he's alive. I let out a breath because of it. Nick's hand squeezes mine, and I squeeze back before letting go and walking up to Shea's bed. He looks like he's sleeping. His tattooed arms are both facing upward, the one to my right has needle marks on it, each one of them picking at my heart, threatening to break it again.

I take a seat in the chair beside his bed and hold his hand, laying my head over his forearm and caressing his Brooklyn tattoo as I cry over him.

"You promised me," I cry in a whisper. "You promised you weren't using. You promised ..."

When the door squeaks open, I turn my head in that direction, blurrily making out his mom standing there.

"Oh, Brooklyn," Maria cries as she walks over to me.

We cling to each other, both of us giving each other the strength we need to get through this for the broken boy we love.

"They're saying he had different things in his system," Maria explains, wiping her nose once we're sitting down calmly.

I shake my head. "He said he wasn't using. He promised," I whisper brokenly, looking at Nick, who hasn't said anything to us the entire time, just staring at Shea. He's standing beside the bed, speaking to him softly.

"Well, he did," Maria says. "He's under so much pressure."

I have a million things to scream to her about that but I don't. Instead I choose to stay quiet for the remainder of the visit, doing what I do best: wallowing. I sit there for what feels like an eternity, but I don't mind because I know death knows no time. Shea is wheeled in and out of the room countless times as Nick and I huddle in a corner, speaking only when

Maria or Darius talk to us as we stare at the center of the room in disbelief.

"Babe, we have to eat something," Nick says finally. My eyes graze over the clock on the wall and the slightly open door, wondering if Father Time will appear through them, not wanting to move in case he does.

"I'm not hungry," I respond in a small voice.

Darius calls out to somebody—I'm assuming the other bodyguard—when we hear chaotic voices down the hall. He steps out and speaks to somebody, my ears perking up at the sound of my brother's voice. I want to find the will to stand, to see him, but I can't, energy doesn't reside in my body.

"Oh my God," Nina screeches as she squeezes her way inside, her bloodshot eyes scanning the room before staying on me as she makes her way over and wraps her arms tightly around me. The false bravado I've been trying to put on for the past couple of hours falls away from me. Leaning into her, I begin to sob loudly again, letting her rock me as she sobs along with me. Soon I feel my brother's arms wrap around us, holding us all together.

"They took him to run tests?" Hendrix asks.

I nod, or try to, beneath them, my chest raking in anguish, not allowing me to respond clearly.

"Yeah, CAT scan, MRI. They wheeled him out a while ago, he should be back soon," Nick responds.

"He's gonna die," I cry as my shoulders shake. "He's gonna die just like Ryan."

"He's not going to die!" Nina says adamantly, stepping away from me and drying the tears from her eyes. Her hair is in a messy bun and her face has no makeup, she looks completely unlike herself. "He can't just die," she says with a troubled frown as her eyes glisten with new tears. Nina's dealt with death, but never like this, never actually had to look at it in the face and acknowledge that it can take your loved ones without your opinion or consent.

"He called me last night," I say, crying again.

Hendrix pulls me into his arms, squeezing me. "It's not your fault, Brooklyn. This is not your fault."

"If I would have picked up the phone …" I start.

"It's my fault," Nick says, making my head snap to where he's standing. He pulls on his hair and walks over to me, pinching my chin and tilting my head to look at him. His ocean eyes are turbulent as he pins me with them, making me see them, making me feel them. "If you're going to blame yourself, you might as well blame me. He called me too, he asked me to go too, so if you're going to believe it's your fault, you might as well blame me for insisting we go to bed early. Blame me for telling you to stop looking at your phone for a goddamn night so that you could rest. Blame life for being so short or drugs for having the ability to give you false hope. But I won't let you blame yourself, Brooklyn, not this time, because whatever happens here, whatever happens with Shea," he says, his voice breaking, "I'm not losing you."

I look at the floor, at my feet, at the T's on my designer flats, training my mind to calm down, my emotions to neutralize, but it's no use. When Nick clasps his hand behind my neck and pulls me into his chest, I lose it again, bawling into him, letting him soak my tears.

"I love you, Brooklyn. I can't lose you," Nick says in a low hoarse voice. "We need to be strong. We need to have faith that he'll pull through."

"He will," Nina cries. "He'll pull through. Shea's too much of a pain in the ass to give up." Her voice waivers and gets lost in sobs, and that's how the nurses find us when they wheel Shea back in. They don't even bother to tell us to leave or that there's a visitation limit. I think our tenacity is painted all over our faces. Until Shea comes back to us, we're not moving. Flowers and balloons with sentiments are continuously brought in, but we don't need to bring any of that for Shea because for him, we are the flowers. We are the reminder that we're here for him. We are the voices of each one of his fans, the ones standing outside of the hospital with signs pleading for him to be okay. And if he would just peel his eyes open, he would see that the family he's so desperately searching for, the people that would never abandon him, have been here all along.

CHAPTER THIRTY-TWO

My eyes open to a darkness that matches my sentiments. Sighing, I inch closer to the edge of the bed, gliding out of Nick's arms and the plush comforter, unable to lie here any longer. Striding past Nick's sleeping figure, I notice the indecent time on the clock before my eyes land on Nick again. I should be sleeping in those sculpted arms right now instead of awake and walking toward the kitchen, but it's no use. The more I toss and turn, the higher chance I'll wake him and he needs sleep too. Once I serve myself a cup of coffee, I walk over to the massive windows of the guest bedroom and sit on the floor in front of the glass. Lowering my cup from my mouth, I run my fingertips over the condensation of the windows, tracing waves over it to clear the haze outside. The day seems to be waking up as foggy as my mind feels, the beauty of the city wrapped up in clouds of grey.

My fingers brush over my phone, the device that's become even more of an appendage in the last two days. I'm itching to call the hospital for an update on Shea. The last time I checked was a couple of hours ago, and even though his mother hasn't left his bedside and the nurse on rotation has my phone number, I feel that I need to call, just in case. The MRI they did yesterday showed a lot of brain activity, which they say is a good sign, but still that little word *miracle* keeps being thrown out there, which scares the shit out of me. It's not that I don't believe in miracles, it's just that I know enough to know they don't come true for everybody. He deserves that miracle, he deserves a chance at life, at love. But so did Ryan. What is it about survival that makes me feel so guilty? Is it the fact that I feel that even though I'm successful, I feel like I haven't accomplished enough? Or is because I have things that Ryan never got a chance to have?

After contemplating but not calling, I decide to crawl into the guest bed and see if sleep consumes me here. I feel bad because Nick has been nothing but great to me and I know he's suffering too, but there's no reasoning with me when the bleakness takes over. There are no answers I can give myself that will be good enough to numb the pain.

When the charcoal clouds begin growing inside of me, letting the darkness saturate all the light I know is there, I shut down. I don't do it on purpose, it just happens. And I hate it. I hate that it happens. I hate losing the wind that normally sails me through the days. I hate losing myself in the stillness of my sadness. Because that's all I become—sadness.

I turn on my side when the door clicks open and Nick appears in the room only wearing basketball shorts. His chest is glistening, his hair is wet, and the smell of the men's Dove body wash he uses hits me, letting me know he just showered. He doesn't say anything as he makes his way over and sits beside me on the bed. Letting out a breath, he begins to run his fingers soothingly through my hair slowly, twirling the ends.

"You have to get out of here, babe," he says, his eyes in pain as he looks at me.

"For what?" I ask, humoring him, even though I don't want to hear his answer.

"Because I need you," he states simply, ruffling the hair on my scalp and laying beside me, turning our bodies toward each other.

Tears well up in my eyes. "I'm so scared," I admit in a whisper, looking into his eyes.

"Me too," he answers back, then grabs my hand, holding onto my fingers and running them over his side, where his song notes lay. "I have something to show you."

He circles his arms around me and pulls me from the bed with him, walking me to the living room. I groan and shut my eyes when the sliver of light coming through the blinds hits me. Nick chuckles knowingly as he sits me on the couch and grabs his guitar.

"You wrote it?" I ask, my eyes darting to his tattoo.

"I did," he responds, tilting his head as he strums the chords of the guitar to a song I haven't heard. The sound makes my throat close with emotion.

"*Yes, I'm someone new. That doesn't mean I'm gonna hurt you. Yes, I'm a mess, that doesn't mean I'm trying to fix you,*" he croons softly. His raspy voice makes me want to close my stinging eyes, but the intensity he's looking at me with makes me keep them open.

"*You could stay in the darkness, let the dark become the day. I say don't wait, come over here. I know I wrote these words,*" he smiles slightly, pausing, "*and that might mean I'm gonna love you. If you should know anythiiing, it's that you light me up. You light me up. You could say that you're too scared, but I'm just as scared as you, please, just see me through, come over here. I'll be heeere, when you're ready for me. I'll be here when you're ready for me. I'll be here when you're ready for me,*" he finishes, letting his voice drift with the strums of the guitar.

I feel like he's singing to the darkness that resides inside of me, the one that doesn't let me just be sometimes, and that makes me cry harder.

Nick puts the guitar down on the floor beside him and catches me when I throw myself into his arms, cocooning myself into a ball as he holds me and kisses my head, repeatedly telling me how much he loves me.

"I'm sorry," I whisper when I finish crying. "That was beautiful. Which verse are your notes on?" I ask, wiping my tears away with the backs of my hand.

He holds my face and kisses my lips softly, deeply, then picks the guitar back up and sings, "*You could say that you're too scared, but I'm just as scared as you, please just see me through, come over here.*"

Through tears, I smile. "That's a great line," I whisper.

"It's Paige's song now," Nick says as he puts the guitar down.

"Chaplin?" I ask, perking up just a little. God, I love that woman's voice. I wonder how she sounds singing the song.

Nick makes a face at me, seemingly reading my thoughts. "Yes, and she sings it better, but I wanted to play it for you."

Leaning forward, I kiss him chastely. "You sing good too," I say, letting him wrap his arms around me.

The phone rings shortly after, making me jump out of his hold and run to it, sliding my finger across it. "Hello?" I say, frantically.

"He's awake!" Maria says, laughing, crying, and yelling at the same time.

I gasp loudly, my heart beginning to beat quickly again. "He's awake!" I announce to Nick, screaming with a smile. "Does he know where he is? Does he remember you? Can he talk?" I ask Maria these questions all at once and then cut off her answers by telling her we're on our way.

I arrive at the hospital feeling as if I'm walking on clouds. I don't see anybody, hear anybody, but this time it's because my heart is bursting with gratitude. I thank God a gazillion times and tell him that I knew he would come through for me, then promise that I'll make it to church every Sunday from now on, and hope I make good on my word. I have to figure out what religion I am before deciding what church I'll end up in, I guess.

"BK," Shea croaks when I walk into his room.

Rushing to his bed, I throw my arms around him, sobbing as I rock him, just like I did to my best friend all those years ago. This time in between I love yous, I say thank you and I'm going to kill you for almost killing yourself as Shea laughs and cries with me.

"You promised," I say hoarsely, not caring that I sound like a belligerent toddler.

"I know. I'm sorry," Shea responds sheepishly.

"I almost want to kill you for putting us through that shit," Nick chimes in, scooting a chair beside Shea and me.

Shea's shoulders slump as he looks at Nick. "Sorry, bro. I fucked up."

"I'm just glad you're okay," Nick says leaning forward and putting his arm around Shea, hugging him tight before letting go to sit down again.

"I'm going to get help," Shea says, nodding his head. "I am. They're keeping me here longer now that I'm awake. I didn't try to kill myself, Bee. You know that, right? I wouldn't do that."

I let out a long, relieved exhale. "But you still almost died. You did die, Shea. They had to pump your stomach. Do you know how fucking scared I was? All I could think about was-"

"Ryan," Shea finishes, holding my hand in his. "I know,

Bee. I'm sorry."

The three of us sit there for a while: Shea holding my right hand, Nick holding my left, and me thanking God for giving us the opportunity to have second chances, because not everybody is this lucky. Nick gets up suddenly and tells me he's going to get us coffee. I smile thankfully before placing both of my hands over Shea's.

"I saw Gia," I whisper, inching my chair closer to his bed. I don't tell him that I haven't seen her around ever since the day he was brought in.

Shea exhales a dark laugh. "My mom called her to tell her I was awake and she said Gia was happy but said she wasn't coming back because she had a tour to finish."

My mouth falls open. "She's just going to go on tour? Without you? Just like that?" I ask in disbelief.

He lets out a dark laugh. "Funny thing about people, Bee, when you're up, they're all over you. When you're down, they don't give a shit about you." He shrugs.

Even though he's completely right about that, it kills me to hear that he feels that way. I hate that Gia is one of those women and I hate that Shea can take it with such ease, probably because he knew that to begin with. Still, I make a mental note to call the bitch and give her hell for this.

"I'm sorry," I offer quietly, lowering my eyes.

He squeezes my hand, making me bring my eyes back to his. "Hey, there's nothing to be sorry for. The only person I need is here." His eyes are sad, but truthful, and although it's supposed to make me feel better, my heart cracks a little more.

I exhale. "Always, Shea. I'm just scared me being here for you won't be enough."

"Moms says Leo and Fern have been coming. They'll be back," he says.

"You know what I mean," I mutter.

"I know," he whispers, tracing my jaw with his fingers. "It makes me happy to see you happy though, BK. It really does."

Blinking my eyes rapidly, I hold his hand on my face to still it. If he keeps talking, I'm going to cry again. "Thank you. It means a lot to hear you say that."

"What are best friends for?" he says with a smile, and it's a genuine smile. I return it. He drops his hand when Nick walks back in the room with two cups of coffee in his hand. "You're a lucky motherfucker, Shadow. You better not fuck this up."

Nick chuckles, shaking his head. "I wouldn't dream of it," he responds, looking directly at me.

The nurse Shea was waiting for comes in and wheels him out to run some tests, leaving Nick and I alone in the room. He sits in the chair opposite of me and places the cups on the table beside us before leaning in and tugging a lock of my hair.

"Have I told you how beautiful you are today?" he asks.

I smile, shaking my head.

"Well, you are," he says. "And you have the most amazing green eyes I've ever seen."

"Thank you," I whisper, thinking the same about his ocean eyes, the ones I now know hold a lot of sharks in it, but I don't care. I'll happily jump in them and let them take a chunk out of me, like they do every day. Tearing my eyes away from him, I look back at the monitors in the room, remembering a time that I was in one similar. I wonder if Shea will really seek help and if he'll be able to stay drug free. I know it's not easy to do, and it scares me that he'll probably want to go right back to his tour.

"Are you sure everything will be okay?" I ask Nick in a whisper.

He scoots his chair closer to mine so that our knees are

touching and cups my face. "No, babe, I'm not, but that's the beauty of life," he says, drawing circles over my cheeks. "The only thing I'm sure about is us."

And then he puts his mouth on mine, and I let myself fall.

Nick,
All I need—AWOLNATION
Love,
Brooklyn

PLAYLIST

I Don't Feel it Anymore (Song of the Sparrow)—William Fitzsimmons

Tell Her This—Del Amitri

Hit the Ground—Paige Chaplin (paigechaplin.bandcamp.com)

Ready—Paige Chaplin*

Sober—Pink

Everlong—Foo Fighters

Farewell—Rosie Thomas

All I Want—Kodaline

Trouble—Ray LaMontagne*

One and Only—Adele

Global Concepts—Robert DeLong*

We Found Love—Rihanna*

Hopeless Wanderer—Mumford & Sons

Dreaming With a Broken Heart—John Meyer

Gravity—John Meyer

Say Something—A Great Big World

Mercury—Sleeping At Last

Homesick—Sleeping At Last

Connect—Drake*

Wrecking Ball—Miley Cyrus

Young and Beautiful—Lana Del Rey

Skyscraper—Demi Lovato

EXTRA

"You know what I love about life?" she asks in a whisper. I turn her in my hold so that I can look at her when she speaks. I love seeing the way her full lips move and her green eyes light up or dim down, depending on what she's talking about. Right now they're dim and that peaks my interest, I never know where her head is when her eyes get that faraway look in them, but I can guess. I don't mind it though, it doesn't bother me that she's a little torn up as long as she lets me help with the stitching.

We've been lying in our bungalow in Maldives for the past two days, away from our chaotic lives. I'd never been here, but she's told me how much my eyes remind her of this water, so I decided to bring her. She's only looked at the water once since we got here, the rest of the time she's spent looking at me. I would pay the fortune I spent getting here to come back here every week just to have her do that.

"What's that, baby?" I ask, my hands moving from her tangled up hair to the curve of her waist. I can't get enough of touching her.

"How beautiful it is, how tragic it is," she responds, her eyes are on mine, but have that distant look in them

"You know what I love about life?" I ask, smiling when she frowns slightly. "Having you in it every day."

I watch her the clouds in her eyes dissipate and her lips curl up as she lets me response sink in. She sits up, letting her body fall against mine, and I catch her.

Shea

3 years later

My hands are sweaty. It always happens right before I go on stage. When the arenas dim the lights and the crowd goes wild in anticipation. That's when the adrenaline kicks in. This is a different kind of appearance, though. This isn't a tour, or a private performance, or a showcase at a radio show where I spit my rhymes and let them praise me. This is probably the most important thing I've ever done in my life (aside from being the godfather of Brooklyn and Nick's little boy). This is me opening up to a group of people who were harsher than any blogger, music journalist, or fellow rapper would ever be. This is me, standing in the front of a shoulder-to-shoulder room full of college kids, not rapping, not singing, but talking about my life.

I had an aha moment a couple of years ago after getting out of rehab for what feels like the billionth time in my life, but was really only the second. I'd done a stint when I was a teenager, a couple of years after I got into the music business. Back then, we'd told the press that I was there to rest, that mental exhaustion and too many responsibilities had gotten the best of me. It wasn't a complete lie. When I got out, I stayed sober for a while, until I didn't. Until I went back to the same ol' parties with the same ol' friends doing the same ol' things.

A few years ago, I was on the last leg of my tour. I performed in Madison Square Garden, a place I'd only dreamed of going to when I was growing up. I had it all. The money, the cars, the ho … women. There wasn't one thing I couldn't get, yet I was unhappy all the time. And me being unhappy meant me getting high. And me getting high meant me overdoing it, because I had no chill. And having no chill led me to waking up in a hospital bed after overdosing. Again. I've heard people talk about waking up from something like that and making a one-eighty because they have this second chance at something they almost lost. I didn't feel like that, though. I just felt lost. I felt heavy. I felt worthless and useless.

A good friend of mine, a girl I'd been in love with once upon a time, one I dated and lost because of my own stupidity and selfishness, told me that I needed to take a good look at my life if I wanted to survive it. She said that I couldn't keep going to the same ol' parties with the same ol' friends doing the same ol' things and expect a brand-new outcome. Unlike the first time I'd gone to rehab, expecting to detox and be fixed, I decided to work at fixing myself. When I got out of rehab, I started going to a therapist. I took up yoga. I went to plays. I did things I'd never been remotely interested in before. And the media took a shit all over my image. They called me phony and soft and said I wasn't the Shea I once had been. And you know what I did when I saw the criticism? I smiled. I smiled because for the first time in my entire life I was the Shea I was supposed to be and I was happy.

Today marks three years to the day I woke up in that hospital bed with no recollection of what had happened and I'm happy to say I haven't abused of any drugs. It's hard to shelter yourself from them when you're in an industry like mine, but I keep my eye on the prize. I have a woman in my life that reminds me every day that I'm fortunate to be alive and fortunate to have her with me. I'm not here to tell you that by getting your life right the demons will go away, because they don't. The demons are always there. You just have to find a way to quiet them.

Amongst the claps, I step off the stage and walk up to a couple of students to take pictures with before I'm hauled out back. I thank the President of the school and a few deans before walking away. As I near the exit, I spot Nina frowning as she looks down at her phone. When she senses me, she looks up at me and smiles, putting her phone away in her purse.

"Good speech," she says. "You should make a career out of this."

A smile tugs at my mouth as I wrap an arm around her and pull her closer. "Maybe I will."

"Who's this mysterious woman you talked about?"

I move my hand down her back, covering her ass. She has the best ass. And pull her forward, flush against me. "Just some girl I've decided I'm going to marry."

"Really?" she whispers, eyes wide. "Tell me more."

I press my lips to the edge of her mouth. "She's beautiful." I kiss the other the other side. "She's funny." I kiss her chin. "So fucking sexy." I kiss her mouth, her lips parting along mine, her tongue dancing with mine, savoring the moment. My cock jumps in my jeans and I groan into her mouth. "And mine," I say, breaking the kiss.

Her fiery, brown eyes meet mine. "Take me home, Mr. Sweet Talker. I haven't been in your bed in two days."

I smile, kissing her one last time before leading her through the door and to the SUV waiting for us out back. The driver opens the door for us and we get into the backseat. Nina's been starring in every huge Broadway play you can think of. Her career took off when she went from understudy to leading lady in A Bronx Tale, and she's been unstoppable since. Never in a million years did I think I'd end up dating Nina, of all people, but it works. She was there for me through the bad and rooted for me in the good. The sparks were always there, even though neither one of us wanted to admit it. Then, Brooklyn set us up on a sneaky blind date and the rest is history.

"Have you spoken to Nick or Brooklyn?" she asks as I reach for my phone. I shake my head and sigh when I see the amount of notifications I have. There's no way I'm going to sort through all of this.

"Nick's in the studio with Lil somebody," I say, scrolling.

"Lil somebody?"

I shrug. "There's always some Lil rapper. I can't keep them all straight."

Nina laughs. "Remind me to never box you in with the Lil rappers."

I put my phone down and cut her a look. "There's nothing Lil about me."

"Hm." She bites her lip. "Two days, Shea. Two days."

I pull her close and kiss her so thoroughly I'm not sure I'll make it to the apartment without fucking her. She breaks the kiss, a blush spreading on her cheeks as she glances at the driver. I kiss her again. It's impossible not to want this girl. I don't know how I kept my hands to myself for as long as I did. We break apart once more.

"It's not my fault you're always on the stage," I say, smiling when she smiles that prideful smile of hers.

"It's hard to stay off stage when I have the hottest man in America in the audience front and center."

I grin and add, "With flowers."

"With flowers." She sighs happily and looks out the window. "Are you coming to tomorrow's show?"

"The two o'clock?" I ask. She nods. "I can't make it."

She gives me a little pout. "Why not?"

"I already told you, babe. I have a meeting."

"On a Saturday?"

I nod, trying on my best sad face, but I'm no actor. I just hope she buys my act and doesn't mess up my elaborate plan. All of us are going to see Nina's performance tomorrow. Her mom, Brooklyn, Nick, Hendrix, Mel, my mom. And after the curtain call, when I normally take her flowers, I'm going to get down on one knee and propose because I refuse to let this one get away.

ClaireContrerasbooks.com

Twitter: @ClariCon

Insta: ClaireContreras

Facebook: www.facebook.com/groups/ClaireContrerasBooks

**Also–please show some love to the very talented
Paige Chaplin:**

www.facebook.com/paigechaplinmusic

Get her music on iTunes or here: paigechaplin.bandcamp.com